HOUR
OF THE
RAT

Also by Lisa Brackmann

Rock Paper Tiger
Getaway

HOUR
OF THE
RAT

LISA
BRACKMANN

SOHO
CRIME

Published by
Soho Press, Inc.
853 Broadway
New York, NY 10003

Library of Congress Cataloging-in-Publication Data

Brackmann, Lisa.
Hour of the rat / Lisa Brackmann.
p. cm
ISBN 978-1-61695-234-1
eISBN 978-1-61695-235-8
1. Art dealers—Fiction. 2. Americans—China—Fiction.
3. Missing persons—Fiction. I. Title.
PS3602.R333H68 2013
813'.6--dc23   2012046282

Printed in the United States of America

10 9 8 7 6 5 4 3 2 1

To my parents, Carol and Bill. Thank you, for everything.

HOUR
OF THE
RAT

★

"Is it just me, or is this bullshit?"

The ducks sit on top of a large metal grill, a skinny rectangle as long as a pool table. Glowing coals underneath. The duck at one end is crispy brown, like Peking Duck. Which I love, but who knows how long it's been sitting here? Moving down the row, the next duck is . . . I don't know, boiled, maybe, the flesh a little greyish. The one after that is raw, I think, its feathers plucked, the naked skin yellow and pimply.

Harrison Wang shrugs. "As a piece, I think it's not terribly sophisticated."

Harrison, who knows from sophisticated, has dragged me along to this art opening. Some new-artists collective way the fuck out in Tongzhou, an eastern suburb of Beijing, in a patchy area of old red brick buildings and white-tiled storefronts between high-rise developments where the buildings are named "Rotterdam," "Bordeaux," and "Seattle."

I mean, Seattle?

The opening is in a tumbledown warehouse across the ring road from the fancy developments, behind a row of cheap restaurants, electronics stores, foot-massage joints and "barbershops." 拆—*chai*, the character for "demolish"—is already slapped up with white paint on the exterior walls.

Inside, it's a dirty concrete slab, some lame performance pieces, big acrylic paintings with a lot of naked butts, cartoon farts, and McDonald's references. It's freezing, which is why I was drawn to this stupid duck thing in the first place, because the lit coals make it warm. Guests and artists mill around, drinking Yanjing beer and eating *yangrou chuanr*, which normally I'd be all over, but the meat on these is so small and gristly that I wonder if it's actually mutton and not dog instead. Or rat.

I was born in the Year of the Rat, and eating my birth animal seems like it would be bad luck. So I stick to the beer.

"Why are we here, again?" I ask.

"I'd heard good things about the painter," Harrison says, flicking his hazel eyes at one of the giant canvases, one where a fat naked guy whose face is done up in Peking Opera makeup lies sprawled across a red Ferrari, his guts spilling out of his sliced-open stomach.

"Really?"

"I agree with you, it's disappointing."

I hold my hands over the grill. They're red with cold, throbbing like I've had them dipped in an ice bucket. I should have kept my gloves on.

Harrison doesn't seem cold. He's wearing a knee-length coat, black, some kind of soft, thick wool, and a black-and-red cashmere scarf. He looks like the centerfold in some men's fashion shoot.

He's my boss, sort of.

I manage the work of a Chinese artist. An important one. Which is pretty funny, considering that I know fuck-all about art. Which is why, I guess, Harrison keeps trying to get me to learn.

"This duck thing is lame," I mutter.

The next duck, predictably, is a dead one with all its feathers still on. Just a whole dead duck. Lying on the grill. Long neck stretched out at a weird angle where I have to think, Oh, they killed it by breaking its neck. The exposed eye looks like dead, rubbery plastic. Some feathers have fallen onto the coals. They smell like burned hair.

"But why is it lame, Ellie?" Harrison persists.

"I don't know, because it's a bunch of dead ducks lying on a grill," I say.

Except the last one isn't dead.

It's wrapped in Saran Wrap sealed with duct tape. Hardly even struggling by now. Lying on the grill, making little duck noises, you can't even call them quacks. Shuddering.

"This is fucking disgusting."

"You don't think that it is perhaps a statement on the reality of what we consume?" Harrison asks mildly. "Stripped of its packaging?"

"I don't care."

I'm going to do one of two things. I'm going to run out of the room, or I'm going to pick up the duck.

I pick up the duck. It quacks and convulses in my arms.

"Hey!"

Somebody—the artist, I guess, some tall guy with glasses, wearing a green Mao jacket over a Polo shirt, a real one, with the little horse (I think it's supposed to be ironic)—comes running over. "You can't do that!"

"I'm responding to the piece, asshole."

He tries to grab the duck, and I kick him in the shin.

"*Saobi laowai!*" he yelps.

"Yeah, your mother, whatever." I've been called worse.

The duck squirms in my arms.

A couple other guys coming running over, and suddenly it seems like most of the crowd has turned toward us.

Hey, it's a better show than the art.

"How much for the piece?" Harrison asks.

"What?" Asshole Artist stutters.

"How much for the piece?" Harrison pulls out his wallet. It's this beautiful soft leather thing that's thin enough to disappear in his back pocket. And yet I'm sure it holds plenty of money.

THAT'S HOW WE END up at a veterinarian's office in Sanlitun with a dehydrated, malnourished duck.

"Stay overnight, I think she is okay after that," the vet says.

Afterward, we go to a rooftop bar where the "mixologist" does a pretty good margarita.

"There's a wildlife sanctuary in Yanqing County that I think will take her," Harrison says.

I stare out the window. There's a great view from here of Sanlitun Village, this upscale shopping mall with edgy smoked-glass buildings, overpriced hamburger restaurants, and all kinds of luxury shops including an Apple Store, where people line up and riot over the latest iPads.

"Thanks," I finally say.

Harrison shrugs. "You were right. It was bad art."

CHAPTER ONE

I SERIOUSLY NEED TO get out of Beijing.

There's the fact that the air is trying to kill me. No joke. The American embassy over in Chaoyang does readings of the air quality in Beijing, since the Chinese government doesn't, or won't reveal the results anyway. A while ago it was so polluted that they ran out of normal descriptions and came up with one of their own, so what went out over Twitter was that the air was "crazy-bad."

Thanks, guys. Remind me not to breathe.

There's also the fact that it's been another long winter, and while you think I'd know what's coming after three years, it still takes me by surprise: months of wind so cold and dry that sometimes I feel like I'm breathing razors. Now that it's the last day in February, temps are getting up above freezing at least, but it's still the kind of cold that settles into your bones and makes my leg ache even more than it usually does.

My apartment's comfortable. There's a central furnace that controls the radiators in the living room and the two bedrooms; the enclosed balconies provide a buffer against the chill. I broke down and got a cheap flat-screen at Suning, and I have a stack of DVDs from my favorite DVD store off Andingmen, every

American movie or TV show you could want. I've got take-out menus from half a dozen restaurants, and right at the end of the alley there's a great jiaozi place and some snack stands, plus there's a tiny store about the size of my bathroom that sells toilet paper and Yanjing beer and a bunch of snack foods, including my favorite spicy peanuts, that's just across from the entrance to my apartment complex.

So it's not like I really have to leave my apartment all that much right now. Or go very far if I do.

It's just that I can only take so much of my mom without a break, and I've about reached my limit.

"Ellie, do you know where's the best place for me to find peanut butter?" she asks from the doorway to my bedroom. "And chocolate chips?"

"Any of the foreign supermarkets'll probably have them," I say. I'm sitting on my bed with my laptop propped on a pillow on my legs. I don't really look up. She's always asking questions like this, and I admit I tune them out a lot of the time.

"Really? Because I went to . . . what's the name of that French one? Carrefour? And they had peanut butter, but it was chunky and I need smooth. And I didn't see any chocolate chips at all."

"I don't know," I mutter. "You could always buy chocolate bars and hit them with a hammer."

"I guess I could."

Now I do glance away from my screen. There's my mom, her streaked, bleached hair rising in a halo of static, wearing a Sunrise T-shirt (I'VE FOUND MR. RIGHT AND HE'S PERFECT! ISAIAH 62:5) and sweats, solid through the middle like a pound cake, the bramble-rose tattoo above her elbow sagging a bit, which is what happens to a tat inked twenty-five years ago.

"Aren't you cold?" I ask, because even with the radiators on I'm wearing a sweatshirt.

She snorts. "Not right now. I've got my own heat." She mimes fanning herself. "Hot flashes."

Like I needed to know.

"The thing is, I want to make my special chocolate chip cookies for Andy," she continues, cheeks flushing.

And that's when I know I've got to get out of Beijing: *That nice Mr. Zhou next door* has become *Andy*.

Given my mom's track record with men, no good can come of this.

"Maybe try Walmart," I mutter, and turn back to my laptop.

I LOVE MY MOM.

Seriously, I really do. She did the best she could do with raising me, which maybe wasn't always very good, but she comes through when it counts, like after I got blown up in the Sandbox, for example, leaving my leg busted in too many places to count and the rest of me not much better.

It's just that a month now, living in my apartment in Beijing? That wasn't what I had in mind when she said she wanted to come and visit me.

"Just to see how you're doing," she'd said, "since you don't have time to come home."

This of course was a lie on my part. I didn't want to come home. Long story.

After a couple of weeks, where I did my best to show her the tourist sites—the Forbidden City, the Summer Palace, the Great Wall, the Silk Market for fake Prada, and the world's largest IKEA store—she showed no sign of going anywhere, other than to the guest room in my apartment by the Gulou subway station, which used to be my office. I finally asked, "So, Mom, when's your flight home again?"

"I'm not sure," she said. "It's really up to you."

"What about work?"

"Well . . ." She hesitated. As I recall, she twisted her hands together. "The job didn't really work out."

IT'S NOT HER FAULT, I tell myself now. She worked hard for years. It's not her fault that the US economy is in the toilet, that she's fifty-one years old and no one wants to hire her for anything. Not her fault that Refinancing Roulette didn't pay off. The condo was a shithole anyway. Sometimes it's even sort of cool having her here, like when she makes tacos, cooking being an activity at which I suck.

But I seriously need some away time from her right now.

"Don't talk to me about Jesus," I said about three days after she got here, Jesus being one of the things that we used to have in common, but that pretty much got blown up along with the rest of my life, in Iraq. Mostly she's been pretty good about it, but every once in a while Jesus slips out.

For example: "You know, that nice Mr. Zhou next door belongs to a church. And I think it's Christian, more or less. They worship Jesus anyway. He invited me to attend their service. Would you like . . . ?"

"No thanks."

Like I'm going to go to some weird-ass Chinese underground house church, featuring Brother Jesus Christ of the Righteous Thundering Fist, or what have you.

Like I'd set foot inside Sunrise, for that matter.

Sunrise is the church that my mom and me used to go to in Arizona. It's a big church, in this fake-adobe complex that always reminded me of an Indian casino. But I still used to believe in it all. Take comfort in Reverend Jim's air-conditioned sermons. Snap my WHAT WOULD JESUS DO? rubber bracelet against my wrist when I needed an invisible helping hand.

HOUR OF THE RAT ★ 9

When people talk about how your faith gets tested, they always say that trials make your faith stronger. What they don't say is that sometimes faith just dissolves like desert sand between your fingers.

"Do you feel like going to Walmart?" my mom asks. "You know, you could use a few things for your kitchen. You don't have a single spatula."

It's fucking cold outside, and so far the lack of a spatula does not seem to have negatively affected my life. "Sure," I say anyway. "Just let me finish some emails."

I should get out of the house, I tell myself. Two P.M. and I've done nothing today but sit on my ass, surf the Net, drink coffee, and eat spicy peanuts and shrimp chips.

It's right about then I hear the underwater gurgle signaling that a contact of mine has signed onto Skype. I don't bother to look who it is. I do have a couple of emails to answer: a request from a San Francisco gallery for a couple of Lao Zhang's paintings to exhibit for a show titled *A Remix of Progress: The Disjunction of the Status Quo*; somebody named Vicky Huang representing some Chinese guy I've never heard of, Sidney Cao, claiming he's a big art collector who wants to arrange "a private viewing" of Lao Zhang's work, and Lucy Wu wanting to know if I can make her opening in Shanghai on March 12. I guess I should do *something* productive today. That is, other than buying a spatula.

I decide to answer Lucy first. Sure, I'll go to her opening. She usually has good wine, and maybe she can explain to me what "the disjunction of the status quo" means.

Besides, Shanghai would be getting out of Beijing, right?

That's when the Skype phone rings.

I switch windows. It's my buddy Dog Turner calling.

"Hey, Baby Doc!"

"Hey, Dog. Hang on a sec. Lemme put on my headset."

Dog twitches on the screen while I untangle my iPhone earbuds.

"Lookin' good, Ellie," he says.

"You, too."

He doesn't, really, but what am I supposed to say? Even with the low-res camera on his computer, I can see the indentation in his skull where the RPG hit. If he sat farther back from the camera, I'd see the arm that wasn't there, but frankly, I'd rather not. I think about that too much, and my own arm starts to hurt, and my leg, which pretty much hurts all the time, although I'm getting better at ignoring it. Thanks in part to the fresh supply of Percocet my mom brought me. When I asked her about it, she just giggled and said, "Well, I still have friends."

In the aquarium light of the computer screen, I see Dog twitching in his chair. Spasms cross his face like sudden ripples on a still pond.

"What's up, man?" I ask. "How's the family?"

"Mostly good." His mouth twists.

"Mostly?"

"Kids are good. Wife . . . I make her crazy." He grins lopsidedly. "You?"

"Fine," I say.

I know something's up with him. We're buddies and all, we keep each other posted, but it's not like we talk all the time. It's hard for him to talk, for one. The TBI, the traumatic brain injury, really fucked him up. Plus, there's the whole thing where we messed around back in Iraq, and even though it didn't really mean anything, I still feel a little weird talking to him too much when he has a wife and a couple of kids. It's almost worse since he got hurt in Af-Pak, because I wish I felt comfortable talking to his wife. Like, if the situation were different, I could say, "Hey, Natalie, what can I do to help?"

Which is pretty fucking stupid, actually. Because there's nothing I can do to help.

"Lookin' good, Ellie," he repeats.

"Thanks."

"I want . . ." He screws up his face again. "I need . . . I have this . . ."

I wait.

"My brother," he manages.

"HE'S IN CHINA, SOMEWHERE," Natalie explains. She's taken over for Dog, who got all agitated when the words he wanted wouldn't come. "We got a postcard a month or so ago from some place called . . . Yang shoe?"

"Yangshuo?" I guess.

"I don't know." She rolls her eyes, impatient. "Someplace with weird-looking mountains."

She's a San Diego girl, I know. A couple years older than me. Thin and tan, with that whole "I jog and do yoga" body and the beginnings of hard lines on her face: around her mouth, outlining her cheeks.

"Probably Yangshuo."

"Whatever." She heaves a sigh. "The thing is . . ."

She glances over her shoulder. Dog is there, hovering, scooting around in an office chair like it's a bumper car, occasionally waving at the screen.

She runs her fingers through her highlighted hair. "He wants Jason to come home."

"So why doesn't he?"

She pauses. Looks sideways for a moment. "Jason has some problems."

"What kind of problems?"

"He's . . ." Her voice drops. "He's not stable. He's on meds. And we think maybe he went off them."

"Meds for what?" I ask. "What's the diagnosis?"

Not like I'm an expert, but when I trained to be a medic, we covered the basics.

"I . . ." She hesitates again. "Manic depression. Doug doesn't like to—"

"What?" Dog says. "What don't I like?"

"He's a little in denial," she whispers. "But it's made Jason . . . He's acted out before. We're just worried about—"

"It's FUBAR!" Dog shouts in the background. "Jason's not a head case!"

"Okay, okay," I say. "So you don't know where he is?"

"No." She glances over her shoulder at Dog, then back to me. "I know it's crazy, even asking you. I tell him China's got a billion people or whatever, but he won't . . . he won't listen."

"Doesn't fucking hurt to ask," I hear Dog say.

I think about it.

"It's not totally crazy," I say.

OKAY, THE ODDS AREN'T great. But it's not impossible.

Here's the thing: China is a big country. *Huge.* With more than a billion people.

But most of them are Chinese.

There are a lot of Westerners who live here, for sure. And tourists. I don't know how many, but enough so that in most popular tourist places it's not like a Westerner is a total Martian or anything. In Beijing no one notices or particularly cares. Yeah, some old auntie might remark to her buddy on the neighborhood committee, "Hey, *laowai laile!*" but it's hard to keep track when there are so many of us.

That said, someone is still watching.

Places like Yangshuo, a major hub on the banana-pancake backpacker circuit, known for its weird, beautiful mountains, "quaint" villages tucked along rice paddies, rivers where you can float down a bamboo raft, sucking down beer—yeah, lots of foreigners go there, for sure. But they tend to congregate in certain establishments.

It's possible I could find someone who'd seen Jason. Who maybe had even hung out with him. Who might have an idea where he is.

WHAT I SAY TO Natalie and Dog is, "Yeah, it's pretty much a long shot. But, you know, send me whatever you got on him and I'll see what I can do."

"Thanks," Natalie says, brushing her hair out of her face again, which I think she's doing because she's tearing up and she doesn't want me to see. "Thanks. It means a lot to Doug. I know you guys are friends. I mean, I know . . ." She blinks rapidly. "He's said a lot of really nice things about you."

"Heh," I say. "Doug's a good guy."

There is a long and somewhat awkward silence. Natalie stares into the webcam, blinking now and then. In the background Dog scoots up to the screen on his office chair, puts his only arm around Natalie's shoulders, and squeezes.

"I'm an asshole!" he says, grinning.

JUST TO CLARIFY, IT'S not because I feel guilty or something that I am thinking about helping Dog out. It's because you help your buddies. That's just the way it is. You help the people who were there for you, is all. And Dog . . . well, yeah, he's kind of an asshole on the one hand. On the other, he was a buddy to me during my first duty assignment in Iraq, in

Mortaritaville. I was as young and dumb as they came, nineteen years old, a good Christian girl.

Maybe he acted like a friend primarily to get into my pants, which I gotta say worked well for him. But when I think about those times now, mostly what I remember is that he was still my friend.

Plus, Yangshuo is supposed to be beautiful. And warm. As mentioned, it's ass-freezing cold here in Beijing, and the air is "crazy-bad."

Then there's this: "Ellie, are you ready to go to Walmart?"

Here's my mom, hovering in the doorway, with a stout Chinese guy standing slightly behind her, his hands clasped in front of him like he's a singer in a choir waiting for his cue.

"Do you mind if Andy tags along?" my mom asks, a little hesitantly. "He needs a few things."

"Yes." Andy nods vigorously. "Socks. And candles."

"Sure," I say. "Fine."

I insist we take a subway there, even though Andy claims to have a car and my mom doesn't understand why we don't just cab it—"But, honey, the taxis are so cheap here!"

"Because if we take a cab, we sit in the same fucking traffic as everyone else, that's why," I say, not for the first time. "And people here drive even worse than in Phoenix."

Plus, I still don't like riding in cars very much. I'm better about it than I was, but I don't like being stuck in traffic, a sitting target. That's how you get blown up. Outside the wire you haul ass.

Okay, I know where I am and that I'm not going to get blown up in a Beijing taxi, probably. Sitting in traffic just makes me nervous sometimes.

We pass the random bronze statues of little kids playing on

the dead grass, the tiny kiosk where the guy makes *jianbing*, which is sort of a Beijing breakfast burrito and one of my favorite foods ever, and trot down the long staircase to the subway.

"*Yi zhang piao,*" I tell the attendant behind the Plexiglas window. I have my *yikatong* card, but my mom hasn't taken the plunge, so I buy her tickets whenever we go someplace. It's like neither of us wants to admit that she's staying here.

"Anal constriction," Andy says in English, carefully sounding out each syllable. "Anal constriction is key."

"Oh, really?"

We put our bags through the X-ray machine that no one pays attention to and head down another set of stairs to the platform. It's not too crowded this time of day. We line up at the shortest queue I can spot, toward the back of the train. I watch the ads for banks, cell phones, and real estate flicker on the dark wall across from us.

"Yes," Andy says. "Anal constriction. And denting naval."

"It's a part of the religious practice," my mom explains. "Kind of like tai chi."

"What does this have to do with Jesus?" I mutter.

"Brother Jesus wants us to be happy," Andy explains. "With anal constriction, you can say good-bye to sad feelings. And take back your youth." He turns to my mom and smiles. "Increases staying power."

She blushes a little as the rush of warm air from the inbound subway hits the platform.

And this is another reason I need a break from my mom: the longer I'm around her and Andy, the more I feel like a pissed-off teenager. As opposed to, you know, a pissed-off twenty-seven-year-old.

★ ★ ★

BY THE TIME WE return from Walmart, with chocolate chips, spatulas, peanut butter, candles, and socks, there's an email from Natalie with an attachment: a photo of Jason.

I stretch my bad leg out on my bed, battered white MacBook propped on a pillow on my lap, and open the attachment.

He's a kid. Younger than me. Longish brown hair. Full cheeks and a backpacker beard. Pretty brown eyes, almost toffee-colored, with flecks of gold in them. A soulful expression, like the dude should be playing an acoustic guitar at some college open mic night or maybe pulling espressos at the local coffee joint.

"What do you feel like for dinner, hon?" my mom asks. "Maybe tacos?" She holds up an avocado. "Look what I found at the Carrefour!"

"Sure. Sounds good."

I go back to my laptop. I have the usual pileup of email in my inbox to deal with.

There's a knock at the front door.

My mom glances over her shoulder and pads off to answer.

The water guy, maybe? Though he usually comes in the early afternoon. The security door to the building is always propped open till later in the evening, so it could be anybody.

I hear a man, his words too faint to make out. And then my mom.

"Ellie," she says, a flat note to her voice. "There's two policemen here to see you."

CHAPTER TWO

I TELL MYSELF NOT to panic.

I'm better about stuff than I was. My heart's pounding, but it's not so bad that I feel like I'm going to throw up. They could be here for all kinds of reasons. Checking to make sure I registered my mom at the local Public Security Bureau, maybe.

I stand up, wincing as my foot hits the floor, and hobble into the living room.

The two men stand in the doorway.

"I said they couldn't come in till you checked their IDs," my mom hisses. "Since I can't tell what they say. I don't think they speak very much English anyway."

The two men are wearing dark blue uniforms with silver buttons, silver wings on their epaulets, and winged bars on their chests. One has his overcoat slung over his arm—the younger of the two men, tall and slender. The other is middle-aged and stocky, with a pockmarked face. He stands behind the first one, looking bored.

"Ellie McEnroe?" the younger one says, only the way he says it sounds more like "Mack-in-arr."

"Yeah?"

"Can you come with us, please?"

"Why?"

"Just for a talk. To have some tea."

I can see the patch on his shoulder. "*Guo Nei Anquan Bao* . . ." something something. My written Chinese sucks. But I'm pretty sure I know where these guys are from.

"We can talk here," I say. "I have all kinds of tea. Your choice."

He hesitates. Glances over his shoulder at his companion, who half raises an eyebrow and makes a tiny smirk. "I don't think," the younger one says, "this is convenient place. Because my English is not very good. So much better if we go talk with my . . . my *laoban*? My boss? So we can understand each other. Just a short talk."

I think about refusing.

When they ask you to "drink tea," it's not exactly official. It's not exactly optional either. It's a way to try to gather information, to intimidate you. But you're not getting arrested.

Yet.

Not that they'd arrest me. I'm not Chinese. They'll just kick me out of the country, if it comes to that.

But I'd rather it didn't come to that.

I shrug. "Okay. I need to use the bathroom first."

Now they step inside. "No time for that," the younger one says. The older one flanks him.

For a moment I think they're actually going to drag me out of here. My heart's pounding so hard I'm starting to shake. I hope they can't see it.

I'm tired of being scared.

"Really?" I say in Chinese. "You want me to liberate myself in your car?"

At that the older one lifts both his eyebrows and makes a little snort.

I grab my canvas bag off the coffee table. Young cop starts to object. Old cop just shakes his head.

Yeah, I'm going to make a phone call, assholes. What do you expect?

Mom follows me toward the bathroom.

"You're not going with them!" she says. "Are you? We should call the American embassy."

"It's just for a talk. Not a big deal."

"Who are they?"

"Domestic Security Department. They're like the . . . the . . . kind of like the FBI."

They're in charge of tracking "subversives," such as democracy activists, environmental crusaders, underground church members, pissed-off petitioners, miscellaneous malcontents—basically anyone with a point of view that isn't in line with the "harmonious society." They have plainclothes spies, a vast network of informants, I don't know how many millions of them.

Not that my mom needs to know this level of detail.

"But why are they here? Why do they want to talk to you?"

"I don't know," I say, though I have a pretty good idea. "It's probably just . . . some of the people I know, some of the artists. They do stuff that's kind of controversial sometimes."

I go into the bathroom, shut the door, and turn on the water in the sink. Get out my iPhone and touch a number.

It rings a few times and goes to voice mail.

Fuck.

"Hey," I say, in English, "I'm going for tea with the National Treasures. Thought you should know."

I hit the red DISCONNECT button. And then I pee. Because I actually need to go.

When I exit the bathroom, my mom is facing the two cops, hands on her hips, like she's daring them to take a step closer.

I gather up my coat and a hat. "Remember that number I gave you?" I say. "The one I put on your cell?"

She nods.

"If you don't hear from me in a couple of hours, call it and explain what's going on. And if there's no answer . . ."

I think about it.

"Yeah, call the embassy."

WE RIDE IN A squad car, heading southwest.

The older cop drives. The younger one sits next to me in the back and tries to make polite conversation. I wish he'd shut up. I need to think. To get my story straight, plan what I'm going to say, what's safe to admit and what isn't.

"Your Chinese is really good," he says. "Really standard."

"Thanks."

"Where did you learn it?"

"Here."

"How long have you been in China?"

"Three years."

He shakes his head. "We learn English in school. I study a long time. But I don't speak it very well."

"Helps to be in the country," I say.

He sighs. "Yes. But I think I won't have that opportunity. Very difficult in my position." He hesitates. "I like American movies and TV shows very much," he says in English. "To practice English. I watch . . . *24. The Sopranos. Sons of* . . ." His brow wrinkles. "*Ah-nah-key.* I am not sure, how to say. They are bad men. Criminals. They drive those . . . those . . ."

"Motorcycles," I supply.

"Yes!" He mimes twisting the handles. "Very dangerous!" His eyes light up, and he grins.

I keep thinking we're going to stop. We pass the local police station. Then monumental government buildings with the state seal attached to the concrete like a giant badge stuck on awkwardly with a pin.

But we don't stop. We keep driving. West, then south.

After a while I have no fucking clue where we're going. The traffic's so bad that the cop takes sides streets, nothing I recognize.

Besides, no one goes to South Beijing unless they're going to the new train station. This far south? I don't even know what's here.

The farther we go, the more it looks like we're not in Beijing anymore, like we've suddenly been transported to a podunk third-tier city in some interior province.

White-tiled storefronts. Cracked plastic signage. Discount malls plastered with billboard-size ads for products you've never heard of, European-looking models advertising watches and shoes, everything greyed by pollution. Vendors who look like peasants with stuff to sell spread out on blankets on the sidewalk: DVDs. Socks and underwear. Barrettes and hairbrushes. Random shit.

"Where are we going?" I finally ask.

"Not far. Just a place . . . that's comfortable. To talk."

And that's when I really get scared. I think maybe they're just going to make me disappear.

No, that doesn't make sense, I tell myself. If they were going to do that, would they send guys in uniforms? Would they do it in front of my mom?

Wouldn't they do it off the books?

I tell myself this stuff until I'm calm again. Calmer anyway.

We turn onto a busy street with the typical iron fence dividing it, so pedestrians can't cross and drivers can't make turns, and for some reason I think about what a pain in the ass those iron fences can be, like they go out of their way to make simple things difficult. We pass trucks stacked with vegetables—potatoes, bundles of celery—that rumble down a narrow street toward some huge grey cement gate with a red badge and gold characters across the top, a guard box on either side.

Finally we get to the end of the block and turn left, into a walled, gated parking lot. In front of us is a large, blocky building, about ten stories high, the façade a combination of faux marble, metal sheets, and green Plexiglas. Red lanterns hang above the entrance.

The pinyin below the characters spells out HEXIE ANXI JIUDIAN. Harmonious Rest Hotel.

We drive past the lobby, around to the back, through a metal gate, into a little service yard. There are rows of dumpsters, a couple of battered electric scooters, a warped ping-pong table, and a clothesline with hotel uniforms hung up, inside out, to dry.

"So we aren't checking in?" I snark.

The younger cop does one of those embarrassed semi-giggles. "Please wait a moment," he says, and gets out of the car. He jogs over to a back entrance and goes inside.

The older cop sits in the front seat and drums on the steering wheel.

Shit, shit, *shit*, I think. Even if this ends up not being a big deal, what are the odds I'll get my visa renewed if I'm getting hauled in to drink tea with the fucking DSD?

The young policeman comes trotting back and opens the car door. "Okay," he says, as cheerful as a tour guide about to show me some special scenic spot, "we can go upstairs now."

IT'S A "BUSINESS HOTEL," meaning stripped down, stained, and frayed around the edges but fairly clean. We enter through the back door, past a curtained room that's some kind of staff facility: I glimpse cleaning supplies, stacks of towels, one hotel worker, a rosy-cheeked girl who hardly looks old enough to be working here, sitting on a metal folding chair, sewing a button on a uniform smock.

We go up three flights of worn carpeted stairs. The air smells like stale cigarettes, the smoke permeating the walls, the red industrial carpet; you'd have to tear the whole place down to get rid of it.

By the time we're on the third flight, my leg is throbbing and I'm just really pissed off, because people keep fucking with me, because I can't catch a break, because my leg really hurts, and I don't even have a Percocet.

Okay, I tell myself, okay. You need to keep it together. Don't lose your temper, and don't panic. Just calm down, listen to what they say, and don't give them any more than you have to.

I've been in worse situations than this, and I got through them.

This is nothing.

We walk down to the end of the hall, to a room like every other room. Room 3310. Young Cop has a key card, and I hear the insect whir as the door unlocks.

It's your basic Chinese hotel room. A bit larger than some of the places I've stayed, in that there's room for two club chairs and a little round table on a raised Formica-covered platform by the window.

A man sits in one of the chairs. No uniform, just a polo shirt and slacks. Middle-aged, a slight paunch hanging over his typically ugly belt with a square gold buckle, fake Gucci or Armani or something. Hair swept back in a Chinese bureaucrat pompadour.

"*Qing zuo,*" he says, gesturing to the other chair.

I sit.

He doesn't say anything. Just sits there and smiles at me. I fidget. Maybe that's the point of the silence.

"You asked me here for tea," I finally say. "I don't see any."

"Ah." He nods. Motions to Young Cop, who quickly scoots over to the desk, where the hot water kettle is, and fills it with a bottle of Nongfu Spring water that's sitting next to it.

"Thank you for your cooperation," he says.

I shrug.

He leans back in his chair, twines his fingers together, rocking them up and down like he's contemplating the universe or something. I stretch out my bad leg, which has started to cramp up and is hurting like hell.

Neither of us says anything. Young Cop busies himself with opening up the complimentary tea bags and putting them into two cups.

The kettle hisses steam, and there's a loud click as it turns itself off. I flinch.

Young Cop pours water into the cups and carries them over. Sets them on the little round table with a rattle and retreats, smiling in that embarrassed way of his.

"You two can go," the man says to the cops.

After that it's just the two of us and more silence. The man sips his tea. So do I.

He's better at this silence thing than I am.

"You want to talk to me," I say. "I'm here. You want to ask me something? Or what?"

"I am just waiting. For my colleague. His English is better than mine." He looks at his watch, a fake—or possibly real— Rolex. "Perhaps there's bad traffic."

So far he hasn't spoken a word of English. Maybe he's telling the truth.

I hear the whir of a keycard unlocking the door.

"Ah. He's arrived." The man turns to me and smiles. "I think you know each other."

The door opens.

That's when I realize: I am so totally screwed.

CHAPTER THREE

"Yili."

"John."

Yeah, I know him.

He's wearing a black leather jacket, a nicer one than he used to wear, a grey sweater beneath it. Jeans and low leather boots. There's a white scar that cuts into one eyebrow, the wisp of a beard on his upper lip and chin. I always thought he was good-looking, and he's better-looking now, something about the way the strong bones of his face have sharpened, how his dark eyes have the quality of banked coals.

Nonetheless, he still creeps me out.

John, Zhou Zheng'an, or whatever the fuck his real name is, hesitates by the door for a moment. Then he walks to the desk. He's light on his feet; the hitch in his step from when he got hurt last year is nearly gone.

Lucky bastard, I think unreasonably.

He pulls out the desk chair and sits.

"How do you know each other?" the other man asks. He repeats the question, just to make sure I understand.

Fuck, fuck, the fucking fuck. What am I supposed to say? What's John told them? None of it? Some of it? Everything?

"Why don't you ask him?" I say. "You already know, right?"

"Yili, it's better if you explain." John stares at me. I can't tell what he's thinking, what the expression means.

I never really trusted him. By the end I figured he was some kind of cop. But this . . . I wasn't expecting this.

If I say the wrong thing, I'll be even more fucked than I already am.

Leniency for those who confess. Severity for those who refuse.

Though if he's told them everything . . . well, I guess I'm fucked regardless. And maybe not just "get kicked out of the country" fucked. More like "go directly to jail" fucked.

My heart starts to thud in my chest, and I'm sweating beneath my sweatshirt. They can tell, I'm sure.

I drink some bitter tea.

"We met last year," I say in English. "At a party. We ran into each other a few times after that. Got attacked during this riot. I thought maybe he was spying on me or something." I don't have to fake a pissed-off glare in John's direction.

John translates, but from the look on Pompadour Bureaucrat's face, I think he pretty much caught the gist in English.

"What reason would he have to spy on you?" he asks, still speaking Chinese.

"I don't know. You tell me."

John winces, fractionally.

Dial it down, I tell myself. "I'm friends with a lot of artists. Seems like you don't always trust them." I speak in English. John translates, accurately from what I can tell.

"Of course we support China's cultural modernization," the man says, continuing in Mandarin. "China aims to become a global cultural force. It's a part of our current Five-Year Plan."

"Maybe you should stop hassling artists then."

He frowns, apparently not understanding "hassling." John translates.

"Ah. But art must still support a harmonious society. Otherwise . . . it would be foolish for the state to encourage it, true?"

"That's not the purpose of art," I mutter in Mandarin, and then I want to laugh, hearing myself trying to make art talk.

"So you think the purpose of art is to disrupt society?"

Oh, shit.

"No . . . I think . . . I think it's just whatever the artist is trying to say."

"But if an artist says disruptive things and causes trouble . . ." He leans forward. "You think this is a good thing."

It's not a question.

"I didn't say that."

"But this artist, this artist you represent . . . Zhang Jianli . . ." Now he leans back. Smiles and stares at me with an odd, satisfied expression. "He causes trouble."

It's not like I'm surprised to hear his name. I was pretty sure from the beginning that Zhang Jianli, my friend Lao Zhang, was the reason I got dragged in here. Still, the wheels turn in my head, too fast, spinning fragments of thoughts, like, Did he do something I don't know about? Did they find him? Arrest him? I try to remember the last time we chatted online, and I can't. A couple of days ago. Not for very long. Not about anything I can even remember.

"I don't know what you're talking about," I say. "He's an artist. He makes art. I help sell it."

"But my understanding is you're not an art expert. Isn't that so?"

I shrug.

"So why? If he's just an artist, why does he have *you* sell his work? Why not an expert?"

"I don't know," I say, which is partly true. I know some of Lao Zhang's reasoning, but a part of it I've never really understood. "I guess he trusts me."

Which is also the truth.

"We just wonder if there's some special reason. Some special relationship you have. Perhaps with the American government."

At that I laugh. "No. No relationship."

"But you're an American."

"So?" I switch back to English. "Doesn't mean I work for the government. *We* don't have to do that." I glare at John. "Maybe it's different in China."

I see a flash of discomfort cross John's face, and I like that I can rattle him a little. "Yili," he says, closing his eyes for a moment, "it is just that your husband—"

"My *ex*-husband."

And yeah, John knows how to piss me off, too.

"Your ex-husband. Works for a company that has government connections. Isn't that true?"

I don't say anything right away. I don't want to go down that road. Don't want to admit what I know. It's a habit with me, not admitting stuff.

"He didn't like talking about his work," I say. "That's one of the reasons we split up."

The main reason, of course, is that he took up with that bitch Lily Ping. But there's no way I'm getting into that discussion right now.

Pompadour Bureaucrat looks interested. Lifts his eyebrows. "You have a difference in values?"

"Yeah, I guess you could say that."

I can see the wheels turning in *his* head, slow and calculating. Like how can he make this into an advantage? Like maybe he can turn me, get me to work for them.

Sorry, dude. I've been down that road too, and I'm not going there again.

"It's possible that we misunderstand Zhang Jianli's intentions," he says. "We want to have a small talk with him. Just to clear up any possible misunderstandings."

I nod and don't say anything. I can play the silent game, too.

Pompadour stares at me. Like if he stares long enough and hard enough, I'm suddenly going to start talking.

But I don't. I drink my tea. It gives me something to do.

"Do you know where we can find him?" he finally asks.

Score one for me.

"Sorry," I say. "I don't."

Which is true.

He frowns. "I find this hard to understand. You manage his art. But you don't know where he is?"

I twitch out a shrug. "He left me instructions to deal with his art however I thought best. You know, maybe show it. Sell it to people who want to buy it."

"But you must have some way to contact him."

That's when the bottom drops out of my gut. Because I do. Not the way that John knows about, the way that used to work, back when John pretended to be a friend of Lao Zhang's.

Pretended to be a friend of mine.

But if John's told his bosses about that . . .

I glance at John. He holds my gaze for a moment. Reveals nothing.

"I have his old email address," I say. "I can give it to you, if you don't have it." Then I shrug again. "Like I said, he left me instructions to manage his work and authority to do that. Until I hear from him and he tells me something different, that's what I'm going to do. There's nothing I've needed to talk to him about. It's not brain surgery, you know?"

Pompadour nods. "I see."

He takes a long sip of tea. "It really would be better for him if we could talk," he says. "And for you."

"Okay."

I let the silence settle in again, waiting for something to break it. It's not going to be me.

Then I hear a little scratching noise at the door, a slither. I turn and see a business card shoved through the crack of the door. I've stayed in hotels like this before, and I know what this is: a business card for prostitutes.

I want to laugh.

"Look, are we done here?" I say.

He appears to consider, all the while gazing at me, seeing if I'll blink.

"For now."

"Good."

I brace myself on the arms of the club chair, which feels too light to support my weight, and stand up. I'm trembling all over, but maybe he can't see that, or maybe he writes it off to my bad leg.

Whatever.

"Thanks for the tea," I say, and hobble to the door.

On my way out, I glance at the glossy card on the floor, at the round-eyed model whose fake boobs are spilling out of her red halter top. I mutter a silent "Thank you" at the image. I'm not sure why.

The cops aren't in front of the hotel door, which doesn't surprise me, because I doubt they would have let the distributor of Chinese hooker cards through. I don't know whether they're waiting out back for me or what, but there's no way I want to get in that car with them again if I can help it. So I go down the long hall, past the back stairway, telling myself, *Just put* one foot in front of the other, until I come to an alcove with an elevator door. I take it down to the ground floor. Walk out to a lobby that's faux-marble floors with a dark wood counter, clocks showing times around the world on the wall behind the counter, along with the current rate of exchange. Two clerks, a man and a woman, hardly more than teenagers, perch on high stools behind the desk, wearing the default navy blue blazers and white shirts. There's a stack of flimsy Styrofoam take-out containers piled on the counter between them, and I can smell the pork and ginger. The girl's giggling about something; the guy suddenly looks up and spots me. Smiles tentatively. He's got to be wondering why I'm there, if he doesn't know already. This is a pretty big hotel, but I'll bet there aren't any other foreigners in it.

"*Ni hao*," I say. I limp on past, not waiting for a response, and push open the Plexiglas doors, heading into the damp cold and the dark.

CHAPTER FOUR

THIS IS SO MESSED up.

I've had almost a year of things being pretty good. Okay, better than pretty good. This last year's been the best year I've had . . . well, in a long time. It's just that even when things are going great, I'm half expecting something to get FUBAR, so it's hard for me to realize that things are great until they aren't again.

I walk down the cracked sidewalk outside the hotel, scanning the street for a taxi. There don't seem to be many here in Bumfuck South Beijing. So I just keep putting one foot in front of the other, following the trail of yellow pavers with the raised vertical ribs. Almost every sidewalk in every Chinese city I've ever been in has these things. Somebody told me they're for the blind. I'm like, Are there really that many blind people in China? But what else would they be for?

"Yili . . ."

"Fuck off, John."

He's pulled alongside me in a silver car, a new Toyota. "Yili, let me give you a ride home."

I shake my head and keep walking. I'm so pissed off I don't trust myself to speak.

"Please," he says. "I need to talk to you."

I halt in my tracks. Throw up my hands. "Okay."

Because I guess I should hear what he has to say. It's probably all bullshit, but I'm better off knowing whatever lie he's going to tell me this time around.

We drive for a while in silence. I stare out the window, at the trucks heaped with vegetables trundling down the road to the big gate.

"They go to Xinfadi Agricultural Products Wholesale Market," he says. "This one market has seventy percent of vegetables for Beijing. Eighty percent of fruit."

"Thanks for sharing."

"Yili, you know I couldn't tell you the truth before."

"What I know is that you *lied* to me. You pretended to be my friend, you pretended to be Lao Zhang's friend. And the whole time you're just some . . . some fucking nark, with your fake tragic-dissident sister and your lies about giving a shit and wanting to change things."

He gives me his squinty-eyed, puzzled look, which I have seen many times, only a few of which when he was actually confused. "Nark?"

"*Spy.* You're a spy. For a bunch of . . . of . . ."

I let my head fall against the seat back. What's the point of even caring? It's not like this is some big surprise.

"It's not so simple," he mumbles.

"Oh, really? You spied on me for the DSD. How fucking complicated is that?"

His hands grip the steering wheel until the knuckles whiten, then relax.

"I don't tell them everything."

You know, I'd like to believe him. I really would. He saved my ass on the road that time—tried to anyway—and got the shit kicked out of him for his trouble. That means something, right?

I wish I knew what.

By now we're approaching the Second Ring Road. Funny, where they took me wasn't as far away as I'd thought. It was just the traffic that made it seem like another city.

"So let's hear it," I finally say. "Your story, whatever you're going to tell me."

He slowly nods.

"They worried about Zhang Jianli and Mati Village. That maybe this place can form the basis of some opposition. Cause some troubles. So, they have people watching them, for a long time. Then, you. They know you spend time with Zhang Jianli. They know about your husband, about the people he works for. They think, maybe the US government helps Zhang Jianli, to do things against China."

"But none of that's true!" I protest. "Lao Zhang's not involved with the American government. And he isn't political."

"Doesn't matter," John says quietly. "He thinks political thoughts, maybe he expresses them in his work, and he brings people together with different kinds of ideas. Maybe this frightens them."

I want to laugh. "Frightens the big bad Party? Really? A bunch of artists doing performance pieces about . . . about stacking up bricks? Walking cabbages on a dog leash?"

"Maybe it's something that they don't understand. And they are nervous." John sighs. "Many things going on right now. The change in party leadership happens next year. They worry, too, about the economic situation. The prices of things, food and houses, the unemployment. The . . . the *laobaixing*, the common people, might get angry."

Food's gone way up the last couple of years, and it doesn't

seem to matter how many houses they build, how many apartment blocks; there are entire empty cities of new houses that no one lives in and hardly anyone can afford to buy.

Yeah, people might get angry.

"Then . . ." And here John's voice drops down a notch. "There are the Jasmine movements."

I'm not surprised to hear him mention them. Ever since people started taking to the streets in the Middle East and overthrowing governments and all, the government here's been a little on edge. China's not Egypt, everyone says, but they're still nervous about it. Especially since someone or a bunch of someones started tweeting and posting, "We want food, we want jobs, we want houses!" And called for people to protest by "taking a stroll" on Sunday afternoons around places like the McDonald's at Wangfujing. Don't carry signs, don't chant slogans, just smile and "take a stroll." And maybe buy a burger.

So the last couple of Sundays, the police have been out en masse, trying to shut down a protest, and then not knowing if one is actually happening, with a bunch of journalists and cameras documenting the whole thing. It's kind of funny in a way: The government freaking out about protests that might not be protests. Chasing ghosts.

A little like performance art, when I think about it.

I feel a shiver, all the way down to my bones.

"Okay, the government's nervous. So you spied on Lao Zhang, and you spied on me. What did you tell your bosses? That we're plotting to overthrow the party? That I'm some kind of spy?"

"No," John says quietly. "I tell them you just wanted to help your friend. That's all."

By this point we've reached the little alley where my

apartment complex is. Of course John doesn't need to ask directions.

"What happens now?" I ask.

"Maybe nothing."

We turn into the *hutong*. Get about halfway to my place and have to stop because a guy with a bicycle cart full of bricks and scrap blocks the road. John hits the horn, a flash of the anger he usually hides coming to the surface.

"Nothing?"

"Maybe they believe you. And me."

"If they don't?"

"Maybe they want to talk to you again."

"Great."

The bicycle cart still hasn't moved, its driver leaning against it, talking to another worker who's loading a couple more bricks on the bed. John lays on the horn, rolls down the window. *"Ni xia ya?"* he yells. Are you blind?

"Cao ni ma de bi," the cart driver says. In other words, "Your mama." He doesn't move.

"Look, you can drop me here," I say, my hand already on the door handle.

"I think I should come up to your apartment. Just to . . . to check things."

"Why? So you can tap my phone or something?"

John punches the horn again. *"Sha bi,"* he mutters. *Dumb fuck.* Turns to me, eyes hard, jaw tight. "Yili, they look at a lot of people right now. Maybe they decide you aren't so important. But if someone watches you for them, you should hope that it's me."

I hesitate.

And think, What difference does it make? If John's going to do something, plant a bug or something like that, he'll do it anyway.

The guy hops on the bike, practically stands on the pedals to get it moving, pulls out of the way.

"Okay. Fine."

We roll up to the gate, where the security guard sits in the box reading a paper and drinking tea and waves us through without a glance.

John parks the car. He hesitates, letting the motor idle, his hand on the key. "Yili," he says, "they maybe don't even trust *me*. That's why . . . it's good how you answered them today. Because this is what I tell them also."

And I'm supposed to believe this?

I don't know if he's playing a game or, if he is, what level we're on.

I BARELY GET MY key in the door before my mom opens it. I see the strain in her face turn to relief in an instant, and she reaches out and gathers me into her arms. "Oh, honey, I was so worried. What happened?"

"Nothing," I say. "It wasn't a big deal."

I don't want to be hugged. Don't want to feel how upset she is. I don't want to feel anything right now.

She glances up, peers over my shoulder. "Oh, who's this?"

"John," I say, stepping out of her embrace. "John, this is Cindy. My mom."

"You are Yili's mother?"

I swear to God, he blushes, like this is high school and we've been on a date and are maybe getting back a little after curfew. "Very pleased to meet you."

He takes a hesitant step across the threshold.

"Well, pleased to meet you, too, John." My mom may be a flake when it comes to the Jesus stuff and the men in her life, but she's not stupid, and the way she's standing, shoulders tilted back, arms crossed, she's suspicious. "How do you two know each other?"

"We met last year, at a party." He ducks his head, convincingly embarrassed, and if I didn't know better, I'd swear he was this nice, awkward guy wanting to make a good impression on his date's mother. "We have traveled a little together."

"Oh, how nice." She gives him a long, appraising look. "I don't think Ellie's told me about you."

"Kind of a crazy time," I mutter.

"Would you like some tea, John?" my mom asks.

I snort. "He likes jasmine," I say. "Excuse me."

I go into the bathroom. Splash some cold water on my face. Sit on the toilet, my head in my hands. My gut's killing me, and my leg hurts like hell, and I wonder if I take a Percocet, is that going to make me puke?

I decide I don't care.

I check my phone. There's a text waiting for me that I missed somehow, probably while I was drinking tea.

RETURNING TO BEIJING TOMORROW, it says. IF YOU CAN MEET, LET ME KNOW.

TOMORROW IS FINE, I text back. THE TEA WAS INTERESTING.

WHEN I COME OUT of the bathroom, John and my mom are sitting at the little table in my living room sipping tea. My mom's smiling and stretching out her hand across the table, like she's going to pat his. John sits in the chair, torso straight, his hands resting parallel to each other on either side of his teacup.

"It was nice of you to bring her home all this way, John."

"Oh, it wasn't so far," John says, smiling and nodding.

"I didn't know that Yili was your Chinese name," she says to me.

"Guess it hasn't come up."

Shit, I think. Are the three of us really going to sit here and drink tea? John, my mom, and me?

Fuck the tea. I need a beer.

I grab a cold Yanjing from the fridge, open it, and sit at the table.

"Honey," my mom says, "you've barely had a thing to eat today." She turns to John. "I was going to make tacos. That's Mexican food."

"Ah. I will let you have your dinner, then." With that he rises. "Yili, may I call you this week? We can . . . go eat dumplings, if you would like."

How am I supposed to answer this?

"Sure . . . if I'm in town," I finally say. "I was thinking about taking a little trip. You know, a vacation. To someplace warm."

John's eyes narrow. "I see," he says. "Yes. Leaving Beijing this time of year can be a good idea. But call me. Maybe I can make some suggestions."

AFTER HE LEAVES, MY mom starts working on the tacos. "Are you really taking a vacation?" she asks as she rubs spices onto the beef.

"I dunno," I mumble. "Probably not. It was just something to say."

"Don't you like him?"

"He's okay. It's complicated."

She gives me a look. "Is he married?"

"No. He had a fiancée, but they broke up."

This, I'm pretty sure, is actually true.

"So how *did* the two of you meet?"

"At a party, like he said."

"Huh." She grabs the big knife and starts chopping, the blade hitting the cutting board with a thunk only slightly muffled by its passing through the meat. "He told me that the whole thing with the police was a misunderstanding."

I don't want to lie to my mom. I'm also not sure if I want to play this game with John, the one where I'm supposed to trust him.

But the last thing I want is my mom freaking out about shit— this tends to make my own freak-outs worse.

"Yeah, it looks that way."

"Well, he seems like a nice young man." *Whack*. A little smile. "And really cute."

My mom likes Creepy John.

Meaning I should stay far, far away from him.

CHAPTER FIVE

"THIS COULD GET COMPLICATED."

I sit across from Harrison Wang, distracted by his sweater. It's this dense charcoal grey, has to be cashmere, and I just want to stroke it.

The sweater, like Harrison, is way out of my price range.

"You think?" I say.

Harrison is a good-looking man. The way that something perfectly constructed out of the best-quality materials is good-looking. You know, like a Ferrari. I've never seen him with a woman—or a man, for that matter—but I'm pretty sure anyone on his arm would be the same kind of expensive: a supermodel built like a gazelle or some genius artist with tragic cheekbones.

We're meeting for dinner at a French-Vietnamese "bistro" in a restored courtyard building not too far from where I live—Harrison's call ("The *bo nhung dam* is particularly good"). Though I'm more comfortable eating jiaozi in some dive dumpling house, I have to admit I'm liking this gourmet lifestyle way more than I should, considering that I don't understand it and I can't really afford it. This place is classy, with worn grey stone floors, antique furniture, and hand-woven tapestries on the walls, smoked paper lamps with yellow light hung on the thick ceiling beams.

And Harrison's right, the *bo nhung dam* is delicious.

As long as he's paying, I guess.

"I'm assuming Zhang Jianli isn't in China," Harrison says. He gives me a look, like he thinks I might know, and he's searching for a hint on my face.

Here's the situation: My friend Lao Zhang, got involved with someone he shouldn't have and disappeared about a year ago. I got chased all over China because of it, and some bad shit happened. The outcome of all said shit being I ended as the manager of Lao Zhang's art. I know he's okay; we have a means of communicating. But I don't know where he is. I don't want to know. It's better if I don't. That way I can't confess or let something slip to people like Pompadour Bureaucrat and Creepy John.

"How come you think that?" I ask.

"Well, if he's in the country, he's very well hidden." Harrison lifts his hand to call the waitress. "I think the Château de Beaucastel," he tells her.

I shrug. "China's a big country."

He turns to me. His hazel eyes catch the lantern light. "Do you know what the largest expenditure in China's budget for the next five years is?"

"Apartments and Buicks for officials' mistresses?"

Harrison doesn't crack a smile. "Internal security. Ninety-five billion dollars this year alone, more than the budget for the People's Liberation Army. And that's only what was announced. All in the name of 'stability protection.'"

"Huh," I say, wishing the wine would get here. My glass is empty, and this discussion is making me nervous.

"If he were a murderer, even a serial killer, he'd be a provincial problem," Harrison says. "Easy enough to disappear in another province, if one is careful. The local authorities don't generally communicate with one another. But if the DSD decides to make Lao Zhang a priority and he's still in China, odds are very good that they'll find him."

I fidget with my glass. "Well, they haven't found him yet."

The wine arrives. The waitress opens it, gives Harrison a taste. He does the swirl, sip, and nod. She pours. Thank God.

"Perhaps they won't."

Harrison lifts his glass. I raise mine as well. We clink. We don't have to say the toast out loud.

I sip the wine, feel the subtle flavors spread on my tongue and fill my mouth and slide down my throat.

Sometimes I wish Harrison hadn't introduced me to good wine.

"The problem is, they don't necessarily have to label Lao Zhang a subversive," Harrison says. "They can decide to go after him from an economic angle instead."

"It's not like Lao Zhang cares about money," I say, but I'm already getting a bad feeling about this.

"Yes, but they can charge him with an economic crime. It's very easy to do, given the ambiguity of tax laws for artists."

"But I'm the one in control of his work," I say.

Harrison nods. "Which doesn't necessarily protect Lao Zhang. They are not much constrained by what's on paper when they want something."

Which means that even Harrison could have a problem. The way he structured the nonprofit I'm officially in charge of, he's pretty insulated from the business of selling Lao Zhang's art. But it still sits somewhere under the umbrella of his business dealings: the venture-capital fund, the real-estate investment company, the stuff he does that I don't really understand.

One thing I do understand: The person square in the crosshairs would be me.

I gulp my wine. Which even trailer trash such as myself can tell is a sin.

"But we've done everything legally, right?" I ask.

Now Harrison does smile.

I get it—that doesn't matter.

"I think for the time being it would be best if you don't try to sell any more of Jianli's work," he says. "Let's not compound the potential problem."

"Okay," I say. "Okay." I'm thinking, So much for the woman who emailed me about the guy claiming to be a billionaire art collector. That could have been some nice commission money if she isn't full of shit.

I'm running the numbers in my head. I have some money stashed, enough to pay for the apartment for the next month and a half, to keep myself in Yanjing beer and dumplings. I have my craptastic disability pension. I can manage without making any commission, for a while anyway.

"What do you think I should do?" I ask.

"Just try to relax. Go about your routine."

My routine . . . that would be what? Eating shrimp chips and drinking beer?

"I was thinking about getting out of town," I say.

Harrison frowns. "I wouldn't try to leave the country. In context it would look like an admission of guilt. They may let you go, but they might not let you back in."

For some reason this irritates me. "Oh, like if I'm getting picked up by the DSD on a regular basis, I'm gonna *want* to stay here?"

"It's up to you, of course," he says mildly.

What he doesn't say is that I knew the risks when I agreed to take this gig on. But I'm pretty sure he's thinking it.

"I wasn't planning on leaving the country," I say, and I sound like a whiny teenager even to myself. "Just, you know, taking a vacation. In China. There's places to take vacations here, right? Like, with air that isn't trying to kill me?"

"Certainly." Harrison gets a little misty-eyed. "I'm partial to Guizhou. Off the beaten path and really spectacular."

"I was thinking of Yangshuo."

"Oh. Well, tourism there is relatively developed. Which has its pluses and minuses. But yes, it's quite beautiful."

He pours us both more wine. "I don't think taking a trip within China would be a problem. The DSD can always find you, if they want to."

I DECIDE TO WALK home along Fangjia Hutong, one of the surviving alley streets that run east-west from Yonghegong to Andingmen. The scenic route. There are a couple of little bars here, and the Hot Cat Club, kind of a dive, but I like it. I like seeing the old, grey, stone buildings with some funky life in them. It's cold, but I've had enough wine so that I'm not really feeling it, plus my leg's aching, and sometimes walking helps.

I cross Andingmen, a big street, dodge a bus and taxis and private cars, walk a ways until I come to Beiluoguxiang Hutong, make a right onto it, going south. Another old street, grey stone buildings trimmed in rotting wood and random electrical wires. I pass a ramshackle bar with chili-pepper Christmas lights draped around the door, jazz music drifting out from within. A sign in the window says YOUTUBE, TWITTER, FACEBOOK, ENJOY WHAT YOU WANT!

All those sites are banned here, hard-blocked by the Great Firewall. That's China for you.

When the revolution comes, it will be fought over kitten videos.

I head down Gulou Dongdajie, East Drum Tower Avenue, a main street that's mostly rebuilt traditional Beijing grey stone buildings, two stories tops, with scalloped arched roofs, past the Mao Live House (a rock club), a string of guitar and music shops, coffeehouses, "Western" restaurants and *chuanr* stands— full as I am, the spicy mutton skewers roasting over charcoal still smell good.

Then I pass the military complex that always creeps me out: huge granite structures, a giant crane hovering over new construction, with trucks trundling smashed bricks from old *hutong* buildings out the gate where a uniformed soldier stands guard. Sometimes I think it's just going to keep growing, taking over the old neighborhood like some malignant tumor.

When I told Creepy John that I was thinking about a vacation, I didn't really mean it. I just wanted to say something, to throw his bullshit "dinner invitation" back in his face.

But I really do want to get out of Beijing. Even if the DSD can find me wherever I go, at least I won't just be sitting around waiting for another knock on my door.

I don't have to even look for Dog's brother, I tell myself. I could take an actual vacation. Go see some cool scenery or whatever.

I take my favorite shortcut, through the Drum and Bell Tower square. It's a plaza ringed by traditional *siheyuanr*, Beijing courtyard buildings, anchored by the Drum Tower on the south end and the Bell Tower on the north. You come here in the day and there are tour buses crammed into the pavement between the two Ming- or Qing-dynasty landmarks (I forget which) and guys on bicycle rickshaws trying to get you to take a *hutong* tour.

This time of night, it's dark. Quiet, except for faint music from one of the bars or the occasional locals taking their little dog out for a late walk. I have it all to myself, the red-washed

Drum Tower greyed by night to nearly match the grey stone Bell Tower across the way.

I love this place. In spite of everything.

I walk through the plaza and head down the alley that leads to Jiugulou Dajie, Old Drum Tower Street, threading my way through bicycle rickshaws parked there for the night.

Maybe I *will* go to Yangshuo. Ask around at some of the backpacker hangs about Jason so I can tell Dog I gave it a shot, like a good buddy should do. Then spend the rest of my time floating down a river on a bamboo raft, drinking beer, which I gather is what you do in Yangshuo.

There's no reason it has to get complicated.

CHAPTER SIX

Except there's my mom.

It's not like I want her to come with me. Part of the reason I need to get out of Beijing is that she's kind of driving me crazy.

On the other hand, I'm not comfortable leaving her here on her own. She's only got another three weeks on her visa, and she's going to need to make a visa run, and I feel like I should be there to help her with that.

Or not. If she fucks up with the visa, then she'll have to go home, right?

"Is that a good idea? Taking a vacation?"

We sit across from each other at my small table the next morning. I'm sucking down coffee and nibbling on spicy peanuts. She's eating granola. ("Are you sure you wouldn't like some?")

I shrug. "Yeah, I think it's okay. I mean, like John said, the thing with the cops was a mistake."

"Well, I know he *said* that."

She regards me with a level look, and I have to remind myself, even with all her crazy-ass Jesus shit and bad taste in men, she's pretty shrewd.

"I'm just not sure. Is it really safe for you to be traveling around on your own like that?"

"Yeah, it's totally safe," I say. Which is normally true. China's a great place for foreigners to travel, even foreign single women.

It's just that my situation isn't exactly normal.

"I'd feel a lot better if you were traveling with someone," Mom says.

"Why don't you come with me?" I blurt.

Oh, shit. Why did I say that?

Her eyes dart up and meet mine for a moment. Then she fiddles with her spoon and won't exactly look at me.

"Well, I don't know. Do you really want me to?"

No, I think, no fucking way.

"Sure," I say. "It'll be fun."

MAYBE IT'LL BE OKAY, I tell myself. As long as she doesn't get into the Jesus stuff, my mom really is okay to be around.

Except if I am in some kind of trouble, if things turn weird, do I want her involved in it?

It'll be okay, I tell myself. If the DSD wants to talk to me again, fine. They don't want to talk to my mom. I don't think.

But how am I going to go out and look for Dog's brother with my mom hanging around?

She's not going to understand why I want to at least try to help Dog, to make an effort. She doesn't know about any of it. About what I did in the war, about why me and Trey broke up—well, she knows about his Chinese girlfriend, which, when I'm being honest with myself, isn't really why we split, but Lily makes a great excuse and something my mom can get mad about on my behalf, because before that all I ever heard about was how wonderful and awesome Trey was, which made telling her we were getting divorced even harder. Like he was always too good for me, but before, I could pretend that I was better than I was, because I'd somehow managed to end up with him.

Now she thinks he's pretty much an asshole. Believe it or not, that helps.

I'll figure it out. I can slip away while she's doing something else, while she's reading her latest serial-killer thriller.

Hey, I could even tell her the truth.

As used as I am to lying, it's not the first option that comes to mind.

"ANDY SAYS HE CAN help us with the train tickets."

I'm sitting on my bed with my laptop, having just sent off an email to Lucy Wu telling her that I don't think I'm going to make her opening after all. Plus, there's another email from this Vicky Huang person, the one who's supposedly representing the Chinese billionaire art collector.

I shrug. "I can do it. It's not a big deal."

"*Dear Ms. Huang,*" I type. "*At the present time, Zhang Jianli's work is not for sale.*"

"Well, I think he'd like to help."

I look up. My mom stands there in the doorway, hands clasped in front of her belly, blushing slightly.

"The thing is . . . he's never been to Yangshuo either, and he'd like to come. I said no, since this was just supposed to be the two of us, but then I thought maybe it would be good to have a man around, and a Chinese person, just in case."

"We don't need a man *or* a Chinese person to take a simple vacation."

I guess I sound pretty pissed off, but you know, this is so fucking typical of her. Meeting some guy, deciding he's awesome after about two dates, and inviting him along for all the family fun.

Next thing you know, he'll be crashing on my couch.

"Well, he doesn't have to come," she says apologetically.

"Whatever," I snap. "I mean, whatever you want."

TWO DAYS LATER THE three of us are on a train from Beijing to Guilin, the jumping-off point for Yangshuo.

"Honey, I can take the top bunk, you don't have to."

"I like the top bunk," I mutter. Which is half a lie. I like that the top bunk feels more private, but climbing up there with my leg is a pain.

"I like top one," Andy says. "You can be on this more comfortable one." He pats the cushion next to him.

"That's okay. I mean, you guys want to be together, right?"

Okay, that didn't sound very nice the way I said it, but it's true. Andy and Mom have been giving each other the look all afternoon, and even though most Chinese don't go for the big public display of affection, they've been holding hands on and off. And now they're sitting next to each other on the lower berth, and he's leaning over and whispering something in her ear.

What a fucking nightmare.

I think, I'll just drink one big beer tonight so I can sleep, and then I won't have to be climbing up and down to use the toilet. Not too many times anyway.

My mom giggles. Andy pats her hand.

And maybe I'll take a Percocet, too.

IT'S NOT LIKE I care that she has sex. I mean, mothers have sex, right? Not exactly a news flash.

It's just this guy, I tell myself. Mr. Anal Constriction.

And every other guy I ever saw her with. And a few I just heard about along the way. Starting with Bio-Dad, aka Drunk

Daddy #1. Thanks for the genetic material, dude. That's about all I can thank him for.

I'm lying on my bunk thinking about all this instead of sleeping, because the fourth passenger in our compartment, the guy on the upper berth across from me, is a middle-aged businessman from Hubei who snores like some kind of asthmatic seal—that is, when he isn't awake and yakking on his cell phone.

You'd think she'd learn. And you'd think I'd stop being surprised.

Across from me, Mr. Asthmatic Seal has settled into sleep again, snorting like a backfiring car engine, providing a counterpoint to the rattle of the wheels on the tracks.

I pull the heavy quilt up around my ears and close my eyes. I always wonder, why a quilt when they almost always overheat the compartments?

Then, from the bunk below, I hear little pulses of breaths, somewhere between pants and coughs, in rhythm.

Do I want to know?

I peer over the edge of the bunk.

In the dim compartment I can just make out the silhouettes of my mom and Andy, sitting straight-backed on the lower berth across from mine, side by side like dolls on a shelf. Panting in unison.

"Denting navel," my mom stops to whisper.

WE PULL IN TO Guilin just before three in the afternoon some twenty-two and a half hours later, most of which I spend trying to sleep and listening to Chinese lessons on my iPod. Andy wants me to come down and sit with them on the lower berth and . . . I don't know, dent navels or something, but I leave my upper bunk only when I have to use the toilet.

I'm not in a great mood. I slept like shit, my leg and hip ache, and I could use a decent meal—shrimp chips and noodles in a cardboard cup didn't cut it. Andy and Mom, though, they're all chirpy, like they'd spent the night in a Hilton and had a full course of room service.

Guilin is in Guangxi, a province in China's far south, between Guangdong and Yunnan. First time I've been here.

It's warmer than Beijing at least. Grey and damp, almost drizzling, but I'm okay in a jacket and a hat.

The Guilin train station looks like just about every Chinese train station I've been in: a big, swoopy roof topped by the giant gold characters for "Guilin," too much slippery marble pavement, too many touts swarming on us like mosquitoes: "Lady, need taxi? Hotel? Go to Yangshuo? Tour Reed Flute Cave?"

"*Buyao. Yijing youle.*" Sorry, dude. We don't want, we've already got.

Mom tugs on my shoulder. "Honey, why don't we take a cab?"

"Because they cost too much and they'll want to take us to their 'special' hotel. Besides, most cab drivers are crazy."

"Andy says—"

"Forget it!" I snap. "We're taking a bus." A lot of the bus drivers are crazy, too, but my logic is at least buses are bigger, in case we crash.

I'm still in my bad mood as the bus to Yangshuo pulls out of the train station's parking lot. It's a big bus, with decent bucket seats and a dirty video screen up in front, which probably means bad Hong Kong movies played at an earsplitting volume for the next hour. Mom and Andy sit next to each other in the seats in front of me. In the seat next to me, I get my backpack. Fucking typical, I think.

Not that I'd be good company or anything.

A few minutes into the ride, it starts getting harder for me to stay pissed off. Because even though Guilin so far looks like your typical Chinese city—green glass high-rises with cylindrical towers topped by what look like giant versions of cocktail umbrellas, stained concrete apartment blocks, white-tiled storefronts, karaoke parlors, half-constructed complexes wrapped in green plastic netting and bamboo scaffolding— there are these weird hills in the middle of it, hills that rise like giant monoliths or misshapen half-formed pottery, and a couple of them remind me of animal silhouettes, almost, and I flash on those sculptures at the Ming Tombs, only furred by green.

Also, the video screen stays blessedly dark and silent.

The farther we get out of town, the more of these hills there are, and even the predictably crazy bus driver's attempts to maneuver around three-wheeled "mosquito" tractors and big blue farm trucks isn't enough to totally distract me from the landscape. It's sort of like the moon, if the moon really were made out of green cheese.

Finally we pull around a broad curve flanked by a massive granite-faced hill, into a town. The first streets are lined with low, white buildings. Lots of cruiser-style bikes ridden by Chinese and Western tourists—you can tell they're tourists by their ambling pace, their relaxed smiles. Farther along I catch glimpses of traditional architecture, probably reproductions, more hills, a small lake fed by canals. There's a hotel in front of the lake, a low green building with a giant TV screen a couple stories high that's playing videos of more of these crazy mountains lit up by lasers and fireworks. Why, I want to know? Aren't the real mountains cool enough?

This is Yangshuo.

Our bus pulls in to a narrow, steep driveway, down to the

parking lot of the Yangshuo bus station, a couple stories of dirty white concrete slabs and a crowd of idling minibuses. Across the top of the building, above a stall selling snacks, there's a red banner in Chinese with an English translation underneath. The English says YANGSHUO TO SHENZHEN MANHOLE TICKETS, YOU CAN ENJOY FREE OF CHARGE IN THE MANHOLE GO TO HONGKONG.

I almost ask Andy what the Chinese actually says, since I still suck at reading characters, but I turn and he's all busy helping my mom with her oversize wheeled suitcase.

Fuck it.

THE HOTEL WE'RE STAYING at is close to the lake, not far from the McDonald's and a place advertising "corn juice." It's cheap enough and it's clean enough, and that's all I really care about. My mom and I are supposed to be sharing a room while Andy has his own, but I wonder how long *that's* going to last.

"What do you feel like doing first, hon?" my mom asks as she unpacks her suitcase. "It's probably too late to rent bikes today, but Andy says the ride over to Moon Mountain is supposed to be really pretty."

"Just taking a walk," I mumble. "Why don't you unpack and do whatever, and I'll meet you guys back here and we'll go to dinner?"

"I wouldn't mind a walk if you want some company."

"Look, I just need a little . . ." I take a deep breath and start over. "Thanks, but I'm feeling a little stressed. It helps me to . . . you know, just think about stuff on my own."

She frowns. "Well, okay, hon. Whatever you need to do."

When in doubt, play the PTSD card, which is what "stressed" is code for. Works with my mom every time.

I am such a shit.

I walk along the lake and the canal and then down to the Li

River, its broad expanse swaddled by fog. It's getting dark, but I can still see the silhouettes of the lunar hills—one that looks like a wizard's hat, another that resembles the big toe of some buried giant poking up through the earth.

It's not totally a lie. I'm better, I know I am, but every time I start to feel okay, something happens, sometimes just some stupid little thing, like some asshole in a bar staring at my rack or a sour smell in a latrine, and it smacks me in the gut, and I'm right back where I was.

Below me an old man wearing a padded peasant jacket and a round straw hat rests a long pole across his shoulders with two fishing birds—cormorants, I think they're called—perched at either end. He's not fishing, he's posing for photos. I see the flash of cameras as a European couple shoots off a few. Probably his last customers of the day. It's almost dark.

I find a coffee place that advertises free Wi-Fi.

I NEED TO GET a hold of Lao Zhang, let him know what's going on. I should have done it before, back in Beijing, but I didn't feel comfortable even using my VPN once I knew the DSD was watching. Stupid, probably. Like Harrison said, they can find me wherever I go. But I feel safer somehow, getting out of town. Being someplace different.

And a random Internet connection with a virtual private network has got to be safer than trying it from my apartment.

I get out my battered laptop. Power it up. Connect to the VPN.

It takes me a few times to get a connection. The government's really ramped up the Great Firewall since all this Jasmine shit started.

Finally I'm in. Over the Wall.

I log on to the Great Community.

It's the same welcome screen as always: the beach, the ocean, rendered in a texture that looks like brush strokes. A three-legged dog splashing in the surf. A giant Mao statue, bleached and faded, half buried in the sand like some sort of Sphinx, seagulls nesting in his outstretched hand. Farther up the beach, the Twin Towers, leaning against each other for support.

He started it as an art project, he told me. And a safe place, for him to work, for me to visit. Like we used to have for real.

It's changed a lot since the first time I saw it. There are others here now, other avatars. Maybe a hundred people. Artists, mostly. Writers. Musicians. Where before there was only a dumpling restaurant and a house, now there is a little village, with a nightclub, a gallery, more houses, crazy constructions that don't fit neatly into any kind of category: windmills cobbled to nuclear plants, castles that morph into trees and mushrooms, crazy-ass shit that doesn't make any sense to me. But then a lot of the art stuff never did.

Some of the avatars I recognize. I've seen them before. I think they might be people I know in real life, but I'm not sure. I don't ask.

They make their art projects, throw parties, have concerts, lectures. Some of it's in Chinese. Some in English. They talk about democracy, and socialism, and deep ecology. Feminism and patriarchy. Sexuality. Death. You can talk about anything you want. Go into private chat rooms and act out whatever you feel like. It's a safe space here.

I don't know who hosts it. No way the servers are in China. It's gone far beyond what Lao Zhang started; there has to be some money involved to support the whole thing. Harrison, I think, is a likely patron. But if he's involved, he won't admit it to me. Just like I won't admit that I know about it.

I wave to an avatar I know, Sea Horse. She's working on

a sculpture in the middle of the town square. By "working" I mean her avatar stands there, sentinel-like, as objects appear—a fat, rosy-cheeked baby and giant ears of corn at the moment—manipulated by the invisible hand pulling her strings.

I think I might know who Sea Horse really is, someone I used to know in the real world, or what passes for it. But I don't ask. No one does here. This is a place where it's safe not just to be who you are but also to be who you want to be.

A lot of the avatars are pretty elaborate. Sea Horse has a mermaid's tail, a glittering silver helmet. Another avatar has angel's wings, his hair wreathed in fire. I haven't bothered with any of that. I'm wearing jeans and a T-shirt, like always.

It's too hard to pretend to be somebody else.

I make my way to my house.

IT'S A STONE HOUSE, surrounded by a wooden deck, against a backdrop of pines. As I approach it, a big three-legged dog lopes toward me, barks, then halts and wags its tail. An orange cat sleeps on the stoop. I cross the threshold, and it starts to purr.

Home.

I go inside, and the place lights up. I sit on the couch, across from the huge picture window that looks out onto the beach, watch the animated waves swell and crash and send up spouts of foam. Occasionally huge goldfish surface, puffing their cheeks, mouths pursed in perfect O's. Dolphins surf in the waves.

If Lao Zhang is online, he'll know that I'm here.

I wait. Order another cup of coffee—I mean, a real cup. The coffee place is decorated like it's French or English or something—uneven wooden tables, puffy chintz cushions, old coffee grinders, prints of gardens and flowers on the walls. The coffee's good, too. They do designs in the foam of their cappuccinos. The other customers, some hip young Chinese, maybe from Hong Kong or Shanghai, a family from France, sit and drink their coffees and chat and laugh, leaning back in their chairs, enjoying themselves. A couple of the kids play a board game, Pictionary, I think. On vacation. Like I should be.

Outside, the fog has thickened into drizzle. I can see the drops suspended in the halo of light from the streetlamps.

Halfway through my second cup of coffee, Lao Zhang knocks on the door.

Monastery Pig, I guess I should say. That's the name he goes by here.

I used to be Little Mountain Tiger, but I changed it. That was a different game, one I want to leave behind.

Now I'm Alley Rat. I was born in the Year of the Rat, and rats are a good sign in China, they tell me: clever and quick and good at surviving. Rats and cockroaches, right?

Lao Zhang's gone for simple in his avatar, too. He's wearing a beanie, a black T-shirt, and cargo shorts. All his work goes into the pieces he creates for this place. Like my house.

A text box appears over his head. YILI, NI HAO.

NI HAO, I type.

My house is a private chat room. I still don't know what the fuck to say after HI, HOW'S IT GOING?

Lao Zhang sits next to me on the couch. SOME GOOD MUSIC LATER TONIGHT, he says. IN THE WAREHOUSE.

COOL, I type, distracted.

HAVE TO USE PASSWORD, BECAUSE THEY HAVE SOME LIVE STREAM. MAYBE VIDEO.

ISN'T THAT RISKY?

MAYBE A LITTLE. BUT I WANT MORE PEOPLE TO COME HERE. TO SHARE THINGS. THAT'S WHY I BUILD IT.

Time was we had a real place to be. An actual village. With

houses made of brick. People made of flesh. We could sit down and eat real dumplings together and drink beer.

But that place got *chai'd*. Bulldozed under. Now there's a cluster of high-rises called Harmony Village Gardens, where nobody lives. The units bought up by speculators or not bought at all. Subsidized by the government, maybe, by bad loans at state-owned banks. A ghost village.

WE HAVE A PROBLEM, I type.

TELL ME.

I keep it short. About me drinking tea with the DSD. About Harrison's fear that they'll charge us on economic crimes.

And about John, whom Lao Zhang knew by another name, before. Who I sure hope isn't here in the Great Community, under a different name entirely.

After I finish, Lao Zhang is silent. Or rather his avatar sits still on the couch, occasionally blinking, which is a default feature for the avatars here.

THANKS FOR TELLING ME, he finally says.

THE MAIN THING IS, IF YOU NEED MONEY, WE CAN'T SELL YOUR WORK RIGHT NOW.

I DON'T NEED MONEY. I AM WORRIED ABOUT YOU.

I get this nice warm flush. Because, you know, some guy acts like he cares about me.

NOTHING TO WORRY ABOUT. I DON'T THINK.

OKAY. And then silence.

Out in the virtual ocean, Chairman Mao surfs an animated wave, wearing baggy swim trunks patterned with marijuana leaves.

I NEED TO CONSIDER, Lao Zhang types.

CONSIDER?

WHAT I SHOULD DO.

THERE'S NOTHING FOR YOU TO DO, I type. I JUST WANTED TO LET YOU KNOW, THAT'S ALL.

YOU SHOULD BE CAREFUL, he types.

No shit.

I COULD LOG OUT from my house, but I decide to leave through the town square. The sculpture that Sea Horse was working on has taken shape. The rosy-cheeked baby has gotten bigger, nearly as tall as the giant ears of corn. And there are bees now, huge bees that buzz the stalks and corn silk. The baby holds up a basket filled with husked corn, except some of the kernels are bulbous. Misshapen. A single bee lies belly-up on the pile of corn, its legs twitching. Other dead bees surround the base of the corn statue.

SEA HORSE, NI HAO, I type. WHAT'S WITH THE BEES?

Sea Horse stands next to the baby, blinking.

YOU'LL SEE, she says.

CHAPTER SEVEN

"Andy says there's a great show we can go to tonight."

"Oh, yeah?"

Andy nods vigorously. "Yes. With lights. And music. On lake."

"By that fellow, the movie director? The one who did the Olympics ceremony, with all the drummers?"

"Oh, right," I mutter.

So far today we've taken a bus to this ancient village called Xingping, which I have to admit is pretty fucking charming—narrow cobbled streets with colored pennants and lanterns strung across them, chickens wandering around, laundry hanging out on poles. You know, the kind of place that looks like a postcard. Kept that way for tourists, I'm pretty sure. My mom stops and buys a bunch of cloth purses shaped like fish—"Oh, look, how cute! See? There's a smaller fish inside for change!"—while Andy insists on buying lunch, the local specialty, "beer fish," and after that we go to a groovy coffeehouse in an ancient building for coffees and dessert.

Now we're on the river cruise back to Yangshuo, on a flat boat made of white PVC tubes, a canvas canopy supported by a shaky aluminum frame, powered by an outboard motor.

And yeah, it's gorgeous. I can't really take it in, it's so beautiful. All the alien mountains, swaddled in fog. Water buffalo and pebbled beaches. Tropical palms and every manner of green. "Those mountains, you see them?" Andy points. "They are on back of the twenty-yuan bill."

I look to where he points: a mountain range that looks like someone went nuts with a soft-ice-cream dispenser, depositing row upon row of these crazy shapes, the greens and browns muting into blues and greys as the ranks recede.

"You see?" Andy says. He's taken a bill out of his wallet. Holds it up in front of my face. "Twenty-yuan bill."

I think, Get that fucking money out of my face so I can see the actual mountains, Andy, because I can look at a twenty-yuan bill anytime.

"Yeah, I see," I say, and take a slug of my Liquan beer. Breathe in the river's mossy scent and tell myself to calm down.

"So what do you think about the show?" my mom asks.

"Why don't you guys go? I have some work I should do."

She pouts. "Ellie, I thought this was supposed to be a vacation."

And I thought the two of us were supposed to go alone, I want to say. But I don't. Because it's not really a vacation for me anyway.

"Stuff happens," I say with a shrug. "I made a promise to . . . you know, to do a good job."

AFTER MOM AND ANDY leave for the light show, I put on my jacket and knit hat, grab my color copy of Jason's photograph, and set out.

The main tourist drag in Yangshuo is called Xi Jie—West Street. It's filled with bars and discos and coffee places with names like Minnie Mao's and the People's Commune Café, complete with Santa Claus in a PLA uniform. There's a Venice

Hotel, a Stone Rose Bar. The street is narrow, most of the buildings two or three stories, a lot of traditional architecture, whitewashed, red-stained wood shutters. Uneven granite paving stones. No cars. By now it's just past 7:00 P.M. The music is already pounding from the discos, the streets thronged with tourists, vendors calling out to "look, come buy!" and holding up their scarves and hats and carved wooden frogs.

The weird thing is, for a street called West Street, there are way more Chinese tourists than Westerners here. Young people, mostly, wearing broad grins. Couples holding hands, cruising the strip. I guess West Street to these kids means it's something sort of forbidden, a little dangerous.

I hate it already. The crowds, the music, the pulsing strobe lights from the discos, the constant come-ons to buy something or drink something or fuck something.

You made a promise, I tell myself. You have to at least try.

I hesitate, then go into the first coffee place I see, show the girl greeter Jason's photo. "Sorry to bother you. Have you seen this young man? I'm a friend of his family. They are worried about him."

The girl, a tiny thing who looks like she's maybe twelve, wearing a sort of sailor suit with very short shorts over tights, makes a show of studying the photo, scrunches up her face and shakes her head. "Haven't seen him. But wait a moment. I can ask my manager."

She retreats into the coffee house, a wood-lined space that reminds me of the inside of a cigar box.

"No, sorry," she says when she comes back. "My manager doesn't recognize him either."

"Thanks for asking," I say, folding the page and putting it back in my canvas bag.

As I turn to go, she puts her hand on my arm for a moment.

"I hope you find him!" she says. "It's terrible for his family to worry."

I wonder where she's from. Where her family is. What they know about her situation. What her situation even is.

If she's lucky, she's from the area. Has a home to go to. A bed of her own. Or works for an employer who provides a dorm room somewhere close by.

Or she sleeps here, in the coffeehouse, after it closes. Wraps herself in a blanket and sleeps on a straw mat, on the floor, beneath the tables.

"Thanks," I say. "I hope I find him, too."

I stop at every open business along Xi Jie. Show people the photo. Watch them shake their heads. If Jason had been here, he was just another foreigner. One who didn't do anything particularly memorable.

I limp down the street. By now I've got a throbbing headache and my leg feels like it's on fire. Percocet, I think. I'm going to sit down and have a beer and a Percocet.

Not on Xi Jie, though. Some quiet side street. At least there's plenty of those here in Yangshuo.

I'll try one last club and call it a night.

Up ahead is a place called the Last Emperor. Lots of red and gold. The same pounding music as everyplace else, Lady Gaga at the moment. Outside, there's a guy dressed in a costume doing his come-ons, a slouched, shuffling sort of dance combined with waving people in. He's wearing a Qing-dynasty-style beanie, a fake pigtail, and a long embroidered robe over counterfeit Levi's and Nikes.

"Come inside! Ladies' night!" he says to me, in English. He's young, with a cigarette dangling from one corner of his mouth, an attempt at a goatee.

"Maybe. But first can I ask you, this man, have you seen him?"

He stops his shuffle. Takes a look at Jason's photo. "Why you want to know?"

"His family misses him."

He lifts the other corner of his mouth in half a grin. "Really?" He hands me back the sheet. "You can ask over there." He points with his cigarette down the side street that empties into Xi Jie across from us. "Place called Gecko. Lots of foreigners like it."

"Okay," I say. "Thanks."

He takes a puff from his cigarette. Grins from both sides. "Then maybe come back here later. For a drink."

"Maybe," I say, and smile back, because he helped me and he's sort of cute, in a slouchy, borderline-delinquent kind of way.

I'm sure not coming back for a drink, though.

I find Gecko easily enough. It's a narrow place sandwiched between a coffeehouse and a pizza restaurant, advertising imported beer, free Wi-Fi, and rock-climbing expeditions. Well, okay. The front is dark wood, with a hanging sign depicting a bright yellow lizard, which I guess is a gecko.

Inside are wooden tables, potted and hanging plants. Photos of mountains and rock climbers. One wall has a rack of equipment—packs, shoes, clothing, metal spikes, a bunch of coiled ropes. The music is groovy Brazilian jazz. And yeah, a lot of foreigners, most with that rangy, "We like fresh air, nuts, and leafy greens!" look.

The waitstaff is Chinese, though. Typical. You don't have to pay them as much.

I sit at an empty table and order an overpriced Sierra Nevada. They don't even offer Liquan here.

The waitress who brings me my beer is young, short-haired, wearing a long-sleeved Gecko T-shirt and a fleece vest.

"Thanks," I say. "Can I ask you a question?"

She nods, smiling, expecting, I'd bet, that I want to know

about rock climbing, or river rafting, or some other healthy outdoor shit they go for around here.

"This man, have you seen him?" I hold out Jason's photo.

She takes it, curious. Crouches down a little so she can scrutinize it under the table lamp. And something in her expression shifts. I'm sure of it. Her eyes dart sideways, like she's looking over her shoulder.

"*Deng yixia*," she says, springing up. Wait a moment. She leaves the photo on the table.

I have a big swallow of Sierra Nevada, feeling this slow burn of excitement. It's something I'm not used to: the sense that I might actually be getting somewhere.

Maybe I'll find out where he is, I think. Or at least that he's okay. Something I can tell Dog, something to make him feel a little better.

The guy who comes over to my table is tall. Blond. Older than me by a decade at least, but built like a basketball player, tall and muscular. Like the waitress, he's wearing a fleece vest, but his is Patagonia, and his T-shirt doesn't have a logo.

"Can I help you with something?" he asks.

His English is flawless, but there's a hint of an accent there. Maybe German, or Dutch, or Scandinavian.

"I don't know," I say. "I'm looking for this guy."

I flip my hand at the paper on the table, the image cracked where I'd folded it. But you can still see Jason, with his dreamy brown eyes.

The guy makes a show of studying it. "I don't think I know him," he finally says.

"You sure about that?"

"Well, no." He smiles at me. He's got a thin face with prominent cheekbones and a high-bridged, long nose, like one of those knight statues you see laid out on top of a medieval tomb. "We have a lot of foreigners who come through here."

"Yeah, so I heard."

"So why are you looking for this one?" he asks, in a deliberately casual way.

"I'm friends with his family. His brother, Dog . . . uh, Doug. They don't know where he is, and they're worried about him."

"I see." He pretends to study the photograph a moment longer. Then pushes it toward me with his long, knotted fingers. Wrapped with scars, from all those ropes they use for rock climbing, maybe.

"Sorry. Don't think I recognize him."

He's lying, I'm sure of it.

"Look," I say, frustrated, "all we want is to know that Jason's okay."

"Jason?" For an instant the guy's brow furrows. Then he composes himself. "Wish I could help."

You fucking liar, I think.

"So what's *your* name?" I ask.

"Erik," he says. "And yours?"

"Ellie. This your place?"

"I'm one of the owners," he says easily. "Will you be in Yangshuo for a while?"

"I'm not sure. Depends on what I find to do around here."

"Well, if you're interested in rock climbing, or white-water rafting, or hiking, just let me know." He smiles. "I'd be happy to set you up."

I WALK OUT OF the Gecko, and I'm so pissed off.

Erik recognized Jason. I'm sure of it. The way he reacted, I'm guessing he knows Jason by another name. But whatever it is, he's not willing to share it with me.

Okay, I tell myself. Calm down. Maybe Erik's a friend of Jason's and he's trying to protect him. Erik doesn't know if I'm really Dog's buddy. He doesn't know anything about me.

I check my watch. It's closing in on midnight. I think, Let's find that quiet bar, have a beer, and then go back to the hotel.

I wander around until I come to a dark side street off the river and a bar called Happy River Crab, where a five-foot-tall plastic crab wearing horn-rimmed glasses and clutching a Chinese flag in one claw greets me by the door. I go inside and order a local Liquan beer. I haven't eaten since lunch, so I order some spicy peanuts as well. Too bad the kitchen's closed for beer fish. I have to admit, Andy had the right idea about the beer fish.

The first beer goes down fast, and I still have some peanuts, so I order a second Liquan and try to figure out what I should do.

Maybe there's some way I can convince Erik that we're on the same side. Get Dog and Natalie on Skype, maybe.

That is, if Erik really is on Jason's side. I mean, how can I know for sure? Maybe something happened. Jason was balling Erik's girlfriend or something. Or there was just some stupid accident and Erik's trying to cover it up.

How can I know?

I take a big swig of beer, and I ask myself, what are my obligations here, really? I mean, I came to Yangshuo. I tried. Trudged up and down Xi Jie asking everybody I saw, ending up with my leg hurting like crazy and my head feeling not much better.

When I leave Happy River Crab, the surrounding streets are quiet, the businesses dark. There's still some action around Xi Jie, I'm sure, but I'm done for the night.

I follow a street along one of the canals.

I'll sleep on it, I tell myself. Maybe go back to the Gecko tomorrow, ask some more questions, see what I can shake loose.

And then I'm done. I've got enough problems in my own life to spend too much more time on somebody else's.

Plus, I still want to go down a river on a real bamboo raft.

I'm thinking about all this and about how I really hope I'm not going to get back to the hotel and find my mom in bed with Andy, except they'd probably go to *his* room, right? And I'm trying to get my bearings, thinking, Okay, I just need to head toward Green Lotus Peak to find my hotel, when I hear the faint flapping of running footsteps behind me, and I start to turn, and someone grabs me around the waist, knocking the wind out of me, yanks me toward him, I feel something, a belt buckle, digging into the small of my back, and he clasps his other hand over my mouth. Tries to anyway. Because I struggle, and his hand shifts, and I bite down on the fleshy part between his thumb and forefinger, deep enough to taste his blood.

"Shit!" he yells, and then I stomp down as hard as I can on the top of his foot. Lucky me, he's wearing sneakers. I'm wearing boots.

"Fuck!" he howls, and then something unintelligible after that, because his grip loosens and I drive the heel of my palm into his groin. He lets go, doubles over, wretching, and I run, as fast as I can, which isn't that fast because of my leg, but fast enough to get away from this fucker.

I run across a bridge, to the other side of the canal, toward the Corn Juice place and the McDonald's that overlooks the lake, stopping finally when I can't catch my breath anymore. I stand there, chest heaving, drenched in sweat, and I start to shake.

"Okay," I tell myself out loud, "Okay."

No one's coming after me. I did it—I got away.

I hope I broke his foot. And that he needs to ice his balls for a week.

Asshole.

I limp toward the hotel, thinking another beer would be nice.

I've changed some since last year. Learned some things. Took a self-defense class, for one. I don't kid myself that I could win against a real pro, but that guy was no pro. I tangled with professionals last year, and I know the difference now.

So what was he?

A foreigner. Maybe British. Young. Not a fighter. A mugger? A would-be rapist?

Maybe so. But what are the odds? I go looking for Jason, I have a weird interaction with that guy Erik, and then *this* happens.

"Way to go, McEnroe," I mutter. "Way to go."

Because, you know, other people, they try to do a simple favor for a friend and it turns out simple. Me, I end up in a fucking clusterfuck.

You think I'd learn.

Back at the hotel, I buy a couple bottles of beer from the cooler in the lobby and hobble up to my room.

My mom is crashed out on the single bed closer to the door, snoring softly. No Andy. Well, that's something.

I tiptoe past her and make my way to the room's tiny balcony.

We have a view of Green Lotus Peak, which is definitely green, but I can't really see the lotus resemblance. It's big anyway. I sit in one of the balcony's cheap plastic chairs. It's chilly and damp, and I turn up the collar of my coat, pull my knit hat over my ears, and pop a beer with the giveaway Yanjing bottle opener I got at a Beijing bar a couple of months ago. Take a long pull and think about what I should do.

Here's another difference between old me and new me: Last year I had to keep going, whether I wanted to or not. I didn't have a lot of options.

This year, you know, I don't *have* to be doing this. Sure, I want to help Dog, but I already gave it my best, and I already have some dude attacking me over it. I think.

I can just pack it in, go back to Beijing, and try to deal with my life. Back to the place where the DSD invites me to drink tea. Where they'll maybe deport me or even throw me in prison, try to get me to betray my friends—an entire fucking arm of the state, with their $95 billion or whatever it is, dedicated to "maintaining security," and me on the wrong side of it.

Where Creepy John is coming home to meet my mother.

Which leads me to another difference.

I used to be scared all the time. I'm still scared, but I'm also really pissed off.

I'm tired of being pushed around. Tired of being scared.

And the guy that attacked me? Not all that scary.

I mean, comparatively.

CHAPTER EIGHT

"ELLIE? HONEY? YOU STILL asleep?"

What do you think? I want to say. Instead I manage, "Huh?"

"Well, it's after nine. Andy thought we could rent bikes and go visit the Big Banyan Tree."

"The what?"

She scrunches her face in a puzzled frown. "It's a famous tree of some sort. I guess it's over a thousand years old. There was a love scene from some big movie filmed there."

"Sounds cool. But I think I'll pass. You guys go ahead."

I grab my pillow and hug it close. I'm feeling seriously sleep-deprived and maybe slightly hung over.

"Ellie, I think we need to talk."

Oh, fuck.

I open my eyes again. There's my mom, still standing by my bed, wearing sweatpants and another Sunrise T-shirt that says PRAY IT FORWARD.

"I know you're upset about Andy," she says.

"I'm really not."

"I don't really blame you." She stands there, twisting her hands together, struggling to smile. "I mean, I haven't always made the best choices when it comes to men."

No shit, Mom.

But that's not what I say. What I say is, "Can we talk about this later? I'm really tired."

"Okay. I was just hoping . . . well, I was hoping this vacation would be a chance for you to get to know Andy a little better. He's . . ." She ducks her head. Her cheeks flush. "Well, I think he's a very special person."

What I want to say is, *Oh, for fuck's sake. You've known this guy how long? A month? More like three weeks? Maybe you should take some time to get to know him better before you come asking me to give a shit.*

What I actually say is, "He seems really nice. Look, I'll catch up with you guys later. Promise. Okay?"

"Okay." She crouches down, gives me a kiss on my forehead. "See you later."

AFTER I GET ANOTHER hour and a half of sleep, after I get up, get dressed, find the nearest coffee place, and have my first cup, I think about what to do next.

I can go back to the Gecko. See if I can corral Erik and get something useful out of him. I'm not sure how I would actually do that. Confront him? Accuse him of setting me up? Would that do any good?

Or I could look for a young British guy with a bad limp and a bloody hand.

It seems so easy when people do this kind of detective stuff on TV, you know?

"*NI HAO.* So is Erik here?"

The same waitress who served me last night smiles— nervously, it seems to me—and shakes her head. "No. Sorry."

There aren't too many customers this time of day. I guess

they're all out rock climbing or what have you. A couple of younger Chinese women checking out a Lonely Planet guide to Tibet; an older Westerner reading a novel and drinking a cup of coffee.

"Do you know what time he's coming in?"

"Sorry, no."

"Gee," I say. "Because he told me I should stop by if I wanted to, you know, go rafting."

"Oh!" She brightens considerably. "Sparrow can help you. I'll fetch her."

SPARROW, NOT SURPRISINGLY, IS tiny. Short, spiky hair, tanned, the beginnings of crow's-feet, with a wiry build that suggests she got that way from doing healthy outdoor activity. A miniature jock. She wears a hoodie that says, in red, CLIMB ON.

"Hi, *ni hao*." She sticks out her hand, American style, though she's as Chinese as they come, pumps mine like she's shaking a cocktail.

"Hi."

"So you want to go rafting? I have space for tomorrow."

"Maybe." I hesitate. "Can we sit and talk about it? I have . . . uh, kind of a leg injury."

We sit at an empty table in the back, next to a bookcase full of travel guides and dog-eared paperbacks. "If your leg is hurt, maybe rafting not a good idea," she says with a frown.

"Yeah. I wasn't sure." I reach into my bag, grab the folded paper with Jason's photo, smooth it out, and push it across the table. "Look, I'm actually trying to find this guy. He's the brother of a friend of mine, and they're worried about him. Do you know him? Have you seen him?"

She stares at the photo. "Looks like David. But David has . . . light hair. No beard."

Score! I mean, hair color can be changed. Beards can be shaved. Easy.

He's calling himself David.

"The colors are a little off in this picture," I say. "You know, it's a photocopy."

"Huh," she says, and the way she says it, I can tell she's drawing back, getting suspicious, wondering why I'm asking her these things.

"Is he around?" I ask.

"Not now. Been gone for a while."

"Do you know where he is?"

She shakes her head. "Maybe camping."

I lean back in my chair and watch Sparrow for a moment. She's staring down at the photo. I don't think I'm going to get anything else from her.

I take a chance. Reach into my bag, get out my card case, and extract a card with my name, my email address, my phone number. I hold it out to her with both hands.

"I just want to tell his family that he's okay," I say. "If you hear anything, if you hear from him, please call me or email me."

She hesitates. Takes the card. Makes a show of studying it, in polite fashion.

"Okay," she says. "I give you mine."

I WALK OUT OF there with Sparrow's card and consider what I've learned. Which is that Jason was in Yangshuo and he's calling himself David. And whatever it is he's up to, it's something worth sending an amateur goon to try to . . . well, I don't know. Scare me? Hurt me? Kill me?

I'm thinking about all this wandering down Xi Jie, trying to ignore the vendors who want to sell me wooden frogs "for give you good luck!" when my phone rings.

I grab it. A number I don't know. My heart starts pounding. Maybe I'm getting somewhere. Maybe it's even Jason.

"*Wei?* Hello?"

"Ellie McEnroe?" A woman's voice. Chinese, I'm pretty sure.

"Yes. Who's this?"

"I am Vicky Huang."

I stand there for a moment, thinking, Who the fuck is Vicky Huang?

"I represent Sidney Cao," she continues.

And who the fuck is Sidney Cao?

"Hi," I say. "How can I help you?"

"I contact you by email. Mr. Cao has interest in buying some Zhang Jianli art pieces."

"Oh, right," I manage. The Chinese billionaire collector. "Look, I'm sorry to disappoint you, but—"

"Mr. Cao is willing to pay top dollar."

"Like I explained in the email, there's nothing for sale right now."

"But how can that be? I hear he has many unsold works."

"It's just . . . um, it's a little complicated."

"No need to be complicated. Mr. Cao has resource to manage all complication."

"Look, I'm on vacation right now. How about we talk when I get back to Beijing?"

"When will you return?"

"I'm not sure."

"When can we schedule this talk?"

"In a couple of days, I promise, " I say through gritted teeth. "It's been nice speaking with you." And I hit the DISCONNECT bar.

Apparently "Vicky Huang" is Chinese for "bulldozer."

"Hey, *lamei*."

I turn. Walking beside me is the doorman from the club last

night, the place called the Last Emperor. He's got his Qing-dynasty robe on, unbuttoned to reveal a T-shirt with a cartoon panda holding a pistol, and he's wearing sunglasses and a Yankees baseball cap. The perpetual cigarette dangles from one corner of his mouth. I don't think it's even lit.

"*Ni hao*," I say, not sure how I feel about his calling me a "spicy sister."

"Thought you said you'd come for a drink last night."

"I wanted to," I lie. "I was too busy."

"Too bad."

I think about it. "I can have a drink now," I say. "But only if you have one with me." And I do my best attempt at a flirtatious smile.

Which, admittedly, sucks.

He grins and says, "Sure."

Well, he did call me a hot number.

It's not dangerous, I tell myself. I'm just going to have a drink with the guy. He gave me a good tip last night, about the Gecko, and I'm wondering if he knows more about it than he said.

We'll sit down, have a drink, and it'll be fine.

"COME ON, A BEER?" He raises his hands, seemingly incredulous. "We make best mixed drinks in Yangshuo. Martini. Cosmopolitan. Long Island Iced Tea. Name your favorite. I make it for you."

We sit just inside the doorway of the Last Emperor. I wish we could sit outside, but it's still a little chilly for that, the leaden sky threatening rain. The decor is kind of what you'd expect: red and gold, a couple of giant hangings of some famous Qing emperor, a huge paper dragon suspended from the ceiling, Plexiglas panels bordering a dance floor that at the moment is dark. A few dead-eyed customers sit around the borders, sipping drinks.

"Well, see, it's the middle of the day. I have to meet my mother later."

His expression suddenly shifts. He almost looks embarrassed. "Ah," he says. "Okay. A beer. You like Budweiser?"

"Not so much. Do you have Liquan?"

"Sure. Okay."

I watch him walk behind the bar and pour the beer. He returns with two full mugs of lager. I hope it's not drugged. He deposits them on the table and sits.

"Cheers," I say, lifting mine.

"Cheers."

Tastes like beer to me.

"What's your name?" he asks.

"Yili. You?"

"You can call me Kobe."

I almost laugh. "Kobe? Like the basketball player?"

"Sure, why not?" He grins. "I aim high."

"Okay, Kobe." I have to admit the guy cracks me up. "Last night I showed you a photo."

Kobe leans back in his chair, adjusts his ball cap, lights his cigarette. "Smoke?" he asks.

"No thanks."

"Smart. They say it's bad for your health."

I can't tell if he's kidding or not. A lot of Chinese people don't know that smoking is bad for you. Maybe because the same government agency that's trying to get people to quit also owns all the tobacco companies.

"Yeah," I say. "Yeah, it is. Maybe you should quit."

"Maybe so." He shrugs. "Then I can eat the baozi made with cardboard, the *youtiao* fried in sewer oil, and the pork that glows in the dark. And feed my kids the milk powder with that chemical in it that makes them sick and die."

He's just rattled off a string of food scandals that have happened in China over the last couple years. He left out a bunch. It seems like there's a new one every day. Like the chicken fed with minerals so they weigh more. The tofu laced with detergent to make it sticky. The fake eggs. Yeah, fake eggs. Don't ask.

"You have kids?" I think to say.

"No. Just preparing for the future." He grins again.

"So the picture I showed you last night. You know that guy, right? David?"

"Maybe I see him around." He takes a deep swallow of beer. "Why you want to know?"

"Like I said, I'm friends with his family. His brother."

"You must be good friends."

"Yeah. I guess we are."

I get the feeling he isn't buying this, which is kind of ironic, given that I'm actually telling the truth.

I pull out my iPhone. Open up the photos. "This is his brother, Doug, and Doug's wife, Natalie. Their kids." I stroke the screen, going from photo to photo. "There's the whole family at Christmas. See, that's . . . uh, David. Those are his parents."

I go through the photos. I come to the one of me and Dog at the FOB, both of us wearing T-shirts and shorts because it was so hot out, him pretending to make a grab at my tit, me laughing and threatening him with a can of Coke. I remember it had been kind of a shitty day up to that point; I'd had to go outside the wire on a run guarding cheesecake for a KBR truck convoy, and it wasn't like anything really bad had happened that time, but it was always like something bad *could* happen next time.

"Yeah, that's us," I say, and I don't want to stay too long on that picture.

"What happen to him?" Kobe flicks a finger at a photo of Dog after he got blown up.

"Accident. That's why they asked me to help. Because it's a little hard for Doug to travel."

Kobe draws on his cigarette. Coughs. "Maybe they *are* bad for me." Stubs it out.

"They just want to know he's okay," I say. "They're worried about him."

Kobe slowly nods. "I don't know where he is," he says. "I haven't seen him for a while. Two months, maybe."

"Why did you tell me to ask at the Gecko?"

"He likes to go there sometimes."

"Any particular reason?"

A longer hesitation. "You know, some of those people who go there, who work there, they're crazy. About the natural environment. They want to . . . to save the pandas." He tugs on his T-shirt, at the pistol-packing panda.

"And you don't?"

"I like pandas that save themselves. That fight back." He grins.

So Jason's a tree hugger? Not Dog's thing, so far as I know, but thinking about the photo of Jason—the coffeehouse soul patch, the dreamy expression—I guess I can see it.

"Is there anyone else you can think of who might know where he is?" I ask.

Kobe takes a long, slow pull on his beer. "Maybe," he finally says.

"Go to this place," he tells me, writing down the name on a napkin. "I think he work out there for a little while."

"Great. Anybody I should talk to in particular?"

A shrug. "Alice, maybe. Maybe Russell."

"And should I tell them you sent me?"

A rapid shake of the head. "No. No, better you don't say."

"Okay."

He fiddles with an unlit cigarette, flipping it across the back of his hand, from one finger to the next. "Just promise me, if you find Daisy, you have to tell me."

"Daisy?"

"A girl," he mumbles.

"Well, yeah, I figured." And it occurs to me: "Your girlfriend?"

"A friend."

Right.

"If I find her . . . what? Do you think something happened to her?"

Because as much as I want to do this favor for Dog, I'm not about to put me, my mom, and even Anal Andy in a situation where there might be people getting killed over it.

Yeah, there was the guy who attacked me, but I don't think he was serious.

"No. Not that." Kobe stares at the table, and I can tell it's killing him to admit this. He'd lost face, but it's more basic than that. "I think she left with him. With David. I call her cell, she doesn't answer. I CQ, just get a text not to bother her."

"Sorry," I say, because I know what it's like to get dumped.

"She thinks he take her to America!" he bursts out. "That's all she cares about, wanting to leave China and go to America. More opportunity there, she says. I say they have economic crisis, why you think more opportunity? I can have more freedom there, she tells me. Freedom for what? To do what? She doesn't even know. It's just a word."

He slumps over his beer. "She thinks she can be a Wendi in the US, that's all."

Sleep her way to the top, in other words.

"Look," I finally say, "if I find her, I'll do what I can. I'll tell her you want to talk to her. But if she's not coming back, she's not coming back. Trust me. It's better to let go."

Yeah, look at me being all "If you love something, set it free!" I'd still rather hunt it down and kill it, you know? But I'm trying.

CHAPTER NINE

So it is that Mom, Andy, and me end up the next day at the Yangshuo Ancient Village Artist Retreat Inn.

I pitched it to them like this: "How would you guys feel about moving to a place that's more out in the country? It's, like, this converted farmhouse. In the middle of some rice paddies and . . . stuff."

"Like where we were today?" my mom asked Andy. "With that big banyan tree?"

Andy seemed to consider. Then he nodded slowly. "The countryside is much more peaceful."

A Yangshuo taxi takes us there, after the driver has sworn that he knows the place and still gets lost a few times, bumping over axle-busting dirt roads where the ruts are almost as jagged as the crazy mountains surrounding us. We go through what definitely looks like an old village: blond and grey bricks, tiled roofs in various stages of collapse, a few open-air stalls selling bottled drinks and snacks, a "farmers' restaurant" advertising beer fish, a ragged basketball hoop where a couple of would-be Yao Mings practice their jump shots. For a while we get stuck behind a farm tractor called a "mosquito" whose engine sounds like a banging hammer on a sheet of tin, until at last it turns off into a rice-paddy path and we continue on.

"*Women daole!*" the cabbie says proudly. We've arrived.

If this is the Ancient Village, I figure we're in the suburbs. There's a tumbledown clump of houses, scattered clotheslines, a woman leading some kind of cow—or an ox, or a water buffalo, like I know the difference—and a baby one of the same variety down the rutted path, copper bells around their necks. Beyond that, rice paddies, surrounded by magician's-hat mountains.

Our cab pulls in to a gravel drive, leading to a complex that might have been a rich peasant's farm once. Maybe even a landlord's.

Several buildings look like they've been restored: a central hall with a Qing-dynasty roof that has the swooping angles of a fishhook, flanked by plain lower wings. Mountain bikes lean up against a railing and a big tree in a courtyard out front. A half dozen Westerners wearing yoga pants hold wooden staffs and do some mutant tai chi routine there. Another group cluster around a potter's wheel. Several more sit at a rustic wooden table with ink brushes, watching a Chinese dude with chin whiskers and long straight hair demonstrate how to draw bamboo. I swear I spot some tie-dye.

"Oh, how cute!" my mom says.

I'm ready to slit my wrists, and we haven't even checked in yet.

"Welcome to Yangshuo Ancient Village Artist Retreat Inn."

The person behind the minimal counter is a young Chinese woman—I'd say girl, but she's probably older than she looks. Her name is Heather, according to her name tag, and when I go up to check my mom and me in, she's texting someone on her cell.

"If you want to rent bicycles, go on Yulong River for rafting, take painting class, study Chinese cooking, all other activities, I can arrange for you," she says after handing me back our passports.

"Great. Thanks."

What I really want to do is pull out my photo of Jason and talk to her about it, but I figure I'd better get Mom and Andy settled weaving baskets or whatever before I start playing Nancy Drew.

The wings are mostly two stories high, built of yellow brick, curved charcoal roof tiles, and old wooden doors and windows. We're on the second floor, in two rooms. They're both pretty big, with double beds and, in one, an extra twin.

"Look," I say to my mom, "if you want to share a room with Andy, I mean, that's fine."

My mom blushes a little. "I don't know if we're really at that point yet."

Great. The one time I want her to sleep with some weirdo and she's getting all Purity Ring on me.

So after lunch at the local "farmers' restaurant" (including beer fish, because Andy's on a mission to find the best beer fish in Greater Yangshuo), Mom and Andy decide they want to try the mutant tai chi class. "Wow, great," I say. "You guys go ahead. I'm going to just hang out for a while."

What I do is, I go up to the front desk. Heather sits behind the counter, going over receipts.

"Is Alice around?"

"She comes later today."

"Oh." Thinking, Okay, on to this Russell guy, then.

"I can help you, though. You want to maybe take river raft?"

"Actually, I'm looking for a guy named Russell. He's . . . he's the friend of a friend of mine."

"Hmmm. A foreigner? Maybe British?"

"Sure. Yeah."

"I think he is working on art space today."

"Great! So where is that?"

Turns out the art space, whatever that is, is a couple rice paddies and a mountain over from the Ancient Village Artist Retreat. "Can I walk there?" I ask.

"Sure! Maybe take you a little while."

"How long?"

"Maybe . . . three-quarters hour?"

What I end up doing is renting a mountain bike.

It takes me a while to get the hang of it—I haven't ridden a bike for fun in years. Lately it's all been about PT, strengthening the fucked-up leg, and my one leg is still way weaker than the other, and it doesn't take long for it to start hurting. But I keep riding, on rutted dirt paths that run along rice paddies tucked among the hills, and I can almost forget the pain, part of the time. It's so beautiful out here that it comes over me like a rush—the crazy mountains, the deep blue sky, the air that smells like . . . well, *air*, instead of exhaust and chemicals.

I pedal down the dirt road that winds among the fields, through another tiny village, following the directions the girl gave me. It's cool out but I'm sweating like crazy. The path turns abruptly to the right, through a narrow pass, the mountains rising on either side of me, and it's so quiet, I think, this can't be China. No one out here but me and the wind.

I come out the other side to more fields, pedal a little further, past a cluster of ramshackle farm buildings, and then I see it.

If this isn't the art space, then I don't know bad contemporary art. Or, I've entered some weird parallel-universe China where it's normal to see a huge deconstructed farmhouse surrounded by some crazy Zen garden with giant sculptures made out of crushed soda cans out in the middle of a rice paddy.

The house itself looks like pictures I've seen of traditional wooden buildings in southern China, except it's like the whole thing was taken apart and buffed and polished and put back together again. It's as big as a barn, with a steep shingled roof, a carved door and window frames. There are a few Chinese workers carrying buckets of stones and two-by-fours, a young European woman sitting on the stoop wearing a gauzy scarf and, I swear, a beret, smoking a cigarette. Maybe she's supervising.

I pedal up to the zigzag wooden walkway, which is framed by smooth stones, and get off the bike. And practically fall over, my leg spasms so bad. I lean my bike against a tree and limp up the path. I wish I had a Percocet. Or at least a beer.

The bottom floor of the house is open in the middle. Maybe it was originally a barn. I hear hammering, an electric drill.

"*Ni hao,*" I say to the European woman.

Her eyes drift up in my direction, like it's almost too much effort to raise her head.

"I'm looking for Russell," I say in English.

"Inside." She indicates with a languid wave of her cigarette.

All righty, then.

Inside, it's light and airy and smells like sawdust. The walls and floors are mostly blond wood, with one end framed in painted white wallboard. An exhibition space, I figure. On the other end, one of the Chinese guys is working on a wooden staircase to the second floor. And back in the corner, there's a slight white guy crouched by a workbench, bolting some piece of electronic equipment onto a shelf built into the wall. He straightens up, retrieves an electric drill from the workbench.

Interesting thing about Russell. He's limping. As I hobble closer, I see that he has a bandage wrapped around his right hand.

"Hey, Russell," I say. "Can I talk to you a sec?"

He looks up. He's got sandy brown hair, already receding, a bony face, a prominent Adam's apple. Which bobbles up and down as he gets a look at me.

He doesn't say a word. He drops the drill and bolts, pushes past me and heads for the exit.

I don't say anything either. I take off after him.

Okay, I'm pretty stupid. Here's a guy I'm reasonably sure attacked me, I don't have any weapons, and it's not like I'm some kind of action hero.

On the other hand, he's freaked out enough by me to run, which feels oddly cool.

I get to the double doors, see him fleeing back the way I came. "Hey!" I call out. "Hey, I just want—"

He keeps running.

I head for my bike, passing the European woman, who hasn't moved and doesn't bother to. Just sits there, smoking her cigarette.

"Nice meeting you, too," I mutter. I haul my sore ass up onto the bike seat and start pedaling.

Russell has a pretty good head start on me, and I'm not that fast on a bike. But he has bruised balls and a bad foot, and maybe he's one of those Westerners who come to China and think it's so cool that you can smoke anywhere you feel like it, because he's in crappy shape and it doesn't take long for him to tire. We're on the path going through the pass that leads back to the Ancient Village, and if he had any sense, he'd run off the road, because even with a mountain bike I'm not going to be able to follow him if he hoofs it up the hill. But he's not thinking clearly, I guess, because he just runs on the path like it's a train track and he can't get off it.

When I'm almost on top of him, we pull a hard left out of the pass and into the next patch of rice paddies and farms, and all of a sudden there's this peasant girl wearing a T-shirt that says TOO SEXY! outlined in rhinestones, driving two of those cow/water-buffalo things, a gigantic one and a half-grown version. And the baby one sees the two of us hauling ass in its direction and just loses its shit and charges at us.

"Fuck!" I yell, swerving around it, barely keeping my balance.

Russell isn't so lucky. I think my front wheel clips his heel, but even if it doesn't, he's already windmilling his arms, stumbling forward as though he's going to take off into the air like some awkward fledgling bird.

Instead he does a header off the path, crying out in a shriek of pain as he lands hard in the ditch.

I hop off my bike, letting it fall on the side of the road.

"Oh, sorry!" the girl says, her hand to her mouth. "So sorry!"

"Not your fault," I say in Chinese.

Russell rolls over onto his back, pulls one leg to his chest, moaning.

"Can I help?" the girl asks, whipping out what I'm pretty sure is a *shanzhai* iPhone, a counterfeit.

"*Mei wenti,*" I assure her. "Your *xiaoniu* is running away."

"*Aiya!*" And she hustles down the path, trying to catch up to her calf.

Meanwhile the big cow stands in the middle of the road staring at me with its placid brown eyes.

"Hey," I say to Russell, who still lies flat on his back, pressing his thigh into his chest. "You okay?"

"What the fuck do you care?" he says between clenched teeth.

"Hello? You're the one who attacked *me*. What the fuck's your problem anyway?"

I scoot down into the ditch next to him. He backs up to get away from me, his shoulders pushing into the dirt and gravel. But aside from whatever's going on with his leg, he's holding his left arm against his chest, like he's splinting it, and as I get closer, I see that his wrist has already started to swell.

"Get the fuck away from me!"

"Fine." I shrug. "You wanna lie in the ditch with the cow, go for it. Seriously, does your paranoia go to eleven? If this is because I was asking questions about . . . about David—"

"He said they'd send people," he spits.

"Who's 'they'?"

His face twists. "You think I'm stupid?"

Well, yeah, but I'm not going to say that.

"Look, the only 'they' who sent me is David's family. They're worried about him."

That's when he reaches behind his hip with his good hand. I back away. Especially when I see that he's reached for a knife. It may be a cheap Chinese knockoff of a Ka-Bar that he fumbles out of its sheath, but it looks sharp enough to do some damage.

I lift my hands. "Okay. Whatever." I scramble up to the road. "Because, unlike you, I'm not a crazy psycho, I'll let someone know you're here."

I pedal back to the Ancient Village Artist Retreat.

When I get there, I turn in the bike to the same Chinese guy who kitted it out for me. *"Hao wan?"* he asks with a grin. Good time?

"Hen hao wanr." Yeah, dude, it was really fun. If you have a weird definition of fun.

I limp into the reception area. I seriously need a beer.

Sitting at the desk is a Chinese woman who looks even younger than Heather. Slight and short, with big eyes and straight hair that cups her chin. She looks like a freakin' elf. Or an anime character. She puts an English textbook facedown on the counter as I approach.

"*Ni hao*. Are you Alice?" I ask.

She nods. "Yes, Alice."

"So I was visiting the art space, and this guy, I think his name is Russell? Do you know him?"

"Yes, Russell." The way she says his name, I can't tell what she thinks about him.

"Well, he had an accident on the road back there."

"Accident?"

"Yeah. He . . . ran into a cow. I mean, he's not hurt badly or anything, he just can't walk very well. So I told him I'd let someone know."

"Okay. Okay, thank you. Thank you very much." She manages a polite smile before she picks up a cell phone.

"When you're done, can I talk to you?" I point toward one of the wooden tables they have set up for indoor dining. "I'll just be over there having a beer."

By the time she comes over, I've drunk half my Liquan and am already thinking about the next one. It goes down like water. Delicious, beer-flavored water.

There's a couple of guests sitting at the tables, checking email on their laptops, drinking coffee. I've found a seat in the corner, away from the others, so it's relatively private. No sign of my mom or Andy. I figure they must be done with tai chi by now. Maybe they've moved on to brush painting.

"Hello," Alice says, standing with her hands clasped next to the empty chair. "Thank you for telling me about Russell. I call the art space. They send someone to go and help him."

"Great." I indicate the chair. "Do you have a few minutes?"

She hesitates. Glances back at the reception desk. No one is waiting there. The few guests in the dining area have their drinks and dumplings and pizzas.

Finally she sits.

"So Russell . . ." I say. "Is he, uh . . . I don't know, a little nervous, maybe?"

"Nervous?"

"Well, he acted like he thought I was trying to hurt him or something."

"Oh." Her eyes get anime big. "He is maybe, how do you say . . . just a little strange."

"*You yidianr duoxin?*" I ask. A little paranoid?

She giggles. "Oh, you speak Mandarin. Yes, he maybe *you yidian duoxin*. Very good with building things, though."

"Okay." So maybe Russell is just a nut and I haven't stepped in some big pile of shit. And if Jason is off his meds, who knows what kind of joint delusion they could have cooked up between them?

"I don't know Russell," I say. "But I heard he's a friend of David's. I'm a friend of David's family. He worked here for a while, right?"

She nods, a small, smooth movement, like her neck's been oiled.

"Do you know where he is?"

She tilts her head to the side. A hitch. Shakes it no.

There's something she's not saying, I'm pretty sure.

"Look, like I've told everyone else, I'm a friend of his brother. I can show you pictures. We just want to make sure he's okay."

"I really don't know," she says, and that part I believe.

"What about Daisy?"

"Daisy?"

"Your friend," I say, and I'm starting to get a little pissed off at this innocent-pixie routine. "She's David's girlfriend, right? They left together?"

She tilts her head the other way. Actually puts a finger on her chin. "I think so, maybe."

"Come on," I say. "You know if they left together or not."

"Okay. They left together."

"How long ago?'

"Maybe . . . almost two months?"

"Are they together now?"

"Maybe not."

"Would she know where he is?"

She gives a fractional shrug. "Don't know."

"Do you know where *she* is?"

Alice takes a moment to toy with the Hello Kitty charm dangling from her cell phone.

"I don't know why I should tell you," she finally says.

Well, shit, how am I supposed to answer that? "Because . . . it won't hurt anything? Because David's brother isn't healthy, and knowing that David's okay would make him happy?"

At that point a couple of Westerners come in and take seats close by—a man and a woman, my age, except all healthy and glowing, wearing yoga pants and groovy eco-spiritual T-shirts.

I switch to Mandarin. "I won't cause Daisy a problem."

"It's not so simple," she mutters.

"Okay, so the complicated part, what is it?"

"Who told you about David and Daisy?" she asks abruptly.

Now it's my turn to hesitate. "Some people in Yangshuo."

"Was it Kobe?" she demands in a rush. "Did he talk to you?"

And that's when I put it together.

"You really like Kobe," I say.

She blushes. "We're friends."

"But he thinks Daisy is a better friend."

"Daisy is foolish. She's not the right girl for him."

"And you think *you* are."

She looks up at me, her dark eyes flashing. "We want the same things. To build something, here, in China. We could have our own guesthouse, our own bar, but he is so stupid about Daisy. He can't please her. She wants a car, a house, he can't give her those things. So she runs off with David. And Kobe still wants her back."

I'm thinking, I hate to burst everyone's bubble here, but there's no way David . . . Jason . . . can give her those things either.

"And if she stays away, maybe you have a chance with Kobe," I say.

All this is making me think, after years of obsessing over a guy who didn't want me anymore, that it's a fucking huge relief to be single and not give a shit.

"You say you're her friend, but you don't want her to come back. I think you're not a very good friend."

Now her eyes brim with tears. "Daisy is my friend," she says quietly. "I want her to be happy."

"*Wo mingbai,*" I say. I get it. "But if she wants to come back, she comes back. I talk to her, I don't talk to her, it doesn't matter."

She bats around the Hello Kitty charm some more.

"If you really are her friend, you want the best for her, right?" I ask. Twisting the Hello Kitty, as it were.

She lets out a sigh, and then she tells me.

CHAPTER TEN

THERE'S NO WAY I'M going to be able to sell Mom and Andy on a vacation where I need to go next.

We're having dinner at a rooftop Italian restaurant in a prosperous village in the shadow of Yueliangshan—Moon Mountain—about a half hour by taxi from the Ancient Village Artist Retreat. I'm burned out on beer fish, so I figure why not ravioli and red wine for a change?

This was one of the first villages in the area to start farmers' restaurants and take advantage of the tourist trade. Now a lot of the farmers have made some money, which they show off by adding upper stories to their skinny cement homes, a third and then a fourth or fifth that no one actually lives in.

Andy sips the wine. Wrinkles his forehead.

"Do you like it?" my mom asks him, a little anxiously.

"I . . ." He turns to me. *"Ni zenme shuo, 'wo buxiguan'?"* How do you say . . . ?

"You're not used to it," I tell him.

"Yes. I am not used to it." He takes another sip. "But I think I can learn to like."

He and my mom smile at each other. He lifts his wineglass. My mom blushes and raises hers. They clink.

This all makes what I need to say next so much easier.

"I've got some bad news. I have to leave Yangshuo. For business."

"Oh, no!" my mom exclaims. "Really? Can't it wait?"

"I wish . . . but . . . it's kind of time-sensitive. So . . ."

"Where must you go?" Andy asks.

"Um . . . near Shantou."

"Shantou." Andy frowns. "But that is . . . factory area. Not very much art."

"True," I say. "But there's this . . . emerging artist working there who's doing some really cool stuff. With . . . recycled electronics. And stuff. And . . ."

I really should have thought of a cover story before I started drinking wine.

"If I go there now, I have a chance to represent him. If I wait, someone else might sign him. And I hear that he's really good."

My mom sighs. "I know that you need to take care of your business. But . . ."

"I can try to catch up with you later," I say. "I don't know how much time you have, Andy. Before you have to go back to Beijing."

Andy takes in a deep breath as he appears to consider. "Maybe three days."

"Oh, that's too bad," my mom says.

Truth is, I can't tell whether she's upset or relieved. She *sounds* upset, but maybe she'd just as soon have Andy to herself for a few days, without me in the way.

Well, fine, Mom, I think. Here's your chance. Have a blast with Anal Andy. Go ahead, do what you're gonna do.

She always does.

I push that out of my mind. I have a mission, you know? I've got something to do. I'm going to find Jason because I told Dog

I'd try, and any problems I have when compared to Dog's seem pretty fucking trivial.

Even if he does have a wife who loves him. And kids he adores. I mean, so what if I don't have any of that?

I can walk. I've got two arms and two legs. I can talk without having to fight my own brain to come up with the words. I can work, and I have a good job. I get to represent Lao Zhang's art, which, even though I still don't know that much about art, I know it's good art, and important, and means something.

Except of course that I can't sell it and the DSD is on my ass waiting for me to fuck something up. To lead them to Lao Zhang. To arrest me if they want to prove their point. That they have the power and I'm nothing.

Okay, so let's not think about that right now. Let's think about the mission. Operation Find Jason.

"Honey, you okay?" my mom asks.

"Sure. Fine." I raise my arm to call the waitress. *"Fuwuyuan! Zai lai yi ping hong putaojiu."* I'll have some more wine.

Forget about all this shit until tomorrow. What else can I do?

I WAKE UP THE next morning, and I'm kind of hungover, but I try to pretend like I'm not. Especially when Mom comes in after her early-morning tai chi session with Andy, all rosy-cheeked and serene, and I'm still lying in bed clutching my pillow and wondering if I have the energy to get up and make a cup of Starbucks instant coffee.

"Do you want to get some breakfast?" she asks.

"Yeah. Sure. Maybe."

Mom sits down in the chair by my bed. "I'm just wondering . . . Do you want me to go with you?"

"No!" I blurt, and then realize that probably sounded harsh.

"It's not a nice place, seriously. You should hang out here and have some fun."

"I just don't want you to go running off because Andy came along," she blurts back. "I guess I shouldn't have told him about the trip. I should have said no when he wanted to come. It's not . . . it's not really fair to you. The whole idea was for you and me to spend some time together and have some fun, and it hasn't worked out that way at all, and I feel really bad about that."

Hah. If she only knew. I don't have a fucking clue what I was thinking when I asked her to come along in the first place. I mean, that was a stupid idea, right?

It's totally better if I do this on my own.

"That's not it at all," I say. "I just have to take care of business, and I won't have time to hang out, and this is a way nicer place for you to be. I mean . . . I wish I didn't have to leave."

This is, actually, mostly true. I haven't even gone down a river on a real bamboo raft yet.

My mom sits there, eyes downcast.

"I was just wondering . . ." she says. "Does it bother you that . . . well, I like having sex?"

So totally not what I need to hear when I'm hungover and undercaffeinated.

Or maybe ever.

"I, uh . . . no."

"Because that's what's led me to make some pretty bad choices," she continues earnestly. "I just . . . you know, I really enjoy it. Always have. It's not about needing a man to pay the bills, because God knows the men I chose mostly sucked at that. That always fell on me, and you know I always tried my best, don't you, honey?"

"I . . . yeah . . . you worked hard," I manage.

"I wanted to make a good life for us." Now she's getting

teary. "I really did. And I didn't do a very good job. And I'm really sorry."

I clutch my pillow, because this is seriously freaking me out.

"Andy seems like a nice guy," I finally say. "If you like him . . . you know, that's cool."

She gives me an odd look. Shakes her head. "Well, I'm glad you think he's nice anyway."

Getting on the train to Guangzhou is a major relief.

I PROBABLY SHOULD'VE FLOWN. There's no direct train to where I need to go. The train leaves in the early evening, from Guilin, and I'm facing an eleven-hour ride to Guangzhou and then a transfer after that.

But I'm actually looking forward to the train. I just can put everything on hold. Get my head together. And I'm not in a hurry, right?

I spring for a soft sleeper, so I can climb up and sack on the upper bunk, drink a beer, watch a movie. I don't have to talk to anybody if I don't want to.

But it's kind of tough, because on the one hand I want to relax. On the other, I don't know if I want to spend too much time thinking about all the weird-ass shit my mom's laid on me.

This is why I climb up to my upper bunk with a big bottle of Liquan premium beer and a Percocet.

Just let me sleep for a few hours.

Operation Find Jason. Oh, yeah. It's on.

SO I FALL ASLEEP in my bunk, and I have this dream that's part dream, part memory.

I'm wandering around in this church place, and in my dream it's Sunrise, even though it doesn't look anything like the actual Sunrise. Instead of bland, dentist-office decor inside of fake adobe, it's this bombed-out collection of tents and weird little condos, almost, with shag rugs like in some of the apartments where I lived when I was a kid. There's a service that I'm trying to find, except I keep getting lost in the tents and the condos, and there's all these people just sort of lying around on the floor. I don't know what they're doing, and they just ignore me.

Then Trey, my ex, is there, and we're holding hands, and that part almost seems real—I can feel his hand in mine, the way it used to feel—and I can't believe we've gotten back together, and I'm happy about it. All the stuff that happened, the bad stuff, it didn't happen or it doesn't matter, and as soon as the service is over, we can be together, the way we used to be, and I want to get naked with him so bad that I can already feel his body against mine.

But first we have to go to the service.

Then we're in the auditorium where the services are held, which instead of being an auditorium is a big tent, like the Morale, Welfare and Recreation tent in the Sandbox where I met Trey. Except instead of soldiers, there's all these Chinese people, including some of the artists I know, and Reverend Jim, the head preacher at Sunrise. Reverend Jim looks exactly like he did the last time I saw him, Hawaiian shirt and all. "Are you reporting for duty?" he asks me. "Are you reporting for duty?"

I run away. The only good thing about this dream is that I can run like I used to, before I got blown up. But I run into this dark room, with orange shag carpet, and it's someone's living room, but not anyone I know, and the room gets smaller and smaller, and then there's no place left to run.

JUST TO BE CLEAR: There is no fucking way I want to get back together with Trey. Signing the divorce papers was one of the few smart things I've done in the last . . . I don't know, decade or so. I'm not even sure if what we had was ever love. But there was a time I felt *something*, you know? I wanted him. Then I hated him.

Now? I don't feel much one way or the other. I guess that's an improvement, right?

GUANGZHOU AT 6:00 A.M. The third-largest city in China and the biggest city in the south. The train station is your typical China nightmare, magnified. It's huge, run-down, and there are so many people shuffling and pushing, carrying their ridiculous huge rolling suitcases, boxes tied with string, overstuffed cheap duffels, striped plastic bags. I elbow my way up the platform, up the stairs, trying to find the subway entrance so I can get to the Guangzhou East train station, a babble of Cantonese washing over me in an unintelligible roar.

I've never been to Guangzhou, but the subway part is easy enough. Line 2 to Line 1. Not as crowded as it's going to be in a couple of hours. I exit at the Guangzhou East stop, thinking I have it wired, except I've somehow gotten off at this gigantic underground mall that's at the same subway stop. Popark, it's called. Most of the stores are still closed. It's the usual luxury shit. Gucci. Coach. A fancy Japanese supermarket. A Starbucks.

Which is open. I go inside.

"Hello. What can I get for you?"

I look at the barista, a slight guy with spiky hair, bright eyes, and a big smile.

"A cup of coffee, please. Medium." I don't bother to order in Mandarin. Who knows if this kid even speaks it?

He brings me my coffee. I sip it.

Different city. Different day. Same Starbucks.

It all starts to look the same after a while. The Guangzhou

East Railway Station? Blocky granite. Blue mirrored glass. I could be in any big city in China.

I FIND MY TRAIN. I'm going to a city called Shantou, in Guangdong, on the southeast coast. One of the original special economic zones, but it never caught on like Shenzhen or Xiamen. This, however, is where Daisy has somehow ended up, and with her, I'm hoping, Jason. Alice gave me her cell number and the address of the place she's working. A toy factory. I guess Shantou is known for its toy factories.

I tried texting Daisy in Yangshuo. Said I was a friend of "David." No response. Alice said she was sure Daisy was still in Shantou. Maybe she was busy. Maybe she just doesn't want to have anything to do with a supposed friend of David's.

It's a six-and-a-half-hour ride from Guangzhou to Shantou. I have a soft seat by the window. No point in getting a sleeper, I figure. I shoulder my backpack up onto the luggage rack and sit. Stare out the window at the passing city, the endless glassy towers, high-rise housing complexes, clusters of shorter apartment blocks, cream and redbrick.

Sometimes the black moods come over me like someone dropped a giant load of sand on my head. It hits me hard, drops me to the ground, but it's soft at the same time, molds to my body almost, and I don't know how to shake it off. I'm weighed down, like I'm drowning in it.

Just because you feel this way now, that doesn't mean you're always going to feel this way. The army shrink told me that. "Feelings are transient," he said. I think he was some sort of weird military Buddhist.

"You let yourself feel them, observe what they are, let them go. And you think of a time when you used to feel different."

I try. I don't have to go back too far, just to when I was riding the bike in Yangshuo. That felt good—that is, until I went riding after crazy Russell and he pulled a knife on me.

I go back further. Think about being with Lao Zhang. Lying there curled up against him on his old couch in his studio. Or sitting there watching him paint. That used to feel like home, almost.

But it's not home anymore, and there's no point in thinking about it. His studio is gone, smashed into rubble like all the artists' spaces at Mati Village. He's gone, and I don't know if he's ever coming back. And if he did?

Sometimes I want to pretend like it was some great love, you know? But it wasn't. I don't think I even know how to feel that kind of big emotion. If I ever did, it got blown up, along with everything else.

We were friends, that's all.

I just want to hole up somewhere and get loaded.

Not an option, I tell myself.

I need to call Daisy again. Set up a meeting if I can.

After that I'm going to go to my hotel, watch some stupid TV, and drink beer. Try not to tip over the edge.

My Shantou hotel, the Brilliant Star Inn, is close to the factory where Daisy works, and it also advertises "convenient traffic." Far from the city center of anonymous skyscrapers and broad avenues, out in a suburb of beat-down concrete slabs stained with dark mold. The hotel is a five-story box painted yellow, topped with tinted glass. It has free Internet, and that's the main thing I care about.

I get there a little before 4:00 P.M. No answer from Daisy when I call.

So I do some more research on Daisy's employer, Furong Wanju Zhizaochang, which means something like "rich prosperity toy factory." Of course they're on the Web. Engaged in the manufacture of "model cars, airplanes, model action figures, lucky chicken, the fashion doll, small farmer series toys, main bubble gun toys, and the UFO maze." Their clients supposedly include Mattel and Disney. "We have always persisted in the business philosophy of first-class quality, sincere services, persistent innovation, leading ideas, nonstop progress, effective integration, humanistic harmony, sustainable development. We sincerely hope to become friendly with all walks of life partner, welcome customers at home and abroad to visit, guidance, and seek common development! Let's join hands to create mutual glory!"

Sounds like a sweatshop to me.

"I think Daisy works till six," Alice had told me. And she swore Daisy was still working there, "in the office. I talk to her a few days ago."

Okay, so I'll just go there, station myself near the entrance, and wait for her.

Alice showed me a photo of Daisy, of the two of them grinning behind the reception desk. Daisy is taller than Alice, has longer hair, a knowing smile.

Alice is cute. Daisy is beautiful. At least that's how it looks in the photo.

THE FACTORY IS SURROUNDED by a concrete wall with an entrance gate of green-speckled tile pillars, shiny gold characters spelling out the factory name fixed on a green-speckled tile arch spanning the pillars. Racks of bicycles and mopeds flank it on either side.

I position myself across the street where there's a little market and a tiny restaurant serving "dry noodles" and tea. They have several outdoor tables, with red-and-white umbrellas possibly swiped from a McDonald's that say I'M LOVIN' IT! I sit at one of those. Order some noodles and tea. And wait.

I'm not there too long before a shift lets out. A steady stream of workers, wearing some kind of factory uniform, red-and-yellow polo shirts that remind me of what the Chinese team for the Beijing Olympics wore. They are almost all young women. Shit, they look like fucking teenagers, most of them.

They come across the street, exhausted and giggling. Mob the market, chatting in dialects I don't understand, buying snacks. Water. Phone cards. A few come to the restaurant and order tea. Linger under the shade trees that break up the concrete monotony. Others go up the block, to the beauty salon, to the little storefronts selling spangled T-shirts, hacked DVDs, maybe even to a suspect karaoke dive—whatever they do to pass the time for not a lot of money.

I sit. Sip my tea. Wait.

Before too long a number of the girls in their red-and-yellow polos go back into the factory grounds. To their dormitories, I'm guessing. Or to the dining hall, where they get to eat their rice and boiled chicken feet that come with the job. Or, who knows, maybe to work a second shift.

I really want a beer.

Later, I tell myself. Later. I'll wait a little while longer, and if Daisy doesn't show up, I'll go back to the hotel, drink a couple beers, get some sleep, and check out in the morning. Head back to Beijing.

Or maybe just go someplace else. Like Tibet. Or Inner Mongolia. See some monks. Ride a fucking pony.

I lift my hand to call the waitress. "*Fuwuyuan. Zai lai yihu cha.*" Bring me some more tea.

And I don't even like tea.

Seven o'clock. It's dark. Starting to get, if not exactly chilly, cold enough for me to zip up my hoodie. I'm thinking it's about time to call this. Tell Dog . . . well, you know, I tried.

That's when Daisy exits the factory grounds.

It has to be Daisy. Even in the dim fluorescents marking the gate, she stands out. Taller than average for a southern girl. Long, thick hair. Dressed in inexpensive office clothes—a blouse, skirt, and little sweater—that she wears like a designer outfit.

She stands there for a moment, checking something in her purse—her cell phone maybe—then glances at the street. Is she waiting for someone?

I get up. I've already paid. Pull the hood over my head, my hand shading one eye, fingers spread so I can see between them, and limp across the street, dodging a few cars and electric scooters.

She doesn't notice me. As I get closer, I see that she's texting, the screen casting a blue-white glow on her face. If anything, the photo doesn't do her justice. This girl is gorgeous. No wonder Kobe's obsessed. Poor Alice doesn't stand a chance.

"Daisy?"

She starts. Looks up.

"Alice gave me your number," I say in Mandarin. "I'm—"

"I don't have time to talk to you."

"I don't need much time. Just a few minutes."

I can see the struggle on her face. Talk to me or not? She looks more irritated than anything else.

"Okay," she says, tossing her head. "I can talk for a few minutes."

WE GO UP THE block and turn onto a street that's almost pleasant, tree-lined, narrow, one- to two-story storefronts that are kind of cute in spite of the white tile facings on some and the bland concrete of others. Couples stroll, vendors sell snacks, old women sit on a stoop playing mah-jongg.

There's a little place Daisy likes, one of those Taiwanese

style *boba* houses, all bright plastic and cheerful green-and-yellow graphics, weird manga sprites on skateboards trailed by icy lightning bolts, holding up cups of product, which are iced teas and shakes served with giant straws so you can suck up the tapioca balls that float in them like chewy shotgun pellets. I really don't like *boba*, but whatever. They have the local beer, Zhujiang. Works for me.

"David and I aren't together anymore," she informs me in English, leaning over her *boba*. She sips. I watch the tapioca balls shoot up the straw, like red blood cells pumped through an artery in one of those biology videos we had to watch in school.

"Right," I say. "Well, I'm sorry it didn't work out."

She shrugs. "It doesn't matter to me. He is not a serious person."

"I don't really know David," I say. "I'm friends with his brother. They haven't heard from him in a while, and they're worried about him."

"Humph," she says, sounding like every young heroine in every bad Chinese comedy I've ever seen. "They should not worry. I think he is fine."

"Do you know where he is?"

She shrugs again.

The thing I'm starting to figure out is that sometimes people will just answer your questions, tell you what you need to know. Other times they want to tell you their story first.

So ask for the story.

"Why do you say David isn't serious?"

She sucks up a noisy strawful of *boba* balls, then stares at me over the plastic cup, chewing on the last few pellets.

"We come here because he say he has business," she finally tells me. "He say we do the business and leave. We stay in this . . . in this cheap guesthouse. Noisy. Dirty. Okay, I can put up with this. I know worse places. Then he say he has to go to Guiyu. He don't know when he comes back. He don't know where he wants to go after. I don't want to go to Guiyu."

"Guiyu?"

"Bad place. Dirty place. Nobody wants to go there." She abruptly shoves her empty drink aside. "Okay, I tell him, I wait for you here. I get some work. When you finish, you tell me."

She tucks a lock of her glossy hair behind her ear, like none of this matters.

"He doesn't come back. He doesn't have real business. He just has stupid dreams."

"Sorry," I say, and I'm not sure what to say after that. I want to know what happened to Jason, but that's not the rest of *her* story.

"So you're working at the factory," I say.

She smiles at me. "Yes. They are always looking for girls."

Now she takes a package of cigarettes out of her purse. Marlboros. Offers me one. I haven't smoked in years, but I'm tempted.

"No, thank you." I have to hold the line somewhere.

She taps one out, lights it, inhales.

"It is a silly job," she says. "I sit on a stool all day, painting toys. Silly. Every day, ten hours, on a stool. Sometimes more. It smells bad, from paint and things. My back hurts. My hands. My head. I hate it."

"But you're not doing that now."

She laughs. "No. One of the bosses from the factory, he watches me. Says he can give me a better job. In the office. So I do that now." She takes a long drag on the cigarette. "He gets me an apartment, too. Not so nice. But better than, than . . ." She frowns. "Better than *sushe*, how do you say that?"

"Dormitory."

"Yes. Better than dormitory."

Not quite two months and she's gone from the factory floor to the office.

I don't need to ask what the rest of the deal is.

"Sounds like you're doing okay," I say.

She gives me a look. Draws on her cigarette, holds it between her fingers, palm up, the smoke curling around her face. She looks like a movie star.

"I can do better," she says. "And I will."

I ASK HER IF she has "David's" cell-phone number, and she shakes her head. "Old one won't work. He must have new one."

"Do you know if he's still in Guiyu?"

She looks at me like I'm pretty stupid. "How can I know?"

Fair enough.

"When was the last time you heard from him?"

"Maybe . . . a month ago."

I try to think of a nice way to ask, *So did he dump you or what?*

"Did he say . . . anything about his plans or . . . ?"

"He say a lot of stupid things," she snaps. "He say what he does is important. He say he can't come back right now. It's not safe. He say he loves me but he is no good for me." She laughs again. "Maybe that second thing is true."

Not safe. Great.

"Why isn't it safe?"

"I don't know," she says, playing with her straw, sounding like a sullen kid.

"Look, I just want to help his family. Is there anything you can tell me? Anything at all? Just so I can let them know *something*?"

She sticks her finger on the top of the straw, then lifts it up, watches the liquid drain out. I want to reach across the table and smack her.

Instead I take a deep breath. There's no point in me getting all worked up over Daisy and her bullshit, over Jason/David and whatever he's been up to. I don't have to be doing this. Nobody's forcing me. I'm trying to do a favor for a buddy, and if this is as far as I get, no one's going to accuse me of being a Fobbit slacker.

While I'm thinking all this, Daisy's apparently doing some thinking of her own.

"Okay." She reaches into her purse—a fake Gucci. Gets out a wallet. Opens that and from an interior pocket pulls out a piece of folded paper.

"This," she says. "This is what he give me." She holds on to it for a moment, smoothing the creases, keeping it neat. Then she puts it on the table in front of me, careful to avoid the ring of water left by my beer.

I pick it up. Unfold it.

There are three names, written in pen, in messy, back-slanted print—

"Modern Scientific Seed Company, Dali
Bright Future Seed Company, Guiyang
New Century Seed Company, Guiyu"

—and what I think are the Chinese translations next to them.

"So what is this?" I ask.

She rolls her eyes. "Names of seed companies."

I am so wanting to smack this girl. "Yeah, I see that, but why did David give it to you?"

"Don't know," she says, doing her best to sound indifferent. "Just something he is interested in. You know, he's always talking about these . . . these bad seeds."

Bad seeds?

"He ask me to keep this paper," she continues. "And if the right person comes, to give it to him." She shrugs. "I guess that person is you."

CHAPTER ELEVEN

GUIYU IS ABOUT AN hour and a half's drive from where I'm staying. After I have a late breakfast, I decide to hire a taxi to take me there. There are buses, but I don't know the territory, and from what I can find out on the Web, it looks confusing and complicated. Guiyu is a collection of villages that just sort of grew together, and though I have an address for New Century Seed Company, it doesn't say which village.

"I need to go to this place," I tell the first taxi driver who stops for me, showing him the paper.

He looks at the paper and shakes his head, waves his hand. "Don't know it," he tells me.

I recognize these gestures. He knows, but he doesn't want to have anything to do with it.

"Do you know where this is?" I ask the next taxi driver.

He looks at my paper. "Sure," he finally says, in heavily accented Mandarin. He looks at the paper another moment, and then he looks at me. "Why you want to go there?"

I get why he asks. I did a little research on Guiyu last night, after I met with Daisy.

"Business," I say.

My answer must be good enough. He nods, and we negotiate a price.

Guiyu is pretty notorious. It's the largest e-waste site in the world, apparently—where old computers go to die and get recycled, scavenged for their valuable components. Copper. Microchips and RAM. Workers, mostly poor migrants, dismantle the units by hand, sort the parts into huge plastic bags of the same rough weave you see in flour sacks and peasants' tote bags, burn the circuit boards to extract metal. There's a *60 Minutes* segment on Guiyu, but I couldn't access it, even with my proxy. Just a few articles here and there, from Greenpeace mostly.

So what's a seed company doing in Guiyu?

And why does Jason care about it?

I searched all three of the names, first using the pinyin. I only got one hit, on Modern Scientific Seed Company. They specialize in "maize seed, rice seed, wheat seed, and cotton seed," along with "spraying tomato powder." According to Modern Scientific's Web site, the company is listed on the Shanghai Stock Exchange; was named "one of the top fifty in Chinese seed industry;" and "it was awarded as High-tech Enterprise and it is the enterprise which abide contract and has high credit level awarded by the State Administration for Industry & Commerce."

"We have established and maintained stable and long-term business relationship with many customers at home and abroad on the basis of mutual benefit," the About Us page concludes. "We warmly welcome friends of the same trade from abroad and home to collaborate with us. Let's sow the seed of good wish and harvest the bright future!"

Right.

The other two companies, I could only find hits in Chinese. I don't read Chinese well enough to make much sense of it, but Google Translate helps me figure out they sell seeds. In the case of Bright Future Seed Company, rice wheat, corn, millet. The one I'm going to, New Century Seeds, has the least information of all. Just the same address I already had and a phone number, which I wrote down. When I called it, I got voice mail. I didn't leave a message.

"YOU A REPORTER?" THE taxi driver asks me. Like a lot of the people here in Shantou, he speaks Mandarin with an accent— it's not his first language. As much as the government's tried to make Mandarin the "national language," you still find plenty of Chinese who don't speak it well. But in cities like this, where there are lots of people from other parts of China, businessmen and migrants and factory workers, most people get by.

He's a young guy, short and slight, the most prominent things about him his teeth and his hair, cut in that shaved-sides, long-top style that resembles a mushroom.

"No."

He nods. "I didn't think so. You don't look like reporter."

We drive awhile in silence. He fiddles with his radio, finding a station playing Cantonese pop. I stare out the window. It's pretty at first. We head out on a busy road that runs beside a broad river. A delta, I guess you'd call it. Onto a long bridge over the water, to a highway on the other side. Across a smaller river. Through farmland and trees.

"So . . . an environmentalist?" he asks.

It takes me a minute to figure that one out—the term he uses translates to "environment protector."

"No."

"Really? Almost all Westerners who go to Guiyu are reporters or environmentalists. You just missed film crew from a foreign news show. The bosses threw them out after a few days."

By now we've been on the road over an hour. The air is

getting really bad, a yellow-grey haze, and I can smell it: Burning wire. Melting plastic.

"A lot of pollution," I say.

"Guiyu is famous for its pollution." He grins. "The world's second-most-polluted place."

"Second-most?"

"First is somewhere in Russia." He shrugs. "I don't remember the name."

We've reached Guiyu proper, I guess. Another anonymous Chinese city with chunky buildings, most of them under six stories, made of cinder block, concrete, and white tile. There are tall plastic signs advertising something about electronics, but I can't read the rest of the characters fast enough to get what.

We continue driving, out of the main commercial district. There are bicycle and donkey carts piled high with woven plastic bags, filled with things I can't see.

I unroll the window so I can see better.

This cart has computer casings. Just empty computer casings. Stacks of cracked beige plastic. The next one, the one hauled by a donkey, has monitors piled five high, barely held in place by black plastic ropes.

Along the street are little workshops. I can't really see what goes on in them. But out in front more piles of electronic junk. Here's a random mound of tangled, twisted wire. Farther along, a hill of telephone handsets. Next, a mountain of keyboards.

I can't take it all in.

People cluster on the sidewalks, like in any other Chinese town. Buy their snacks, walk arm in arm, scold their kids, do their business.

"The place you want to go, what's the address again?"

I tell him.

"Ah, okay."

We drive out of this center—whatever it is—down a road lined with fringes: dilapidated storefronts, more piles of junk. Now we've reached a canal, or a stream. The water is black. There's trash floating on the oily sludge. A couple of teenagers hang out on a little arched bridge over it, leaning against the faux-marble rail. We pass weed-choked fields, remains of rice paddies. Smoke from random fires forms low-hanging clouds. The air is so thick with chemicals that my nose and throat feel like I've been snorting chili powder.

None of this is helping my bad mood.

"I think it's up here," the cab driver says.

Another cluster of buildings, more solidly built, like it's the town center in another village. A broad dirt street. There are huge mounds of . . . I don't know, electronic crap, everywhere. Plastic. Cathode tubes. Metal scraps, partly covered by a ripped blue tarp.

"Here," the cabbie says. He points across the street, to a two-story building, grimy white tile with pink accents.

"You're sure?"

He shrugs. "It's the address."

"I'll go ask."

I sling my daypack over my shoulders and get out. The front of the building is open, except there are thick, round iron bars, like a prison, that run from from top to bottom into the surrounding structure. Workers sit in a row facing the street, six of them, four women and two men. I can see their heads and torsos above the low wall that frames the opening. Smoke billows from inside, blown out by a couple of industrial fans embedded in the wall.

As I approach, I can see that they're sitting on squat wooden chairs, cheap bamboo folding ones, like you'd take to the beach. The smoke is coming from little iron barrels. They've got circuit boards on top of them that they're holding in place with tongs, and I have this weird flash of this church camping trip I went on once, when we toasted marshmallows over a fire pit.

The double doors are open, all the better to let the smoke out, I guess. I step over the threshold.

"*Ni hao,*" I say loudly, so they'll hear me over the fans.

A couple of the women look up. One is middle-aged, her face wrinkled and weathered, from sun or—who knows?—maybe exposure to toxic chemicals. She wears a nice striped blouse and tailored slacks, like she's dressing for an office job. The other is young, with a long, thick ponytail held in place by a scrunchie and two sequined barrettes, wearing a fashion hoodie that has KITTEN! stenciled across the chest, and an appliqué of an anime cat holding a ray gun.

"Sorry, I don't want to trouble you," I say in my best polite Mandarin. "But I'm looking for this company. I thought it was this address."

I have the piece of paper that Daisy gave me, and I hold that out in my hand.

Kitten Girl stands up, as does Office Woman. The two of them study the paper.

I glance around. Past the first row of circuit-board campfires are other workstations, if you can call them that, thin wallboard stretched across plastic milk crates, covered by plastic bowls, surrounded by plastic bins, small ones like you'd buy to organize your office supplies, large ones like you'd use to do your laundry. Each one holds different pieces of plastic or metal or wire: transistors, capacitors, relays, microchips.

"This is the address," Kitten Girl says. "But no seeds here." She giggles, like it's a really funny notion.

Office Woman frowns. "*Shi.* But . . . I think sometimes . . ." Then she shakes her head. "*Buqingchu.*" Not clear.

"*Weishenme buqingchu?*" I ask. Why isn't it clear?

"I've seen boxes with that name come here," she says. "I think maybe is a mistake."

"Do you think anyone here might know?"

"Maybe. *Xiao deng,*" she says. Wait a moment.

I hear a honk from outside. The cabdriver has rolled down the passenger window. "Hey!" he calls out.

I hobble over to the cab.

"I need to get back to Shantou," he says.

"*Weishenme?* I thought we had an agreement."

"Sorry," he says. "Family problem. If you want, I can take you back with me."

I hesitate. I'm thinking what are the odds anyone here is going to tell me anything useful? Plus, my chest hurts, my throat hurts, and my head's pounding, just from trying to breathe.

"How hard is it to find a cab back to Shantou?" I ask.

"Not hard. You go to downtown, plenty of cabs there. You can take local bus to downtown. Easy."

I guess I must look pretty pissed off, because then he says, "Okay, when I drive through Guiyu, I send a cab back for you." He catches my look again. "Really! I promise!"

I shrug. "Okay. Whatever." And I pay him.

A waste of time, I'm pretty sure. But I've come all this way. I might as well see it through.

I hang around outside the workshop, upwind of the exhaust fans, though I'm not at all sure that the air is any better out here than it is in there. Thinking, if I wanted to get something to eat, would that be a good idea? Could you trust any food prepared in this place? Probably I'd be better off buying nuts or chips, something packaged. Maybe a beer, as long as it's not local.

It feels like I'm there a long time, but it's probably only ten or fifteen minutes before a man comes out of the workshop. He's short and squat and bald, and I don't like the pig-eyed look he gives me.

He stands there, his fists clenched like stones.

"You looking for New Century Seeds?" he asks.

Is this a trick question?

"I am," I finally say. Thinking, okay, nothing's going to happen to me here, right? On a street, in broad daylight, with a couple people on the sidewalk, going into another workshop, stopping at a snack stand to buy Cokes.

"Not here," he spits out. "Old address. They moved."

I can't place his accent. I'm not that good. Not proper Mandarin, but I don't think he's local either.

"Oh," I say. "Do you know where . . . ?"

"No."

I can't say it's unusual for a business to come and go so quickly. Happens in China all the time. And who knows how old Jason's information was?

"Okay. Thank you."

I start to turn, to walk away, to think about where that bus might be, so I can get back to Shantou. Back to my life. Such as it is.

I stop. It's like I can't help it.

"I'm looking for a foreigner," I say. "An American. His name is David. Have you seen him?"

The guy's piggy eyes narrow to slits. "You his friend?"

My heart pounds hard in my chest. I should have kept my mouth shut, I can tell. I swallow, and my throat's raw and swollen, like there's rocks in it.

"No. I'm his family's friend."

He says nothing. Then he gives a little shrug. "Don't know him. Not here."

I manage a smile. "Thank you," I say again. "Sorry to bother you."

We stare at each other a moment longer. Then I turn and take a few stumbling steps down the street, the muscles between my shoulders clenched, waiting for a blow.

But nothing happens. I keep on walking.

Okay, I think, okay. That was dumb. There's something going on here, and I don't know what it is, but I'm pretty sure that I'm lucky to be getting out of here in one piece. I'll tell Dog what I know, and he can do whatever, report it to the American embassy or hire someone professional. Someone else can figure it out. I've done my duty, I've been a good buddy, no one's gonna argue that. I'm just going to get my fool ass back to Beijing, see what kind of life I've got left, and take it from there.

I've been walking without really looking where I'm going. Now I take a moment to see where I am.

Ahead of me the buildings thin out, looking more derelict, less permanent. I hesitate. I'm trying to remember how we got here, and I can't be sure, but I don't think this is the way back to beautiful downtown Guiyu.

On the other hand, if I go back the way I came, I'll run into Mr. Piggy, and I know I don't want to do that.

So I keep walking. I think I see a sign for a local bus up ahead. Maybe that will take me back where I need to go.

Or maybe another taxi will magically appear to whisk me back to Shantou.

I'll just keep walking, I tell myself. Long enough for Mr. Piggy to think I'm out of his business. Walk to the next town if I have to. This is China, and it's not like I'm walking into wilderness here. There's always another town down the road.

Just keep walking and it'll all be fine.

My leg's throbbing. My mouth's beyond dry. Next snack

stand I come to, I'll buy a Coke or something. And take a Percocet.

But I'm not seeing snack stands. Instead I'm walking out into the country. Into polluted, brackish rice paddies. Pungent smoke rises on either side of me, from burning trash, I guess. There aren't any solid buildings anymore. Now there are shanties with roofs made out of tarp, walls of the same wobbly blue tin fencing that surrounds every construction site in China. The most solid things are the piles of electronic scrap flanking the road, mountains of computer casings, of monitors, of circuit boards.

Mud, and ash, and plastic.

Workers sit on plastic stools in the shanties, burning circuit boards, stripping wire, sorting transistors. A few of them glance up as I pass, some curious, some wary. A motorcycle rumbles by, then a battered truck, its bed loaded high with electronic scrap. No magic taxi.

The sky's the color of lead. I don't know if that means rain or if it's just from the crap in the air.

Fuck, I think. How long am I going to have to walk to get out of this?

Another car, some beater VW or Chinese Chery, hurtles down the road. Unlike the last couple of cars, it pulls off to the shoulder, screeches to a halt.

Three guys clamber out. Two of them have metal rods about a yard long and two inches thick. And they're all heading toward me.

I want to run, but I don't. I can't run that fast. But mainly it's like I'm frozen in place, a scared little rabbit about to be some tiger's lunch.

Flight or fight. I do neither.

"What are you doing here?" one of them shouts, the one without a rod.

"I'm just leaving," I manage.

"This is forbidden area! You're not allowed!"

By now they've closed the gap. They form a semicircle around me. To my back is a wall of junked monitors.

"I didn't know," I say, lifting up my hands. "I just want to find a bus to Shantou."

"Give me your backpack," he says, but before I can even decide what to do, one of the other guys swings his rod and smashes it into my bad leg, right above my knee.

A bolt of white shoots across my eyes, and I crumple. I can't even scream, it hurts so bad. I land against the wall of monitors, throw my hands up to ward off another blow. The first guy shouts something, I can't understand what, and another one of them starts yanking at my backpack, and I lash out with my fists, trying to connect, and he wrenches the backpack off, pulling one of my arms so far back that I think it's come out of its socket, and then I scream because I can't help it, and one of the guys with the rods hits me again, in the ribs this time. I curl into myself because there's nothing I can do, no way to fight back, and I'm just waiting for the next blow.

Instead I hear the zip of my pack being opened.

I open my eyes, and the first guy has my laptop out.

Then something truly weird happens.

"What are you doing?" I hear a man shout—at least I think that's what he says. His accent's so thick I can barely understand him. "You can't do that!"

"Mind your own business! You should get out of here, if you know what's good for you."

"*Cao ni ma de bi!* You think you can just do what you want, treat people like dogs? You think you own the earth and sky?"

This guy, whoever he is, his voice is shaking with rage.

"You think *you* can tell *me* what to do?" says Thug #1, sounding like he's on the verge of laughing.

I can make out Thug #1, standing there with his back to me, his fists clenched, looking like he's going to beat the shit out of this new guy.

Except it's not just one guy. Behind him are others. I can't see them clearly, but there are about a half dozen men and women clustered around him, some hesitant, some furious, ready to take up metal bars of their own and kick some ass.

"*Haode,*" Thug #1 finally says. I see his shoulders bunch in a shrug. "*Chou tu,*" he adds under his breath. Filthy peasant.

Then he takes my laptop and hurls it into the pile.

I slowly sit up as the three of them get in their car, reverse it in a grinding of gears, and head back the way they came.

I try to focus on the crowd that stands a few yards away, in a ragged semicircle of their own. I can't really see their faces. "Thank you," I manage. Several of them shift back and forth, mutter words I can't make out, and suddenly I'm not sure if I'm any better off than I was before.

Then a man steps forward. His arm is still raised, and he's holding something in his hand—a brick.

I scuttle back against the monitors.

"You all right?" he asks. "Are you hurt?"

It's the guy who yelled at the thugs, I'm pretty sure. I think he's in his forties, but it's hard to tell—he's average height, with a shaved head, sharp cheekbones, and the kind of no-nonsense wiry build that comes from a life of hard work.

"*Hai keyi,*" I say. Meaning I could be better, but I could be worse.

I try to stand. Not going to happen. The pain from my bad leg leaves me gasping against the pile of monitors.

The man takes another step toward me, hesitates, then turns his head and yells out something I can't understand. A woman steps forward. "She can help you," the man says to me.

She's about the same age as the guy, angular, blunt-cut hair streaked with grey, deep crow's feet and brow lines etched on her face.

"Give me your hand," she says.

I reach out with my right, or try to, but my shoulder hurts like a motherfucker, and I have to lean there a moment longer and catch my breath until my head clears.

So I give her my left, same side as my fucked-up leg, and somehow get to my feet. The woman has me drape my arm over her shoulder.

"You can walk?"

"I can." I laugh a little. "Maybe." It's more like I can hop.

We take a few steps this way, my good arm over her shoulder, her arm circled around my back, me not able to put much weight on my bad leg. She shouts something that I can't understand to the man.

"*Hao le,*" he says, and trots off.

The woman points toward one of the stalls across the street from the monitor mountain. "You can wait there a little."

Wait for what?

"You need doctor?" she asks.

I nod, because I guess I probably do.

Then I remember my laptop. "*Wo . . . wode xiao diannao.*" My little computer. I can't exactly remember the Chinese for "laptop."

"Where is it?" she asks.

I take a look around me, at the endless piles of electronic scrap, and I laugh.

Another person in the crowd, a kid, scrambles over to the

pile. Roots around in the junk. "This one?" he shouts, holding up a laptop.

Who the fuck knows?

I nod anyway.

CHAPTER TWELVE

Turns out we're waiting for a tractor.

I sit on a little plastic stool beneath a blue tarp, in one of the makeshift workshops where they're dismantling monitors, and I try not to breathe too much. One of the workers brings me a Coke from someplace, which I figure is probably safe to drink. I wonder why they're being so nice to me, but all I say is, *"Ganxie nimen"*—Thank you very much—and use the Coke to wash down a Percocet. I know sometimes I take the things when I'm really stressed out or just because it feels good, but right now I take it because I'm fucking hurting.

What the fuck was all that? I try to think, but it's hard, it's like my thoughts are tangled up in barbed wire, my head throbbing with the pain in my leg.

Something's going on with New Century Seeds. I'm as sure as I can be about that without actually knowing what it is. And it's easy to figure that the guys who attacked me are connected to that. But I can't know for sure. With all the unrest going on, maybe they're just touchy about having foreigners around.

Maybe there's something they don't want me to see. But it doesn't necessarily have to be about New Century Seeds.

While I sit, I try to boot up my laptop. Turns out it really is my laptop, but the casing is cracked, and when I power it up, there's some sad whirring and then nothing but a grey screen.

The kid who retrieved it sidles up to me. He's . . . I don't know, maybe twelve? Skinny like the couple who rescued me. Oversize head. Bucktoothed. Wearing sneakers a size too large, laces flapping.

"Broken?" he asks.

I nod.

"*Pingguo?*" Apple?

"*Shi.*" It's an old MacBook, a white plastic slab that's taken all kinds of abuse and still works. Well, up till now.

"Can I?" the kid asks, reaching out his hand.

Sure. Why not? I hand him the laptop.

He opens it. "Late 2006 one. I can fix," he says solemnly.

"Really." I'm skeptical.

"Really!" He makes a fist and thumps his skinny chest.

Right about then the guy with the brick shows up in a *tuolaji*. It's this crazy farm vehicle, a cross between a truck and a tractor that looks like it's built out of scrap and rubber bands: two-stroke engine mounted in the front, thrusting out over two small wheels, a little truck bed in back, with a long, skinny metal beam connecting them, like it would snap in half if you jumped on it hard, something a kid would build out of Legos. The engine turns the front wheels by what looks like a giant vacuum-cleaner belt. The guy steers it with these long handlebars, his seat a cracked green vinyl cushion.

"*Lai, lai!*" he calls out. Come, come!

"My parents," the kid says, pointing at the woman who helped me and then the guy on the tractor. "I fix the computer for you. Okay?"

"Maybe later," I say. I mean, it would be nice, but I'm not

about to leave my laptop with this kid, even if it is just so much electronic junk, like everything else here.

The kid turns to his mom, rattles off something I don't understand. She replies, and I don't understand her either.

"Okay!" he says to me. "Later. I fix it." The kid grins. "We have parts."

SO HERE I AM sitting in the back of the little truck bed, which I'm guessing recently transported chickens, with the woman, whose name, I think, is Lau Mei Yee. Aside from the fact that I have a hard time understanding her Mandarin, the engine on this tractor is so loud that it's like rounds of gunfire, shot off fast and right next to my ear.

"He is a good doctor!" she shouts. "Wa Keung see him before. My husband. And Moudzu, our son."

"Oh. What was wrong?"

"Feiyan," I think she says, which means pneumonia. And she says something else that might mean bronchitis, which I know only because I got that the first winter I lived in Beijing.

Now that the Percocet's kicked in, I'm thinking there isn't much point in seeing the doctor. What's he going to say? *Oh, your leg's fucked up.* I mean, what else is new?

But they picked me up in their tractor, you know? So I sort of feel obligated.

It feels like we're going farther out into the country, which is fine with me, because I want to get as far away from that fucking place and Mr. Piggy and his thugs as I can. They have to be his thugs, right? Probably not a coincidence that I go looking for New Century Seeds, mention "David," and people try to beat the shit out of me.

Or it's just how they welcome foreigners who might be journalists or environmentalists in these parts.

I lean back in the little truck bed and think, Okay, this is now officially above my pay grade.

We've rumbled into another village—or city, I can't tell which. Slightly less electronic crap lining the road. Open storefronts with things like tractor parts and hardware, sacks of fertilizer, feed. A farm town.

"*Zai zheli,*" Mrs. Lau says, pointing to a two-story, white-tile-faced storefront with red banners above the entrance and a white canvas curtain with a red cross hanging in the doorframe.

Wa Keung stops the tractor, and Mei Yee helps me out.

I stagger onto the curb, stumbling and almost falling against her, as Wa Keung pulls away. I guess he has to find tractor parking.

The inside of the clinic has smudged whitewashed walls, cheery health posters with cartoon doctors dispensing advice and pills. It's a small room, stuffed full of about two dozen people sitting in plastic chairs, a dozen others leaning against the walls, waiting.

"I really feel better," I tell Mei Yee. I don't feel like waiting in this airless little room. Some of these people look really sick. There's all kinds of coughing: horrible, phlegm-filled fits that sound like death rattles. Some of them are skeleton thin, pale. Others have barrel chests, bloated bellies. I remember enough of my medic training to make good guesses on some of them, but it's not exactly a shock that you'd have a lot of respiratory and heart disease here. Have to figure the cancer rates are pretty high as well. And the kids. I don't like seeing the little kids, their heads too big, their ribs jutting out, their skin tones pale and jaundiced.

"The doctor knows you are coming. You don't have to wait long."

Now I really want to leave. When you're a military medic,

one of the things the training emphasizes is triage: You sort the casualties according to priority for treatment. Treat the serious first, leave the less urgent for later, and if there are too many patients, put aside the ones who who'll probably die or take up too much time to save.

There're all kinds of people here who need help more than I do.

I open my mouth to object, and as I do, a door opens and a woman comes out with a clipboard. She's middle-aged, stout. Takes a quick look around the room and waves in my direction.

With Mei Yee's help, I hobble over, face burning red, not wanting to look at the people who've been waiting in this room for God knows how long, who are really sick, who might be dying. They don't complain, don't stand up and yell and demand an explanation. They just sit, or stand, and wait.

It's not right, and it's not fair. But I go anyway.

The clinic isn't big. There's a short hallway. On one side a room about the size of the waiting area with a half dozen beds in it, all occupied. On the other side, a couple of closed doors, and then one that's open, an exam room from the look of things.

A middle-aged man wearing a white coat sits on an adjustable stool there. When he sees me, he rises. His hair is thick but shot with grey. His eyes have dark pouches under them. He gives me a nod of a bow and smiles, indicates a padded table. I get myself on it, with a little boost from Mei Yee.

"Hello," he says in English. "I am Dr. Chen. I understand you have some leg injury."

I nod.

"If you can . . . take off the trousers, I can have a look."

I feel myself flush. I don't like people seeing my leg. I don't like looking at it myself. But that's why I'm here, right?

He steps out of the exam room. I'm hoping he's going to

help someone else. The middle-aged woman with the clipboard comes in. I unbutton my jeans. She helps me get them off, me gasping from the spasms that travel from my ass down to my toes.

After she drapes a sheet across my lap, the doctor comes back in.

He bends his head over my leg, studying the ridged white scars, the withered dent in the quad where a chunk of muscle is missing.

"Ah. You have an old injury?"

"Yeah," I say. "There's a rod in there, in the femur, and some screws."

There's also a wicked-looking, purpling lump on the side of my leg, above my knee.

"How did this happen?"

I shrug. I don't want to get into it. "Accident."

Mei Yee launches into an explanation in the local dialect. I can't understand it, but she pretty much acts it out for him, holding an imaginary rod in her hands, swinging it down, so I guess I'm busted.

"Ah. I see."

The doctor probes around the area with his fingers, and he's gentle enough, but I feel these weird electric shocks, almost, sparking up and down my leg.

"We don't have X-ray here," he finally says. "For this you must go to county hospital. But I think first ice, raise up. We can put on, the . . . the . . ." He can't come up with the word he wants. "The bandages. To . . . to tighten it."

"Compression bandage," I supply.

"Yes, yes. This. But I think also you should take a rest. Try not to stand or to sit too much. Instead to lie down and raise up. And to walk now and again, for preventing . . . the clot."

"Okay. Sounds good." Like I needed a doctor to tell me any of this.

"Because . . . the blow maybe hit the . . . the screw you talk about. Can maybe cause a problem. You must take care." He gives my leg a final look. "This was bad injury, before."

"Yeah," I say.

They have me lie down on one of the beds with a big ice pack on my leg for a while, and in a way I'm glad that the lady next to me is too sick to feel like talking much, because I sure don't feel like talking to anyone. After that the woman with the clipboard wraps a compression bandage around my thigh and fits me with a pair of crutches, so I guess the visit isn't a total waste of time. I also get a bunch of pills, which I put in my backpack and probably won't take, given that I'm not sure what they are or what they're for, and the quality control of Chinese medicine, like a lot of things in China, is kind of variable.

Plus, they probably aren't painkillers.

Then I get the bill—a hundred yuan, about fourteen bucks. I pay it, plus "a charitable contribution to village health" of another hundred kuai, thank the doctor and the woman with the clipboard and crutch it outside, the coughs from the people in the waiting room following me out onto the cracked concrete slab.

Mei Yee waits for me there on the nonexistent sidewalk, texting on her phone.

"You better now?" she asks.

"*Yue lai, yue hao.*" Getting better and better.

"Wa Keung come and pick us up. Take to our home."

"You're too polite. It's not necessary. I should go back to Shantou."

She covers my hand with hers. "Come to our home. Have

a rest." She grins at me, her smile revealing tea-stained teeth. "Moudzu can fix your computer."

AND THAT'S HOW I end up in the back of the tractor again, this time with my leg propped up on a couple bags of fertilizer. I really don't want to go to these people's home, but I can't think of a polite way to refuse, especially after all the trouble they went to, saving me from getting my ass kicked and all.

Besides, it wouldn't hurt to try to find out a little more about what's going on around here.

I know I should just give up on this whole thing. Haul my gimpy ass back to Beijing and . . . I don't know, deal. With the business I can't run. With my mom, who's going to see me on crutches and freak out or, alternatively, is so busy practicing navel denting with Anal Andy that she won't even notice.

That's the thing. I like having a mission.

Yeah, it's helping a buddy, but it's more than that. It's having a puzzle to solve. Having something to do. Something that matters.

And maybe they'll have beer.

YOU CAN STILL SEE some of the original structure of the Laus' farmhouse: blond brick with the texture of sand, crumbling in places, peaked grey tile roofs. Concrete smooths over the brick on a couple of the walls, and stuck on the walls here and there are little block-shaped rooms made out of cement, with flat tin roofs. Topping off the whole thing is a satellite dish, which I'd bet is aimed toward Hong Kong. There are outbuildings, sheds and a barn, and though it's getting dark, I can catch glimpses of fields behind the house, other farmhouses in the distance.

"Welcome, welcome," Mrs. Lau says, clasping her hands, her head bobbing up and down.

I shake off her offer of help and manage to hop over the beam across the threshold with the aid of my crutches. I'm thinking I can get by with just the one of them, really. My leg hurts, but it feels better than it did. Give me a couple of days and I'll be as good as . . . well, as good as I was before this happened.

Inside, the main room has battered whitewashed walls decorated with posters, mostly of Chinese folk figures: the woman who holds up a lantern in one arm and a rabbit in the other; a big, red-faced dude with a fancy outfit and a sword; plus a print of the *Mona Lisa*. In some places the flooring is old stone—who knows how old? I can see the wear from centuries of footsteps. There's a battered wooden table and a couple of chairs; a newish-looking TV across from a couch; a refrigerator; a water dispenser next to that; and a chest of drawers that's painted white with gold trim and curlicues, with books stacked on top of it. I glimpse the kitchen off to one side, one of the add-on rooms, and a tiny bedroom, the entire space taken up by quilts and whatever kind of mattress is beneath them.

"You like to drink something? Some tea? Coke? Maybe beer?" Mrs. Lau asks.

Score.

"Thank you, I very much like to drink beer."

I settle myself on the couch.

"Wa Keung and I make dinner," she says after opening a bottle and pouring a measure into a plastic cup.

"Please don't go to any trouble."

"Just something simple. Wa Keung is very good cook. Better than me. You want to watch TV?"

"That's okay."

She switches it on anyway. Oh, great, a Chinese soap. Cue the giggling ingenue and the inevitable crying child. I dig into my backpack for a Percocet. It's been . . . what? A couple of hours since the last one?

"Moudzu!" Mei Yee yells. "Come in here!"

Moudzu emerges from a room across from the bedroom.

"You can fix the computer?" she asks.

He grins and nods. "Sure. Very easy. I already get parts." He stands there in his outsize sneakers, waiting for me to hand it over.

I'm not crazy about letting him have my laptop, but if he can really fix it, maybe it's worth the risk. I try to remember: Is there anything on the hard drive that might get me in trouble? Anything about the Great Community? I'm careful about how I log on, using the VPN and all, but maybe there's some cookie, some hidden file, something that you could find if you copied the hard drive and dug deep enough.

"Do you need to take it someplace?" I ask.

"No," he says, his grin getting broader. "You want to see? I show you."

Better than watching TV, I guess. I push myself to my feet with one of the crutches, grab my cup of beer in my free hand, and follow him.

Moudzu's lair is one of the newer additions: a spare concrete block. But that's not what I notice when I part the curtain made from a patterned sheet and peer inside.

It's dark, lit up by battered computer monitors and a bunch of blinking diodes, from modems, from power strips, from who knows what. The computers sit on a makeshift desk consisting of a detached door propped on top of crates against one wall and another ad hoc desk made out of a shipping crate against the other. One monitor has a game going on, explosions and flashing swords, another a series of chats against a background of noisy, cluttered Flash animation—for some reason a couple of cartoon rabbits drinking cans of cola. There are anime and gaming posters on the wall that I can just make out in the dim, bluish green light. Books are piled everywhere there aren't computers or pieces of computers. Between the desks and the bed, there's about six inches of clearance through which to walk.

Moudzu switches on a lamp that shines down on the larger, door desk. Aside from the two monitors, there are a bunch of electronic parts and components, a couple of portable hard drives, and what I think is an internal one, some circuit boards, rectangles of RAM. Now I can see that the crates holding up the door are subdivided into plastic bins, like they had at the workshop that was New Century Seeds, with additional bins beneath the desk.

Moudzu rummages around and holds up a small Phillips-head screwdriver. "I can fix."

I am a little fuzzy because of the Percocet and the beer, not to mention the fucking weird day I've had, and also maybe a little more euphoric than I should be to make a decision like this, but as I try to think it through, I figure there's really no way these guys can know who I am and what may or may not be on my computer.

"What do you think is wrong with it?" I ask.

"Motherboard. And you need new screen."

I watch for a while, sitting on the bed with my bum leg stretched out under the smaller desk, the one made from the shipping crate, Percocet spreading through my veins and nerves and muscles like warm, narcotic honey, as Moudzu expertly takes my laptop apart, removing a series of tiny screws with his magnetized Phillips head, lifting off the top case, and sticking his fingers in its electronic guts. The scents of garlic and scallions and meat drift in from the kitchen.

Moudzu retrieves a pencil-thin soldering iron from one of his bins.

"So you like computers," I say by way of small talk, an activity at which, admittedly, I suck.

He nods, focused on the components strewn across the desk, the soldering iron in his hand.

"Is this the kind of work you want to do in the future?"

He smiles but doesn't look at me, touches the tip of the soldering iron to a coil of solder and the edge of a circuit board. "Not only this."

The smell of singed metal fills the room. He holds the soldering iron down a moment longer to seal the connection, lifts it up with a flourish.

"I want to be like Steve Jobs," he says. "Make new Apple. Something better." He grins. "Maybe I call my company Peach."

AFTER THAT IT'S TIME for dinner. Too much food, which happens just about anytime a Chinese person invites you to his home and which always embarrasses me. Dried noodles with meat and spices, chicken in bean sauce and ginger, fried rice cakes with shrimp, pumpkin stuffed with sweet taro, and a lot of vegetables. Wa Keung must have picked some of this up while I was at the doctor's; they couldn't have made it all so quickly.

"Really good," I say, and it is.

"We grow a lot ourselves," Mei Yee says. "The rice and the vegetables. We also have chickens and a few pigs."

Wa Keung shakes his head. "But crops don't grow the way they used to. In the southern fields, many things die or don't grow right. We had eggplant last year, and most of them were shaped strangely. Couldn't sell them. Afraid to eat them."

"What do you think causes it?" I ask, although of course I already know the answer.

Wa Keung snorts and laughs. "The workshops, of course. The pollution. They were supposed to clean it up in Guiyu, but all they've done is move it to other places, closer to us."

"People get sick now, all the time," Mei Yee chimes in. "Everyone knows someone with cancer. Everyone."

Great, I think, looking at the delicious food on my plate. Who the fuck knows what's in this stuff, how safe *any* of it is?

I eat it anyway. You know, to be polite.

WA KEUNG POURS A round of *baijiu*, for everyone but Moudzu. Clear grain alcohol, ranging from pretty smooth to furniture-stripping, depending on how much you spend.

"Drink, drink," he says, noticing my hesitation. "A little bit is good for you. Anyway, you cannot drink the water here." He waves at the dispenser by the refrigerator. "We have to spend money on water from out of town."

I sip. The stuff burns my throat.

"We've had enough," he says. "The guy, the one who hit you, his bosses—they take people's land. Beat people. Poison our crops. Get rich and give us nothing. That farmer, the one who bombed the government offices in Fujian, he had the right idea."

He pours himself another shot of *baijiu* and tosses it back.

"Yeah," I say. "I can see why you're angry."

"So you're a reporter?" he asks. "An environmentalist?"

I shake my head, reluctantly.

The disappointment shows on both his and Mei Yee's faces, though they quickly cover it up with smiles.

I had a feeling, you know? That they didn't just rescue me and take me to the doctor and stuff me full of food and have their kid fix my computer because they're nice people, though they seem nice enough. They're looking for justice, for someone to pay attention to their problems, for things to be put right. I don't know how much news coverage even does for situations like this, but sometimes, if the central government's sufficiently embarrassed, *sometimes* the problem gets addressed.

And then moved somewhere else, out of sight.

"Why you come here, then?" Mei Yee asks flatly.

"Looking for the brother of a friend," I say. I tell them the story and pull out my photo of Jason.

They haven't seen him.

"Environmentalists come all the time to Guiyu," Mei Yee says. "Not so much out here."

"I understand," I say. We sit in silence. Wa Keung drinks more *baijiu*. I have another glass of beer.

Then it occurs to me: These guys are farmers. They grow things. Like, from seeds.

"*Ni zhidao Xin Shiji Zhongzi Gongsi?*" I ask. Have you heard of New Century Seeds?

Wa Keung frowns. "Sure," he says. "Sure, we just plant some."

I TELL WA KEUNG I can walk, and I follow him outside with the aid of my crutch—between the Percocet and the beer, I'm feeling pretty good.

We go out behind the house, and Wa Keung points to a paddy cut into the hill that I can just make out, water glinting under the moonlight.

"Rice," he says. "First time I try this kind. Sprouting now. Seems good enough."

"So it's just normal rice?" I ask.

"No, they say it's special kind. They tell us in conditions like this it grows better than normal rice."

"Conditions like what?"

He turns his palms skyward and spreads his arms. "Like all of this. The pollution. The bad air and dirty water and poisoned earth. They say the rice will still grow, no matter what."

Prickles rise on the back of my neck. I'm not even sure why. I mean, rice that can grow in bad soil, that's a good thing, right?

"No matter what? How can it do that?"

"Not sure. They say it's 'scientific process of development.'" Wa Keung shakes his head. "I don't know. I'd rather grow same rice we grow here for generations. But last year's crop hardly worth growing. Old rice can't live here anymore."

There's something buzzing in my head, about Jason, about him being into the environment, about a seed company in the middle of a toxic-waste dump.

Jason may be off his meds, but something's not right here.

"Do you think this new rice is safe?" I ask. "My meaning is . . . if it can grow in these conditions . . ."

Do you really want to be eating something that can grow in poisoned ground?

He shrugs. "Who can say? Nothing is safe here. But we still have to make money. We have to eat. What choice do we have?"

Wa Keung drives me in the *tuolaji* to a bus stop in the town where I saw the doctor, where I can catch a bus back to Shantou. He and Mei Yee made the polite offer that I should stay at their place for the night; I just as politely turned it down. I'm not the person they hoped I was, and they've already done enough for me. Besides, I want to get back to Shantou, to my hotel, to my own room and my own bed, temporary as it all is.

Before I go, Wa Keung tells me a little more about the New Century "Hero Rice" seeds.

"They say you can't save seeds and grow from them the next year," he tells me. "That you need to buy the seeds each time."

"That sounds a little complicated," I say.

"Maybe it's not true. Maybe that's just what they want you

to think, so they can make more money." He grins, and for the first time I can see that he's Moudzu's father.

"Rice is rice," he tells me. "If it isn't processed, you can grow it. Of course we'll try to use what we grow. Why should we pay them over and over again?"

We go into a little shed tacked onto the main house, stuffed with random junk—a broken chair, a stack of empty plastic buckets, a battered suitcase—and he aims a flashlight to show me the bag the rice came in, which they'd been using to store some of Moudzu's computer parts. It's a couple feet high, white woven plastic with a red, gold, and black stencil on it of your basic Chinese proletariat hero thrusting a hoe into the air, rice growing triumphantly in the background. NEW CENTURY HERO RICE! it says, in Chinese and English.

Is this some kind of joke?

Wa Keung dumps the components out onto the floor—a bunch of old keyboards, mostly.

"Here," he says, folding the bag up and holding it out to me. "You can have it if you want."

I stuff it into my daypack.

"Do you know any reporter?" he asks, "who maybe is interested in our story?"

"Maybe," I say. I've met a couple anyway. "When I return to Beijing, I can ask."

He smiles and nods, but I can't tell if he believes me. I don't know if I believe myself.

The other thing I do before we leave is pay Moudzu some money for the parts and trouble he took to fix my laptop. Because, what do you know, it boots up fine now.

"You should get new one," he informs me solemnly. "This one very outdated. Most people don't bother to fix."

"True," I say. "True."

★ ★ ★

I TAKE THE BUS back to Shantou and a taxi to my hotel, the Brilliant Star Inn. I'm managing with one crutch and trying to juggle the other as I enter the minimal lobby: a small room with a red-cushioned couch framed in fake chrome; a glass-door cooler filled with water, sodas, beer, and energy drinks; shelves with sundries for sale that are mostly packaged underwear and Pringles chips and, with a nod to Shantou's international reputation, radio-controlled crawling soldier toys and Barbie rip-offs called Spank Me Girl!

Behind a reception counter covered with walnut-grained plastic veneer is a friendly hotel worker representing the colors of the Brilliant Star posse—a bright yellow jacket with purple stitching that claims her name is LaToya.

"Oh, are you hurt?" she asks. "Do you need help?"

I manage a smile. "I'm fine. Thank you." I gesture toward the cooler. "But I'll take two bottles of beer."

She insists on carrying the beer and my spare crutch up to my room, which is on the third floor. "Did you have an accident?" she asks. "Do you need a doctor?"

"A small accident. I already saw a doctor. Thank you."

Truth is, once I hang the Do Not Disturb sign on my door, lock it, and gingerly position myself on the bed, which is your basic cheap Chinese-hotel "Is this a mattress or a sheet of plywood covered by a polyester pad and a sheet?" kind of deal, I realize that I feel pretty crappy. I mean, I'm used to my leg hurting. It hurts a lot of the time. But this is on a different level, the kind of pain I felt years ago, when the injury was fresh. And my chest hurts, too, and my throat, and the insides of my nostrils, like everything's been rubbed with sandpaper and bleach. And I wonder, how the fuck do people live in that place? People like Wa Keung and Mei Yee and Moudzu? How do they get up every day and do what they have to do? How does a kid like Moudzu believe he's going to become the next Steve fucking Jobs?

I crack open a beer and I drink, thinking sometimes it's better not to know how the world really works. The less you know, the more you can pretend that you have a shot of beating the odds.

I lift up my bottle of Kingway beer. "Go Peach Computers!"

That makes me laugh. I laugh and laugh, and then I pound a few more slugs of beer. I'd open the other bottle, but it's all the way over on the desk by the TV, and I don't think I can go that far.

At some point I manage to put the empty bottle down on the pressboard nightstand and turn off the light.

CHAPTER THIRTEEN

I SLEEP PRETTY CRAPPY most of the night, the pain in my leg waking me up when I stay too long in one position, until finally I take another Percocet at around 5:00 A.M., and that knocks me out for a while.

Until my phone goes off. The default ringtone I use for unknown callers is, System of a Down's "Hypnotize."

I fumble around for my phone. I feel like someone's dropped a skip loader of cement on me. "*Wei?*" I manage.

"Ellie McEnroe?" A woman, clipped, forceful.

"Yes?"

"This is Vicky Huang, representing Sidney Cao. Have you returned to Beijing?"

"I, uh . . ." Something about the sharp edge of her voice penetrates the haze in my skull, and then I remember. It's the woman fronting for the supposed billionaire who wants to buy some of Lao Zhang's work.

"No," I say, "not yet."

"Do you have a date for returning?"

"It's complicated. Look, Ms. Huang—"

"Mr. Cao is very patient man. If we can only schedule this talk, that will satisfy him for present time."

I stare at my phone. It's possible I'm misinterpreting due to a Percocet hangover, no coffee, and Vicky Huang's English as a Second Language lack of nuance, but I feel like she's about to order someone to come and break my kneecaps if I don't cooperate.

Which is ridiculous, right? We're talking about *art* here.

"Vicky. Look. I keep trying to tell you, I can't sell you any of Zhang Jianli's art right now. I mean, nothing you say to me is going to make a difference."

"Why?" she demands. "Why can't you sell to us?"

"I can't sell to *anybody*." My heart's pounding from a rush of anger. Get a grip, I tell myself. You can't tell her the truth—make something up. "We're reorganizing. The . . . the business structure. We can't sell anything till that's done, and we get a . . . a new business license."

"What is your time frame for this? Mr. Cao is a powerful man. He can aid you in securing any necessary permits."

Sweet cartwheeling Jesus, this woman is like the fucking Terminator.

I open my mouth to tell her to kindly fuck off, and then I stop. So much stuff happens in China because of *guanxi*—personal connections. If this guy really is a big-deal billionaire, maybe he has some pull. I mean, I doubt he can call up the DSD and tell them to lay off, but who knows? It might not be a bad idea to hear what he has to say. Or to at least not piss him off.

"I very much would like to talk to Mr. Cao," I say. "But I had a small accident, so I have to rest for a few more days."

When in doubt, play the *xiuxi* card. Rest! It's like the catch-all excuse in China—no matter what kind of deep shit you're in, just say you need a rest and, weirdly, people will often leave you alone.

"I am sorry to hear," she says, not sounding particularly

sorry. "Where will you be resting? Perhaps we can arrange a meeting."

"Yangshuo," I say without thinking. I mean, I have to say *something*, and it's not like I can explain a vacation in Shantou, or in scenic Guiyu.

"Ah, yes. Very beautiful." The slightest of pauses, and I think I hear the clicking of fingers on a keyboard. "Perhaps in two days?"

"I'm not sure about that. Let me call you when I . . . when I've had a chance to rest."

The clicking stops. "Three days is also a possibility."

"Okay. Right. I'll call you. Really."

Oh, man.

So here's my dilemma: What do I do now?

I've told Vicky that I'm in Yangshuo, which of course I'm not. So should I go back there? Or should I stay far away? Maybe get my ass back to Beijing. Because I don't know who Vicky Huang and Sidney Cao really are. They could be . . . I don't know, DSD informers. Or crazy art stalkers. I mean, who knows?

I slowly haul my gimpy ass out of bed, and man, do I feel like shit. My leg is killing me, and my hip hurts on the other side, and my back, too, probably because I've been walking funny. I heat up some water in the little electric kettle, rip open a Starbucks VIA. I suck that down, and then I make another one.

Okay, I think, okay. I am sort of awake. My head doesn't hurt too much. I can handle this. Or at least think it through.

I boot up my battered laptop, log on to the hotel's free Internet, and start searching for Sidney Cao.

It takes me a while, and I find a lot of irrelevant crap, but there's a Sidney Cao based in Anhui who started a company called Happy Village Ltd that does something involving chemical products. And yeah, he's loaded. In addition to his business, he's built shopping malls, housing developments, and he's cited in a Web magazine devoted to "the business of luxury and culture in China" as having recently begun to collect Chinese art, both ancient and modern, in a big way. Art and Bordeaux wines.

That's got to be my guy.

I check Vicky Huang's emails, and sure enough the domain is happyvillageltd.cn.

Okay, he's for real, then. So what makes the most sense?

I mull it over.

I don't think I have to worry about him if I decide to go to Yangshuo. He seems legitimate. But I could also just go back to Beijing and arrange a meeting from there. It's not like I'm obligated to go to Yangshuo.

But that's where a part of me still wants to go. Because I haven't completed the mission yet: Operation Find Jason. I know a little more than I did, or at least I think that I do. I know that Jason was interested in New Century Seeds and that there's something pretty shady about them.

The rice will still grow, no matter what.

Maybe I can use that information to find out more from his friends in Yangshuo.

Even as I think this, there's another part of me that's going, *You fucking idiot.* You're not going to find out anything, and what's the point anyway? Whatever the problem is, you're not going to be able to fix it.

But there's the idea that I can give Dog an answer. That I can give *myself* an answer. You know, figure things out. Solve the mystery. The End.

Yeah, right.

★   ★   ★

I'm not crazy about it, but I decide to fly to Guilin. It costs more, but my leg hurts a lot, and I'm not feeling all that great in general, and I just want to get there. So I buy a ticket, rise up at stupid o'clock the next day to catch the one plane from Shantou to Guilin, and I get into Guilin around nine-thirty in the A.M. I stagger around the airport with my daypack and my duffel and my crutches and find the bus that goes into Guilin proper. Take that to the train station and find the bus to Yangshuo. I do all this in a fog of hurt and narcotics and lack of sleep. None of it feels real, except for the shooting pain every time I step on my bad foot.

"This sucks," I mutter as I rest my head against the window of the Yangshuo bus. I stretch my leg out as much as I can. At least no one claims the seat next to me, and I doze a bit as the bus bumps along down the road to Yangshuo. I don't even open my eyes when the driver lays on the horn and swerves around whatever car or taxi or *tuolaji* might be in his path.

I get into Yangshuo about noon. I check into my hotel, which is tucked in an alley off Xi Jie. It's a backpacker dive called Maggie's Guesthouse. The lobby is a jumble of mismatched furniture, old travel and music posters, kids sprawled out working on their laptops. I picked it because it's close to the Gecko, and I don't want to walk far in the shape I'm in.

Yeah, I plan on going back there. Yeah, it's probably a stupid idea. But that guy Erik knows something, I'm sure he does. And so does Sparrow, who might even be a better target. She was nicer anyway.

But I'm too tired to go there right now. I ache all over, and my leg feels swollen against the compression bandage. I should take a look at it, I guess, but I don't want to. Instead I have a Percocet and stretch out on the hard bed. I swallow a couple of aspirin, too, for the inflammation. I stare at the ceiling, at the water stains and peeling paint and think, *Seriously, what the fuck are you doing?*

Attacked twice, in two different cities. All of Jason's friends, if they really are his friends, acting like they're in some mafia and took a vow of silence, treating me like I'm some kind of cop or something.

What is there about this situation that I'm missing? Aside from Jason?

Then I think: Jason.

I've researched the seed companies. I've researched Sidney Cao and Vicky Huang. The person I haven't checked out is Jason.

I start Googling. And it doesn't take me long to find out just how FUBAR the situation really is.

IT'S ABOUT 10:00 P.M. in San Diego. If that's past anybody's bedtime, too fucking bad. Because if I have to make an actual phone call, I will.

Somebody's up, though—Dog's Skype icon is green.

Sure enough, when I ring, he picks up right away. Like he's been sitting by the computer waiting.

His face lights up when he sees me.

"Hey, Baby Doc! You got . . . you got news?"

"I'm working on it. Listen, is Natalie around?"

That gets him worried. His forehead wrinkles, his eyes squeeze shut for a second, his lips draw back before he can get the words out. "You can . . . tell me."

"Look, as far as I know, Jason's fine. This is something I gotta talk to Natalie about."

He frowns. Then bellows, "Hey, Nat!"

I wait for Natalie to sit in the computer chair, adjust the

earbuds. She smiles at me, showing her slightly crooked teeth. She looks exhausted, but maybe that's from the blue glow of the computer screen.

"Hi, Ellie," she starts. "Doug said—"

I cut her off. "So you left out a few things."

Her eyes dart to one side, then back to me. "It's complicated," she says.

"Really? Complicated? Like, the part where Jason's an ecoterrorist?"

CHAPTER FOURTEEN

Yeah. An ecoterrorist.

That's what the spokesman of the company whose property he vandalized called him. I'd write that off to corporate asshattery, except it looks like the FBI is saying the same thing.

Here's what I found out:

Jason was in some group of environmental activists who went from posting their manifestos online and protesting in front of companies who'd committed ecological sins to more serious shit: "monkey-wrenching" they called it at first. Minor acts of sabotage, like chaining themselves to trees and slapping bumper stickers on SUVs that said things like YOU ARE DRIVING A DEATH MACHINE!

Then it escalated.

There's this one company in particular that Jason and his buddies targeted, a corporation called Eos. I'd heard of them, vaguely. They're "as good as nature can be," or something. But I never knew exactly what it is that they *do*.

Turns out they make chemicals. Plastics. Fertilizer.

And seeds.

Hybrid seeds, which Wikipedia tells me are seeds produced by cross-pollinated plants. I'm not sure what that means, but the seeds are trademarked, meaning Eos owns them. Eos also makes genetically modified seeds, GMOs. Gene-spliced crops created to resist their own herbicides. So you can drop a shitload of Rescue Ride!® weed killer, also made by Eos, on the crops and not kill the plants but kill all the weeds. They also make a potato that contains its own pesticide. Which sounds kind of creepy, but they claim it's perfectly safe.

The articles I found about Jason don't have a lot of information about why he and his friends think Eos is such bad news. Mostly the articles are about their "criminal activities," not about why they did what they did.

But what they did includes trying to set fire to some Eos experimental crops. Which is what got Jason on the FBI's Ten Most Wanted List.

"You didn't think this was something I needed to know?"

"I thought—"

"It's bogus!" Dog yells in the background. "He didn't!"

"I don't fucking care if it's bogus!" I snap. "You got me running around looking for an *ecoterrorist*? Me and the fucking *FBI*?"

That's when the hard lines in Natalie's face get harder. "The way I see it, you owed me one."

Bitch.

Okay, she has a small point. Me and Dog did fuck around a few times. But, like, that's all on me? Didn't *he* have something to do with it?

"Doug wants to find his brother," Natalie says, her voice cold. "And Doug and I are a team." She tosses her streaked blond hair. "You can do what you want."

★ ★ ★

NOW I REALLY HAVE to decide.

Once you start calling somebody a terrorist, things escalate to a whole different level. I know that from experience.

Jason's looking at twenty years in prison, at least, and for what? For setting a bunch of plants on fire?

And of all places, he flees to China. Not the best choice, if you ask me.

I've met some pretty sketchy Westerners living here, it's true. People who are running from something, who get lost in plain sight, almost. Creepy English teachers you wouldn't want around your daughter. Scam artists living from rip-off to rip-off. Somehow they manage.

Seems to me the best thing that could happen to Jason is that he *doesn't* get found.

Dog and Natalie insist that he didn't do what he's accused of doing. That he was part of the group but not into breaking the law. "He comes home, we fix it," Dog says. I don't know about that.

What I do know is that I pretty much don't trust anything that's a lot bigger and stronger than me.

Call me bitter. Whatever.

Given what's going on with the DSD, given the shit that's happened to me in the past, the last thing I need is to get involved with any kind of "terrorist," whether he really is one or not.

A COUPLE OF HOURS later, me and my crutch are hobbling down Xi Jie, heading for the Gecko.

Okay, yeah, I'm stupid. But I figure I'll just try to make sure Jason's okay. And if I end up finding out where he is, if I talk to him, I'll tell him what Dog wants, and he can decide for himself.

"Hey! Hey, *lamei!*"

It's Kobe. He trots up to me, unbuttoned Qing-dynasty robe flapping, black fedora pulled down low on his forehead.

"What happened to you?"

"A little accident."

"Ah." He falls in alongside me, now and again jogging in place to keep from getting too far ahead. "So did you travel, see some sights?"

He's trying to act casual, but I know what he really wants to talk about.

I stop. "Yes, I saw her."

Kobe stands there in front of me. The expression on his face, a mix of hope and fear and God knows what—love, I guess—it just makes me feel like shit.

"She . . . how is she?"

"Miss! Miss! Look, come buy!"

We're standing in front of an open-front store with tables outside covered with carved wooden frogs, cloth hangings, souvenir T-shirts, embroidered tote bags.

"She's . . . she's okay."

"Look, see?" The shopgirl is holding up a wooden frog, and she takes the stick piercing its belly and starts rubbing the carved ridges on its back, and it sounds like it's chirping.

Kobe turns to her and snaps off something in the local dialect that I don't exactly understand but the gist of which is "Bother someone else right now!"

The shopgirl snickers. Strokes the frog in his direction.

He ignores her. "So what's she doing? She's working, she's still in Shantou?"

Is she still with "David"?

That's what he really wants to know.

"Yeah," I say. "She's working. She's doing well."

He stares at me, his eyes pleading. "Did you . . . did you tell her . . . ?"

"Miss, look," the shopgirl says to me. "You need this, right? Better than what you have."

I turn to her, and she's holding up a walking stick. Carved dark wood, with a metal badge tacked right below that, stamped with the characters for Yangshuo and one of those crazy mountains.

"You stupid bitch, you didn't hear me?" Kobe snaps.

"*Hundan,*" she says, grinning at him. Slacker.

"Daisy told me to tell you she's fine," I say. "And she hopes you're doing well."

Which is a lie. Daisy didn't say anything about Kobe at all. When I mentioned him, she just rolled her eyes.

"She's not with David," I tell him. "But she's happy where she is. She's not coming back. Not for a while anyway."

Kobe stares down at his Nikes. "Okay," he says. He shrugs. "Okay."

He composes himself. Looks up at me. "Stop by later and have a drink." He adjusts his fedora. "If you want."

I watch him go slouching down the street toward the Last Emperor.

"Come on, miss," the shopgirl says, holding up the walking stick. "Come on! I give you good price."

I sigh. "How much?"

Mission to Gecko, take two: I go back to Maggie's Guesthouse and drop off the crutch. The walking stick isn't exactly as good a substitute, but it works okay and it's better camouflage—I'm hoping I can walk into Gecko and it's not so obvious that I'm hurt. Not that I'm too scary when I'm healthy, but I think about those nature movies with the wounded antelope and the lions, and I don't want to be that antelope, you know? It never ends well.

I hesitate for a moment outside the door, staring at the bright yellow lizard on the signboard. Then think, Whatever. I'm going to a tourist joint in Yangshuo, and it's barely even dark out. I mean, what can they do to me, right?

I push open the door and walk inside.

I swear, it's like one of those cheesy westerns where the saloon musician stops playing the piano and everyone turns and stares.

Well, not everyone. There are more customers here than there were the two times I came before, and a lot of them are indifferent. They're drinking their beers or coffees, eating pizza and nachos, talking about their next rock-climbing or river-rafting or cool authentic-Chinese-village excursion, and I'm just another *laowai* coming in for a stale microbrew or mediocre espresso.

But there are a few people who mark my entrance, who look up and stare when I walk in. The waitress who served me before. Sparrow. And Erik.

Erik stands behind the bar counter, in midconsultation with the waitress, looking at a list on a clipboard.

I limp up to the bar. "Hi, Erik," I say.

"Do I know you?"

"Yeah. Pretty sure we've met."

"You were interested in a river cruise, right?"

I pull out the New Century Hero Rice sack from my canvas messenger bag and drop it on the bar. "No. This."

He looks at the bag, smooths out its wrinkles, seems to consider the heroic figure in his overalls and Mao cap and thrusting hoe. "Is there some reason I should care?"

"I don't know. You tell me. I'm pretty sure that David does."

Some movement at the corner of my field of vision makes me glance left.

Sparrow, staring at me, taking a step forward. Then she ducks her head and retreats, back to the station by the rock-climbing equipment and the river-rafting posters.

Erik stares at the rice bag a moment longer, and then he looks up at me. "It's interesting that people you talk to end up getting hurt."

"It's interesting that people I talk to pull dick moves like trying to mug me and sticking a knife in my face. Or is that just how you guys like to say hello?"

"People attack when they're threatened," he says.

"You think I'm a threat? Seriously?" I laugh. "Wow. I guess I should hang out around you and your buddies more often. You're making me feel all empowered and shit."

I pick up the rice sack. Fold it and stuff it back into my messenger bag. "I know I'm kind of repeating myself here, but all I'm trying to do is find out if David is okay so I can let his family know how he's doing. The rest of this I don't give a fuck about."

Now I see something, a real emotion, flash across his face, but I'm not sure what. Anger?

"Maybe you should," he says.

"But you're not going to tell me why." I shrug. "Whatever."

I take one of my name cards out of the pocket of my bag and lay it on the counter. "If you wanna enlighten me, here's my phone number and my email address."

Then I turn my back and walk away.

So maybe that was dumb, giving Erik my information. But here's what I figure: He's a foreigner. The odds of him having some kind of juice here in China aren't that great. Maybe he's the guy who pushed Russell to attack me or maybe not, but there's a big difference between him trying to jack me up and being able to bring the DSD or the Public Security Bureau down on my ass. If he's involved in something sketchy, he's not going to go out of his way to call attention to it.

Unless, of course, he's fronting for someone else who does have the juice.

I shudder a little, the muscles between my shoulder blades twitching, and I tell myself, Don't be paranoid. And what's done is done.

I pause for a moment at Sparrow's station. She's making a show of rearranging the brochures on the wall.

"*Ni hao,*" I say.

"Hello," she says, not meeting my eyes.

"So about that river rafting . . ."

Now she stops shuffling pamphlets. Gives me a quick look. "You have my card," she says in a low voice.

That's right. I do.

I DON'T CALL HER right away, not with Erik probably still hanging around. Besides, I'm feeling like I need to lie down. My leg really hurts, it feels warm and swollen beneath the compression bandage, and I'm thinking ice, elevate, and some aspirin.

When I do get back to my little room at Maggie's with a bag of ice from their café, I take off my jeans, sit on the bed, and contemplate the bandage. I really don't want to take it off and see what I'm dealing with. But I was a medic once, and I know how things can go wrong, and given how fucked up my leg was—all the surgeries, then the blow, and the pain I'm having now—it could be a DVT, a deep vein thrombosis. The danger with a DVT is a blood clot can form, dislodge, and travel to the lungs, which I'm really not in the mood for.

I unwind the bandage.

There's my leg, crisscrossed with scars, the indentation on

the quad where no amount of PT can make up for the chunk of muscle I lost. And there's the bruise from where that asshole hit me, a deep purpling red. I have this flash of something that happened, something I saw that was really bad, back when I was a lil' ol' 91 Whiskey medic, but I push that out of my head. No fucking point going down that road again.

There's generalized swelling as well, but there's no way I can be sure what it's from—maybe just, you know, because the guy hit me and I fell, and I've been walking around like an idiot since it happened.

I take some aspirin and a Percocet, make a pile of the extra pillow and a rolled-up quilt, put a towel over my leg and the ice pack on top of that, and I lie down. I switch on the TV, landing on a Chinese game show that seems to be a rip-off of *America's Next Top Model*, which is weirdly compelling, especially when they do a photo shoot where they're dressed up like Red Guards and *qipao*-wearing class traitors, except with kohl outlining their eyes, their arms and legs posed like displaced puppets in front of deconstructed Qing-dynasty sets.

After the ice melts and the Percocet kicks in, I retrieve Sparrow's card from the bottom of my little canvas bag.

It says SPARROW in English on one side, Chinese on the other. There's a phone number. And an address in Chinese. Something about birds.

I tap out the number.

"*Wei?*"

"Is this Sparrow?"

"*Shi.* Yes."

"This is David's friend."

A pause. "*Wo xianzai meiyou kong.*" I don't have free time now. "But if you want, you can visit me at the sanctuary tomorrow. It's very interesting. For tourists."

"Oh, yeah?" I look at the card again. There's the character for "bird." After that, one I don't know, then the character for "prohibit," and then another I don't recognize with the radical for "animals."

"Thank you," I say. "I'll check my schedule."

After we hang up, I open the Pleco Chinese Dictionary app on my iPhone and trace the characters. "Birds." The next two are "prohibit hunting." Which means "sanctuary."

Bird sanctuary.

CHAPTER FIFTEEN

"ELLIE? HI, HON. IT'S Mom. Just checking in to see how you're doing. I'm back in BJ, no problem. Your apartment's fine, except I wasn't sure if I should tip the water man. The guy that brings the dispenser bottles? Can you let me know? In case he comes back? Anyway, hope you're doing well. Give me a call when you get a chance. Okay? Bye. Love you!"

I stare at the phone.

Okay, I heard it ring, I picked it up, I saw that it was my mom calling, and I was going to answer it, but I was just moving kind of slowly. I'm not feeling that great, and I didn't have that much to drink last night . . . did I? Just some beers, on top of Thai food. Which isn't sitting too well either. I slept . . . twelve hours. More. Not like me.

Probably the Percocet. I've been taking a lot of it.

Is it really such a good idea to go out to Sparrow's bird sanctuary? I'm pretty sure it's not smart.

What the fuck is wrong with me?

Because I know I'm going to do it anyway.

I stand up and test out my bad leg. It feels better, I tell myself. I probably don't have a DVT. Probably.

I make a cup of instant coffee, suck it down with a couple of aspirin, take a shower, and get dressed.

By the time I get out the door, it's around noon. Not too cold, but grey and on the verge of drizzling. I should eat something, I guess, maybe just some *jiaozi* or pizza or something.

As I stand on the little street off Xi Jie, my phone rings. Vicky Huang.

I don't want to answer it. But I've put her off I forget how many times already, and at least I'm in Yangshuo, where I said I'd be.

"Miss McEnroe? This is the third day. Are you available for a meeting?"

I'm so not up for this. I'm still so tired I can barely see straight.

"I . . . uh, sure. I have an appointment right now, though. Maybe later? Like, for dinner? I mean, are you actually in Yangshuo?"

"We have representatives. What time?"

"Seven?"

"Location?"

"I . . . uh . . . look, can we, like, figure this out later? I'm running kind of late. And if there's a restaurant you like, feel free to name it, 'cause I don't really know."

A pause.

"I will research and call you in the afternoon."

"Great. Looking forward to it," I lie.

I head down the alley, in the opposite direction from Xi Jie, because I am really not in the mood for the crowds and the wooden-frog vendors. Though, actually, I bet my mom would like one of those frogs. They're supposed to be good luck; they attract money or something. She'd be into that. I could buy her one of those and maybe a Yangshuo T-shirt or one of those embroidered bags.

I hesitate, and then I turn toward Xi Jie.

And see two guys up the block, staring at me.

Dark sunglasses. Zipped windbreakers, one with a white logo that says US POLO TEAM. Slacks. They turn away, pretending to have a conversation, like they're considering checking in to Maggie's Guesthouse.

Forget the frogs.

I want to turn and run, but that isn't an option.

Besides, this isn't a country road. This is the middle of the tourist zone in Yangshuo.

So I pretend I haven't made them. I keep walking back to Xi Jie.

I mean, what are they going to do? It's not like they can kidnap me off the street, right?

As I pass them on the left, I think, well, yeah, actually, they *could* do that. This is China. If they're DSD . . .

I keep walking.

By the time I walk the remaining half block to Xi Jie, my heart's beating double time and I'm sweating like I'm running a race in a heat wave.

Who needs coffee when you've got adrenaline?

The tourists are out, Chinese and foreign, surrounding me in a comforting blanket of . . . well, potential witnesses. And there are enough foreigners up here where I'm not going to stand out, so maybe I can hide in plain sight. I weave through the crowd, taking a moment to glance behind me like, I hope, a clueless tourist, praying that maybe I just imagined I've got two Chinese rent-a-goons on my tail.

Unfortunately, no. There they are, pretending like they don't see me pretending not to be looking for them.

Okay, I think. Okay. I'm just going to keep hobbling down the street here. Look for a cab. If they have a car, they'll need some time to get back to it, and maybe that will be enough time for me to lose them.

Here's the problem: There aren't very many taxis in Yangshuo. None here on Xi Jie, which is pedestrians-only on this stretch. I need to walk up to the intersection, then hang a left and go up to whatever that big street is, where the buses run.

Okay.

"Miss? Bamboo raft?"

A tiny woman in traditional clothes, from whatever "ethnic minority" lives around here, thrusts her laminated tourist brochures in my face.

"No thanks."

"*Impressions* show? See Ancient Village? Rock-climb?"

"*Buyao!*" I snap. Then think.

"Oh, you can ask those guys behind me," I say. "They want a bamboo-raft trip. Don't believe them if they say no. They are looking for a good deal."

"Ah, okay, okay."

Off she goes, like a lamprey seeking a shark.

Up ahead on my left is the Last Emperor. And I think maybe I've got the wooden frogs on my side, because slouching by the entrance is Kobe, fedora pulled low on his forehead, unlit cigarette dangling from the corner of his mouth.

"Hey, *lamei*." He puts on a smile, but I don't think he's really that happy to see me.

"Kobe, *ni hao*. Listen . . . uh, can I use your bathroom?"

"Bathroom? You sick?"

"No, I . . ." I glance over my shoulder. There's Mr. US Polo Team and his buddy in the generic windbreaker hovering on the corner, letting the tourists flow around them. I guess they weren't tempted by a cheap bamboo-raft ride. "These two guys, they're following me. I don't know why. Something I saw in Shantou, or Guiyu, and . . ."

He frowns. "Police?"

Technically, the DSD aren't police. "I don't think so."

Now Kobe looks past me, trying to spot my tails. Hesitates. Maybe he's trying to decide if it's a good idea to get involved.

"Okay," he says. "Sure."

"Is there a way out the back? I need to catch a taxi."

He nods. "Past the bathrooms. At the end of the hall. That door, it should be open. If anyone asks, tell them I said it's okay. If you don't see a taxi on Pantao Road, go up to the traffic circle on the way to Moon Mountain. You can find one there."

"Thanks." I stand there for a moment. He's wearing the T-shirt with the pistol-packing panda, I notice. I feel as if there's something else I should say. It's like I want to apologize, and I'm not sure why.

"Thanks, Kobe," I say.

He shrugs. "No problem. Come back sometime. I make you my special drink."

As I hobble inside, as fast as I can manage, I hear Kobe engage the guys behind me, telling them, "We have two-for-one drink today! Margarita! Sex on the Beach! Here's a discount card!"

As before, the place is mostly empty, the dance floor dark. A waitress drops a pizza on a table where two stoned-looking Westerners sit; another waitress leans against the bar, texting on her phone. I head toward the back, to the hall where the bathrooms are. To my right is the kitchen, smelling like stale grease and ammonia. Ahead of me is the door.

"Hey, *ni buneng jin nar qu!*" You can't go there.

It's a middle-aged woman wearing a stained apron, her hair tied up and tucked under a baseball cap with a Chanel logo, waving her hand at me as I try to duck out the back door.

"Kobe said I could," I say in Mandarin. "Because these two men, they're bothering me."

She follows the tilt of my head, looks over my shoulder into the bar. "Okay," she says gruffly. "Go quickly."

"Quickly" in my case is relative, but I walk as fast as I can, out the back door, into a little cement alcove crowded with reeking trash cans and a couple of bikes locked to the rusting rail. Up the three stairs, slick with grease, to the street above. Follow that to a broad avenue. Okay. Here's a bus stop, in front of a Li-Ning sporting-goods store. I'm on Pantao Road. I head up the street toward the traffic circle, on the way out of town. I don't see any cabs. I think if I don't see one soon I'll duck into a store or a restaurant. Stay there or sneak out another back door. Staying is sounding good, because my leg's really hurting, swelling against the bandage, and I think I'd better ice and elevate it, but mostly what I'm passing are shops, with open storefronts or glass windows, not great places to hide, and I see a hotel, but I think I'll have to show a passport there, and if these guys are DSD . . .

A taxi. Letting off a couple of girls in front of a *shanzhai* Juicy Couture boutique. I don't even ask the driver if he's available, I just slide into the backseat.

"Moon Mountain," I say. Not that I want to go there, but I don't have Sparrow's card handy, and what I mainly want to do right now is get the fuck out of town.

"MOON MOUNTAIN"—*YUELIANGSHAN*—IS called that because of the crescent-shaped hole in the middle of it, like someone took a giant Christmas-cookie cutter and punched it out. It's where Mom and Andy and me went to the Italian restaurant . . . was it a week ago? It feels like a lot longer.

First thing I do, I switch off the GPS in my phone. Think

about it some more, and then I turn the phone off. They might be able to find me that way, depending on who these guys are.

I wasn't really thinking too much when I told the cabbie to bring me here. It was just a place I knew that was down the road from Yangshuo proper and easy to get to. But as we drive, passing a fancy resort on one side of the road and then a huge billboard for a NEW SOCIALISM COUNTRY MODEL VILLAGE on the other, I realize that it's not a bad destination. There are a fair number of tourists who come here: Chinese tour groups in buses who arrive for lunches of beer fish at farmers' restaurants and leave afterward to go on to their river cruises or whatever, Europeans who like the "boutique hotel" where the Italian restaurant is. There are public shuttle buses that run up and down the main road outside the village, and where there are a lot of tourists, odds are there might also be a few taxis.

"You can stop here," I tell my driver. I pay him and get out. I figure just in case those guys back in Yangshuo made this cab, better I should switch for the trip to Sparrow's sanctuary. I'm feeling all James Bond for having thought of this.

Especially because I'm not thinking too clearly. I'm really not feeling all that great. Aside from my leg, I'm dizzy, hot. Those aren't DVT symptoms. I don't think. Probably just because I haven't eaten. And I'm having a little trouble catching my breath, but that makes sense, considering that strange men are following me and I'm freaking out, right?

I should breathe into a paper bag or something.

I ignore the vendors selling flower garlands, pass the group of Chinese students on their cruiser bikes, posing for photos, walk on by a three-story farmers' restaurant still crowded with Chinese tour groups, and go down the dirt road with stalls and shops on either side until I come to a cab parked outside some kind of paintball business called War Game (in English), with huge signboards depicting camoed soldiers with infrared goggles and M1s, plus photos of happy customers blasting the shit out of each other.

I shudder and approach the driver, who drinks tea from a glass jar.

"*Ni hao,*" I say. "You working now?"

SPARROW'S PLACE IS ABOUT a half hour away from Yueliangshan, first up the main road, through a town that straddles the highway, then down a series of smaller roads and dirt paths that run through tiny villages and rice paddies and tombstone-shaped mountains. I have no fucking clue where we are. I'm not sure I care at this point.

The driver has to stop a couple of times to ask directions, once in a tiny village with a rutted muddy path for a main road, a second time as we bounce between rice paddies, shouting out to a farmer taking a break under a tree next to his fields.

Finally we come to a pass between two hills, then a turnoff into a stand of trees. There's a chicken-wire fence and a ramshackle gate and a sign hung on the fence post with a painted bird—some kind of phoenix, I think—with long, brightly colored, curling tail feathers.

"Here," the driver says.

"That's a phoenix, right? *Zhe shi da luan.*"

He shrugs. "Could be."

The *zhegu* turns into a *luan*—I got that in a fortune once. A little brown bird changes into a phoenix, soaring high above the clouds. You'd think this would be a good thing, but it isn't necessarily. It just means big changes. Sometimes good, sometimes bad, depending on your actions.

Story of my fucking life.

I pay him and hobble down the path.

It looks like an old farm, a couple buildings of worn, blondish brick and curved, blackened roof tiles. There are some other, newer structures: more chicken wire, like cages, some with tin roofs. I hear things—birds, I guess—a sort of low chuckling, an occasional caw, clacking and trills. I *think* that's what I'm hearing anyway. I'm drenched in sweat, and I'm pretty sure it's not hot out.

"Can I help you?"

It's a young guy, Chinese, tall and thin, with glasses.

"Yeah, I . . ." I have to stop for a minute. I wipe my forehead. "I'm here to see Sparrow."

He looks me up and down. Like, I don't know, there's something funny about me. Maybe that I'm kind of leaning on my souvenir Yangshuo walking stick because I suddenly can't stand up straight.

"*Xiaoma!*" he yells. "*Kuai lai ba!*"

I don't exactly pass out, nothing that humiliating, but what happens is my vision blurs to white and there's this hollow roaring in my ears, like a low ocean tide, and there are hands grasping my arms and guiding me down the path, and as I glance to one side, I swear I see this huge white bird with a red crown, like it's wearing a skull cap—a phoenix maybe—walking alongside me, tilting its head now and again like it's studying my face, trying to talk to me, almost.

"Hey, hi, bird," I say.

CHAPTER SIXTEEN

I END UP LYING on a couch in an overstuffed office—or is it a clinic?—in the main farmhouse anyway, with my leg propped up on a couple of pillows and a rolled blanket. Apparently I did not hallucinate the white bird, because it's followed us into the room and stands by the couch like some kind of bleached plastic lawn flamingo. There are other birds in here, too, in cages— some little songbirds, a duck, and is that a parrot on a perch?

"You should not be walking," Sparrow says. "You need to rest." She hands me a bottle of water.

"Yeah, yeah," I say. I dig through my backpack for a Percocet and some aspirin, and then I think more of that on an empty stomach probably isn't the best idea.

I take another look around. The interior walls are plastered, crumbling in places. There are paintings hung on the walls, traditional Chinese watercolors, of birds. Copies of famous pieces, probably, the kind you buy from "art students" who approach foreigners at the Forbidden City or Tiananmen, claiming they're from the provinces and their professor is having an exhibition, will you come and take a look?

The paintings are pretty, though. Good enough copies at least.

Hanging up among them are big colored posters, birds of the world, birds of China.

The big white bird stands next to the couch staring at me. I wonder what kind it is. Maybe it's on one of those posters.

"Is that a . . . a crane?"

Sparrow smiles and nods. "Yes. His name is Boba. He is hungry. Have you eaten?" she adds politely.

"I, uh . . . not exactly."

Pretty rude of me, but I know I need to eat.

"Oh! I can make you some noodles. Do you like?"

"Anything is fine. Please, don't trouble yourself."

Sparrow rushes off. The young guy, the thin man with the glasses, pulls up a folding chair and sits next to me. His name is Han Rong, "But please call me Harold."

"Harold. Do you work here?"

He laughs, a little nervously, it seems to me, but maybe it's just that weird politeness disguised as social awkwardness you get in conversations here sometimes. Like you've stepped in something and you don't know what.

"No. Just volunteer."

"Oh. So I guess you like birds." My lame attempt at a joke.

"I think they are okay. An important part of natural environment," he adds.

"So you volunteer. For a long time?"

He hesitates. "Just a month or two."

Jason/David left not quite two months ago.

It's possible that I'm a little paranoid. Okay, maybe a lot. Life just keeps giving me reasons.

"What else do you do?"

He sits up straighter and smiles. "I am a student."

"Really. What do you study?"

"The natural sciences." He spreads his hands in a little wave around the room. "So this is extending my learning."

"I see."

I hear a few random chirps from the caged birds and a cackle from the parrot. Boba still stands by the couch, staring at me with his black, reptilian eyes. Then he stretches out his long neck and starts rooting around in my hair.

"Oh! Maybe he likes you!" Han Rong exclaims.

Either that or he's looking for nest material.

I EAT THE BOWL of noodles that Sparrow made for me, probably one of those giant Cup-a-Soup things that everyone eats on the trains, but it's good enough right now, and after I'm done the dizziness recedes somewhat, and I tell myself probably there's nothing seriously wrong, I was just stressed out and tired and needed to get off my feet.

While I eat, a couple other volunteers wander in and out, a teenager with the English name of Sophie, chubby and serious, with pigtails like a younger girl, and a man who I'm guessing is a little older than Sparrow, rugged like a laborer, wearing a sweat-stained T-shirt and a sullen look, a grain sack slung over one shoulder.

"The feed, where do you want it?" he says to Sparrow, with a wary glance at me.

"Here is good."

As she says this, she's crouched down in front of one of the big cages, checking on the inhabitant, one of those fishing birds. I check my dictionary. "Is that one a cormorant? *Yizhi luci?*"

Sparrow nods.

"What's wrong with him?" I ask.

"The owner, when they fish, they tie a cord around the neck, near the throat. So the bird cannot swallow. This owner doesn't know how to take care of the bird. So he ties too tight. It gets an infection. Very bad."

"And he brought it to you?"

The guy who carried the grain sack snorts. "We liberate it," he says with a grin.

Sparrow blushes. "We don't steal it. We offer him a payment. Tell him a little money better than a dead bird." She rises. "Are you feeling better? Do you want to see the sanctuary? Or maybe you should rest a while longer."

By now it's getting late into the afternoon, and though maybe I should rest, I figure it's my best chance to talk to Sparrow privately.

"I'd love to see it," I say.

I'LL ADMIT WALKING IS still not a lot of fun. These weird pings that feel like electrical shocks almost, running up and down my leg, the spasms in my back, the pain in my hip, and those, I figure, are just because I'm not walking normally, but the leg pain, it's got to be nerve pain, right? Like the doctor said, maybe the guy hit one of the screws in my leg and the swelling is impinging on a nerve. That would make sense. Odds are that's all it is.

Given all the shit I've been through with my leg, that had better be all it is.

"This is our biggest cage," Sparrow says.

We've walked down a path from the main farmhouse that leads toward what looks like an old rice paddy. I don't know enough about rice to tell if they're growing anything there or not, but bordering it is a big chicken-wire enclosure that makes a dome around a gnarled tree, nearly twice as tall as I am and about the size of a basketball court in length and width. There are a couple of wooden structures in it—big birdhouses? Some tin trays and what looks like a pond. And birds. Big waterfowl like Boba. Smaller ones, doves, chickens, ducks. A bunch of little ones, I don't know what they are. Some of them are obviously injured: limping, crooked wings flapping; a big one that I can see from here has a mangled beak. A few act almost like they're drunk, walking and flying in wobbling circles, as if they're tied to a pole.

"Wow," I say. So far my plan to get Sparrow alone hasn't worked. We've had a little entourage trailing us every step of the way: Han Rong and then Sophie and the macho guy toting grain sacks. It's like they're all tag-teaming, keeping watch, and I don't know what that means.

"So what's wrong with them?" I ask. "The birds, I mean."

"Many things. Some of them injured. By people. By boats. Even cars. Others, they are sick. Parasites. Diseases. Some of them, they are poisoned, we think, with heavy metals. That's why they act that way, why they can't fly straight."

Sparrow kneels by the enclosure, where a large crow has trotted up to greet her. It has a feather in its beak.

"*Xiao Heizi . . . Ni xihuan huasheng ma?*"

She reaches into a pocket and pulls out a peanut. Xiao Heizi—whose name means "Little Black One"—pokes its beak through the chicken wire, pushing the feather out toward Sparrow's hand, releasing it onto her palm. She holds the peanut between her thumb and finger, and the crow snatches it in its beak.

"We trade gifts," she explains.

I glance around. Sophie and Han Rong are a few yards away. Macho Man totes another big bag of feed over one shoulder, heading toward another chicken-wire cage and shed.

"What about David?" I ask.

"What about him?"

I'm still not thinking that straight, I guess. Before, I'd kept hoping I could ask a simple, direct question and find out what I want to know, which is where the fuck *is* the guy, but I know by now that isn't going to happen. So instead I ask a vague one and get a nonanswer. Great.

"Did he volunteer here?"

"A little." She rises. Meets my eyes for a moment, then looks away. "I'll show you."

I follow her down the path. Boba follows me.

It's colder now, or I'm just catching a chill, and I take a moment to zip up my jacket. I can see my breath on the air, mist surrounding the cone-shaped hills, lighter grey against a dark grey sky. It feels like rain is coming. There's a sudden flapping of wings behind us, maybe from the birds that can't fly straight.

The path we're on leads to the cage and shed where Macho Guy was headed, I think, but I don't see him. Maybe he's inside.

I stop for a moment. I'm not sure I want to go any farther.

Sparrow half turns. "This way," she says, gesturing toward the shed.

It's a big shed, more like a small barn, really, surrounded by another chicken-wire fence. The door is closed. The front of it is featureless. Blank. I shiver in my jacket.

Sparrow opens the gate. "Come on, we just go inside."

"I, uh . . ."

I've already been attacked, twice. Jason was here, and he's vanished.

I just blundered out here like it was safe. Like it was a refuge. But what do I know about her? What do I know about any of these people?

Now Sparrow stops and looks at me. "You okay?" She seems genuinely concerned. Or she's a really good actor. "You need to rest again?"

Remember the wounded antelope. You don't want to be one.

"Oh, no, I'm fine. Just . . . uh, it looks like it might rain."

"Maybe so." She hesitates. "You don't have to see this," she says. "Just, you ask about David."

I have a bunch of thoughts, like David's dead and rotting in there, or maybe maimed, or he's crazy and chained up to keep him from running away, or . . .

Well, fuck.

In for a penny, in for a pound or whatever.

Sparrow pauses by the door of the shed. "Okay, when I open, come in quickly," she says.

She opens the door. I hesitate. And stumble into the dim interior. The door closes behind me.

I smell it before my eyes can adjust.

The unmistakable odor of cat piss.

Something bumps against my calf.

"Holy shit!"

"You don't like cats?" Macho Man asks.

CHAPTER SEVENTEEN

"I, uh . . . wow. This is a lot of cats."

The shed/barn/cathouse—whatever you want to call it—is crawling with cats, or hissing/jumping/purring/meowing with them. I can't begin to count. There are shelves along the walls where they perch, ceiling beams they drape themselves on or pad across, a giant cat tree in the middle of the room that stretches up to a beam with platforms jutting out.

"I just built that," Macho Man says. "The cats love it."

The cats obviously love *him*. We've caught him in the middle of pouring kibble into feeding stations. Several cats rub and lean against his calves.

"I made an outside area, too. You want to see?" He points toward the back of the cathouse.

"Sure. I guess."

I follow him. He opens the door. Several of the cats dash for the exit. There's a yard there, screened in with chicken wire all the way to the top of a mostly-dead tree that looks like it was struck by lightning. Two cats, a white one and a ginger, scramble up the trunk.

Sparrow has crept in behind me, so quietly that I took her for another cat at first.

"So . . ." I try to think how to ask it. "You're a bird sanctuary. And . . . cats?"

Sparrow shrugs.

"We rescue them," Macho Man says proudly. "Somebody post on Weibo that a truck passes by here with many cats. To sell to restaurants, for meat. So we go up there and block the road. Fifty of us. Argue with him for hours. Finally he releases the cats to us."

Weibo is Chinese Twitter. It makes the authorities crazy, but microblogging's so popular that they're afraid to shut it down.

"We pay him," Sparrow explains. "Also, Kang Li is very persuasive."

Macho Man, Kang Li, grins. "I just tell him to think of his karma. Better to release so many cats than to kill them."

"So now we have cats," Sparrow says with a sigh. She gives me a sudden, sidelong glance. "You want one or two? Take them home to Beijing?"

"I . . . well, let me see how things go the next few months. My situation is a little . . . unclear."

Kang Li, the tough guy, scoops up one of the cats, a coal-black one that's all long legs and skinny tail. He flips it over, holding it like a baby. *"Mao mao,"* he croons, scratching its belly. *"Ni tebie lihai!"* You're especially fierce!

"So . . . David," I manage. "How does he fit into all this?"

"He help with the cat rescue," Sparrow explains. "Block road. Take video. That's where we meet."

I think about this. "Video?" I ask.

"YOU KNOW WHY I like cats?" Kang Li leans back in the chair, sucks down his beer. "Because they are affectionate yet independent."

He leans over and scratches Boba's head. Boba blinks his reptile eye, stretches his long neck, and flaps his wings, which I guess means he likes it.

"Here it is," Sparrow says. She's booted up her computer. I push myself to my feet and hobble over to her desk, which is stacked high with paper, books, a dirty teacup, and a couple of rubber-duck bath toys.

On the monitor is a video posted to Youku, which is like Chinese YouTube, except with more censorship and less copyright protection.

There's a two-lane road where a small truck faces off against a weird assortment of vehicles: a newish Buick, a couple of Chery sedans, a beater PLA Jeep, even one of those crazy "mosquito" tractors. A bunch of people stand on the road waving signs, and I recognize Sparrow and Kang Li. Kang Li is at the head of the crowd, confronting the driver, who's red-faced and furious, shaking his fist, and I think he's going to take a swing at Kang Li, but he doesn't. Kang Li just stands there, calm but alert—energized. He gets off on this kind of thing, I'm guessing.

The video's been edited, actually cut together pretty well, and the next shot is of Kang Li with his arm around the driver, calming him down, and another woman I don't recognize talking earnestly to the driver.

Shots of the crowd watching the confrontation.

And shots of the inside of the truck: stacks of bamboo cages with cats crammed into them. You can hear them crying, hissing. Terrified.

Time passes. It gets dark. The activists sit on the road. No one's going anywhere. Shots of activists with their signs and candles.

Finally a cheer goes up from the crowd. Kang Li and the other woman and the driver smile and nod and do little head bows. A deal has been struck.

Next we see the people passing the bamboo crates from person to person, loading them into the cars and the tractor. And in one of those shots I'm pretty sure I see Jason, lending a hand with the loading, his hair longer and darker than in the photo I have of him, his face framed by a backpacker beard.

The final shot: Kang Li with a cat in his arms. The titles read, in Chinese and English: "Yangshuo Friends of Animals—Love cats, don't eat them!"

"That's a good cat," Kang Li says. He's come over to peer at the monitor. "A French lady who has a restaurant in town took that cat. She has three now. Donated a lot of money for the rescue, too."

"So David made that video?" I ask.

Sparrow nods. "Yes. Very good with the camera and the . . . the edits."

"Can you send me the link?" I ask.

I SIT ON THE couch, elevating my leg again. Kang Li brings me a beer. I'm starting to like Kang Li. I mean, how can you not like a guy who's tough, gets gooey over cats, and brings you beer?

Sparrow, meanwhile, sits in front of her computer with a neutral smile. I'm not getting her. I had the feeling, last time in the Gecko, that she knew something, that she wanted to talk to me, but either I was wrong or she's not ready to share.

"Did David ever talk to you about seeds?" I ask.

She frowns. "Seeds?"

"Special ones. GMO. Uh . . ." I'm not sure if she knows that term in English, and I don't know it in Chinese, so I look it up on my phone. "*Jiyingaizao.*"

"*Ah. Wo mingbai.*" She hesitates. "Maybe. Maybe he has this interest."

"So he talked to you about it?"

"Sometimes."

"What did he have to say?"

"Just that . . . such things are damaging. To the natural environment. To animals. And people."

I watch her. She doesn't want to meet my eyes. "What do *you* think?" I ask.

"I don't know enough, maybe."

"Well, *I* do," Kang Li says loudly. "They're dangerous. Come on, look at this country. You can't trust the food, you can't breathe the air, and we should let them make a fish tomato?"

"A fish tomato?"

"*Dui!* Take gene from a fish and put it in a tomato. You Americans tried that."

"We did? Why?"

He shrugs. "Maybe so it can swim?" Then he grins. "Supposed to keep it from freezing, I think."

"*Zhen exin,*" I say, because it really seems pretty disgusting.

"I hear you want to make new kind of fish! Take gene, put in *guiyu. Samenyu,*" he adds, off my blank look.

"Salmon?"

"*Dui.* Corn, hay, rice." Kang Li ticks each one off on his fingers. "They change them so you can use . . ." He turns to Sparrow. "*Zenme shuo 'nongyao'?*"

"Pesticide," she tells him.

"Pesticide," he resumes, "and not kill the plant. But then other weeds become stronger. Must use more and more *nongyao,* pesticide. Too much poison, already a problem in China. We don't need more."

"And now you have the superweeds," Sparrow says hesitantly.

"Yes. The *nongyao* can't kill them. Crowd out other crops."

"Some even have this . . . this *dusu* inside, this poison, to kill insect that eat plant."

"And that's supposed to be okay for us to eat?" I ask. Because it sure doesn't sound okay.

"Maybe." Sparrow gives a tiny, eloquent shrug. "Or maybe cause organ failure. Maybe cancer. Allergies. Make animals sterile. Many health problems. Or just not so nutritious as natural food." She no longer sounds hesitant. "Perhaps factor in death of bees. With no bees, what will happen to food supply?"

"Plus contaminate other crops," Kang Li puts in. "So you don't have original kind anymore. Just changed."

"And once changed, we don't know how the plants develop. Mutate. Could change into something else."

"Something we can't eat," I say slowly, getting it. "Or something that might kill us."

Sparrow nods. "We just don't know."

I remember something else, something that Wa Keung told me about the New Century Hero Rice.

"I've heard you can't save seeds and grow from them the next year," I say. "That you need to buy the seeds each time."

"*Ah, yinwei zhezhong zhongzi bufayu?*" Kang Li asks. The type of seeds are. . . ?

"*Bufayu?*" I ask. It's a word I don't recognize.

"Sterile," Sparrow supplies. "Not necessarily *bufayu*. But buying seeds every year, this is not new. You know hybrid seed?"

I nod. I read the Wikipedia entry anyway.

"Farmers for many generations breed for example two different types of rice to make a better one. But this kind not stable. Second generation not as good as first. By third or fourth, maybe they don't grow at all."

This stuff is making my head hurt. "So how's that different from GMOs?"

"GMO more unpredictable. These kinds not bred by farmer. They change plant DNA, in laboratory, even put in DNA from other species."

"Like the fish tomato?" I guess.

"Yes," she says, nodding hard. "*Just* like that. Because with the gene . . . the gene splicing, you can have the . . . the *tubian*. The mutation. They even try to create seed that fail completely, after first generation. Because maybe second generation already no good."

"So the farmer would *have* to buy new seeds from the company every year," I say, now getting it. "They'd have no choice. And there's no bad second generation to worry about."

"Maybe." Sparrow gives me a narrow-eyed look. "So you have an interest in this topic?"

"I have an interest in finding David, like I told you," I say. "And he's interested in this topic."

Truthfully, I have to say, the whole thing is making me queasy. I mean, it can't be good for you, eating plants with a poison inside them, can it? Or that sterilize themselves. Or that have added fish genes. I keep picturing tomatoes with fins. That can't be a good idea.

I notice that Sparrow's still watching me, and I'm pretty sure there's something she's not saying.

"We have dinner now," she finally does say. "Please, join us."

I'm really not sure if it's a great idea, but I stay for dinner. It's Sparrow, Kang Li, me, and Han Rong—the other volunteers have gone home. We sit at a folding table that, before the meal, held stacks of papers, books, and boxes of seed and veterinary supplies. No beer fish but plenty of beer, plus tofu, vegetables, rice, and some pumpkin dumplings that are really awesome. We eat, and we chat, and I get asked the typical questions: How long have I been in China, where did I learn Chinese, am I married, do I have children?

Kang Li holds court, even though I'd thought that the sanctuary was Sparrow's project, not his, but then a lot of guys are like that, and it's not as if he's totally acting like he's in charge, more that he enjoys talking and drinking beer and pontificating about stuff—for example, the Chinese government: "Corrupt, useless cowards, they don't care about protecting environment, just approving projects to keep enough people working so that there aren't more 'mass incidents.'" Or Chinese businessmen: "Completely immoral, most of them. All they care about is making money, and fuck everyone else." Or Chinese people in general: "*Mamu*, you know that term?—too numb to care about others. This country can never be great until social-relations reform." Or America: "Hypocrites, don't you think so? All that talk about human rights and the environment, but you invade other countries and don't sign Kyoto treaty." Or Communism: "a failed experiment." Capitalism: ditto. And cats: he's in favor.

All the while Sparrow sits there contributing the occasional word, sometimes smiling, sometimes seeming annoyed, but it's that kind of affectionate annoyance where I'm wondering, Are these two a couple? Family? Or what?

As for Han Rong, he mostly smiles, laughing at Kang Li's jokes and giggling at his more outrageous remarks, the sort of nerdy guy who deliberately flies under the radar and goes out of his way to act like Mr. Nonthreatening. I'm not buying it, but maybe that's just because I'm paranoid.

He looks a little old to be a student, I think.

After dinner is done, Sparrow and Han Rong clear the dishes while Kang Li and I continue to drink beer. I know I have a decision to make, and I'm really not sure what the smart thing to do is.

I don't think I should go back to my hotel, to Maggie's Guesthouse, even though I'm paying for it and I've got a bag there. Mr. US Polo Team and his buddy already have it staked out.

Maybe another hostel out here somewhere, I think. Just for the night. And I'll decide what makes sense to do tomorrow.

"Could I use your Internet?" I ask Sparrow. "To look for a hotel?"

"Oh, but that's not necessary," she says quickly. "You can stay here if you'd like." She ducks her head behind her hand, seemingly embarrassed. "This couch is not the best bed, but you are welcome to it."

How safe is it for me here? Is it worth sticking around to try and figure out what it is that Sparrow isn't saying? Or is that another one of my really bad ideas?

At that moment Boba trots over to me, his toenails clicking on the concrete, and stretches out his long neck, like he wants his head scratched.

"Thanks," I say. "Thanks, I'll take you up on that."

Look, they rescue birds and cats—I mean, they can't be dangerous.

I'VE HAD BEER, AND I've had Percocet, so I fall asleep in spite of the lumpy couch, my leg propped up on its back cushions, and my general paranoia. It occurs to me, before I drift off, that I really need to think a little more about some of the shit I do. You know, take a ruthless inventory or whatever.

I'm having some dream where there's all these people sitting at a long table, including Reverend Jim from my churchgoing days, wearing his Hawaiian shirt, and he's saying to me, "All of us are different aspects of God, and separateness is just an illusion," and I'm thinking, Well, that's easy for you to say.

Then there's this honking, like a car horn that got stuck, and I'm really pissed off—it's like, turn off your fucking horn, asshole.

And then I wake up and realize that it's Boba making all the noise. I grab the flashlight I stashed under my pillow, 'cause I'm not totally stupid, flick it on, and there's Han Rong with his hand in my backpack.

"What the fuck," I manage.

CHAPTER EIGHTEEN

"OH," HAN RONG SAYS. "I'm sorry."

"You're sorry?" I yank the backpack away from him. "Why are you messing with my stuff?"

"I . . ." His head swivels back and forth. "Maybe I made a mistake."

"You think?" I aim my flashlight at his face. "So what was it you were trying to do?"

"Just . . ." He tries to smile. "Maybe it's a little complicated."

"Yeah, I'd say so."

Boba stretches his neck out and pokes his beak in my face. I guess he wants attention, and hey, he deserves it. I scratch his head.

"That bird, he really likes you," Han Rong says, with a nervous giggle.

"Don't change the subject. What were you doing with my stuff?"

That's when Sparrow and Kang Li come stumbling into the room, her wearing an oversize T-shirt, him wearing boxer shorts, both with major cases of bed head.

Couple, I decide.

"What's going on?" Kang Li barks.

"I caught your friend here going through my backpack."

"What?" Kang Li wheels around in Han Rong's direction. "Are you some kind of thief?" he yells in Chinese.

"No, I . . . I can explain."

"Yeah, that's what you keep saying," I snap.

At that point Sparrow steps forward, reluctantly. Runs her fingers through her hair. "He can," she says with a sigh. "Maybe I should make some tea."

WE ALL HAVE OUR tea, which is to say Sparrow and Han Rong. Kang Li and I split a beer. I'm jittery. An adrenaline rush will do that. We sit there, me on the couch, with my best friend Boba standing sentinel, Han Rong, Sparrow, and Kang Li on two folding chairs and one secondhand armchair that looks like it was salvaged from a dumpster, pulled into a semicircle across from me.

"Okay, so explain," I say.

Sparrow and Han Rong exchange significant looks. Kang Li, meanwhile, looks almost as frustrated as I feel.

"Xiaoma, what's going on?" he asks.

"We don't know who she works for," Sparrow tells him. She turns to me. "We don't know if we can trust you."

"Look, you want to search my bag, search my bag," I say. "You're not going to find anything one way or another. It's like I told you, like I keep telling all of you—I'm just trying to find David so I can tell his family he's okay. Maybe get him to come home to see his brother. That's it. The rest of this, it isn't my business. I'm not going to go running to the authorities because you're rescuing cats. I'm just a *laowai* with a little business representing artists."

"Artists?" Sparrow asks. "What kind of artists?"

"Chinese artists. You heard of Zhang Jianli?"

Kang Li and Han Rong shake their heads. I didn't really expect them to know who Lao Zhang is—it's not like *I* could have named a contemporary Chinese artist before I got involved with him.

Sparrow's forehead wrinkles.

"You know who he is?" I ask, surprised.

"I heard of him."

I shiver a little in the cold of the farmhouse. Coincidences make me nervous. Nonetheless, I get out my wallet and extract a business card and hand it to her in proper two-handed fashion. "I can show you the Web site if you want," I say.

Sparrow studies the card. Looks at me. "Why don't you tell her, Han Rong?" she says.

"I work for Chinese biotech company," Han Rong says, clutching his teacup, for warmth maybe. It's chilly in the farmhouse, and both Kang Li and Sparrow have put on sweats. "I take leave from my job recently. I . . . have some problems with the work we do." He stares into his cup. A good imitation of contrite.

"Like what?" I ask.

"Just . . . you know, the safety, it is not so clear from results. We need more time to test. But there is a big rush to get this new rice into market."

"Rice?" I fish through my backpack and grab the New Century Hero rice bag. "Like this one?" I toss it at him.

He puts down the teacup. Picks up the sack. Unfolds it. Studies the label.

"Yes, I think so. You see this?" He rises, comes over to where I sit on the couch, points to a string of letters and numbers in smallish print on the back of the sack. "With the 'XE'? Stands for Hongxing and Eos."

Hongxing = Red Star. And Eos . . . that's the American company Jason has a bug up his ass about.

"So this rice . . . this is made by an American company?"

"In part. It is . . . a partnership. A joint venture. Hongxing is Chinese side, Hongxing Nongye Chanpin." Han Rong bows his head. "This is company I work for."

I try to figure it out. I wish I were smarter, or faster, or at least more awake. But I'm none of those things, so I just ask the stupid question:

"So how is David connected? Or am I wasting my time out here?"

Han Rong hesitates. "I come here, to Yangshuo, to get away from stressful situation. Enjoy time in nature. I meet Sparrow and David at the Gecko. We begin to talk, about problems in the environment. You know, China's environmental problems are relatively serious," he adds earnestly.

No shit, I think. "Yeah, so I hear."

"I start to talk to David, about my work, about the concerns I have," he continues. "David is very knowledgeable on this subject. Especially about our American partner, Eos. He tell me he is involved before in criticizing their activities. He tell me also they are very dangerous. They have spies who work for them, who can cause trouble for people. That's why . . . that's why I look in your things."

"'Cause you thought I might be a spy for Eos?" I laugh. "Right. Like if I were a spy, I'd leave the evidence in my bag for you to find."

Kang Li slams his beer bottle down on the desk. "Why didn't you tell me about any of this?" he says to Sparrow in Mandarin, and he sounds pretty pissed off.

"Because you like to talk too much," she snaps back. "You go on Weibo, go on Youku, you say whatever you think, you don't care if you get in trouble—"

"I'm not going to get in trouble—"

"You don't know that! Besides, sometimes you can accomplish more by saying less."

"I'm not criticizing the government! I'm talking about protecting the natural environment!"

"Sometimes I also think you are completely naïve."

"No one can say anything," Han Rong announces in English, sounding anxious. "Not yet. Not until we have proof."

"Proof of what?" I ask.

"Many GMOs not approved for use in China," Sparrow explains. "Han Rong thinks Hongxing and Eos selling them anyway. This Hero Rice."

"This company, this New Century Seeds, it's not a legal company. Not registered," Han Rong says. "Hongxing and Eos set this up to sell seeds, get them in the marketplace."

"Why?" I ask.

"Because once GMO rice in the environment, easier to get official approval. It is like . . . how do you say?" Han Rong smiles. "Easier to beg forgiveness than ask permission."

"They can say, 'Look, this product is being used, there are no problems,'" Sparrow tells me. "Even though we can't say for certain if there are long-term bad effects or not."

"And if there is contamination, if farmers grow this rice by mistake, then Hongxing and Eos can say, 'We own these seeds,'" Han Rong adds. "'This . . . product.'"

I think about this. "Wait a second. You work for these guys. And you don't have proof?"

Han Rong's eyes do this little shifty thing, just for an instant, but I catch it.

"I don't have it," he says.

"And you can't get it?"

"I can't be involved," he says frantically. "You know how things are in China. My company has government connections.

They can cause a lot of trouble for me. Besides," he adds in a low voice, like a cartoon conspirator, "is much easier to pressure the foreign partner."

Eos.

I'm starting to get it.

"So you told David about the project. You gave him the information about the fake companies."

He smiles, a big beaming one, and nods. "Because David is foreigner. He says he can talk to foreign media. Help put pressure on Eos."

"Jesus Christ," I mutter. Of all the things Jason could and should be doing, going after his old nemesis, in China, is pretty much the opposite of a good idea.

The kid is obsessed. Completely out of his mind. And this guy Han Rong took advantage of it.

For some kind of noble goal?

I don't know. Color me suspicious.

"Where's David now?"

Han Rong shakes his head. "Don't know. Last I hear, he go to Guiyu. Since then nothing."

I glance over at Kang Li and Sparrow. She sits there, eyes downcast, seeming to stare at her hands clasped in her lap.

"You should have told me," Kang Li tells her in Chinese, glowering. He stands, pounds down the last slug of his beer, and stalks out.

Sparrow sighs. "Maybe," she mumbles.

So AFTER THAT I sleep. I mean, might as well. If I'm being played by Han Rong, I figure he's already made his move. "Good night," he said after Kang Li flounced off, trailed by Sparrow a few minutes later.

"What are you doing here?" I asked him.

Han Rong smiled at me, bobbed his head. "Just taking a rest. Helping with the birds."

Right.

WAY, WAY TOO EARLY, Boba sticks his beak in my ear. Makes little chuckling noises. Kind of like a giant white chicken rooting for seeds. Or bugs.

"Shit, bird," I mutter.

Not that it really matters, because a few minutes after that, Sparrow creeps in. Okay, "creeps" isn't fair. She's not being sneaky, I don't think—she's just light on her feet, someone whose footsteps don't echo.

"*Zao hao*. You want tea? Nescafé?"

"Nescafé. Thanks."

By the time Sparrow brings me a chipped mug full of caffeine, sugar, and non-dairy creamer, Kang Li has shuffled in, scratching and yawning.

"*Zao hao*," he mumbles, taking a seat in the decaying armchair. The fabric used to be some sort of gold brocade, blackened now and worn out in places, with hints of stuffing peeking through the frayed threads.

I look for hints about what happened between them after their fight last night, and I can't really tell.

"Good morning," I repeat.

I sip my Nescafé, they have their tea, and none of us says anything for a while.

"Can we give you a ride anywhere?" Sparrow finally asks.

I think about this. "Thank you," I say. "Maybe back to my hotel. If you don't mind."

KANG LI VOLUNTEERS TO drive me. But first he needs to see to the cats and do a few other chores. "No problem," I tell him. It would be nice if we could make it to Yangshuo before noon so I can save myself another day's charge at Maggie's, but it's not going to break me if we don't.

Sparrow, meanwhile, checks on the birds needing special treatment in the main farmhouse.

I follow along behind her.

She crouches down at the cage with the injured cormorant, the fishing bird with the infected neck.

"How is he doing?" I ask.

She sighs and shakes her head. "Maybe not so good."

"I'm sorry," I say.

I watch as she reaches in and grasps the bird at the base of its skull, applies some kind of ointment to its oozing neck, squirts something—water? medicine?—down its gullet with a plastic syringe, coaxes it to eat what smells like mashed-up fish. The bird lowers its head, like it's embarrassed, not willing to eat.

"*Chi yidian*," Sparrow whispers to the bird. Eat a little.

"Do you trust Han Rong?" I ask.

"Not really," she says.

KANG LI DRIVES ME into town in his vintage PLA Jeep. He drives like he does a lot of things—with swagger, one hand on the wheel, other arm draped casually across the seat back.

"Han Rong, he's okay, I guess," Kang Li says. "He comes to sanctuary a few days a week, works a little. Best thing he does? Gives money. I think this is really why Sparrow has sympathy for him."

"Ah." Well, that explains a lot. You got a guy who pitches in, says all the right things, and, most important, helps pay for the birdseed and kibble. Maybe you're not inclined to look too closely at his story.

And who knows? Maybe it's even true.

Kang Li shrugs. "Hard to keep the place going. Always short of money. Sparrow worries."

I nod, distracted. We're just pulling in to Yangshuo, and I'm more than a little nervous about going back to my hotel. I've got stuff there, and if I don't check out, God knows how many days of charges I'll pile up before they give up on me. But who's to say that those two rent-a-thugs, Mr. US Polo Team and his plain-wrap pal, don't still have the place staked out?

I glance over at Kang Li. He's got his aviator shades on, his careless, confident vibe, and I think I understand what kind of guy he is: the kind who gets off on a little action.

"I have a small problem," I say.

"Sure, I can wait." Kang Li grins. I told him about my mystery stalkers, and, just like I figured, he's into it.

I direct him around the back of the hostel. It's on an alley, with an overflowing dumpster and a rack of cruiser bikes and a minuscule parking lot, two of the three cars there double-parked. "Ten minutes," I say. All I'm going to do is run up to my room, get my duffel bag, and check out.

The back entrance to the hostel is unlocked. I head up the sagging wooden stairs to the second floor. Swipe my key card. The Do Not Disturb sign is hanging on the doorknob where I left it.

Inside, it's dark, the blackout curtains drawn, the lights turned off. I never really unpacked, so all I have to do is grab my duffel from the chair by the desk and TV where I left it. So I do that. Head downstairs. Approach the battered front desk, where a girl with dyed blue hair sits and stares at her monitor.

"Hey, *ni hao. Wo xihuan jiezhang.*"

I push my receipt for the deposit across the counter. She nods, picks up a walkie-talkie, calls for a *fuwuyuan* to check out my room and make sure that I didn't leave anything and/or steal the television.

While she's doing all this and toting up the figures, I stand there anxiously, the nerves in my back and shoulders twitching like whiskers on a mouse.

I owe less than the deposit I'd left. She hands me a night's worth of yuan, a hundred fifty and change.

"Okay, thank you very much, please come visit us again!"

"I will, thanks," I say, jamming the money into my jeans pocket. "Very nice hotel!"

And I am out of there. I walk as fast as I can, which is not very—daypack on my back, duffel on my shoulder, Yangshuo walking stick helping me balance—open the back door to the tiny parking lot, and I notice two things: First, Kang Li and his Jeep aren't there. Second, a new black Buick is, and leaning against the driver's door reading a manga is US Polo Team.

I close the door. Fumble for the dead bolt. Lock it. Scramble as fast as I can back into the minimal lobby. Blue-haired girl looks up and smiles.

"Sorry!" I say. "Wrong way!"

Fuck, fuck, fuck. Did he see me? And Kang Li—*fuck*. I thought I'd read him right. Guess not. What the fuck do I do now?

Out the front. Look for a taxi. Ditch the duffel if I have to.

I shouldn't have gone back. So what if they have my passport number? My visa? So I get into trouble and pay them a bribe later. Like I'm not in worse trouble now?

I push open the Plexiglas door. Step outside. Look toward Xi Jie. And see Plain-Wrap Windbreaker, stationed by the lamppost.

He lunges toward me. I stumble back.

"Hey!" I hear behind me. I half turn. And there's Kang Li.

Who takes two steps up, balls his hand into a fist, swings, and connects with the guy's jaw.

Windbreaker staggers, Kang Li kicks him in the side of his knee, and he goes down, hard.

"Come on!" Kang Li yells. *"Lai, lai!"*

He gestures over his shoulder, and there's the Jeep, parked way illegally, two wheels on the sidewalk.

I throw the duffel into the back and scramble into the passenger seat as Kang Li vaults into the driver's seat, just like in the movies, and jams the key into the ignition.

"Where to?" he asks as we bounce off the curb, brakes squealing.

CHAPTER NINETEEN

"I wait for you, and I see the Buick. The guy in the jacket. Just like you told me. So I move the Jeep to the front. Hope you find me."

"Good plan," I manage. We're weaving through traffic on the main road out of Yangshuo, and I seriously don't know how he missed the middle-aged couple on the tandem cruiser bike and the kid on the skateboard.

"Who are these guys?" Kang Li asks. "What you do to piss them off?"

"Wish I knew."

We swerve around a bicycle cart loaded with a mountain of Styrofoam packing, and now we're on the highway heading back to Guilin.

"You think it has something to do with this . . . with these seeds? The thing that Han Rong and David— *Sha bi!*" He waves his fist as we screech around a tractor that crawled onto the road and barely chugs into gear. "Some people should not be driving," he mutters.

"Heh. Yeah."

"So where you want to go?"

I think about this. "Guilin, I guess. If that's not too much trouble."

"No trouble. We can be there in half an hour."

The way he drives, probably so.

Kang Li glances at his rearview mirror. His face scrunches up in a frown. "That the same car?" He points a thumb over his shoulder.

I look behind me. The Jeep has a roll-bar frame with a battered canvas roof, a scratched plastic "window" in the back, and it's hard to see through it. I check the side mirror. And see a new black Buick, moving out from behind a bus, trying to pass it.

"Same kind of car," I say. But I can't be sure. Buicks, for whatever reason, are prestige cars in China. There are a lot of them here.

The Buick nestles in between the bus and a taxi, which is the car right behind us.

"Huh," Kang Li says. "Let's find out."

He glances to his left and suddenly spins the steering wheel hard in that direction, and we cut across the oncoming lane, right in front of a military truck, and barrel onto a small road that leads into a little town, but I have my eyes closed and am not sure of that part for a moment.

"Holy shit," I gasp.

We're flying down that road, and now I open my eyes and can see the town, built mostly of that yellow brick they use around here, interspersed with white tile and concrete, and as we pass, a couple of panicked chickens flutter into the air and a mom yanks her kid back away from the street, and we careen around a corner, barely avoiding a guy selling yams off a cart.

"You see him now?" Kang Li asks.

I look. Fuck if the Buick isn't following us.

"Yeah."

"*Cao dan*," he mutters. He steers hard right, and the Jeep goes up on two wheels as we take the corner onto another narrow street. Through the gaps in the low buildings, I can see fields, and before too long the buildings fall away and we're bouncing down a rutted dirt road bordering rice paddies. We turn again, onto an even bumpier lane that turns to mud as it suddenly runs downhill into an even smaller village. The Buick is still right on our ass. We nearly take out an old guy on a bike and we kick pebbles onto a couple of old aunties shucking corn out on a stoop, and then we're through that village and into more fields. The road's even muddier now as we barrel along, the Buick behind us, and I think, okay, maybe this was why Sparrow didn't tell Kang Li about the whole David–Han Rong thing, because this is insane, and that's when Kang Li pulls the Jeep off the road and heads into a flooded field. The Buick follows. The Jeep chugs and churns and keeps moving, oversize wheels throwing up wads of mud.

The Buick? Sits there. Stuck. Wheels spinning in the muck. We pull away, leaving them behind.

Kang Li pumps his fist. "*Diu na ma!*" he shouts, grinning.

"Hoo-ah!" I yell back. "That was awesome!"

"*Zhen niubi!*" he agrees.

We're at the end of the field now, and with a grinding of gears the Jeep crawls up onto another tiny road. I look back at the deep gashes our tires made through the field. "I hope we didn't trash his crops too much."

"Not planted yet. Besides"—Kang Li shrugs—"let the guys in the Buick pay."

Works for me.

"To Guilin?" he asks.

I nod. "Sounds good."

★ ★ ★

I ASK KANG LI to drop me someplace with wireless, close to the train station.

Here's the thing: Sure, planes are faster. But when you buy a plane ticket, you have to show your passport. Trains? Just hand over your cash.

I don't know who those guys are, who they're working for, but if they're at all connected, I'd rather not leave them an easy way to figure out where I'm going.

Which brings up the question: Where do I go now?

I figure I have three choices. Back to Beijing. Or to Guiyang, capital of Guizhou, or Dali, in Yunnan, where the other two seed companies from Daisy's list are.

Beijing is probably the sensible choice.

I haven't decided, I tell myself. I'll think about it for a while, and then I'll make a decision. Based on . . . you know, rational shit, like the train schedule and what makes the most sense for me to do.

Yeah, right.

THERE'S A HOSTEL WITH a bar and a café about ten minutes' walk from the station, advertising free Wi-Fi. Kang Li drops me off at the curb. On it, more accurately. "Get you close," he says.

So it's only a couple of yards, but I appreciate it. My leg hurts like hell, from sitting in the car, from the kidney-rattling chase through the rice paddies.

It's no big, I tell myself. It's just pain.

"Thanks," I say. "Thanks a lot. I mean, that was . . . that was . . ."

Kang Li waves a hand, brushing my appreciation aside. "*Mei wenti,*" he says. Not a problem. "It was good fun."

We get out of the Jeep. Kang Li grabs my duffel from the back. "I'll take it inside for you."

"No need. It's not heavy."

He hands the duffel to me, and I sling it over my shoulder.

"You sure you don't know who they are?" he asks.

"I really don't." I hesitate. "I don't think they know about me visiting the sanctuary, whoever they are."

Unless they're connected to someone at the Gecko. Someone who saw me talking to Sparrow.

I push the thought aside.

"You should still be careful." I fake a smile. "Sparrow needs you to take care of the cats."

He grins. "I will. *Bie jiaoji.*" Don't worry.

I GET A TABLE at the bar/café. One wall has money from all over the world plastered to it. Another is fake brick. It's just after 1:00 P.M., so I order a beer and a pizza and get out my laptop.

Of course I've got a ton of emails, and I tell myself not to get sucked into those, though I do take a minute to read the one from my mom ("*Back in Beijing, the apartment's fine, except the toilet in the guest bathroom isn't flushing and there are some pretty bad smells, so I just have the door shut for now*"). I note that I have a couple from Vicky Huang, and I think, Shit, I was supposed to meet with her, or with Sidney Cao, or with somebody, while I was in Yangshuo, but that's going to have to wait.

I look for the email from Sparrow with the link to the video she showed me, the one that Jason helped put together.

I watch it again.

There's that one glimpse of Jason, loading the crated cats into a car.

How is this going to help me?

I check out the links on the video. Here's one for Yangshuo Friends of Animals. I click on it and find their website. In Chinese, of course. It would help if I read Chinese better, but I don't. So I just scroll down until I come to a post with photos, photos of cats, in bamboo cages. The truck. The rescue. This is it.

And here's the embedded video.

I go to Babelfish, an Internet translator. It's not perfect, but in a pinch it will give you a quick and dirty translation of a web page.

And at the bottom of the post it says, "Thanking for the production of video element to Wolf Child."

I look up "wolf" on my handy iPhone Chinese dictionary. "Wolf child," *langhai*, has its own entry. It doesn't just mean "baby wolf." *Langhai* is a term for a human child raised by wolves.

What did Dog say about his and Jason's parents? I try to remember. It wasn't like we talked about things that much, back in the Sandbox. Our whole "relationship," if you want to call it that, wasn't exactly about sharing serious emotional stuff. He mostly gave me shit, and we occasionally messed around.

Everyone's parents are fucked up. I suddenly hear his voice in my head, saying that. I remember, when he said it, we were hanging out in the dining hall, having gotten our tacos and a Coke in his case, a mochaccino in mine. The air-con was working that day, I remember, because I'd gotten a chill off all the sweat that had soaked my clothes. I'd just read some email from my mom, about some guy she'd been seeing and how it hadn't worked out, and I was bitching about it, like, how could she keep making the same stupid mistakes over and over again?

"Most of them shouldn't have kids, but they do, and here we are." Dog leaned back in his chair, laughed a little. "People do the best they can. Sometimes it's not good enough."

★ ★ ★

So, Wolf Child, AKA Langhai. I do a search on Youku for users with that name. And what do you know, there he is. With five videos posted. Including the Yangshuo cat rescue.

"You fucking idiot," I mutter.

Okay, maybe not totally. All you have to do to get a Youku account is provide a name and an email address, and that stuff's easy enough to disguise. Hotmail, Yahoo!, a host of others, you don't have to give your real name.

But still. The guy's a fugitive. He fled to China, which was stupid enough. And he's left a video trail.

Here's one from Guiyu.

I click on it.

Shots of the countryside. Music underneath, some kind of weird techno stuff that makes me nervous. But he's good at this. The video is powerful. The smoking fields. The mountains of electronic scrap. The blackened streams.

And people. Workers surrounded by clouds of toxic steam. Their arms covered with rashes. Children, little kids, standing in front of piles of wire and keyboards.

Text crawls across the screen, in English and Chinese, saying things like, "Guiyu is the largest e-waste site on earth." "Guiyu's children have a seventy percent higher rate of lead poisoning than average." "Guiyu's water is undrinkable."

And then shots of a protest, a mob of farmers from the look of it, surrounding a government building, holding signs and clenching rakes and hoes in their fists. "The pollution has spread beyond Guiyu, killing crops and contaminating farmland."

Huh, I think. In China stuff like this gets "harmonized" pretty fast, scrubbed right off the Internet, but on the other hand there are so many "mass incidents" in China that it's hard to catch them all, and Langhai hasn't had a ton of hits on his videos yet.

The truth is out there, but if no one sees it, does it matter?

I look at the titles of the other videos: "Beautiful Yangshuo" and "Dangerous Seeds." I watch the second one. Most of it's a compilation of still images, shots of fields and corn and the occasional PowerPoint slide. The narration is in Mandarin, with English and Chinese subtitles. It's a sort of brief history of GMO plants and why they should scare us, a summary of the stuff I read and the things that Sparrow and Kang Li and Han Rong told me at the sanctuary.

The Mandarin speaker is a woman—Daisy, maybe? I can't tell. We talked mostly in English. Maybe some other cute Chinese girl he's met along the way.

Okay, call me bitter. But a guy like Jason, good-looking, American, he's going to find Chinese girlfriends pretty easily.

The last shot: a graphic of a Chinese proletariat hero brandishing a hoe, a field of golden rice. "New Century Hero Rice."

I get that prickly feeling, the one that's part fear and part connection, like I've stumbled into an electric current.

"Is this a hero or a traitor?" the woman asks.

The most recent video, posted just two weeks ago, is called "Dali Scene."

Dali, in Yunnan, the province on China's southwestern border. The second location on Daisy's list of seed companies.

THERE ARE TWO TRAINS daily from Guilin to Kunming, the capital of Yunnan, one at 3:30 P.M. leaving from Guilin North, the other at about 4:45 P.M. from the main train station close to the hostel. From Kunming it's easy to get a train or a bus to Dali.

Yeah, I'm going to Dali. Yeah, I know it's a stupid idea. But I've come this far, I might as well keep going, right?

Right.

I could probably make the 3:30 P.M. train if I hustled, but when I go to check train tickets at the handy hostel travel desk, they make a call and tell me that the only sleeping berths available are two upper soft sleepers and one upper hard sleeper, and I really don't know if I can manage the climb up to either of them right now.

There's a lower soft sleeper available on the 4:45 P.M. train, and for a small surcharge they'll buy the ticket for me and bring it back to the hostel.

So that's what I decide to do. I hand over the money for a ticket. I hang out in the bar/restaurant. Have another beer, then some coffee. Watch "Beautiful Yangshuo" and "Dali Scene." The Yangshuo video includes footage of the Yangshuo Ancient Village Artist Retreat Inn, and I wonder if they paid for it, paid Jason/David/Langhai to shoot the piece, because it sure is a good advertisement for them—the video's really well done. Maybe he's putting some of these pieces up on Youku so he can get work from them.

And that's when it occurs to me: These video sites have messaging.

Maybe I can send Jason an email.

I sit back, staring at the last frame of "Beautiful Yangshuo," and consider.

If I write him, tell him I'm Dog's friend, tell him how worried his family is, how much it would mean to Dog to hear from him, that would be doing my duty, right? Completing the mission. No need to go all the way to Dali.

Then I think, But I wouldn't know for sure that he's okay. That he believes I am who I say I am.

I mean, I guess I could try to get Sparrow to vouch for me. That is, if I can trust Sparrow. If Sparrow can trust me.

I should just bag it. Except I already bought the train ticket.

I figure I might as well go. My leg's feeling better, so I'm not so worried I'm going to drop dead from a blood clot. And what am I going to do back in Beijing, other than deal with my mom and Andy, a toilet that won't flush, and the DSD?

Besides, Dali's supposed to be beautiful, and I never got to float down a river on a bamboo raft.

CHAPTER TWENTY

WE GET INTO KUNMING at 10:35 A.M., and I have less than an hour to catch the train to Dali.

No big deal, you'd think, but this is China, where most times you get on a train it's like an escape from the fucking Nazis or something: mobs of people carrying crazy amounts of crap, pushing, shoving, determined to get on that train first, which can be kind of scary, going through gates and up and down stairs. For a lot of Chinese, if you're going any distance, the train is how you go. If you're a migrant worker, one of the tens of millions traveling for work, especially if you're trying to get home one of the few times a year you have a holiday, you pray you can get a train ticket.

I've learned never to travel during those times.

But even though this isn't one of those times, the train I'm trying to catch is hard seats only, and that scene can be pretty Darwin.

I'm wiped out. I didn't sleep too much on the overnight train, a combination of some snoring business dude, pain, and nerves. I made myself a double Starbucks VIA before we pulled in, and that's hardly put a dent in my exhaustion.

Kunming is supposed to be a cool city. I've heard a lot of

great things about it. They have really nice weather, a hipster-foreigner ghetto, lots of pretty scenery. But the Kunming train station is freaky. I have to go downstairs to buy my ticket to Dali—you can't buy tickets for a train that doesn't go through your departure city, don't ask me why—and I've never seen so many *nongmin*, peasants, camped out in a train station before, sleeping on the ground, propped up against their faded plastic bundles, sitting there, waiting for . . . I don't know what. Wearing their patched clothes, their cast-off T-shirts, faces tanned and thickened by years of sun. Staring at me like I'm a total alien.

I'm looking for the ticket window. My leg hurts, my duffel's slipping off my shoulder, and I really need to pee.

"*Xiaojie. Xiaojie. Qing ni, bangzhu wo. Bangzhu wo xiaohai.*" Help me, miss. Help my little child.

I turn to look, and there's this beggar lady crawling toward me on her knees, clutching a filthy kid in one arm, her other hand outstretched. "*Qing ni, bangzhu women.*"

I so do not have time for this right now. I give her my best blank look and keep walking.

And she grabs my leg.

"Please, please," she sobs. "Please help me and my child!"

The pain is so intense that I don't even scream. I just do a face plant, my cheek hitting the slick marble pavers, the shock only barely absorbed by my outstretched hand, my duffel bag landing with a whump to one side.

"*Cao ni!*" I yell. "Get your hands off me!"

The kid starts to wail. I shake my head, wait till the white spots in my vision clear, push myself up to a sitting position.

A crowd has gathered around us—*nongmin*, mostly. They stand there, arms clasped behind their backs, staring like they're watching a play, maybe one called *Foreigners Do the Strangest Things*.

"You've never seen a foreigner before?" I yell at them. "What are you all, *zhutou*?"

"Sorry," the woman whispers. "Sorry."

I look at her, and she's sitting there with her blackened clothes and her howling baby and a frightened look, and suddenly I don't care if it's a scam, if she's run by some boss of an organized beggar ring; it's just sad and horrible, and I want to get away, go someplace where I can pretend this stuff doesn't exist.

Ha-ha. Good luck with that one.

I try to stand up, and I can't. The people in the crowd shuffle their feet. Mutter at one another. Point. A couple of them get out cell phones and snap pictures.

Fucking great.

I drop my duffel. I can't stand up with the weight of it on my shoulder. I push myself to my feet, slowly, with my Yangshuo walking stick. Try to blink the pain away. Adjust my daypack and grab the duffel strap.

The beggar woman scrambles to her feet. Then she does this totally weird thing—she puts her hands under the duffel and boosts it up, so that I can easily adjust the strap pad on my shoulder.

The baby has stopped crying. Its face is smeared with dirt, I notice. I wonder, did Mom put the dirt there before they came out of whatever hole they're living in, so the kid would look more pathetic?

The baby stares at me, dark eyes the color of coffee beans.

I reach into my jeans pocket and pull out a couple of wadded-up twenty-yuan notes and give them to the woman, because I'm such a fucking idiot.

And of course I miss the fucking 11:20 A.M. train to Dali.

S o . I B U Y A ticket for the next available train, which doesn't leave until 11:30 P.M. I score a bottom bunk on a hard sleeper—

it's a seven hour trip, and even if I can't sleep, I figure it's better I should be able to stretch out my leg. I check my duffel bag at a locker, and I hobble back outside, to the chaos of the station and of Kunming in general, and somewhere past the giant black plastic policeman robot—I'm not sure what it does, but it looks like some pervy child of Robocop and a Legos man—I catch a taxi.

"Where do foreigners like to go in Kunming?" I ask the driver.

He starts going on about the Stone Forest and then some other theme park an hour or two outside of town that, if I understand him correctly, involves dwarves, which is kind of tempting, but I shake my head and lift up my hand. "Just want to go someplace close by. I have a train to catch later."

"Maybe Wenlin Jie."

It's a street near the university. There's a lake not too far from here, he tells me, "Very beautiful. Very peaceful. You can go there and drink tea if you like."

On the ride from the train station, Kunming looks like the other second-tier cities I've seen: too much traffic, the same banks and shopping malls, and big glass and plastic fronted buildings. More trees, maybe. The weather's not bad for this time of year—shirtsleeve appropriate—and the air smells pretty much like air, as opposed to soot and chemicals.

I lean back against the bench seat, my leg and wrist throbbing.

By the time we get to the university district, to Cuihu, Green Lake Park, everything seems to slow down. The buildings are smaller. There are more trees. People stroll, like they're not in a hurry to get anywhere.

Wenlin Jie is a little street lined with small businesses, including a place called Teabucks. If I didn't so need coffee, I'd stop there. The taxi driver takes me a few blocks farther, and I can tell that we've entered a *laowai* ghetto. I see an ice-cream parlor, a pizza place, a wine store, and a head shop. Most of the people on the sidewalk are Chinese, but there are plenty of foreigners around, too—students and backpacker types mostly, plus a few older Westerners who give off that long-term-expat vibe.

There's a place on the corner called Salvador's advertising coffee. "You can stop here," I tell the driver.

Inside, it's dark wood. Nice music. Two levels, with computer terminals and a makeshift travel library, a glass case displaying their T-shirts, coffee, juices and all kinds of other organic products. Vegetables. Meats. Cheese, even. There's an explanation on the menu about how all the employees get health care and free English lessons and actual paid vacations. It's like I've suddenly been transported to Berkeley or something.

I order a cup of "fresh-brewed coffee" with an espresso shot, plus a breakfast quesadilla. Boot up my laptop. Since I've had my phone off all this time, I figure I'd better at least check my email.

The coffee is good. The quesadilla is excellent. This isn't a bad place, I'm thinking. Maybe I should move here. Set up shop. It's cheaper than Beijing, and I've heard that a lot of artists are buying second homes around Kunming.

I'm thinking this when I hear the Skype orchestra hit signaling a contact request.

It's Vicky Huang. That's the name that comes up, anyway, in a little box requesting that I add her as a contact. No photo, just a blank icon.

I mean, this behavior really is reaching stalker level.

I think about ignoring it. But there's that whole, not wanting to piss off a Chinese billionaire factor.

I make sure the video camera on my laptop is off, and I accept.

Thirty seconds later, the Skype phone rings.

"*Wei?*"

"Ellie McEnroe?"

Her camera is off too. But I recognize that voice.

"Yes, this is Ellie."

"Vicky Huang." She says it like she's Bond. James Bond. "I cannot reach you by phone."

"Yeah, sorry. I, uh, dead battery."

"Are you in Yangshuo?"

"I . . ." I'm trying to think fast, and it's hard. I'm only on my first cup of coffee, and thinking fast is not something I do well anyway.

"No," I say. "I'm really sorry. I had . . . a family emergency, and I had to leave suddenly."

Silence on the other end.

"I see," she finally says.

"Look, I really do want to meet with you." I really do, because blowing off Chinese billionaires is really not a good idea. "I just have some personal business I need to deal with."

"For how long?"

Like I have a clue.

"Around a week," I say.

Another pause. "All right," she says. "Then we will speak next week."

JUST MY LUCK: My sleeper car is filled with fucking hipsters.

Chinese artsy types. Western backpackers. A whole carload of ironic T-shirts and soul patches. It's a big rolling party the minute the train pulls out of Kunming at 11:40 P.M.

I got a little bit of sleep while I hung out in Kunming, at a bathhouse mostly, where I also splurged on a massage and spent some time in the steam room. You can hang out for hours in these places. There are separate sides for men and women, and then meeting rooms for both; you can wrap up in a bathhouse robe and fall asleep in the lounger chairs if you want to, so that's what I did.

"Just leave the leg alone," I told the masseuse. It doesn't look as swollen, I told myself. The bruises are dark purple, but greening around the edges.

"We have acupuncture clinic, you can go have treatment," the masseuse said, and I had the time. When I finally come out of there, I'm feeling pretty good. Better anyway.

Not good enough to party all night on the train to Dali, though.

I apologize to the goateed Chinese guy in the porkpie hat and his girlfriend wearing the cat's-eye glasses and a LEI FENG FOREVER T-shirt that I can't share my bottom bunk with them because I need to stretch out my leg. They offer me some *baijiu* and the backpacker couple across from me ask if I'd like a beer, so I have a little *baijiu* and a beer to be polite, and then I try to sleep, in spite of the noise and the lights. At about 3:30 A.M., it finally quiets down, and I doze a bit, just enough to feel really out of it when the train pulls in to Dali at 7:30 A.M.

I GO TO THE old town. There's a new city, which is where the train station is, but, you know, it's a typical Chinese city, where you can only tell where you are by the street signs. It's not where the tourists go, and it's not where "Dali Scene" was shot. I can tell that as soon as I get off the train. What people think of as Dali is actually a half hour's drive north. I found that out from the hipsters on the train.

Modern Scientific Seed Company is in Xiaguan, the new city. But there's no way I'm ready to tackle that right now.

Instead I share a taxi with the couple from the train and head to Dali proper, to my room at the Dali Perfect Inn, which, according to the booking website, "features a traditional Bai Minority architectural style while applying modern management methods. It is a glamorous and attractive place to rest!"

More to the point, the Dali Perfect Inn is featured in "Dali Scene." I'm guessing Langhai stayed there, or if he didn't, maybe they know where he is.

I'm dozing off in the car, but when I open my eyes now and again, I see flashes of an immense lake, mountains, deep blue skies. Then an old-fashioned city wall, stark white in the glaring sunlight.

"Ming dynasty," Porkpie Hat Guy tells me.

They get dropped off on a quiet section of a street close to the lake, lined with traditional buildings, grass growing out from between the grey roof tiles, by a produce store with vegetables and fruits spread out in plastic tubs and a bar with a bright yellow door, called Lazy Bastard.

"We're going to Cheeky Monkey later," Lei Feng T-Shirt Girl says. "Maybe see you there?"

I force a smile. "Yeah. Sure. Maybe."

The Dali Perfect Inn is west, toward the mountains. It's cool and crisp out, hat and jacket weather and nothing like the overcast damp of Yangshuo. We wait at an intersection for a mob of Chinese tourists to pass, all wearing identical turquoise baseball caps, led by a guide, a woman barely into her twenties, with a giant pennant and a battery-operated bullhorn. It's not even eight-thirty. "Tourists like to walk on this street, Fuxing Lu," the driver explains. "Go from south gate to north gate." I tell myself to avoid Fuxing Lu.

The road we're on slopes gently upward. We pass another

narrow street lined with traditional houses turned into pizza places, coffeehouses, bars. "Yangren Lu," the driver says. Foreigner Street. Most of the people I see on it look Chinese, though. A riot of sloping triangular roofs, wooden shutters of red and gold, painted eaves, carved signboards against a sky that's a deep, sharp, almost desert blue.

You want to talk quaint? This place is quaint on steroids.

Finally we arrive at Dali Perfect Inn.

It's a small building tucked away on another narrow street, two stories of weathered grey stone and wood. It looks old, but you never know for sure in China; they create fake old stuff all the time. You know, after they knock the real old stuff down.

"Room number twenty-one, here is key, and you can have a breakfast until nine A.M."

I look around the lobby. It's elegant, almost, with world clocks set in carved panels, Ming-dynasty-style furniture, stone floors. You can find plenty of cheaper hotels in Dali, less than the Perfect's thirty dollars a night. Not quite the backpacker dive I'd figure was Jason's kind of place. But the kind of place that looks like it has the money to sponsor a video.

"*Zhege lüguan, zhen piaoliang,*" I say. Your hotel, it's very pretty. "I saw a video on Youku recommending it."

The woman behind the counter is slim, young, wearing what I guess is Bai traditional dress—this red tunic thing with white sleeves and an embroidered trim. She smiles.

"Oh, yes, 'Dali Scene.'"

"That's the one. It's a very good video." I hesitate, not sure how far I should push this right away. "Do you know the person who made it? Because maybe I would like to hire him to make a video for me."

Her forehead wrinkles. "I myself don't know. But my manager, I can ask her later."

"Thank you," I say. "Thank you very much."

It's a start, I guess.

I limp up to my room. It's on the second floor. There's this covered walkway that runs alongside the rooms, with stone arches and a beamed ceiling, making a horseshoe shape around a central courtyard. When I get to my room, it's all wooden shutters, wooden furniture, a bed with a carved wooden frame, a canopy, and embroidered pillows on top of a puffy quilt.

Fucking quaint.

I kick off my shoes and collapse on the bed.

When I wake up, it's late afternoon, I have a headache, and I'm hungry.

I make myself an instant Starbucks coffee, stand in the shower for a while, dress in jeans, a semi-fresh T-shirt, sweater, and jacket. I head outside.

After Yangshuo the light still feels bright here, the shadows sharp-edged. The wind has picked up, and I zip my jacket against the chill. I'm thinking pizza. Or . . . I don't know, a burger. The street parallel to this one is full of all kinds of restaurants, outdoor cafés, some with free Wi-Fi, each with its carved wood, arched roofs, and postcard-ready façade.

"Ganja? Ganja?"

I turn. There's a little old lady wearing traditional clothes, a tunic and this black headdress with embroidered flowers and beadwork hanging off the back. She's about five feet tall and has sidled up next to me. She mutters again, "Ganja? Ganja?"

You know, I'm kind of tempted, because I'm starting to feel hungover all the time from the Percocet I've been taking. Also constipated. Maybe a little ganja would help, but even though pot's not a super big deal in China, I can't afford the risk.

"Xianzai buyao," I say, and continue my search for a likely restaurant.

I SETTLE FOR INDIAN food, and after I've eaten, I do what I do in every place I've been: find a coffeehouse/bar advertising free Wi-Fi, order a beer, and get out my laptop.

I sip my beer—I splurged for an imported Sierra Nevada—and check my email.

Spam. Messages from various artists. One from Torres, another buddy of mine from the Sandbox.

One from Dog Turner.

"Hoya baby doo hows it going? Any joy yet on my bro? if you see him tell him to get his ass home ok?"

I hesitate. I'm using the VPN, but I still feel uneasy. This whole thing, it's another one of those situations that feels way bigger than me, where there's stuff going on that I don't know about, stuff that could come back and bite me on the ass.

Your basic iceberg of shit.

I mean, if Jason really is this wanted guy, considered a terrorist to boot, just because I'm using a VPN, that doesn't mean that Dog's end of the communication is secure.

"Hey, Dog," I type. *"Sorry, nothing to report. Have been tied up with business stuff. Not sure I can really help. Let's talk next week, okay?"*

I feel like shit, because I'm lying. There's plenty of things I could tell Dog. And he's going to read the email, and he's going to think that I'm being a Fobbit, afraid to go outside the wire, afraid to take a risk to help a buddy.

Then I think, I'm such an asshole, because I'm more worried about what he's going to think about me than how he's going to feel about what I said.

Next an email from Harrison.

Dear Ellie,

I hope this finds you well and that you are enjoying your vacation.

The possibility that we may be facing some of the complications we spoke about during our last dinner is looking more likely. I'll see what I can do on my end. There's no immediate crisis, but the situation is complicated. If you have a chance, give Lucy Wu a call. She can fill you in.

Best,

Harrison

Great. Fucking great.

Finally, the latest from my mom:

Once upon a time, there was this girl who had four boyfriends.

She loved the fourth boyfriend the most and adorned him with rich robes and treated him to the finest of delicacies. She gave him nothing but the best.

She also loved the third boyfriend very much and was always showing him off to neighboring kingdoms. However, she feared that one day he would leave her for another.

She also loved her second boyfriend. He was her confidant and was always kind, considerate and patient with her. Whenever this girl faced a problem, she could confide in him, and he would help her get through the difficult times.

The girl's first boyfriend was a very loyal partner and had made great contributions in maintaining her wealth and kingdom. However, she did not love the first boyfriend. Although he loved her deeply, she hardly took notice of him!

One day the girl fell ill, and she knew her time was short. She thought of her luxurious life and wondered, I now have four boyfriends with me, but when I die, I'll be all alone.

Thus, she asked the 4th boyfriend, "I loved you the most, endowed you with the finest clothing and showered great care over you. Now that I'm dying, will you follow me and keep me company?" "No way!" replied the fourth boyfriend, and he walked away without another word.

His answer cut like a sharp knife right into her heart. The sad girl then asked the third boyfriend, "I loved you all my life. Now that I'm dying, will you follow me and keep me company?" "No!" replied the third boyfriend. "Life is too good! When you die, I'm going to marry someone else!" Her heart sank and turned cold. She then asked the second boyfriend, "I have always turned to you for help and you've always been there for me. When I die, will you follow me and keep me company?"

"I'm sorry, I can't help you out this time!" replied the second boyfriend. "At the very most, I can only walk with you to your grave."

His answer struck her like a bolt of lightning, and the girl was devastated. Then a voice called out, "I'll go with you. I'll follow you no matter where you go."

The girl looked up, and there was her first boyfriend. He was very skinny, as he suffered from malnutrition and neglect. Greatly grieved, the girl said, "I should have taken much better care of you when I had the chance!"

In truth, you have four boyfriends in your lives:

Your fourth boyfriend is your body. No matter how much time and effort you lavish on making it look good, it will leave you when you die. Your third boyfriend is your possessions, status and wealth. When you die, it will all go to others. Your second boyfriend is your family and friends. No matter how much they have been there for you, the furthest they can stay by you is up to the grave. And your first boyfriend is your soul. Often neglected in pursuit of wealth, power and pleasures of the world. However, your soul is the only thing that will follow you where ever you go. Cultivate, strengthen and cherish it now, for it is the only part of you that will follow you to the throne of God and continue with you throughout Eternity.

Thought for the day: Remember, when the world pushes you to your knees, you're in the perfect position to pray.

Below this my mom has added, *"Andy says he knows some guys who can take care of the toilet!! XOXOX, Mom."*

I order another beer and call Lucy Wu.

CHAPTER TWENTY-ONE

"Oh, it's nothing so serious."

I hear glasses clinking, conversation, jazz playing underneath. I'm guessing Lucy Wu is at some nice bar or fancy party.

"Just . . . wait a moment." She moves somewhere quieter. "The authorities came to the gallery, that's all."

"That's all?"

A pause. "They asked me some questions about Lao Zhang. If I knew where he was. If I had any contact with him." In the background someone laughs. "I don't, of course, and I told them that. Then they asked if I could provide them with sales records for the last year. I told them I could."

"And . . . ?"

"They left. For now."

I can picture her elegant shrug. Lucy Wu is one of these perfectly groomed, perfectly dressed, delicate, sexy Chinese women who make me feel like a big hot mess.

In spite of that, I kind of like her.

"Who were they?"

"Shanghai police." Another pause. "That's who they said they were anyway."

The implication being: who the fuck knows who they really were?

"I get it."

"It's all so disagreeable. I'm just trying to run a business. Support art." I hear footsteps, the sharp click of heels, like she's pacing. "The government talks about promoting China's culture in the Five-Year Plan, and *this* is the sort of thing they do. I'm a gallery owner, that's all. An art dealer. Not some kind of dissident."

She sounds pretty pissed off.

"Yeah," I say. "So what are you going to do?"

Lucy sighs. "Well, I have some business in Hong Kong. I think I'll go ahead and attend to that. Then maybe I'll visit my cousin in Vancouver for a while." She laughs shortly. "That is, if they let me leave the country."

WE TALK A LITTLE longer, and Lucy confesses that she's had a Canadian bank account for years, "just in case."

"You know, you can't always depend on things here," she says, sounding a little defensive.

"Yeah," I say. "I know."

"Of course, you have an American passport. You can always go home if you want."

"Yeah. Right."

IT'S DARK NOW. STILL early, just after seven, and I'm not sure what to do with myself. I settle up and hobble out onto the street. Take a walk. Test out my leg. It feels better, I tell myself, but the pain's still pretty bad. I'm running low on Percocets, too. The majority of my stash is back in Beijing.

Yeah, I could go home. Back to the States. But what would I do there? I've been following the news. The recession. The unemployment. What kind of work could I possibly get? What would I do with myself?

I have a life here. I have work. Friends. An apartment. Where my mom is currently living. And if I go home, what's *she* gonna do?

Fuck it. I need a drink.

I WALK FOR A while, the farthest I've walked since that asshole in Guiyu took a whack at me. It's cool out, but not freezing or anything, and I'm fine in my jacket and a knit hat that I bought off a blanket from some guy near the Beijing Forestry University. I need my Yangshuo walking stick for support, but I'm feeling pretty good. The walking helps get me out of my own head, a little anyway.

This is a pretty town. Not a lot of traffic. I find myself heading east, toward the lake. The street looks familiar, like maybe I saw it from the taxi this morning. Where the hipster couple from the train got dropped off. A few bars and coffee places stuck in between local businesses and houses. Quieter than the main tourist drag near where I'm staying.

Except this place. I can hear the music thumping faintly as I approach. An old building, decrepit façade painted black.

There's a signboard with a cartoon monkey grinning over his shoulder, red ass cheeks thrust out like an invitation.

The Cheeky Monkey.

That's where the hipster couple said they'd be tonight, I remember.

I hesitate outside the door. I still don't do well with a lot of noise. It makes me nervous. And the hipster couple, I mean, they were nice enough, but it's not like I'm dying to see them again.

On the other hand, I could go in there and have a couple

of beers. It's something to do. And tomorrow I'll question the manager at the Dali Perfect Inn, see if she can tell me anything about video director Langhai, maybe even go to the new city and check out the Modern Scientific Seed Company.

Or not.

Because a part of me thinks I'd better punch out. Deal with my own shit. Of which there is much. Turn over the leads I have to Dog, or to Natalie anyway, and let them decide what to do.

But in the meantime I could have a beer, I guess.

I grab the door handle, feel the rough carved wood against my palm and fingers, open it, and go inside.

The smoke hits me more than the music does; the air is blue with it. The walls of the bar are painted black, with Day-Glo graffiti on them, lit up by black lights. The place is pretty small, like a *hutong* bar, with a combination of small sprung couches and old wooden chairs. The music's not bad. Modern trance stuff, British, I think.

I push my way up to the bar. Not too many customers this time of night. A couple Western hippie/backpacker types, a young Chinese woman wearing a sixties-style polka-dot dress, her girlfriend in rolled-up Levi's and slicked-back hair. The waitress is Chinese, the bartender some burnout European guy dressed in black, with big gold earrings. "What can I get you, love?" he says.

I look at the beer list. "Erdinger, I guess." Thirty kuai, which is nuts, but at least it's a big bottle.

He pours, I pay, and I hobble off to a solitary armchair in the back of the bar. I sip my beer and let the music wash over me. I seriously don't know why I'm here.

After a few minutes, Polka-Dot Dress and Levi's drift over. "Hello!" Polka-Dot Dress says. "Where are you from?"

"Beijing. *Ni ne?*"

She giggles. "Oh, you speak Chinese! So many foreigners speak Chinese now! We are from Shanghai."

The two of them settle down in chairs next to me and strike up a conversation. Levi's is an "independent filmmaker working on story of two lesbians in relationship and one marries gay man to satisfy family demands." Polka-Dot is a fashion designer. "We come here because Dali very artistic place. You can meet all kinds of people."

They seem nice. It's nice talking to them. One of the backpackers comes over, a guy from Germany. The bar starts to fill up, not that it takes much in a place this size. Porkpie Hat Guy and Lei Feng T-Shirt, the couple from the train, arrive. "Hey, *ni hao*! You came!" The backpacker buys a round of the local Dali beer for the table. I'm thinking, you know, this is . . . nice. I can meet people, and hang out, and enjoy myself. I'm feeling like a member of the human race for a change.

And that's when Russell from Yangshuo walks in the door.

I spot him right away. Weaselly dude with greasy hair, his cheekbones and Adam's apple overwhelming his chin. And he's limping. A lot. Worse than me. He has an actual cane. His head swivels around, like he's looking for someone.

Me, apparently.

He limps over. Stretches the corners of his mouth in an attempt at a smile.

"Hey. Ellie. Glad I found you."

"Russell, right?"

"That's right."

He sits in the chair next to me that the backpacker guy just vacated. He has to juggle the cane to pull out the chair, because his free wrist is wrapped in an elastic bandage.

"How did you know I was here?" I ask.

"Dali's a small place." The smile again. "American, good-looking girl, I asked around."

Oh, brother. "I didn't tell anyone I was coming to this bar. I didn't even *know* I was coming to this bar."

"Like I said, small town. And a little luck."

I try to think it through.

If I could figure out that Jason had a connection to the Dali Perfect Inn, no reason someone who actually knew him wouldn't be able to as well. Russell could have started there, I guess. Tracked me to the Indian place. And from there . . .

"This bar is in all the guidebooks," he's saying. "You know, your Lonely Planets." His lip curls a bit as he says this.

But how would he know I was in Dali?

I shrug. "Okay, whatever. What do you want?"

He leans toward me. Ducks his head. Lowers his voice. "You want to find David, right?"

I lean back. I don't like this guy in my face. I nod. "Yeah."

"What if I could take you to him?"

"IT'S A FARMHOUSE," HE says. "Outside town a bit. I'll take you there."

"A farmhouse. You pulled a knife on me, and you want me to go with you to a 'farmhouse.'" I make the finger quotes. "I may not be Einstein, but I'm not fucking stupid."

"You fucking drove me into a ditch," he half snarls. "And you—" He thinks better of it and shuts up.

"Stomped on your foot when you tried to mug me? Yeah. I'm real sorry about that."

I watch him try to calm himself down.

"Look, we didn't know who you were," he says. "The . . . the people we're up against, they have . . ." He looks around. Lowers his voice. "They have spies. Everywhere."

"Uh-huh. Okay."

And I thought *I* was paranoid.

"So who is it you're up against?"

"*You* know."

"Not offhand."

He leans in close. "Eos."

Eos. Naturally. "And New Century Seeds?"

Russell nods.

"Why are you coming to me now?" I ask.

"We checked you out," he practically whispers. His mouth is next to my ear. I can still barely hear him over the music. "Your story, I mean. That you're a friend of David's family."

"I checked out, huh? Interesting."

Because there's no way my story could have "checked out"—I never gave Russell, or Erik, or Alice, or *anyone* "David's" real name or the names of his family.

The only person who could verify it is David/Jason himself.

So either Russell is a big liar or he really is in contact with Jason.

"I'm not just gonna go with you to some farmhouse," I finally say. "I mean, why should I trust you?"

"I thought you wanted to talk to David." He sounds surprised.

"I do." I hold out my hand. "Give me the address. Write it down. Name a time. I'll meet you there."

HE DOESN'T WANT TO do it, but in the end he doesn't have much choice. Because I'm totally willing to hit the eject button on this mission and head home. Russell, on the other hand, seems really hung up on my going to this farmhouse. Which all by itself is a reason I'm not so enthusiastic about going, because this guy is a weasel, and not in the cute little pet ferrety sense.

Finally he gives in. Scribbles something on a piece of paper. "Okay," he says. How about ten-thirty?"

"Okay."

"Come by yourself," he hisses. "Or there'll be trouble."

I shrug, to cover a shudder.

You don't have to go, I tell myself.

How did Russell know I'd gone to Dali?

Here's the thing: the Chinese government's finding a foreigner most places in China, not a surprise. There are ways around it, but, for example, I have to show my passport every time I register at a hotel, and you've got to figure they have some means of tracking you with that.

Russell, though, wouldn't have that information—that is, unless he's working for the government.

I try to figure out the implications of that scenario, and it makes my head hurt.

Otherwise, if Russell really is a friend of Jason's, then he could have known about Jason's list of seed companies. Those were three locations: Guiyu, Dali, and Guiyang, in Guizhou. So he had a one-in-three chance of getting it right, and if he's in contact with Daisy, a one-in-two, because Daisy could have told him that I'd already gone to Guiyu. And maybe he could make an educated guess that I might choose Dali over Guiyang, given the video evidence. No films by Langhai from Guiyang or Guizhou, not yet.

On the other hand, Russell really doesn't seem that smart.

Erik, though . . .

I have this sudden flash of him sitting across from me at the table, studying Jason's photo like he's analyzing a poker hand.

Yeah, he's smart.

★ ★ ★

I CAN'T FIND A regular taxi, so I end up in one of those three-wheeled motorcycle carts, sitting on a bench covered with fake fur under a canopy of orange-and-pink-dyed fabric strung up on skinny metal tubing that looks like it couldn't bear the weight of a shower curtain. The driver is a woman who resembles one of the pot-selling grannies without the traditional dress—instead her round, wrinkled face is shaded by a New Orleans Saints baseball cap.

We head west, up into the foothills. The lights thin out, the houses, too, until it's nothing but darkness, the occasional house with a lit window, a few passing cars.

"*Daole*," the driver says. We've arrived.

A crumbling stone wall, a glimpse of peaked roof with weeds growing in the shingles. Dim lights. Faint music.

"Can you wait for me?" I ask. "I can pay you."

She shakes her head. "I'm off work now. Going home."

"So if I need to get back to town?"

"I think maybe foreigners come to this house all the time," she says with a little grin. "So I think you can find a taxi."

"Okay," I say. "Thanks."

I pay her and get out. My heart's pounding in my throat, and I have to steady myself with my Yangshuo walking stick.

I am not nearly drunk enough to be this stupid.

First thing I do is switch my iPhone back on, GPS and all. This is one of those situations where maybe I'd rather have certain people find me than just disappear off the radar and end up . . . I don't know, as pig food. 'Cause you know pigs will eat anything, including people. And I think I hear pigs. Snuffling. Snorting. Or maybe that's the music.

I open up the splintering wood gate. It's so dark that I can barely see a foot in front of me. I wake up my phone, use it as a flashlight. There's probably an app for that, but I don't have it.

There's a dirt path that leads up to what seems to be the main building, a grey shape in the dark. The roof I saw before is just some kind of shed or barn or something. Maybe abandoned. This doesn't look like an active farm, from what I can see. There's an ancient blue farm truck, though, and a newer lime green Chery parked off to one side, on the border of an overgrown field.

Holy crap, what a tremendously stupid idea this was.

Why am I doing this? What the fuck's wrong with me?

I take a moment and go into my contacts on the phone. Hesitate, then find one. My finger hovers over the number. I don't want to call it. But just in case.

As I approach the door to what I guess is the farmhouse, a dog starts barking like a pit bull in a crack den.

And the front door of the farmhouse slams open.

"*Shei laile?*" someone yells. Chinese. A skinny silhouette backlit by interior light. The dog at his side lunges forward. The music is louder now, with the door open. I'm thinking it might be Radiohead.

"*Ni hao,*" I manage. "I'm, uh . . . Russell invited me to come."

The figure hesitates. I still can't make out his face. The dog growls.

"Okay," he finally says. "*Qing jin.*" Come in.

When I get inside, I feel a little better.

It's another converted farmhouse with whitewashed walls, now covered in a combination of graffiti murals and posters. There's a Western guy, not Jason, with a knit cap, a Plastered T-shirt, and a backpacker beard, sitting next to a lanky Chinese girl wearing embroidered bell-bottoms and a fake-fur jacket. There's the Chinese guy who opened the door—glasses, shaggy hair, red Li-Ning soccer jersey. A couple of guitars and a beat-to-shit drum kit, a battered amp. Empty beer bottles on flimsy tables and the floor. Folding chairs. Fast-food containers. Overflowing ashtrays. A strong scent of pot.

It's familiar, at least. I've been in a lot of rooms like this. And it's generally worked out okay. Most of the time.

I put my phone back into my jacket pocket.

"Is Russell here?" I ask.

The Chinese guy nods. "Yeah. Sure."

The Western guy takes a hit off a joint mixed with tobacco and coughs on the exhale. "Hey, Russell!" he yells. American. "You got someone here looking for you."

The Chinese guy indicates a chair. "You can sit if you'd like." I sit.

The Chinese girl hangs out by the American guy, leaning against him, taking a hit off the spliff. The Chinese guy paces. His dog, which is some kind of yellow mutt with a curled tail, noses his leg, whines.

"*Zou, zou, zou,*" he mutters, grabbing the dog's rope collar and hauling him toward the front door. "Go!" he says, one more time, and shoves the dog outside.

I sit there, my daypack on my lap, throat parched, wishing I had a beer. Or a Coke. Or something.

Mainly I wish that I was somewhere else. Like on a bamboo raft, floating down a river. Or in my hotel room. A train. Anyplace.

From across the room, Russell emerges from a dark doorway, beers in hand. "Hey, Ellie," he says, teeth bared in an attempt at a grin. "You made it. Beer?"

"Sure," I say. "Thanks."

"This is Ellie," Russell says to the others. "She's a friend of David's." He turns to me. "Right?"

"A friend of his family," I say, taking a long pull on the beer.

"Where is he anyway?" the American guy asks, his voice slurring. "I haven't seen him in a while."

Russell jerks his head, shoots the guy a look. "He'll be here. I just talked to him."

"Oh. Cool." He mimes a drum pattern. "Be good to play a little."

The Chinese guy paces in short, sharp angles. He's amped. I can see from here that his pupils are dilated. *Bingdu*, amphetamines of some sort, I'm guessing.

"When's he coming?" I ask.

"Few minutes, half hour," Russell says with a shrug. "No worries, he'll be here."

The American guy stands up, wobbling, with the Chinese girl on his arm; goes over to the drum kit and almost falls onto the stool; picks up some sticks and tries to play in time to the music. The Chinese guy keeps pacing.

"Hey, is there a bathroom I can use?" I ask.

The Chinese guy stops pacing for a moment. He points at the door where Russell came in. "That way."

I push myself to my feet with my Yangshou stick and limp back there.

The door leads outside. There's a small cinder-block building that I'm guessing is an outhouse. I have a real flashlight in my daypack, one of those agro LED models I picked up at the Pearl Market. I get it out and turn it on so I can see what I'm doing.

Sure enough it's a squat shitter, framed by grey brick. I go inside. Squat and pee, hoping I'll be able to get up again, the pain in my leg like someone's stabbing me in the thigh, over and over. Maybe Russell, with his *shanzhai* Ka-Bar.

While I'm doing this, the yellow dog slinks inside. I hear a low growl.

Great.

I use my Yangshuo stick to boost myself up, my jeans still puddling around my ankles, the dog showing its teeth and growling.

"Fuck, dog, come on!" I mutter. "Your boss invited me inside. Doesn't that count for something?"

The dog sits back on its haunches. I can't really see its eyes in the dark, but I think it's watching me. I tug my jeans up over my ass.

Funny thing, the outhouse smells like shit, obviously, but that's not all I'm smelling. I fumble the last button on my jeans and look around.

It seems pretty straightforward. Low ceiling. A latrine and a faucet that drains into an iron sink. I look behind me, aiming my phone to cast whatever dim light it can.

There's a wall and a tiny window, like a vent. I'm not tall enough to see into it. But there's a tin bucket by the faucet.

I grab it, turn it upside down, get my good leg on it and haul my ass up.

My eyes are just at the level of the little window. From what I can tell, there's another room at the back of the outhouse. I aim my flashlight.

Some bags piled against the back wall. Bags about a foot and a half long, a foot wide.

My first thought is New Century Hero Rice. But these bags are burlap, from what I can see. No logo.

I press my nose up against the window. Breathe in deep.

I'm not sure, due to the ambient odors, but I think what I'm smelling in there is ganja.

Maybe this is where the local grannies get it.

I lower myself, sneaker sole catching on the rim of the tin bucket. Get my balance. Turn toward the door I came in, and the dog is there, waiting. I shine my light at it. It's like one of those bad flash photos, where the object lit up in front doesn't look real.

"Okay, dog," I say. "You don't bite me, I won't hit you with my stick. How's that sound?"

I inch my way forward: flashlight in one hand, stick in the other.

When I reach the door, the dog shakes itself and trots away.

Back inside, American dude is still banging his drums. The Chinese guy's picked up one of the guitars and strums at it like he's jerking off. The girl sits back in one of the folding chairs smoking a cigarette.

"Hey, Russell," I say. "So when's David getting here?"

Russell frowns. He's sitting in a chair next to the girl, hunched over like a letter C.

"Soon, like I told you."

"See, thing is, I can't really hang out here much longer. I got stuff to do."

Russell uncoils and fishes a phone from his jacket pocket. Stares at it for a moment.

"I'm not getting a good signal here," he says. "I'll go outside and call him."

He gets up. Hobbles to the front door.

I wait. Sip my beer. Feel my heart pound. Watch American dude and Chinese guy whaling away on the guitar and drums. I think they're trying to play "Smells Like Teen Spirit," but it's hard to tell.

After a few minutes of this, I stand up, and smile at the Chinese girl. "Be right back."

"Where are you going?"

The way she says it, a little flat, not smiling, if my nerves weren't already pinging all over the place, they're ratcheted up another couple of notches now.

I pat my stomach. *"Wo you yidianr bushufu."*

Funny phrase in Mandarin. You say it when you're feeling sick, but it literally means, "I'm a little uncomfortable."

Yeah, I'm definitely not comfortable.

I go out the back again, toward the outhouse.

I don't want to use my flashlight. There's some ambient light, from the farmhouse, from the moon, but the paths are uneven, so I use my stick to feel my way.

I don't see Russell. Don't hear him. But based on how he scrammed outside when he checked the time, I don't like it.

And that's when I hear a car motor.

The sound echoes off the hills, and I can't tell for sure where it's coming from, but I figure it's probably on the road I took to get here. I freeze a moment and listen, see if it recedes and fades and goes on down the road, but it doesn't. The car idles for a minute. Then it's back in gear.

Heading up the path to the farmhouse.

I hesitate. Maybe it's Jason, at long last.

But maybe it's not.

Hide.

Not in the outhouse. I've done that, but not with a couple kilos of pot. I look around, try to see what the landscape is, where I can go, and I can't, really. That low, flat stretch to my right, that's probably an overgrown field, not a good choice.

Past the outhouse, that dark mass, that's the hillside.

I think if I can get up there, up high, maybe I can see who's coming.

If I can get there in time.

I jog as best I can, pain shooting up my leg with every step, past the outhouse, past another shed, and the car's getting louder, and I can see the headlight beams now, and I scramble past a woodpile, into the shadow of a large tree, and from there I head up the hill, stumbling on rocks and ruts of a trail that's hardly even there, that disappears into weeds and grass.

I keep going, and it's steep enough so I'm grabbing onto roots and bushes with my hands, and finally I get to another tree and I stop, latch onto the tree trunk, hug the rough bark.

I turn and look down the hill. There are two cars pulling up to the farmhouse. The light from the headlights of the second illuminates the first.

White. Blue band on the side. Blue-and-red light bar on top. Oh, fuck. Police.

CHAPTER TWENTY-TWO

I can see a couple of cops drag the Chinese guy and the American guy out of the farmhouse, into the glare of the car headlights, their hands cuffed behind their backs. The cops push their heads down and shove them into the backseat of the cruiser. Then the Chinese girl. They put her in the other car. I can't tell if her hands are cuffed or not.

No Russell.

That asshole. I knew he was up to something.

Two more squad cars pull up. Four more cops. Eight of them altogether. Two of the new ones go into the farmhouse. The other two start checking out the grounds, LED flashlights casting glowing bluish beams. Looking for evidence, maybe.

Or looking for me.

I want to run, but I'm not good at that, and I'm scared that if I try to head farther up the hill, they'll see me, they'll hear me. So I stay where I am.

I don't know how long I sit there clutching the tree trunk. The cars with the Chinese and American guys and the Chinese girl leave. The cops come out of the farmhouse, carrying stuff in bags. I don't know what. The cops with the flashlights check out one of the sheds and then the outhouse. I hear one of them shout.

That's when I hear a low-pitched growl, then frantic barking. The yellow dog.

I can see the shadow of the dog standing near the outhouse. See one of the cops reach down to his hip. Lift his arm up.

The gunshot is so loud. It echoes off the hills. The dog yelps; it seems to jump straight in the air. I press my cheek into the tree trunk. I don't want to look anymore.

Shouts and laughter from the cops.

Then there's a rustling noise. Getting louder.

I open my eyes. I can't exactly see it, but there's a dark shape, and it's heading in my direction.

The fucking dog.

Flashlight beams pour light on the hill.

I clutch the tree trunk. Shrink into myself. Oh, shit.

I can hear the dog's panting breaths now. I turn my head and see it standing there, head lowered, hackles raised, a low growl in its throat.

I stare at it.

Down the hill I hear another shouted sentence from one of the cops. The flashlight beams sweep in an arc, hit the tree. Then turn back toward the outhouse and the farm.

The dog stands there a moment longer. Then slowly settles onto its haunches.

I don't move.

WE SIT THERE A long time.

I risk a peek down the hill now and again. See the cops going in and out of the main building and the outhouse. Sometimes carrying things. Taking breaks, leaning against the squad cars and smoking cigarettes. My leg throbs, but I'm too scared to move it. The dog sits like a sphinx, watching me.

Now my leg's getting numb. Just hold on, I tell myself. Hold on until they leave.

Finally I hear a car start. Tires on dirt and gravel. The other car's still there. The two cops hang out. Smoke more cigarettes. Why the fuck don't they leave?

I can't take it anymore. I've got to move.

I stare at the dog. I clutch my calf with both hands—my leg's so numb it feels like wood. Stretch my leg out in front of me. It's cold, and then it's like somebody hits me with a stun gun. I bite my lip, swallow the moan in the back of my throat, nerves firing like popcorn. Breathe, I tell myself. Breathe.

When I open my eyes again, the dog hasn't moved. Neither have the cops.

It gets cold. At some point I curl up on my side, turn up the collar of my jacket, tuck my hands into my armpits. I can't stop shivering. I think, Fucking catch me already. Just take me someplace warm.

I hear rustling. Panting. A warm body presses up against my belly and chest. The dog.

Eventually I doze, the dog's head tucked under my chin.

I don't exactly wake up. I never really sleep. But there's warmth on my face and light on my eyes, so I open them.

The yellow dog is curled up against me. The sun hits a red splash on its shoulder. Blood.

I lie there a little longer.

The dog is alive. It's still warm. It's breathing. I can see its flank rise up and down.

Okay, I think. I have to sit up. I have to figure out what I'm dealing with. Besides, my hip hurts like a motherfucker where it's pressed against the hard ground. I need to move.

Please don't bite me, dog, I think.

I push myself up. The dog shifts and whines. Then it rolls and sits in its sphinx position. Raises its head and stares at me. It has these light brown eyes, almost gold.

"*Ni hao*, dog," I whisper. "You're a really nice dog. *Hen piaoyong*." Very brave.

The dog's tail thumps weakly. I'm not sure what to do. We never had pets when I was a kid, and I didn't have any when I was married either.

"Okay, so we're friends, right? You're not going to bite me?"

Or bark? Because this, too, would be bad.

I look down the hill.

A layer of mist swaddles the farm, blurring all the hard edges, breaking up the morning light so it sparkles in places. The police car is still there. Nothing seems to move. It's like a video on pause, except for an occasional ripple of breeze.

I squint, try to focus on the police car. I can't tell if there's anyone inside it or not. I figure wherever they are, they're probably asleep. Maybe they decided to go inside the farmhouse for their *xiuxi* break. Cops here don't get paid enough to stay awake standing guard over something like this. Whatever this is.

Okay, I don't know for sure. Given my involvement with Lao Zhang and Creepy John and the DSD, who the fuck does know? But if I had to guess, I'm figuring Russell set me up, for whatever reason. Lured me up here, where he knew there was a substantial quantity of pot, and then called in the bust. Maybe he was working with that girl who was hanging out, maybe not.

And, you know, there's no evidence tying me to whatever little drug action was going on here, and pot is not a hugely big deal in any case. But *that* amount of pot . . . any amount of bullshit evidence . . . depending on who's paying who off . . .

Not good.

I can't risk going down the hill. I mean, unless I just want to give myself up and fight the bullshit charges. I could do that, I guess. Call in some favors.

But the thought of getting locked up someplace. Of being in a jail.

I think of a cell from another time, in another place, of scabbing yellow paint over concrete, of bare lightbulbs in rusting metal cages, and I can feel the acid panic rise in my throat.

I look around. I think I see the faint tracings of a path heading north. Away from the farm. Away from Dali. Going to . . . ?

I have no idea. But I don't really care.

The yellow dog rests its head on its front paws now, still staring at me, but its eyes seem dull, half open. Maybe it's in pain. I can't tell how bad the wound on its shoulder is.

The longer I stay here, the more likely it is that the cops are going to wake up, that more of them are going to come or that someone is going to see me up here.

I have to risk it.

"Please don't bark, dog," I whisper.

I grasp the handle of my Yangshuo walking stick, staring at the dog. The dog stares back. I hear the faint rumbling of a growl.

"I'm not going to hit you, dog," I mutter. "Promise. Okay? Just gonna stand up and walk out of here. Good dog. *Hen haode gou.*"

I stand up in increments, pushing myself to my feet with the stick, my butt up against the tree trunk, and if it weren't for the tree, I don't know if I could do it, that's how stiff and sore I'm feeling, my leg muscles locked in spasm. All the while the dog watches, almost thoughtfully, it seems to me, like it's trying to decide what to do: Bark? Bite? Run?

I make it to my feet. Stand up as straight as I can, feeling my back muscles clench and release.

"Okay, dog," I whisper. "I'm going now. Okay?"

It lifts its head.

I back away. Toward the mountain path. The dog watches me.

Finally I turn my back on the dog. Walk onto the path. The way rises ahead of me, and all I can see is the point where it hits the horizon and blue sky.

I haven't gone very far when I hear rustling grass, panting, the four-legged trot behind me.

Keep walking, I tell myself. There's nothing else you can do.

The dog closes in as I reach the top of the rise. I can hear its panting on my heels. There's no cover. If anyone down on the farm is looking up here, they'll see me.

Don't bark, dog. Please don't bark.

Below me the path slopes around and down in a steep arc. I can see the lake from here, and it's so big that the opposite shore is lost in the morning mist.

I scramble down the path. The dog follows.

By now I'm out of sight of the farmhouse. I take a moment to stop, to turn around.

The dog stops as well. Tail lowered, like it's scared. Blood staining its shoulder.

"Why are you following me, dog?" I turn back to the path. I can see clusters of buildings here and there along the lake, something that looks like a village in the distance, a broad road, maybe even a highway, heading north.

I could catch a taxi, I think. Get on a bus. Just drive north, to wherever. Zhongdian, maybe. The government's renamed it Shangri-La. The next stop on the banana-pancake backpacker circuit, where I won't attract much attention. I can crash at a farmhouse. Some place off the grid that isn't going to ask for my passport or, if they do, is just going to make a copy and turn it over to the local PSB. A place that isn't hooked into some kind of central foreigner-tracking system, that isn't going to know that the Dali cops are after me for a bogus pot bust.

There are still places like that in China, right?

I actually don't know.

"Fuck."

I pick my way down the path with the aid of my walking stick. The adrenaline's wearing off, leaving me feeling like I fell off a moving truck and hit the pavement hard. The dog still follows. When I stop, it stops. Hangs back. And when I start walking, it does, too.

We walk for a long time.

It's pretty, I guess. Evergreen trees and bushes with tiny pink buds. The big mountain behind me, capped with snow. Another day I might appreciate the scenery.

The sun burns off the mist. Midmorning. I check the time on my phone—9:07 A.M. I've been walking for a couple of hours. My leg's hurting so bad that every time I step, I just want to cry.

I have to stop.

I lower myself and sit in the shade of a banyan tree.

What's the point, I think? Okay, so maybe I can get out of Dali without getting arrested. Abandon my stuff in the Dali Perfect Inn. Not like I have a lot of stuff there. I have my laptop with me, which is the most important thing, and I didn't leave a credit-card deposit this time, just cash. So I'll lose that, but whatever. Worth it to avoid a couple nights in jail.

But how long can I run? If I make it back to Beijing, will the whole thing just go away? Like it's some local problem, like . . . I don't know, a traffic ticket?

I look up, and the dog sits there, a few feet away.

"Hey, dog," I say.

Its tail wags, hesitantly.

"I don't know what you think I'm gonna do. I don't have any food, okay?"

The tail thumps harder.

"So . . . what? We're friends now?"

The dog inches forward. Practically crawls on its belly.

I stretch out my hand for it to sniff—that's what you're supposed to do, right? The dog cringes. Like it's afraid of getting hit. So I reach out my hand palms up. The dog gives my fingers a tentative sniff, then a nuzzle. I pull my hand back. Pat the ground next to me. The dog slinks over. Finally rests its head on my good thigh. I give it a scratch behind its ears. It has a yellow face with a darker muzzle, a ruff of fur around its neck, a feathered tail. Kind of skinny. Needs a bath.

And then I think, Great. I'm friends with a dog. What am I supposed to do with it?

An injured dog at that. I look at the shoulder, and it's hard to see exactly what's going on with the wound because of the fur, but it looks to me like the bullet went in and out and took out a small chunk of flesh with it, maybe the size of a quarter.

"Okay, dog," I finally say. "I need to get going."

I push myself to my feet and start walking.

The dog follows, at my side now.

Fucking great.

WE WALK A COUPLE of hours. The trail is rutted, steep in places. The weather's okay at least, cool but not cold, with a breeze that gathers into gusts of wind sometimes. I get pretty thirsty, though. I'm guessing the dog does, too, its mouth open, its tongue hanging out, panting almost in time to its steps. Limping now, and I think, Ha-ha, of course I attract a limping dog.

Occasionally I glance at its shoulder. Rusted blood mats the yellow fur, with bright red seeping beneath it. I'd like to do something about that, I think. If I had a razor and some disinfectant and some bandages, that would help, and I could do the stitches if I had to. Could I get an anesthetic? Antibiotics are pretty easy to find here, if it needs that.

Just to be clear, it's not that I really care about the dog. I'm not a dog person. Except it kept me warm last night, and I guess I feel a little obligated.

At last we make it down to the road.

Now that we're here, I'm not sure what to do. We stand there, the dog and me, at the side of the road. Some cars rush past. A beater Chery. A Buick. A local bus.

Bus, I think. All we need to do is find a stop. Or maybe wave one down. That might work.

A part of me feels like, what's the point? I'm going to get caught eventually. I always feel like I'm going to get busted for something, when it comes down to it.

Then I think, Get a grip. If this was the DSD or Creepy John doing some weird-ass shit, or even some of the other creeps I've butted heads with the last few years from my own country, I'd have plenty of reasons to freak. And this whole thing with Eos, and Hongxing, and New Century Hero Rice—*something's* going on there. Something a whole lot bigger than me.

But Russell? Erik? Setting me up for some cheesy pot bust?

Don't quit, I tell myself. Keep playing.

It's a local problem, and local police in China are really bad at coordinating with different provinces, from what I've heard. All I need to do is get the fuck out of Dali and out of Yunnan and back to Beijing. I'll deal with it there.

Or, maybe, head southeast to Shenzhen, then to Hong Kong.

Get the fuck out of Dodge altogether, before the bust catches up to me.

Except there's my mom, back at my apartment. With Andy, and a toilet that may or may not flush.

"Fuck, dog," I mutter. "Why isn't this shit ever simple?"

The dog sits back on its haunches and thumps its tail. I stretch out my hand. It pushes its nose into my palm, and I give it a scratch behind its ears.

"Oh, okay, I get it. It *is* simple. For you."

We keep walking north. To the right is the lake, deep blue shifting to slate grey when the clouds blow over it, sunlight hitting the water in fan-shaped beams.

I'd heard there were lots of artists designing and building second homes around here, and now I get why. This would be a nice place to live.

That is, if I wasn't wanted by the Dali police.

I'm thinking about all this, the dog on one side, the lake on the other, spacing out the way I tend to do, taking in the light glinting off little waves, the sharp blue of the sky, the panting of the dog.

I *don't* take in the silver Toyota pulling up alongside me until it slows and the passenger window rolls down.

"Yili. Please get in the car."

CHAPTER TWENTY-THREE

MY HEART SLAMS INTO my throat. I don't even know how I feel when I place the familiar voice and look over and see Creepy John leaning toward the passenger window from the driver's seat.

He opens the passenger door.

"What do you want?" I manage.

He sighs through gritted teeth. "Just, please. Get into the car."

"Why? What are you going to do?"

"Try to fix this mess you are in. For first thing. For second . . ." His eyes drift down. His head cocks back. "What is that?"

"A dog. Duh."

The dog cocks its head back, too. Bares its teeth. A growl rumbles in its throat.

I'm liking this dog.

John does his squinty-eyed look, but this time it's like he's getting a headache, for real. "Why you have dog?"

"Long story."

"Doesn't matter," he finally says. "Just get in car."

"What if I don't?"

"Then maybe you get arrested here and go to prison," he snaps. "You want to go to prison?"

I stand there at the side of the road, the dog pressing against my leg, the wind kicking up, carrying a smell that's like a giant aquarium, moss or algae or something.

I mean, what am I going to do? What are my choices here, really?

"The dog comes too," I say.

So maybe I'm pushing it, but I honestly don't give a fuck at this point.

"We need to go to . . . to a . . . an animal doctor," I manage in Mandarin.

"*Shouyi?*" John supplies.

"Yeah. That."

"Yili . . ." he starts.

We're driving down the road along the lake. I don't have a clue where John plans to take me. The dog lies in the backseat on one side, head resting on front leg, wounded side up, which is good because it's not bleeding all over John's new upholstery, which I have a feeling would piss him off.

"Or get me some drugs and bandages if you want," I say. "Whatever. But I need to do something for him." Or her. I still don't know.

There's no reason he has to go along. No reason he can't stop the car and dump the dog by the side of the road. It's not like I have any kind of power here. Not even a little.

"Okay," he says. "Okay. We find someone."

We drive north. Mountain on the left, lake on the right. Past little villages, creeks that empty into the lake, green fields, I don't know of what.

I think about New Century Hero Rice.

"So how'd you find me?" I ask.

He gives a half shrug, like it's not even worth answering.

"Come on," I say. "My cell phone? My passport? How?"

"Not very hard," he finally says. "We watch you, you go to train station, they see what ticket you buy, what train. Hotels report to local PSB. Easy for us to ask. We lose you a while in Yangshuo but find you again in Dali."

"'We'?"

"Just . . . you know, people. Some are . . . are officers. Others just . . . we pay them." He shrugs again. "Many people work for DSD these days."

"Huh. Like guys in polo shirts, driving a Buick?"

John frowns. "Buick? I don't think so."

Whatever.

"Why are you going to so much trouble? Don't you guys have better things to do? Stop monks from lighting themselves on fire or arrest people cracking jokes on Twitter?"

His hands tighten on the steering wheel. "You know why."

"Lao Zhang? I told you, I don't know where he is."

"Why didn't you tell me you were leaving Beijing, then?"

He actually sounds hurt. Which is kind of funny and pretty bizarre.

"I can't take a vacation with my mom?"

His head whips around, and he glares at me. "Vacation? You go to Guiyu for vacation? Without your mother? And she goes back to Beijing anyway."

We hit something, a pothole, the car bounces and shimmies. John yanks the steering wheel to compensate. The tires squeal. The dog yelps from the backseat.

"I had some business to take care of," I say.

"So you come here to do business with those guys, those guys with all the ganja? I did not think you were so stupid." Now he just sounds pissed.

"No! No. I didn't know anything about that. I was going there to meet someone else. He . . ."

I could tell him, I guess. Maybe he could even help. I mean, if there's anyone who could probably track down a runaway foreigner, it's Creepy John.

But I just don't know what the consequences of that would be. For Jason/David. For me.

Trust Mr. Double-Dealing Secret Agent? I don't think so.

"It's a long story," I say. "But it's got nothing to do with Lao Zhang. It's personal. Not anything you'd care about."

We get to some village that's pretty cute: a lot of white with grey stone trim, black and white and grey nature scenes painted under the peaked roofs, carved wood and raw brick. Not a lot of white-tile disease. Middle-aged ladies wearing traditional dress: deep blue shifts and blouses under them, dark head wraps, sashes embroidered with pink flowers and butterflies.

"Bai people," John says. I see a couple of Western tourists wandering through the narrow lanes, taking pictures with their iPhones.

No veterinarian, though.

We finally find a medical clinic. The doctor there, an older man, at first he doesn't want to have anything to do with the dog, but John whips out his credential and a wad of cash and the doctor starts bobbing his head up and down and clasps his hands together and smiles like he can't imagine a better way to be spending his time.

The dog doesn't want to go with him. It whimpers and hugs my thigh. "It's okay, dog," I whisper. "I'll come with you, all right?"

I make sure the doctor gives it a painkiller before he starts doing stuff. I scratch behind its ears and help hold it down when he shaves the fur around the wound, douses it with antiseptic, and loosely stitches it up. "Might need drain," he says. "I give antibiotic injection, but hard to say."

He doesn't ask what happened to the dog. Just bandages it up and hands me a bottle of antibiotics at the end.

"Two times a day," he says.

"*Xie xie.*" I pocket the pills. Hesitate. "Is it a boy or a girl?"

He laughs a little. "Girl. You can have *xiao gou* if you want." Puppies.

"*Wo . . . wo buyao,*" I say. I don't want.

I mean, I don't even want *one* dog.

AFTER THAT, I'M THINKING, I should get the dog something to eat, but it's not like there's a Petco here. Maybe we can just stop at a restaurant, get some chicken or beef, or something.

"To feed dog?" John asks with a hard sigh.

I shrug. "He . . . she . . . I don't know when the last time she ate was."

John checks his watch. "Okay. Lunchtime anyway."

You can tell that this village gets tourists. We find a courtyard restaurant with an English sign that says WELCOME FOR YOU TRY XIZHOU SPECIAL FLAVORS! ENJOYING IN RETROSPECT THE EVERLASTING! John manages to squeeze in his Toyota out front, in the narrow lane.

I order the local fish and something called a *poshu*, a "roasting round flat cake by the wheat flour with all good color, joss-stick, and flavor," that features "ethereal oil layering." It's supposed to be good for "go out to labor or tour of holding." It all tastes pretty good, if not ethereally everlasting. But even though I haven't eaten since last night, I'm not feeling much like eating. There's the dog, lying in the back of John's car, with the windows cracked. She seems pretty lethargic—doped up, I have to figure—so I'm hoping she doesn't pee all over his new upholstery.

And there's John, sitting across from me. Eating with a sort of angry efficiency.

We don't talk. We just eat, in record time, leaving with a take-out order of some plain beef-and-rice dish that I figure will be easy for the dog to eat.

I try to pay. John won't let me.

When we get back to the car, I open the take-out container and put it under the dog's nose. She sniffs at it. Her tail thumps a little.

"Don't you want to eat any of it? Come on, it's got ethereal flavors."

She lifts her head enough to nose at the beef and rice. Takes a couple of slurping bites. Lays her head back down, tail thumping weakly.

"Okay, good dog," I say. "You can have more later."

I close up the Styrofoam take-out container. Tie the flimsy plastic bag. John stands behind me, and I can feel him watching. I don't have a clue what he's thinking.

When I try to stand up, my leg's buckling and I have to brace myself on the car seat, and even then I'm wobbling like one of those plates on top of a Chinese acrobat's stick.

"Here," John says. He circles his arm around my back, tucking his hand more or less in my armpit, and I, reluctantly, thread my arm across his back, my hand resting on his ribs. He slowly hoists me up. His hand remains there for a moment, beneath my arm, his fingertips grazing the side of my tit, then falls away.

We stand there next to the car.

"Did you hurt yourself?"

"Yeah. In Guiyu. Getting better, though."

★ ★ ★

I'M NOT SURE WHERE I expect us to go, and truthfully, I kind of space out for a while, something I still tend to do if I get too tired or too stressed out for too long—"dissociate" is the technical term.

Or maybe . . . I don't know, after everything that's happened, I'm finally feeling like I can afford to relax. Like right now I'm kind of safe.

That's when adrenaline rushes through me like an electric shock.

Safe? With Creepy John? What am I smoking?

I look out the window, try to get my bearings. We've been driving north, away from Dali. Now we're heading east, around the north end of Erhai Lake. *Erhai* means "Ear Sea," I think, because the lake is kind of shaped like an ear, and it's a big freaking lake. We're heading around the top of it. The road is dirt now, rutted, and there are wind turbines up on the hillside, and I can't tell how much of the bumping is from the road and how much is from the gusts of wind.

"Where are we going?" I ask.

"Some place quiet," he mutters, hands gripping the steering wheel.

"Why?"

"So you can rest. So I can . . . so I can decide what to do."

My heart thumps hard in my chest. "What do you mean, 'decide what to do'?"

He winces now, scrunches up his face like he's in pain. "Just . . . just how I can fix things."

Okay, I think, okay. He's not going to hurt me. He's not. He saved my ass before. He took my dog to a doctor and bought it lunch.

It's not your dog, I remind myself.

And when it comes down to it, I have no idea what John really wants.

AS WE CURVE AROUND the top of the lake and head south, the road smooths out again. Beams of light stream through breaks in the cloud like some giant flashlight, the peaks of the little waves on the lake sparkling where they hit. There are rusting boats now and again tied up at rotting wooden posts. We blow by some Westerners on bikes struggling against the wind.

"So you really don't know where Zhang Jianli is," John finally says.

"No. I really don't." I summon up the energy to get pissed off. "I thought you were supposed to be his friend."

"I . . ." He looks ashamed, and maybe he actually is. "I just have to tell them *something*. They think *you* know. And I don't want . . ." His voice trails off. He stares straight ahead.

"What?"

"I don't want you to have trouble, that's all."

He turns to look at me, which I wish he wouldn't do, given the cyclists and farm trucks and motorcycle carts on the road. "Just tell me what you are doing. Then I can say it has nothing to do with Lao Zhang and they will leave you alone."

"It's personal. Meaning it's none of their fucking business."

Or yours, I want to say, but I don't.

WE PULL IN TO this village by the side of the lake. Traditional buildings in white and grey, trimmed with wood, that look like they've been fixed up. A finger of land that juts out into the lake and a tiny island.

Yeah, pretty fucking quaint.

"We can stay here for a while," John says.

I shrug. Whatever. "Okay."

AT THE EDGE OF town, there's a couple of crazy modern buildings, all hard angles and glass. Artists' homes, I'm guessing. We end up at one of them, which turns out to be another boutique hotel.

The room the receptionist points us to looks out over the lake. Glass, slate, and wood. A king-size bed. Hand-woven carpets. Contemporary paintings on the walls, splashes of red against white and grey. I'm still no expert, but they go with the room, I guess.

John and I stand there in the center of the room. The dog settles down by my side. I'm surprised they're letting the dog stay here. But maybe John showed them his badge or something.

"So what now?" I finally ask.

"You can have a shower and a rest if you want."

"You?"

His eyes don't meet mine. "Just got to take care of some things. I come back later."

He looks at me for a second, gives an awkward little wave and leaves, shutting the door gently behind him.

"Well, shit, dog, what do you make of that?"

The dog yawns.

"Yeah, he's kind of a freak, huh?" I lean over and give her a scratch behind the ears. I'm not sure what to do.

I could take off, I guess. See how far I could get. But it feels kind of pointless. He'll just find me again.

I guess I could take that shower.

I STAND UNDER THE water for a long time. It's a nice bathroom, grey slate floors like the rest of the room, copper-clad sink, a shower with stone-studded walls, which have to be a bitch to clean but look very cool. I let the water pound my neck and shoulders for a while.

When I come out, I don't really want to put my sweaty T-shirt and grimy jeans back on. There's a white terry-cloth bathrobe hanging on a hook by the door. I put that on instead.

The dog's sound asleep on the carpet by the bed. I limp past her, to the wall of windows overlooking the lake.

There's nothing but a narrow stone walkway separating the window from the shore. Clouds have turned the water practically the color of the slate floor, with ridges of white where the wind has kicked up tiny waves, like frosting.

As I stand there, a big white bird flaps down and lands on the walkway, almost in slow motion. It takes a few steps, lifting its legs and putting them down with a weird sort of hesitant precision. Like it's testing the ground ahead. It looks like Boba. I wonder if it's the same kind of bird. A crane, or whatever.

Fuck, I'm tired.

I pull back the comforter on the bed and slide under the sheet. I swear, the mattress feels like a cloud.

I WAKE UP WITH a jolt. The dog, barking. It's dark but there's a light on. Someone standing in the room.

"It's just me," John says.

I let out a held breath and sit up. "It's okay, dog," I say. I reach out and find the scruff of the dog's neck; she's standing guard next to the bed.

John's dark against the entry light. I can't see his face. He's got a duffel bag slung over each shoulder, a sack in his hand.

I switch on the lamp on the nightstand. "What time is it?"

"Just after seven."

I smell food.

"Some dinner," he says.

One of the bags he's carrying is my duffel—olive canvas, from my deployment. His is black. He drops them on the luggage rack by the wardrobe.

"You picked up my stuff?"

"Sure."

"Thanks."

"No problem. Are you hungry?"

I nod. "A little."

He stares at me for a moment, and I remember that I'm not wearing anything except the hotel bathrobe. "I . . . uh, give me a minute to change."

I find the baggy drawstring pants I've been using for pajamas and a cleanish T-shirt, the one from the Mati Village coffeehouse I used to like, with Lei Feng holding a steaming mug of coffee. I change in the bathroom. The pressure bandage I've had wrapped around my leg lies on the floor in the corner. It reminds me of a shed snakeskin, like I used to see sometimes when I was a kid and I'd ride my bike out in the desert. I pick the bandage up, but I don't try to put it back on. My leg feels a lot better, I tell myself. Instead I roll it up neatly as I can and put it on the shelf where the towels are stacked.

When I come out of the bathroom, John has the food laid out on the little table pressed up against the window overlooking the lake. Dumplings and some green vegetables. Vinegar peanuts. And a couple bottles of Dali Beer.

"Looks great," I say.

"I have this for the dog," John says. He holds up a bag of Iams kibble and a leash and collar.

"That's really nice of you." I don't know what else to say.

★ ★ ★

HE RIPS OPEN THE dog food and pours some onto the empty sack that had carried our dinner. The dog digs in, seeming to like this better than the ethereal-flavor beef, or maybe she's just feeling better than she was. "She probably needs some water," I say. John frowns. It's like he'd thought of everything but he hadn't thought of that, and it bugs him.

Finally he grabs one of the hotel teacups and fills it with water. "Not so good," he says. "I find something better later."

After that we both sit down at the little table.

I eat a couple dumplings. Drink some beer.

"So the . . . the thing in Dali," I say.

John shrugs. "I take care of it."

"What does that mean?"

"I tell the PSB they make a mistake. That you have nothing to do with these guys."

"Oh, yeah? So it's over? I don't have anything to worry about? Or are you gonna keep this in one of your files, just in case you need me to do something? Help you find Lao Zhang, maybe? Or fuck over some other artist who says things you don't like?"

A muscle in John's cheek twitches.

"This problem you have in Dali is just a local thing," he says. He sounds calm. Cold, almost. "It did not go any further than here. And it is gone now. You want to go back to Dali, to Lijiang, to anyplace around here, you can. The local PSB understands now you are a friend to China. You won't have any troubles."

I really don't know what to say to that. I drink my beer. John pours me more and then refills his own glass. Downs it and opens another bottle.

"Why are you doing all this?" I finally ask.

He puts the bottle down. "Because we are friends."

The way he looks at me—steady, serious, not putting on one of his confused, clueless acts—I almost believe him.

WE FINISH EATING. THEN we drink the rest of the beer. It's not until we're on the last bottle that I start thinking about the other times I've drunk beer with John.

Both times turned out pretty weird.

"Are you tired, Yili?" he asks, watching me.

"A little."

He stands. Tidies up the take-out containers and the paper plates, stuffing them in the plastic bag and tying the bag shut.

I look around, at the big room, the king-size bed. And I think, What the fuck? Are we going to be sharing this bed?

My heart starts to pound, and I'm not sure why. Because yeah, he's creepy, but he's also pretty good-looking.

I stand up, too, bracing myself on the table.

John tosses the bag in the trash.

"I, uh . . . I need to give the dog her antibiotic," I say.

He nods. "I will let you sleep."

With that he slings his black duffel over his shoulder and heads to the door. So I guess he has his own room. I follow. You know, to be polite.

He pauses by the door. "Tomorrow . . . I can take you someplace. Wherever you need to go. If you like."

"Thanks. I . . ." The truth is, I don't have a clue what I'm going to do tomorrow. "Anyway, thanks. For . . . you know. Helping me with the dog."

We're standing pretty close together, but I still don't exactly expect it when John leans over and kisses me.

He does it fast, presses his lips against mine and then draws back. Like he's nervous. The clueless, slightly awkward guy I met at that party a year ago.

I don't know why, but it pisses me off.

"That the best you can do?"

His face darkens. He takes a step closer; we're standing toe-to-toe. And then he kisses me for real, his body up against mine, my tits against his hard chest, his one hand tangling in my hair, the other running down my back till it cups my ass.

And yeah, I guess this is what I wanted.

I WANT THE LIGHTS out, but he wants one turned down low. "Because you are beautiful," he says softly, "and I want to look at you."

"I'm not." Hearing him say that makes me get teary, which is stupid, and I know it. But I'm a mess. I don't like looking at myself, especially my leg. Why would anyone else want to look at me, unless he's some kind of freak?

"You are wrong," he says. "And I can prove it to you."

We're lying on the bed, and he rocks back, resting on his calves and heels. His dick is standing at attention, like a good little soldier. Not the biggest one I've ever seen, but it's nice. Trim and hard, like the rest of him. I like the neat black hair around it, too. I reach my hand out.

"No, Yili," he says.

"No?"

He stretches out next to me, his face close to mine. "You know about Dao?"

"Taoism?"

"Yes."

His fingers start tracing light patterns all over me, from the crease of my jaw down to the hollow of my neck, onto my nipple, along my ribs, and it's making me crazy.

"I . . . uh, just, *ren fa di, di fa tian, tian fa . . .*" It's this Taoist rhyme I learned in Chinese class.

"*Tian fa dao,*" John supplies. "*Dao fa ziran.*"

Man follows Earth, Earth follows Heaven, Heaven follows the Way, the Way follows Nature.

"Yeah. That," I manage.

"You know what Taoists believe?"

"Uh . . ."

"Taoists believe that man is yang. Man must preserve essence."

"Essence?"

"*You* know," he whispers.

I can guess.

"Women, women are yin. Men only have so much yang essence. But women, women have always their yin. In this way women are stronger than men."

His hand moves lower, and I am not feeling strong.

"Taoist say it's very good for man to . . . to get yin from woman. But she only release yin if he pleases her. So he should be inside her as long as he can. And please her many times."

"Are you a Taoist?" I ask.

He grins. "I practice."

AT ONE POINT THE dog starts whining and comes over to the bed. "It's okay, dog," I tell her, but she keeps whining. Maybe she only understands Chinese. "Uh, *dou hao. Xiuxi! Shuijiao!*" Finally she settles down again. Which is good, because John does not seem to be settling down anytime soon.

He gets my yin once, twice, and it's not until we're trying something called "Mating Cicadas" (it's a lot better than it sounds) and a third dose of my yin that John's jade stalk gives it up inside my red pearl.

"Wow," I finally say.

"I can do better," he tells me.

★ ★ ★

I MANAGE TO GET out of bed, clean myself up, put my pj's back on, because even though John's seen pretty much all there is to see of me, I still don't like being seen. The dog's lying on a rug near the bathroom. When she sees me approach, she looks up and thumps her tail. "Good dog," I whisper. "*Hao gou.*" I hold out my hand, and her wet nose nuzzles my palm.

By the time I get back to bed, John is sound asleep. I settle in next to him.

I lie there, exhausted, but not quite ready to sleep.

I just had the best sex of my life, with Creepy John.

And he doesn't even snore.

CHAPTER TWENTY-FOUR

I WAKE UP BECAUSE the dog barks.

I lift my head, and I see John and the dog by the door. He has the dog on the leash, and the dog is doing this excited hopping and circling, from her back to her front legs. She barks again. A happy bark.

"Sorry!" John says in a low voice. "I just take her outside. For walk. I already give her antibiotic," he adds.

"Thanks."

After he closes the door, I fall back on the bed. I'm so sore I feel like I've been to fucking Taoist boot camp. Or Taoist fucking boot camp. Ha-ha.

I lie there for a while, but I can't sleep. I think, John will come back soon. Do I want to be lying here in bed when he does? For another round of yin exchange?

I haul my ass out of bed and into the shower.

As I stand under the water, I think of all the reasons why sex with Creepy John was a truly bad idea.

Okay, I'm not completely irresponsible. I know I have this tendency to occasionally hook up with guys I don't know very well. So I'm on the pill. And I also insist on condoms.

Well, most of the time. Last night being an exception.

I've had the hepatitis B vaccination series, so that's good. There's a lot of hep B in China. HIV, though . . . and there's a lot of HIV here, too.

He's with the DSD. He's not going to have HIV. I don't think.

And, he's with the DSD. Which I am pretty sure is one for the "truly bad idea" category.

On the other hand, it's slightly less creepy than if he were just some crazed stalker dude. Right?

How can you be so fucking stupid? I ask myself.

By the time I come out of the shower, pressure bandage rewrapped, dressed in my jeans and a fresh T-shirt, John has returned with the dog.

"Breakfast," he announces.

Croissants and coffee. On a tray. Un-fucking-believable.

"They have all this at the hotel," he explains, setting it up on the little table. "From European bakery. And very good coffee."

"You like coffee?"

"Before, not very much. But lately I like more and more." He smiles at me.

The dog, meanwhile, nuzzles my legs and then sits on my feet.

"She is very affectionate," John says.

"Yeah."

"Please, sit. Have coffee."

I feel this sudden rush of . . . maybe not anger, but irritation. I don't want to do anything that John tells me to do.

Except I really want some coffee. And maybe a Percocet.

Is it too early for beer?

I lower myself onto the chair and pick up the cup of coffee. I read somewhere that a study in Japan showed that rats get happier just from smelling coffee. I take a deep breath before I sip.

John sits across from me, holding his coffee cup in his hands. He looks younger somehow. Boyish. A bounce in his step like the dog's.

Maybe it was all that yin he got last night.

"So where do you want to go now, Yili?"

I shrug. I don't really know, and I don't feel like talking about it.

John tears off a piece of his croissant. Hesitates.

"If you tell me a little more, maybe I can help."

"Look, just fucking lay off me, all right?"

He sits back in his chair. I'm not sure how to read the expression on his face. Is he pissed off? Is he hurt? I can't tell.

"Okay, last night? You satisfied your curiosity," I say. "Fine. So did I. But you think that means we're suddenly all friends and I'm going to trust you? How stupid do you think I am?"

Now he's angry, and I can tell. He slams his mug on the table, coffee splashing over the sides. "What do you think this is, Ellie? What do you think?"

We stare at each other. I focus on the white scar that cuts across his eyebrow.

I want to say something awful, something nasty, something so mean that he'll fuck off and out of my life forever.

But I can't.

"I don't know," I say.

AFTER BREAKFAST WE TAKE a walk: me, John, and the dog. We walk on the brick path that runs along the lake—a promenade, I guess you'd call it. There's one of those grey stone "traditional" fences to keep you from falling in, like you see everywhere in China: square posts with flowers carved at the top, a rail and a slab below, with geometric cutouts. It's beautiful, and quiet, and we don't fill the silence by trying to talk. What's there to say?

But finally I have to say something. I guess I owe him, given that he got me off of the Dali's Most Wanted Foreigners list.

Unless he was the one who set me up . . .

But no. I don't really think that. I don't know how I feel about John, exactly. But I don't think he'd do that to me.

"I'm just doing a favor for a friend, that's all. I didn't think it was going to get complicated."

He frowns. "Complicated how?"

"I'm still not sure. But it's not like . . . I mean, it's just a bunch of foreigners, mostly. Nobody's doing anything against China."

Of course, neither were my artist friends, last year. But they were Chinese, and it's not the same.

"Why don't you want me to help you, Ellie?"

The question drops in the air like a stone.

"Just . . . It's something I should do myself, that's all."

"Why?" He sounds more frustrated than angry. "Why you have to do everything by yourself?"

I stop walking. I don't know why. I lean against the stone railing and look at the lake. Wonder if the white bird is out there somewhere.

"I guess because I can't find anyone to do it with me. No one I can trust anyway."

I have to give him credit. He doesn't say some stupid bullshit like, "But you can trust *me*." He doesn't say anything at all.

The dog whimpers a little and settles on my feet. I scratch behind her ears. I'm not really sure what dogs like, but she likes that.

Eventually the three of us start walking again.

"If you want to stay in this room some more time, you can," he tells me.

"Thanks."

We stand inside the hotel room: me, John, and the dog. The room's been cleaned. The bed made. Fresh sheets.

"I go back to Beijing, then," John says. He hesitates. "I think you are just on vacation. If anyone asks me."

I look at him standing there, head tilted down, hands hooked in the pockets of his jeans like a sheepish kid.

"There's something you could do for me," I say. "I mean, you don't have to. Just if you want. And if you don't want to, if it's too much trouble . . ."

"Tell me," he says.

I don't want to say it. Because it's like I'm attached and I don't want to give her up.

"The dog. Can you take her back to Beijing? Make sure she gets her medicine? You can take her to my apartment, to my mom. Just let my mom know what she needs to do. To take care of her."

I swear it's like the fucking dog is psychic. She looks up at me. Her eyes are big and gold. She thumps her tail.

"Sure," John says. "Sure. I can do that."

"And you won't . . . you won't sell her for hotpot in Guangzhou. Right?"

John draws back. He looks offended. "Of course not." He holds his hand out, so the dog can sniff it. "The tradition of eating dogs is old-fashioned and uncivilized. China needs to abandon this, as part of modernization."

"And cats?"

"Certainly we should not eat cats. They do not even taste good."

THE DOG CLIMBS INTO John's silver Toyota without much fuss and curls up on the backseat.

"Be good, dog," I tell her, even though I'm pretty sure she doesn't understand English. "I'll see you soon, okay?"

She nuzzles my hand, thumps her tail.

John stands by the open door of the driver's side, hands clasped in front of him, like he doesn't know what do with them. "Don't worry. I will take good care of her."

"Thanks."

"If you have any troubles, call me."

"I will."

We stand there for a moment. Then he nods, gets into the car, and starts the engine.

Who *is* this guy? I still can't figure him out.

I watch the car pull away, hear the dog whine and bark once, twice. Then the car turns down a narrow lane, and I can't see it anymore.

Now what?

I GO BACK INSIDE the hotel room and look around. It's a nice room. Nicer than the places I usually stay. Maybe I'll take John up on his offer. Stay here a few days longer.

And do what?

I made a big deal to John about how I had this thing I needed to do, something I had to do by myself, without him. How I had to help a friend.

But what can I actually *do* about it?

I make a mental list.

I can go back to the Dali Perfect Inn, see if they have any contact info for Jason/David/Langhai. I can search the Web to see if he's uploaded any new videos. And I can go to New Dali and check out the Modern Scientific Seed Company.

I fall back on the bed with a sigh. I really don't feel like doing any of this, except for maybe the Internet search, because I don't have to go anywhere to do that. But after getting on my high horse and telling John I was on this big fucking mission . . .

I guess I have to try.

I make myself a cup of Starbucks VIA and boot up my battered laptop. Go to Langhai's stream on Youku.

And fuck me if there isn't a new video.

I settle back in my chair, heart thumping, fingers twitching, and I grin, because I've been hunting this guy and here's a trail of bread crumbs. I click on the video.

Another field of grain, manipulated so the sky is dark and the grain glowing yellow, outlined in black.

"The Truth About Eos in China," the title says. In English.

"This is what you need to know," a man says. American. He sounds young. Ragged, on the edge of exhaustion.

Jason?

"Eos has a joint venture with Hongxing Agricultural Products. They're working on developing GMOs for the Chinese market. Especially rice."

There's a shot of a bag of New Century Hero Rice. The farmer smiling, raising his hoe like a rifle.

"They're putting this stuff on the market illegally. Without permission. Hiding what they're doing in places like Guiyu, where no one would think of looking."

Shots of Guiyu. Of tainted fields surrounded by smoking electronic scrap. Of the New Century Seeds storefront, the electronics workshop where I ran into Mr. Piggy, who subsequently arranged to have my ass kicked, I'm pretty sure.

"In Yunnan, one of China's breadbaskets."

I think I recognize the landscape, the green fields and hills around Dali. Then a shot of another storefront, in the middle of a typical Chinese city street. The camera lingers on it long enough for me to take in a cartoon graphic on the window—a dancing tomato tangoing with an ear of corn. The supered title reads: "Modern Scientific Seed Company. Dali, Yunnan."

"Eos has its people working in the US government, in the

Department of Agriculture, in the FDA, making sure their products get approved with minimal oversight." A slide of names and positions. Most of them I don't recognize—I mean, who knows the names of deputy directors of the FDA and US Trade Policy Committee members?—but isn't that one a Supreme Court judge? *"It works the other way, too—Eos employs former congressional and White House staffers as lobbyists—they've spent hundreds of millions of dollars on lobbying and campaign contributions."*

A photo of some old white dude, with a name beneath it and FORMER SECRETARY OF DEFENSE NOW ON BOARD OF DIRECTORS.

"And in China? Who knows how it works?"

A slide of the Great Wall with a big red question mark supered over it.

"These people are trying to control the global food supply," he says urgently. *"I know that sounds crazy."*

Yeah, well, kind of. I get that the stuff they're making maybe isn't safe. But control the food supply all over the world? I mean, nobody can do that.

It's like he's reading my mind.

"They own the patents. If their stuff contaminates other crops, they can claim they own those, too. That the farmer owes them money. That the farmer has to buy their seeds."

More PowerPoint slides. A list of citations. Things like "Eos Sues Farmer for Patent Infringement." "Farmer Claims Eos Corn Contaminated His Fields."

"There's a tipping point that happens," Jason says, because it *has* to be him, right? *"Like with soybeans in the US.* GMO soy is *ninety percent of all the soybeans planted in the US. Ninety percent! And if GMOs get a foothold here? In China?"*

In China, where they barely regulate food safety. Where restaurants use sewer oil and pork glows in the dark. Where milk powder poisons babies.

"We won't have a choice anymore. They'll own us. All of us."

He's manic-depressive, right? Paranoid. A criminal.

I know *you* are, but what am I? Ha-ha.

"I don't know if anyone will see this," Jason says. *"I'm putting it out there, hoping somebody does. I have proof. I can prove it all."*

AFTER THAT I LOOK around the elegant room, and I realize that there's no way I'm going to stay here.

It's too bad. It's nice. Quiet. And this has got to be one of the most comfortable beds I've ever slept on. But I want to pick up those bread crumbs. Even if Jason's crazy, like Natalie says and like he kind of sounds on that video. Maybe especially if he is.

Maybe even more if he's not.

I can go to both the Dali Perfect Inn and Modern Scientific Seed Company today and, if I don't learn anything, get out of Dali tonight. I'm not sure what time the train to Kunming leaves, but there are long-distance buses going there every couple of hours.

Besides, being here by myself . . . it doesn't feel right.

I miss the dog. Maybe I even miss Creepy John.

I DECIDE TO GO to the Dali Perfect Inn first. It takes about as long to get to the old town as it does to get to the new city from Shuanglang, at least according to Google Maps; I just have to go back the way I came, west and then south around the lake. I figure it's better to start there, at the hotel, where there are less likely to be thugs with iron rods.

The front desk arranges a car and driver for me. I have another cup of coffee while I wait for it to arrive. Sit on a terrace overlooking the lake. Watch the birds and the clouds and wonder how I got here.

★　★　★

"Oh! We thought you checked out!"

I'm back at the Dali Perfect Inn, and it's still fucking quaint. The same girl stands behind the counter as when I checked in a couple days ago: slim, young, wearing a Bai Minority costume. She looks kind of nervous. I wonder if the PSB paid her a visit.

Then I realize that John did.

"Yeah," I say. "Change of plans. And I wish I could stay a little longer, because this is a very nice hotel."

"Thank you," she says, nodding rapidly.

"But I'm still trying to find the person who made the video. 'Dali Scene.' You said you could ask your manager?"

She bobs her head again. "Yes, certainly. Please, wait a moment. I will ask her."

I sit in one of the Ming-dynasty chairs, stare at the world clock telling me that it's 8:49 A.M. in Moscow.

At 9:02 A.M., Moscow time, another woman appears: middle-aged, in a sweater and slacks.

"Yes, I remember the foreigner who made the video. Very nice young man."

"Great! Do you have a cell-phone number for him? Because I want him to make a video for me."

She nods. "I found the number for you." Hands me a slip of paper with a number written on it.

"Thanks," I say. "Thanks very much."

She hesitates. Smiles. "Will you be staying with us now? We have very nice room available."

"I'm not sure," I tell her. "I might be leaving town. But thanks for that."

I stand outside the Dali Perfect Inn and dial the number. And get the China Mobile recording: *"Ni hao! Nin suo boda de shi konghao. Qing chazheng hou zaibo."*

The number you dialed is no longer in service. Please check the number and try your call again.

I take a taxi to Xiaguan, to New Dali, to the long-distance bus station. It's a cement building painted peeling white and blue with a couple of buses parked in a small lot, on a narrow street, on a block that looks like any other third-tier Chinese city: cluttered, grimy, cracked plastic signs. I check my duffel in to a locker there, and find another taxi to take me to Modern Scientific Seed Company.

TURNS OUT IT'S A storefront on another typical block, wedged between a paint store and a place that looks like it's selling mostly doors.

I stand on the sidewalk across the street. Unlike the New Century Seed Company in Guiyu, this place has a sign, and the characters above the entrance, according to my trusty Pleco dictionary, actually *do* say MODERN SCIENTIFIC SEED COMPANY.

There's a cartoon graphic of dancing ears of corn and tomatoes stenciled on the window.

The seed company in Jason's latest video. I'm positive.

So he made it as far as here. Across the street at least. About where I'm standing right now.

You never know, and that's the only thing that's for sure. You never know what you're going to step in. What's going to be safe and what isn't.

I take a deep breath, and I walk across the street.

AN ELECTRONIC DOORBELL SOUNDS as I push open the door, so loud that I jump.

Not cool, McEnroe.

Inside, it's almost like a small showroom. Shoe-box-shaped. Cement floors. Plastic photos lit from behind on the walls of green fields, a factory complex, and various crops, with slogans like "Creating Green and Harmonious!" and "Harvest Happiness!" There's a counter at the back with a computer sitting on it, a lone woman wearing a white smock, like she's working in a hospital or a pharmacy. Older than me. Hair pulled back in a tight ponytail. She's staring at me.

I smile. Nod. Walk along the wall, looking at the pictures of various seeds and crops. Cartoon ear of corn carried by happy baby. "Lihai 231 Hybrid," it's called. The dancing tomatoes. "Jingli 88." Something green with stalks that's rice or wheat or hay, like I can tell, called "Zhongcheng 351."

By now my circuit has brought me to the back counter. The woman who sits there smiles tightly. *"Wo keyi bang ni mang ma?"* Can I help you?

"Ni hao." I hesitate. I'm not sure what to ask. Do I pull out my photo of Jason/David/Langhai?

Maybe I should, you know, have an actual *plan* the next time I do something like this.

"I hear you sell a special kind of rice," I finally say.

She keeps smiling. "We sell several special varieties of rice. For different circumstances."

"This one is called New Century Hero Rice. Do you know it?"

She frowns. A cartoon kind of frown, almost. Put it up on the wall next to the dancing tomatoes.

"Burenshi." Don't recognize it. "I can search our products."

She starts tapping on the keyboard. I glance around and see a surveillance camera, one of those black domes encased in white plastic, tucked in the corner of the ceiling.

Okay, I tell myself. Okay. These cameras are everywhere. It doesn't mean anything.

The woman shakes her head. "We don't have that brand,"

she says. "Sorry. But I can ask my manager to recommend the proper kind." The smile is back. "Depending on your circumstances."

I start backing toward the door before I even think about it. "Thank you," I say. *"Wo kaolü hou zai jueding."* I'll consider before I decide. *"Zai jian!"*

Another step. I turn around. Just get to the door, I tell myself, the muscles between my shoulders clenching.

Get to the door. Open it. Walk outside.

By the time I reach the sidewalk, I'm sweating like crazy. My heart's pounding. Nerves in my bad leg lighting up like they're on fire. I gulp in a breath. Then another.

Okay, I tell myself. No one's coming to get me. It's okay.

I'm a fucking head case. What makes me think I can do this kind of shit anyway?

Bus station.

Even though I'm a head case, even though there are no guys with iron bars chasing me, all I want to do right now is get to the bus station and get out of town.

Five hours from Dali to Kunming and I'm stuck on a bus playing a Hong Kong comedy at a volume that rattles the cheap speakers. I tilt the seat as far back as it goes, prop my feet up on the footrest. Close my eyes and try to figure out why I freaked out in the Modern Scientific Seed Company showroom.

Well, there's the fact that, as mentioned, I'm a head case. Plus, the attempted mugging, getting beat up, followed, framed, Jason's video, and having amazing sex with Creepy John.

I mean, it's all pretty unsettling.

But that whole setup. An empty display room. The woman on her computer. The way she looked at me. The surveillance camera.

What was it? There weren't any actual seeds there, at least that I saw. It didn't look like the kind of place that farmers would go in to buy their future crops. Though what do I know about how Chinese farmers do business? Next to nothing. Maybe they go in there and look at all the pretty photos and place their orders over the Internet or something.

A corporate branch office, maybe.

Why was it on Jason's list?

He had to have gotten those names from Han Rong, right? Han Rong, who claims to be a dissatisfied employee, but who doesn't have any evidence of his own to bust Eos.

The whole thing stinks. Like a rotten fish tomato.

I GET INTO KUNMING around 9:00 P.M. I'm sore, I'm tired and I'm hungry. I check in to a hotel near Wenlin Jie, the cool area near the university where I hung out before. Limp down the street and find a restaurant specializing in Yunnan food. There's all kinds of people out and about: students and tourists and locals, wandering down the narrow street that smells faintly of spices and sewage, gathering in clusters around the open-air bars, eating ice cream, drinking beer.

I sit and eat. Spicy beef with crispy basil and something called "Grandmother's potatoes," which is sort of like fried mashed potatoes but better. Wash it down with a Dali beer.

After I settle up, I'm feeling pretty good, so I wander down the street until I find a bar that looks decent. Well, actually, it looks kind of tacky, with silver walls and Plexiglas tables and red and blue floodlights, but it's not crowded, which is what makes it look decent to me right now.

I take a seat at the bar, facing the street. Order an overpriced tequila shot and another Dali beer.

There's one more name on Jason's list. Bright Future Seed Company, in Guiyang, the capital of Guizhou Province.

I've never been to Guizhou. I don't know very much about it, only that it's poor and supposedly beautiful and that it's located between Yunnan, where I am now, and Guangxi, where Guilin and Yangshuo are.

Just east of here.

I don't know, I tell myself. I don't know. Does it make sense for me to go there? I mean, what are the odds that I go to Bright Future Seed Company and all my questions are answered?

That I find Jason.

Because that's why I'm doing all this, right?

I'm thinking this, and I'm tired, and I guess I'm a little buzzed. Because when my phone rings, I flinch, and I grab it, and I hit ANSWER, even though it's an unknown number.

I don't stop to think about what that might mean.

CHAPTER TWENTY-FIVE

"ELLIE? ELLIE MCENROE?"

A woman's voice.

I don't recognize her at first because she sounds nervous, almost panicked, as opposed to being her usual pain in my ass.

"Yeah?"

"It's Vicky Huang."

I have a moment of panic myself, thinking, Weren't we supposed to talk in a week? Has it already been a week? I try to count up the days.

"Sorry to call you so late," she says.

I think that it hasn't been a week, it's been . . . what, three days? Four? And yeah, it *is* pretty late, like almost midnight. And all the time zones are the same in China, so she doesn't have *that* excuse.

"Uh, that's okay," I finally manage. "What can I do for you?"

A hesitation. "I just need to know . . ." Another pause. "Do you negotiate to sell Zhang Jianli's work to another collector?" Her words come out in a rush, like they're propelled by a small explosion.

"No. Why would you think that?"

A brief, nervous laugh. "So sorry! It is only that . . . Mr.

Cao, he . . . he is very anxious to secure certain pieces. For his collection. He is very serious about his collection."

She sounds like he's going to take it out of her hide if he doesn't get what he wants.

"I promise you. I'm not negotiating with anyone. I've just been on vacation. That's all."

At that moment the waitress swings over. *"Zai lai yi ping pijui,"* I tell the waitress, because I really need another beer if I'm going to have this conversation.

"Where are you now? Mr. Cao is very anxious to arrange a meeting."

"I'm in Kunming . . . Look, I'll be back in Beijing in a few days. Tell Mr. Cao not to worry. Nothing's being sold right now. And I'm sorry we haven't been able to meet."

Because as much as I hate apologizing to this pushy bitch, I can't afford to piss off a Chinese billionaire potential investor.

"I've had some personal business, that's all. It doesn't have anything to do with Zhang Jianli's art."

"I see," she says.

I can't tell for sure if she believes me, but she sounds calmer anyway.

Man, people are freaks.

I sit there a while longer, sipping my beer. I think about checking my email. I haven't done that since I left Dali, and there's free wireless here.

I have my laptop with me, like I always do—no way I trust leaving it in a hotel room. No matter how careful I am about using VPNs, about clearing my browsing history and running spyware and virus scans, about deleting anything sensitive off my hard drive, I just don't know enough about how all that stuff works to be sure. Besides, one thing I do know is, people can put all kinds of spyware and key-logging software on your computer if they have access to it, and even on a Mac that stuff can be hard to find.

For all I know, that kid Moudzu back in Guiyu could have bugged it when he fixed it. I mean, I don't think so, but how can I know for sure?

No Great Community, I tell myself. Just email.

When I log on, there's a message from my mom.

Hey, hon, hope you're having fun. Things are okay here. Andy's friend got the toilet fixed. It's been really great having Andy around, since you're not here. It's nothing I planned on or expected, but I think things might be getting serious between us. Will you be home soon? Love, Mom.

I lean back in my chair, sip my beer, and think about ordering another tequila shot, even though I know I shouldn't. I mean, what am I supposed to say to this? "Way to go, Mom! So happy you found another crazy boyfriend!"

While I'm trying to decide what to drink and what to write, I launch Skype. Dog Turner's account is green.

It's 12:45 A.M. here, 8:45 A.M. in San Diego.

Not that early for most people, I guess.

As I stare at the screen, the Skype phone rings. Dog Turner. I hesitate for a moment. I don't know what to say to him.

I could just not answer it, I guess.

"Fuck it," I mutter. I'm going to have to talk to him eventually. Might as well get it over with.

I hit ANSWER. But it's not Dog's face on the screen. It's Natalie's.

"Ellie, hi. Thanks . . . thanks for picking up."

She looks like shit, but then just about anybody lit up by a computer screen looks kind of sickly.

"Hey," I say. "Give me a second. Let me get my earbuds in."

It's more than the blue computer light, though. Her eyes are red-rimmed, the lids puffy. Her streaked blond hair has taken on the texture of straw.

No Dog in sight.

"Hi," I say after untangling my earbuds. "How's . . . Is everything okay?"

Because suddenly I know that things aren't okay at all.

"Doug's in the hospital," she bursts out. "He had—they aren't sure—a seizure, maybe a stroke. He just . . ."

"Oh, shit. How is he? I mean, is he . . . ?"

And I don't know how to finish the question. Because no matter what, he isn't okay.

"They're running tests." She swipes the back of her hand across her eyes. "I don't know, I'm sure he's fine, it's just . . ."

She can't finish.

"I'm really sorry," I say.

She looks up at me.

"Is there any word about . . . about Jason? Because Doug's just so . . . he's so emotional about it. That was what— I mean, he was going off about it, before he . . ."

She has to stop again.

Fucking great.

"Yeah," I say. "Yeah, I'm working on it. I can't promise anything, but I have a few leads."

It's like the strain in her face suddenly dissolves, like someone had been pulling a rubber band as far as it could stretch and then let go. "Thanks," she says. "Thanks. Even if you don't . . . At least I can tell him you're doing something. It really helps."

AFTER WE DISCONNECT, I order the tequila shot. And I think, fuck, Dog. Why did you mess around with me when you had someone like Natalie at home, who cares so much about you?

I didn't know.

If I'd known, I never would have done it.

At least I hope not.

SO YEAH, I DECIDE to go to Guizhou. To Guiyang, to check out the last of the seed companies on Jason's list.

It's not like I think I'll find Jason. It's not like I think I'll find out anything at all. It's just that I can tell Dog and Natalie I tried. That I did everything I could do. Followed the last lead through to its conclusion.

I mean, what else am I going to do? Go back to Beijing and meet with Sidney Cao and Vicky Huang about art I can't sell? Or hang out with my mom and her new boyfriend, Anal Andy?

And Creepy John. He should be back in Beijing by now. With my dog.

Don't think about that now.

A soft sleeper to Guizhou costs less than thirty-five bucks from here. I can afford it.

I hit REPLY to my mom's email. *Hi,* I type. *Glad things are going well. I have something else to do but should be home in a couple days. Make sure you check the date on your visa. It expires soon, right? If so, you can go to Hong Kong or Korea to renew it. Ask Andy to help with the travel. See you soon.*

THERE ARE PLENTY OF trains from Kunming that go to Guiyang, and I find a seat on one that leaves at 12:30 P.M. the next day and gets me there around 10 P.M.

I find a cab. From the car window, Guiyang's just another second- or third-tier Chinese city: lots of strange grey and tan high-rises faced with fogged mirror glass, shorter white-tile-fronted buildings with blackened grout, apartment blocks with sagging, rusting balconies. Overhead in places there's these crazy dull metal tubes that look like giant hamster trails—elevated roads, I guess. And even in one of China's poorest provinces, a luxury mall advertising Gucci, with promises of Armani to come.

My hotel is in the same building as a seedy mall that smells like grease, the entrance to it around the corner, across from sagging grey and brown apartment blocks. There's no hotel lobby here, just a security guard sitting behind a desk, then a couple of elevators in a hall with warped linoleum floors scarred by cigarette burns.

The hotel takes up the twenty-fifth to the thirtieth floors. It's not bad. Some Japanese chain. A lot of brass plating and red-flocked wallpaper. Everything feels undersized: A tiny lobby. Narrow halls.

"Zhege lüguan, you meiyou yige jiuba?" I ask the desk clerk. Does this hotel have a bar? Because after ten hours on the train, my leg is just killing me, even with a Percocet.

"They have one on the fifth floor," she tells me. Her Chinese is hard to understand; the accent, or dialect or whatever it is, is pretty thick.

"Xie xie." I start to head to the elevator, and then I think about the mission. I extract the piece of paper from my wallet, the one with Jason's seed companies.

"Do you recognize this place?" I point to Bright Future Seed Company. The last name on the list.

She studies the paper. "No, don't recognize. The address, this place is on west side of city. Perhaps past long-distance bus station." She smiles. "Maybe not a famous Guiyang business."

THE BAR IS DARK, with wood-slat benches, Formica tables, a couple of aquariums. I sit underneath the spray-painted mural of a screaming bald guy, drink a Snow Beer, and try to ignore the Mandarin pop and cigarette smoke. There's a skinny young bartender with long hair that flops over one eye, wearing a stretched-out white V-neck, a table of college-age kids, I think—a few years younger than me anyway—drinking beers and colas and eating snacks that, if they're anything like what's on my table, taste like jicama dipped in chili oil.

Works for me.

I'm pretty sure I'm the only white girl for miles. At least I'm the only one I've seen in this bar and this building.

So what do I do?

I order my second beer and think about it.

Just go there, I guess. Take a look. See what happens.

If it seems too sketchy, I'm not going to make the mistake I made in Guiyu. I'll just stay in the cab.

I DON'T MAKE IT into a cab until just before 2:00 P.M. the next day. I slept in this morning. I was tired, and also I ended up hanging out a little with those guys at the other table, and two beers turned into four. They were nice, and I need to do that, make an effort to hang out with people. That's what the army shrink told me, back in the day: "It's easy to get overwhelmed by too much external stimulation. But try not to isolate."

He'd be proud of me. I think about the last couple of weeks, and whatever it is I've been doing, it hasn't been isolating.

The cabdriver looks at the address and considers. "Long way. Maybe forty-five minutes."

"*Mei wenti,*" I say. No problem. I have the room reserved for another night; it's cheap enough. I figure this last mission, to Bright Future Seed Company, isn't going to take too long. I'll check it out and cross it off my list of stuff I need to do. I'll have a nice dinner someplace and see if I can get on a train to Beijing tomorrow. Maybe even a plane, if it's not too expensive. Because even though I don't know what I'm going to do about all the crap on my plate waiting for me in BJ, a part of me kind of wants to get back there and . . . I don't know, maybe deal with it.

Not Creepy John, I tell myself. No way. That whole thing is just too weird. Even if some parts of it make me really horny.

He works for the DSD. You can't trust him. Plus, he's a freak.

Think about something else. Like the dog.

I wonder how she's doing.

Probably my mom and Andy are taking her for walks. I can picture the two of them doing that. Walking the dog. Holding hands.

They've got to be screwing each other by now. I mean, they've already dented navels.

The cabdriver wasn't kidding—this is a long drive. Just getting across Guiyu took longer than I would have thought. Traffic in the city sucks. This is a poor province—who knew there'd be so many cars here?

Now we're on a highway heading west. Mountains rise on either side. The road is pretty good, the traffic not bad, but then there's nothing much out here. At first half-built housing developments—high-rises swathed in green nets and bamboo scaffolds. Broad, empty streets. Then not even the half-built communities, just billboards advertising the modern, luxurious lifestyles to come: GOLDEN FORTUNE ESTATES, RISEN PHOENIX WATERFRONT MANSIONS.

We take a turn off the main highway, onto a frontage road, pass a factory of some kind—maybe cement?—then a string of small businesses, low storefronts framed in white tile. A restaurant. A car-repair place. A new-looking Sinopec gas station.

Then, finally, a long building with a tin roof. No sign. No windows in front. A couple of cars parked on one side.

"I think this is it," the cabdriver says.

A nondescript warehouse in an isolated area. Fucking awesome. It's like the cover of those paperbacks my mom used to read, with the chick in a nightgown running through the castle carrying a candle, and I'm the stupid chick dripping the candle wax.

"You sure?"

"We can ask."

I really don't want to go knock on that door and ask.

Across from where the cars are parked, there's a small building, your basic white tile and cement. Two businesses, it looks like. On the left is cigarettes and booze, one of those state-owned stores that are everywhere. The other, I can see a glass-topped freezer and a soft-drink cooler, so I'm guessing snacks and sundries.

The driver has the same thought I do. He pulls the car up to the store.

"Ni deng wo, hao buhao?" I ask. Can you wait for me? Because I so do not want to get left out here by myself.

He nods. *"Wo kending keyi deng ni."* He can wait. Which makes sense, since I haven't paid him yet.

It's raining, not hard, but it's cold out, too, colder than Kunming anyway. Feels like mid-forties. I turn up the collar of my jacket, glad that I'm wearing my knit hat.

I decide to go into the snack store. I could use some water. There's a middle-aged woman behind the counter, small, stout. Ordinary, except her hair's done up in this fancy bun, these swooping, shining waves, some kind of silver comb holding it together.

Must be an ethnic-minority thing.

I grab a bottle of water from the cooler and put it on the counter. *"Ni hao. Duo shao qian?"*

"San kuai."

I give her a five-yuan note, get two coins back. "Please, can

I ask, that building over there . . . Do you know, is that Bright Future Seed Company?"

"Yes," she says. "Bright Future Seed Company."

I don't know what to ask next. Or if I should ask anything at all.

"So . . . I can buy seeds there?"

She frowns. "*Bu qingchu.*" Not clear. "I don't think you can buy seeds. Not too many people work there. Maybe is just a storehouse?"

"Okay. *Xie xie.*"

Now what?

I exit the store, and I think about what to do.

A part of me really wants to be all action-movie heroine. Just go kick down the doors over there and see what's up.

Except I suck at kicking down doors. And I'm pretty sure that it's a really bad idea to try.

A truck trundles by on the frontage road, stirring up dust and spewing diesel.

I'll take a couple pictures with my iPhone, I decide. Document it. Tell Natalie everything that's happened and everything I've found.

There are other people I could ask to help. Harrison. Maybe even Creepy John. But I'm not going to do that until I tell Natalie exactly what the risks of asking them might be.

I'm thinking about all this, staring at the road. I see a motorcycle cart, a three-wheeler with a wooden bed. The engine sounds like a series of exploding fireworks. It's not going very fast. Those things rarely can.

There are iron crates on it. Crates full of dogs. Crammed in there like livestock. Barking. Whimpering. I can hear them, their cries fading as the cart disappears down the road.

They eat a lot of dog meat in Guizhou, I heard.

"*Ni hao!*"

I just about jump out of my skin.

I turn, and standing there is this girl. Well, woman. Young woman. She's wearing a white blouse and a blue smock, like a work uniform.

"Can I help you?"

"I, uh . . ."

She's smiling at me. She's cute, looks like an ad for a product, like she's about to dissolve into giggles. Glossy black pigtails with pink-and-white plastic ponytail holders shaped like . . .

"I'm looking for Bright Future Seed Company," I manage.

"Oh," she says, sounding delighted. "Yes. You've found it."

Hello Kitty. That's what the ponytail holders are shaped like.

She reaches out her hand, like she wants to shake.

Her other hand comes out of her smock pocket, and she's gripping something, something pink.

And then this wave of pain knocks me off my feet. Like those guys in Guiyu with their iron bars are somehow beating on every part of me all at once, and everything spasms. I can't control myself, I feel like something slams into me—a car, maybe, that's all I can think of.

And I'm on the ground, looking up at the girl with the Hello Kitty ponytail holders.

I hear shouts—the cabdriver, I think, then the girl: "We have a doctor! I'll call the doctor!"

And I try to object, say, "No, no, don't leave me here! Don't—" and it slams into me again, this pain, and a part of me watches the rest of me curl up and writhe and convulse, and that part thinks, must be a taser or something like that.

But that part of me can't do a fucking thing about it.

CHAPTER TWENTY-SIX

I CAN'T MOVE.

Then my muscles start coming back to life. I try to sit up—because I should sit up, right?—and Hello Kitty, the pink thing she's holding, she moves her finger, and I'm struck by lightning again, out of control, losing my shit. Screaming. But there's still this part of me that's detached, flying above it all, trying to think it through.

When they tase you to say hello, you have to figure it's not going to end well.

I'm lying on my back in this little room. Some other guys came from somewhere—the warehouse, it must have been—and carried me here. And there's these wires, I can see them, like spiderwebbing, rising from my arm and my stomach.

If I try to move, if I try to talk, if I try to do anything, she pushes the button again.

So I don't move. I don't talk. I just lie there. And wait.

I don't have to wait too long before two new guys enter the room. They're a step up from the first two, who look like your basic rent-a-thugs. These guys are dressed better. One Chinese, one Western.

I don't recognize the Western guy, but I know the type.

Forty-something. Gym muscles under the nice coat, belly going soft. Hair cut down to stubble, to minimize the bald spot.

Hello Kitty hands him the Taser. Funny, I think. It looks like a video-game controller. Like a bright pink Wii.

He kneels down next to me.

"Ellie McEnroe. I've heard about you."

American. "Nice things, I hope." My voice is raw. It hurts to talk.

His thumb hovers over the trigger. I cringe.

He grins. "Good girl. We understand each other."

The Chinese guy jerks his head at the rent-a-thugs. "Bring two chairs," he snaps. One of them hustles off.

American guy rocks back on his heels. "Okay, here's the deal. I'm going to ask you a couple of questions. You're going to answer me. We're clear on that?"

I nod.

"Where's Jason Turner?"

Oh, fuck. I'm screwed. I tell him the truth: "I don't know."

His thumb twitches. I'm shaking now, so hard it's like he's already pushed the button. He laughs.

"One more chance," he says. "Where's Jason?"

I squeeze my eyes shut. "I don't know."

By the time I can move again, the thug's come back with the chairs. The American and the Chinese guy sit in them, the American's chair pulled up to me, practically touching me, the Chinese guy's farther back.

The American nudges me with his foot. "Hey," he says. "You with us? Want to try again?"

"I . . ."

The Chinese guy looks bored. He lights a cigarette. He's got a sharp haircut, wears a snappy black jacket. Probably Armani or Gucci or whatever the fuck.

Part of me just wants to shut down. Curl up in a ball and they can do whatever the fuck it is they're going to do. Because even if I wanted to, I can't answer him.

"I . . ." I clear my throat. Try, I tell myself. Say something. "I'm friends with his brother. We served together. In Iraq."

I wait for the shock. It doesn't happen. Instead the guy is watching me. Listening.

He's ex-military, I'm willing to bet. That's the only thing I've got to play. So I play it.

"Jason's brother . . . he got blown up pretty good. TBI. Lost an arm, too. He's pretty messed up."

The American nods. He knows this already.

"We're buddies," I say. "You know how it is. He heard Jason was in China. Asked me if I could find him. I said I'd try."

"Okay," he finally says. "So how'd you know to come here? And to Dali?"

"Jason's girlfriend. I . . . I met her. In Shantou. He left her a list. She gave it to me."

"And how'd you find her?"

Fuck. I can't think straight. I don't know what's safe to say. What isn't.

He pushes the trigger.

"Yangshuo," I gasp, when I can talk. "Dog had a postcard. From Jason. So I went there. That's where they met. I just . . . I just asked around."

He leans back in his chair. Crosses his arms over his chest. Sighs. Tilts his head toward the Chinese guy. "I think it's pretty clear where the leak came from," he says. Then he turns back to me.

"We don't let little terrorist fucks like your pal Jason interfere with our business. It's not acceptable."

"Okay," I say.

"And we don't take kindly to people stealing our intellectual property and trying to make a profit off it."

"I, uh . . . okay."

"So if you want to make things right, you better tell me, right now, anything else you know. Where you got your information, who your sources are, and anything you know about where Jason Turner is."

I'm so fucked up right now I can't even think. I have these flashes. About Langhai and his videos. About Han Rong, who I'm pretty sure is not to be trusted, and his fellow weasel Russell. I wouldn't mind ratting those two out to these guys. They've got to be from Eos, right? And maybe Hongxing.

I close my eyes.

I see Boba and the birds. Sparrow, and Kang Li, and the cats.

Whatever I say, I don't want to lead these guys back to them.

"It's like I said. Jason sent a postcard. From Yangshuo. I went there. Asked around. Found out about Jason's girlfriend and where she was. It wasn't hard. You could do the same thing I did."

The American guy sits in the chair. He stares at me. His finger brushes the trigger of the Taser.

I stare back. I can't tell if he believes me. And I don't know what I'll do if he hurts me again.

Finally he tosses the Taser on the floor.

"Whatever," he says. He stands up. The Chinese guy flicks his cigarette butt onto the floor and rises as well.

"After we're gone, take care of the trash," the Chinese guy says to the thugs. "Away from here."

Hello Kitty follows them out.

Now it's just me and the thugs.

It's weird. Here's these two guys, and they're looking at me with dead eyes. Like one time I went to a restaurant in Beijing and ordered a fish, and the waiter took the fish out of the net by the tail and slammed its head against the concrete floor right in front of me.

I'm the fish.

I don't know why I'm so calm. They're going to do something, they're probably going to kill me, and it's like I'm already feeling dead.

Outside, I hear a car start. The engine rev. Then fade away.

"I'm friends with a man in the DSD," I say. "He's my lover, in fact. If you hurt me, he will find you."

I think the guy on the left, maybe there's a flicker of doubt in his eyes. I'm a foreigner, and messing with foreigners can be a pain in the ass. Messing with the DSD an even bigger pain in the ass.

"I have money, too. More than they're paying you."

The other guy stoops over. Picks up the pink Taser and hands it to the one on the left. Trots out of the room.

"I'm telling the truth," I say. "My lover works for the DSD. He knows I'm in Guiyang."

I'm wondering how many charges one of those things has. Because this guy, he may be a thug, but he's not very big, and he's kind of scrawny. I'm pretty sure I'm taller than he is.

Could I do it? Could I kick him in the nuts and run?

I'm not even sure I can stand up.

"I'm telling the truth about the money, too. I can pay you."

His eyes flick down, then up; he shuffles his feet. He's nervous about this. I'm getting to him.

"You don't want trouble, right?"

That's when the other guy comes back. He's carrying a large bag, woven plastic. The kind the migrant workers carry their stuff in. Like for flour, or rice.

That and a length of rope.

Take care of the trash. Away from here.

I'm not dead, I'm not dead yet, and I don't want to be.

"Wait," I say. "Just wait. You don't want to do this. You don't want the trouble. Listen to me, it's not worth it. He'll kill you. I'm telling you the truth—"

The little guy looks at the Taser, almost curiously. Like, how do I work this?

Pushes the button.

I can't see anything for a while.

I'm aware of the other guy kneeling down by my side, fumbling with the sack and the rope. Then I hear something, a car engine, a screech of brakes, a door slam.

He lets out a curse, drops his stuff, springs to his feet. "Wait here!" he yells—at least I think that's what he says. He's speaking in dialect, and besides, there's a buzzing in my ears and I'm dizzy and sick, like something's pulling on my eyes from behind, hollowing out my gut.

But when I hear the gunfire, I know what that is.

The other guy drops the Taser and runs.

The adrenaline clears my head some. I push myself up with my arms so I'm sitting, try to stand, but I'm still too weak, too dizzy.

More shots.

I crawl to the chair. Brace my hands on either side of the seat. Stand up. Fucking stand up.

I'm about halfway there when two men burst into the room.

The guys Kang Li and I left in a rice paddy: US Polo Team and his buddy, from Yangshuo.

CHAPTER TWENTY-SEVEN

THEY'RE VERY POLITE.

One of them helps me to my feet. The other picks up my backpack, which was sitting against the wall across from the door.

They guide me out of the little room and into the next one: bigger and vacant, except for bare metal shelves and a few odds and ends—a computer monitor here, empty file folders there, an abandoned desk, a couple of deflated plastic grain sacks scattered on the floor.

And a dead guy.

My little buddy I thought I could bribe. Lying on his back by a bank of shelves. They shot him in the neck and in the chest. I can see blood still pulsing from the wound just under his throat.

Maybe not all the way dead, but he will be in a minute or two.

The other dead guy is sprawled facedown by the door.

"*Lai, lai,*" US Polo Team says. Come, come.

I'm not going to argue.

THE BLACK BUICK'S OUTSIDE, pulled close to the entrance. No license plates on it, I notice. Smart. I wonder what the woman in the snack store is doing right now, if she called the PSB or if she's just hunkered down behind the counter waiting for all this shit to blow over, like a storm. I wouldn't be surprised if that's what she's doing. Stuff like this, who wants to get involved?

The second guy, Windbreaker, helps me into the backseat, goes around to the other side and slides in next to me. US Polo gets behind the wheel, and we peel out.

I sit there. Stare out the window. *"Women qu nar?"* I finally ask. Where are we going?

"Jichang." Airport.

"Okay."

That's when I start to shake. I don't know if it's nerves coming back to life or just the whole "I almost died" experience, but whatever it is, I can't stop.

"Yao he shui?" Windbreaker asks.

I nod. Sure, I'll drink some water. I love water. He hands me a bottle stashed under the seat.

I'm guessing they're DSD. People working for John, even though he acted like he didn't know who they were when I asked him about them. Whatever. I don't care that he lied. I don't care that they killed two guys. All I can think of right now is, I'm alive and those guys aren't. Tough shit.

AT SOME POINT WE pull over onto a shoulder, in the shadow of a giant billboard advertising FAIRY LAKEFRONT ESTATES—THE BRIGHT FUTURE AND RICH LIFE AWAIT! and Windbreaker takes a set of license plates out of the trunk and attaches them to the front and rear of the Buick.

As he gets back into the car, I wonder why would the DSD even care if someone gets their license numbers?

Okay, I think, okay. Whoever these guys are, they still saved my ass. They're being pretty nice to me. And I'm too fucking wiped out to panic. Much.

WHEN I START SEEING signs for the Guiyang Airport, we don't head toward the passenger terminals. Instead we follow directions to "Cargo and Freight."

We pull alongside a big, corrugated tin-clad hangar, Shining Star Aviation.

Poised at the hangar exit leading out onto the tarmac is a private jet. You know, like a Gulfstream, one of those things. There's a movable boarding ramp leading up to it. And waiting at the foot of the ramp is a cute young woman wearing a retro flight-attendant outfit that looks like something out of an old magazine. Back when they were called stewardesses. Sky blue, white gloves, peaked hat, short skirt.

"Welcome!" she says with a bright smile. "Welcome you to fly with us!"

She helps me up the stairs, backed up by Windbreaker because I'm still feeling pretty wobbly, and she leads me to a leather seat. Windbreaker and US Polo sit a couple of seats behind me.

It's pretty fancy. Like I said, leather seats. A couch across the aisle. A wash of red on the walls, interspersed by walnut inserts and paintings. And though I still don't know as much about Chinese art as I should, I'm pretty sure I recognize a piece, one of Gu Wenda's "Fake Character" series.

Well, that's weird.

Maybe it's a *shanzhai* rip-off.

"Please fasten your seat belt—we will take off soon! I can help you if you need."

"No thanks." I mean, I think I can fasten my own fucking seat belt.

Truth is, my hands tremble so bad that I have a hard time getting the tongue in the buckle. Finally the flight attendant leans over and fastens it for me.

"*Xie xie,*" I say.

Not too long after that, the whine of the jet engines picks up and the plane taxis out onto the tarmac. We pause at the beginning of the runway, gathering power, like some big cat bunching up its muscles, and then we spring.

Up into the air.

AS SOON AS WE start to level off, the flight attendant's back.

"May I serve you something to drink?"

Yeah, I guess I could use a drink. "Sure. Thanks."

"What kind of drink you like? Chivas Regal, Grand Mariner, cognac? Maybe Johnnie Walker?"

"I, uh . . ." I can't even take it in. *Just bring me something,* I want to say.

"Oh, maybe you prefer wine."

"Sure. Wine sounds good."

The bottle she brings out is Château Lafite Rothschild—"*shi zhende!*" she says. The real thing. I remember Harrison saying to me, not too long ago, "No one serious is buying Château Lafite Rothschild anymore—too many counterfeits. The real collectors have moved on to burgundy."

This one tastes pretty good.

"Can I bring you anything else? Something to eat? Maybe foie gras? Or sushi?"

Sushi?

"No thanks."

I drink some more wine.

"Whose plane is this?" I finally ask.

She beams. "It's Mr. Sidney Cao's, of course."

Sidney Cao.

"Of course."

I DRAIN THE FIRST glass of wine, barely tasting it. Try to think it through.

Sidney Cao? Billionaire art collector Sidney Cao? That would account for the Gu Wenda on the wall. But the other stuff? Guys with guns who follow me around and kill people?

I try to remember the source of Cao's wealth. Chemicals, wasn't it? Something like that. Could he be . . . I don't know, the CEO of a rival seed company? A passionate environmentalist?

"More wine?"

"Sure. Thanks."

I take my time with this glass. It really is pretty good, though I don't know how well it would go with sushi. I'd try the combo and find out, but my gut's still in knots. I don't think I could eat anything. The wine's about all I can handle.

About halfway through the glass, I can't hold my head up anymore. I lean back against the seat. My eyes feel like someone's rubbed them with sand.

"Do you want to take a rest?" I hear the stewardess's voice in my ear. "Still some time before we land."

I nod. I figure she'll bring me a pillow and a blanket. Maybe a chocolate mint.

She pats me gently on the shoulder. "Come with me."

She has to help me up, and my feet hurt so bad the first few steps that I'm hobbling like a little old lady.

We go down the aisle past the US Polo Team, who's watching a DVD, a Harry Potter movie it looks like, and Windbreaker, who's tilted back in the chair, jaw hanging open, asleep.

Beyond them is another compartment. The stewardess opens the door.

It's dark, except for a night-light. But I can see an actual bed, fluffy white quilt, plumped pillows.

She rushes ahead and expertly flips down the quilt and sheets. *"Xiuxi yixia,"* she says. Rest a little.

I collapse on the side of the bed. Somehow manage to kick my shoes off. She helps me with the shoes, I think. I fall back against the pillow.

"Where are we going?" I finally think to ask.

"Xingfu Cun," she says.

"I don't know it. Where's that?"

"It's the home of Sidney Cao," she says brightly, pulling the quilt over me. "Have a rest. You can call me if you need anything."

I think I nod, but by the time she's closed the door behind her, I'm pretty much passed out.

WAY TOO SOON, I hear the stewardess: "Miss! Miss! Sorry, but you must return to seat now. Time for landing."

"Can't I land here?" I mumble.

The last thing I want to do is get up, but I do and hobble back to my seat.

By now it's close to sunset, and as the plane descends and banks, I get a look at the landscape below me. I see rows of houses, ranks of high-rise apartments, laid out in loose circles, like some giant amoeba. Then larger buildings, crazy shapes: gold globes and a lopped-off pyramid that looks like some kind of Mayan temple.

The weird thing is, hardly any cars. Hardly any lights. Where's the neon?

Then the lights of the runway.

IT'S A SMALL AIRPORT. A little terminal building. A

couple of hangars. I glimpse a couple of other small jets inside one of them.

It all looks brand-new.

In no time at all, two young men in blue uniforms that look like the flight attendants'—well, no skirt, but chevron-peaked caps, gold buttons and white shirts—have positioned the boarding ramp.

Windbreaker in front, US Polo team behind, gripping the rail so I don't tumble and take Windbreaker down with me, I make my way down the stairs.

Waiting there in the shadow of a gleaming BMW SUV is a woman. She's small, a little chubby, with a huge pile of teased black hair and a lot of eye shadow, wearing a snug pink cashmere sweater, a pencil skirt, and bright pink stilettos.

It's maybe not the best look for her.

She steps forward, extends her hand. Her long pink nails match the shoes.

"Vicky Huang. Welcome to Xingfu Cun."

CHAPTER TWENTY-EIGHT

"I HOPE YOU HAD a comfortable flight."

"It was great," I say.

"Mr. Cao is very anxious to meet you. He has invited you for dinner."

"That's . . . uh, really nice of him." I mean, what else can I say?

Vicky Huang looks me up and down. Her nose wrinkles. "Your clothes are a little dirty."

"Yeah. Sorry about that. The rest of my stuff's in Guiyang."

"Ah. I arrange for pickup." She reaches into her designer handbag, which I think is Versace (I only know this from hanging out with Lucy Wu) and pulls out an iPhone in a gold rhinestone case. "Of course your things won't arrive in time." Her finger pauses above the touch screen. She looks me up and down again. "For now we can go shopping."

"So . . . that was a lot of trouble you went to . . . to, uh . . . pick me up."

Vicky Huang gives a little shrug and cranks the wheel of the SUV hard to the left, like she's taking a turn on a NASCAR track. "Mr. Cao wants to speak with you. He is tired of delays." She doesn't bother to look for oncoming traffic, but then there doesn't seem to be any. Xingfu Cun looks brand-new and, so far, pretty much deserted. A ghost city.

I try to think of what to say. How there are two dead people back in Guiyang and it seems like maybe something we should discuss. But I don't know, maybe that's not my problem. It's not like *I* killed them.

"What does he want to talk to me about?" I finally ask.

She draws back, surprised. "But I think you know." Makes a hard right. "However, now that you are here, you can discuss business with Mr. Cao himself."

I lean back in the leather seat. Maybe I should be scared. But I'm just too tired to care. And anyway, we're going shopping.

The thing I saw when we were landing, that I thought looked like a Mayan pyramid? Well, I think that's where we are now, and it's more like some kind of . . . I don't know, Egyptian . . . thing, or maybe Babylonian—a ziggurat? Is that what they call them? And it's gold. And flanked by huge statues of winged lions, and there's a fountain out in front the size of an Olympic pool, with more weird animal statues, elephants and panthers and horses, spewing water according to some complicated sequence timed with changing colored lights. We passed the giant egg-shaped things on our way here, those and blocky black granite buildings with the red-and-gold seal of government.

There's hardly anyone here. A few cars parked at the government Death Star. A couple of cars in a huge lot out in front of the giant gold whatever-the-fuck-it-is place we've arrived at.

But no cars on the broad asphalt streets. No people either.

Vicky Huang pulls her BMW up to the front of the pyramid thing, all the way up to the expanse of sparkling pink granite pavers that spread out in a semicircle in front of the entrance: a small plaza, flagpoles spaced around the curve. Actually, she parks with one wheel up on the low curb. I guess the No Parking sign doesn't count.

"We are here," she announces.

I get out of the car, and now I can hear recorded music: "The Blue Danube"—which is what the animal fountain's timed to. The flagpoles have flags of a bunch of countries hung up on them, like a mini–United Nations. Highest of the flags is the red banner and gold stars of the People's Republic. Next to that is one I don't recognize—sky blue background, stylized gold sun, and green grass.

Cao can mean "grass." It can also mean "fuck." Depends on your pronunciation.

Vicky Huang doesn't wait for me. She heads toward the wide Plexiglas entrance—huge double doors and windows on either side.

I limp after her.

There are mannequins in the windows, high-fashion ones wearing what I'm pretty sure are designer clothes, posed with their arms and legs at crazy angles, against a black-and-white backdrop that I think is supposed to be a city and cars. There are a couple of sparkling snowflakes suspended on wires. One of the mannequins is missing a hand.

The broad doors slide open, triggered by our approach.

Yeah, a mall.

Inside, it's three stories high. I can see escalators going up and down between the floors. There are stores—signs for them anyway. Coach. Li-Ning. Nike. Louis Vuitton. Armani. North Face. Gucci.

Mostly, though, there are empty spaces where the stores should be. Steel shutters and unfinished walls. No customers.

Music plays. And right now, just my luck, it's "My Heart Will Go On."

Vicky Huang looks over her shoulder, making sure I'm keeping up. "Follow me."

We walk a ways, past a Häagen-Dazs. Actually, it says "Hagen Das," so I'm assuming it's not a real one. A lone worker lounges behind the counter, a young girl in a white-and-blue uniform, texting on her cell phone, ghostly in the bright fluorescent light.

Maybe there's a *shanzhai* Starbucks around here, too. Because I could really use a cup of coffee.

But Vicky Huang has other ideas. She turns right, into another wing of the mall, which is just as deserted as the first one.

At the end of it, though, is some kind of larger store. Like, if I were at a mall in the US, I'd figure it was a department store, a Macy's or a Nordstrom or something.

I'm not sure what this is. But it's open. There are a lot of clothes, hanging on racks. Shoes. Handbags. Low, classy lighting. Thick carpets.

"*Ni hao, ni hao! Huanying nimen!*" Two young, cute salesclerks, wearing expensive-looking black dresses, gold jewelry, and heels, come rushing over like we're movie stars or something. Well, I figure we're their only customers of the day, and I'm guessing they know Vicky Huang. A guess that's confirmed when she says, "We need to find clothes for her." She points a finger at me. "She has dinner with Mr. Cao."

"Oh!"

This, obviously, is a big fucking deal.

"*Qing zuo, qing zuo!*" Please sit. I do, on a leather couch between a purse display and a rack of skirts.

They start bringing over outfits. Each more ridiculous than the last. Short, sequined dresses. Fuzzy tight sweaters. "I think this is good," Vicky Huang announces, holding up an off-the-shoulder dress that looks like something a Greek goddess would wear—that is, if she were a hooker—and a pair of gold strappy high heels.

"No," I say. "No. Sorry. I can't wear that. I . . . I have an injury."

The two salesclerks and Vicky Huang surround me, studying me. "I think you would look very nice," one offers timidly.

I shake my head. Stand up. "Let's take a look."

We wander around the store. I hate this kind of shit. You know, I hang out with artists. I wear jeans and T-shirts most of the time. And the price tags I glimpse . . . crazy.

Here, though, here's some stuff that might be okay. I pull out a black jacket. Kind of a suit coat, long and narrow and sort of slouchy. Some skinny black pants with a low rise. A white blouse that's pretending to be a men's dress shirt, except it's not. Black leather ankle-high boots.

"*Hen lihai*," one of the salesclerks says. Fierce. Sometimes that's a compliment.

I TRY THE CLOTHES on. As usual, I don't look at myself in the fitting-room mirror when I'm half undressed. Seeing my leg, the other scars, I just can't.

But once I get the clothes on, I take a look.

I look . . . not bad. Maybe even . . . I don't know, kind of cool. Like I could be playing in a band or something. Or hanging out at one of Lucy Wu's fancy openings. The black jacket hangs just so. The white blouse is open just above my bra, showing a little cleavage. I have nice tits, it's true.

"Let me see," Vicky Huang demands from outside the curtain.

I step out, reluctantly.

Vicky Huang looks me up and down. The salesgirls flank her.

"*Keyi*," she finally says.

"*Zhen ku!*" one of the salesgirls whispers, giggling.

Pretty cool, in other words.

I WHIP OUT MY credit card, but Vicky Huang won't hear of it. "Not to worry," she says. "This is Mr. Cao's business."

I put up the polite argument, but I don't argue too hard. The stuff's Armani and Marc Jacobs. The money this outfit costs would pay my rent in BJ for like two and a half months. And my rent ain't cheap.

I can tell that Vicky's stalling for time; she retreats to a corner of the shop and makes a hurried phone call, and then we end up chatting with the salesgirls, who ask if they can get us anything, water, tea, cola. "Coffee would be great," I say. I mean, why not? And they find a pretty awful cup somewhere, Nescafé, probably, but I drink it anyway.

As the salesgirls bag up my purchases, Vicky Huang turns to me.

"Before you dress for dinner, maybe you would like to have a shower."

I'm not sure it's a request. Besides, I stink.

"Yeah. Thanks. That would be great."

And of course we end up going to a fucking spa.

THE TWO OF US ride the escalator into the basement. It's deserted, of course. More empty storefronts, unfinished and open, with framed entrances and nothing inside. There are signs for a Carrefour supermarket and a Watsons down at one end, but no actual stores. Maybe it's just a promise. Or a wish.

At the other end is the spa. Spring Victory Wellness Center. Well, okay.

I'm pretty sure the workers got here about five minutes ahead of us. They wear white smocks and white caps, like nurses. One of them opens the door for us, and as we enter, I see a girl rushing around lighting scented candles.

White walls, white towels, greenish glass. The scent of eucalyptus.

"This way, miss!"

I FOLLOW THEM. I have a bath. I sit in a steam room. I let them give me a massage, a facial, plus do this crazy thing with a milk bath and sea salt and a loofah. I draw the line at them giving me a hairstyle like Vicky Huang's.

By the time all this is done, I'm so relaxed that I just want to sleep for a week.

Instead I put on my new outfit and agree to wear a little mascara, eye shadow, and lipstick. After I've done all that, I exit into the lobby, where Vicky Huang waits.

She gives me the once-over. "Good," she says. "I think you are ready to meet Mr. Cao now."

Maybe I should be a little more nervous. Vicky Huang seems to be. As she drives, she's leaning forward, jaw clenched, hands clutching the steering wheel tight. But after everything that's happened, I don't have the energy. I feel like someone's wrung me out and hung me up to dry.

Stay frosty, I tell myself. You don't know what you're getting into here.

We drive a ways through the broad, empty city. Past banks of twenty-story apartment buildings, some finished and empty, some half built, then farther out, where there are rows of houses, three, four stories tall, on narrow lots, circling an artificial lake. Empty. Then a golf course.

Finally we arrive at a gated compound surrounded by a stone wall. Two guards man the gatehouse, wearing the same sky blue uniform as the flight attendant and the airport workers. The gate, this huge white wrought-iron thing, slides open.

We head up a very long drive.

In front of us on a rise is a French palace.

I don't mean that it looks kind of like a French palace, the way that some Chinese buildings kind of look European. I mean, it's this huge, fucking French palace! Down to the white marble and the gold trim and the big fountain out in front with winged horses and Neptune and Venus or whoever the naked man and woman are supposed to be, and fat cherubs shooting jets of water out of their asses.

"The home of Sidney Cao," Vicky Huang says proudly.

She parks in the big gravel drive, next to a fire-engine-red sports car, which looks like something Batman would drive. "Lamborghini Aventador," Vicky says. "First in China." She smiles. "You don't even have one in America yet."

There's a butler at the door, of course. Dressed like an English butler on a PBS show. "Welcome, welcome," he says in English. "Please, come inside."

Inside, it's even crazier.

The entrance hall is, like, acres of white marble and gold trim. White marble stairs. White marble columns. Paintings on the walls, all kinds of . . . I don't know, Renaissance things. Or whatever's after the Renaissance. Dudes in ruffles and long, curly white wigs. Women with even bigger white wigs and huge skirts holding weird little dogs. Statues in alcoves. More cherubs. Roman busts.

This is so over the top that I think it might be on another planet.

THE BUTLER GUIDES US down a long hallway. More paintings and murals on the wall, like of forests and wigged people riding horses and hunting deer. Fancy-ass carved chairs that you'd never want to sit in. "Isn't it beautiful?" Vicky Huang says in a hushed voice.

"Yeah. It's really something."

Finally the butler pauses at a set of large wooden double doors. Pushes one open for us. *"Cao Xiansheng. Ninde keren daole,"* he announces. Your guests have arrived.

I follow Vicky inside.

It's a wood-paneled room lined with bookshelves, a thick carpet, leather chairs, and a big wooden desk. Also, an actual fucking deer head on the wall. Like we've gone from the Palace of Versailles to one of those English movies starring the Queen.

Rising from his desk chair is Sidney Cao.

"Huanying, huanying!" Welcome!

I guess I don't know what I expected, but probably not this. Sidney Cao's a normal-looking middle-aged guy wearing a golf shirt, slacks, and a designer belt—Gucci, with the interlocked Gs. He has receding hair, high and bony cheekbones, a prominent nose with a bump at the bridge, and crooked front teeth.

He comes out from behind the desk and extends his hand to me. I take it.

"Thank you for coming!" he says.

Then he does this little bow, kisses the back of my hand, straightens up and grins.

"I, uh . . . thanks. For inviting me, Cao Xiansheng."

"Please, call me Sidney," he says in English. Then, "Have you eaten?" he asks in Chinese.

FOR DINNER IT'S JUST me and Sidney, and I think we're back in France. Pâté. Oysters. Little tart things with sweet onions and cheese. Baby lamb chops. I lose track pretty fast.

There's too much food, and it arrives too quickly, carried in by a young . . . waitress? Maid? Along with bottles of French wine, three of them, that Sidney holds up and announces as they are brought to the table by the butler guy: "This one very rare. Very rare! Come, you must try!"

Yeah, okay. But for once I'm trying to be smart. The last thing I need is to get bombed off my ass in the Palace of Versailles. At least not till I figure out what's going on. So I sip and I nibble and I nod as Sidney narrates the names of the dishes, the origins of the ingredients, the complicated preparation, and, especially, the quality. "Lamb from New Zealand! Fed just on grass. Like my name! *Cao!* Means 'grass'!" He laughs.

The dining room, maybe they were going for medieval: tapestries on the wall of knights and ladies playing lutes, and I think I spot a unicorn. We're seated at one end of a long formal table with silver candlesticks and way too many little plates and pieces of silverware. Sidney doesn't really seem to know what to do with them all either. "This kind of eating, I am still not expert," he confesses. "But I enjoy trying new things."

"Great," I say. Me, I'm trying to figure out how to steer the conversation around to maybe the two dead guys in Guiyang. "So I'm not that familiar with your business," I finally say. "I know you work with . . . chemicals?"

Sidney waves that off. "Business not so very interesting. I no longer worry too much about it."

"I see," I say, even though I don't. "But . . . you're interested in . . . seeds?"

"Seeds?" He frowns. *"Ni weishenme wen wo?"* Why do you ask?

"I, uh . . ." My heart starts thumping hard. Like maybe I just stepped in it. But if I have, it's too late now. "Well, I was at a seed company. When your . . . your workers picked me up. And I thought . . .”

“Ah. I just wanted to make sure . . .”

The waitress maid has entered with a fresh platter. Sidney Cao claps his hands. “Time for cheese course!”

WE EAT SOME CHEESE. There are a bunch of different kinds: some hard, some runny, some stinky. There’s also more wine, and port.

“So you like cheese?” Sidney asks.

“Sure. Yeah. I like it fine.”

“I think this is a Western taste. I am trying to learn to like. But still not very sure.”

“Sidney, can I ask you a question?”

He smiles. “Of course! You can ask me anything you like.”

“Why did you bring me here?”

He doesn’t say anything. Just frowns.

So I plunge ahead. “I mean, you went to a lot of trouble. And I really appreciate it. But . . . it was . . . kind of extreme.”

He leans back in his chair. Sips his port. He seems truly puzzled. “For the art, of course.”

“FOR A FEW YEARS now, I collect art,” he explains as we walk down another overdressed hallway. “First I buy old Chinese painting and calligraphy. Tang Ying. Shen Zhou. Qi Baishi. Because this is my culture, and I like this work. Then European. Vermeer. Goya. The impressionists. I have Monet, I have Cézanne. Very beautiful. I like them very much.”

We’ve come to what looks like an elevator, with shiny brass doors. Sidney pushes the button.

“Then I think I should buy more modern things. Picasso. Warhol. Jackson Pollock. Other works of this nature. Maybe I don't understand as well, but I know they are important to the development of artistic tradition."

The doors slide open. Sidney gestures for me to enter and follows me inside.

"And then I hear more and more about new Chinese artists," he continues as the doors close. "Many becoming famous. Work selling for big money. But mostly foreigners buy this work." He pushes the DOWN button. "I decide since I am Chinese I must support my countrymen and keep some of this art inside China. Because, you know, in the past, foreigners take art out of China all the time. They are like robbers."

I know enough about this stuff now to know that a lot of foreigners *were* robbers, pretty much. I mean, you can't live in Beijing for more than a week without hearing how the "Anglo-French forces" looted and burned the old Summer Palace. But there's also the part where, during the Cultural Revolution, Red Guards smashed the "Four Olds" of traditional Chinese culture, which included a lot of art. And how some contemporary Chinese artists are getting rich while others are hassled and censored, even arrested.

But, I'm thinking, not the time to get into that whole discussion, right?

The elevator opens onto a short hall, which compared to everything else in this place is pretty plain: white walls, painted concrete, I think. Soft lighting, grey carpet. No windows. We might be belowground. I can hear the hum of circulating air.

"This just temporary," Sidney says.

At the end of the hall are two Plexiglas doors. Sidney opens one and gestures politely for me to enter.

As I do, the lights come up.

White walls. Paintings. Sculptures and smaller pieces in center exhibits.

A gallery space.

"Wow," I say.

"Do you like?" Sidney asks. He sounds almost anxious.

"I . . ." I take a few steps in. It's huge. I can see another gallery beyond this one.

Not a gallery. This is a fucking museum.

"It's amazing." And I mean it.

This first gallery is the traditional Chinese art he talked about. Landscape scrolls. Porcelain vases. Horse statuettes. Calligraphy. The next, Renaissance and neoclassical European. After that the Impressionists, then into the moderns. All the artists whose names he rattled off, he's got their stuff hanging on the wall.

He's even got a Warhol Mao.

Finally, the last gallery: contemporary Chinese art.

Yue Minjun. Ai Weiwei. Fang Lijun. Zhang Xiaogang.

I can't begin to add up what this collection is worth. I don't know enough to even start. But I do know that what this guy has in his basement is better than most museums in China. Maybe most museums in the world.

From behind me Sidney says softly "So, you can see why I must have work by Zhang Jianli."

By Lao Zhang.

CHAPTER TWENTY-NINE

"This cigar is from Cuba! You can try it. With this rum, very good."

"I, uh . . . sure. Thanks."

We're back in the library, or study, or whatever this room with the giant dead deer head on the wall is supposed to be. Vicky Huang has joined us. She's not sampling the cigar, but she just knocked back a shot of Cuban rum like a pro.

I think about all that wine we left on the table. I bet someone on the kitchen staff is having a nice night.

I'm still trying to take it in, that this guy had me followed all around China and even killed people so he could buy art that he likes. Or is obsessed with. It's kind of hard to tell.

I guess if you've got this much money, so much that you've built an entire fucking city that no one lives in, hey, why not?

"So," Vicky Huang says, getting out her iPad, "now we can arrange for private viewing of Zhang Jianli artwork."

"To complete the collection," Sidney says, clasping his hands.

How can I explain the situation? "No" doesn't seem to be a word in either of these guys' vocabularies.

Instead I stall.

"It's an amazing collection. I've never seen anything like it. Not in somebody's house, I mean."

Sydney smiles proudly. Sips his rum. "I think maybe it is my life work," he says.

Yeah, I think. A life's work in an empty city that no one will see.

"And I really want to . . . you know, support that. So as soon as I can sell you some work, I promise you're first on the list."

Both of them stare at me, their expressions frozen, Sidney's in midsmile. The skin prickles between my shoulders.

I'm remembering that this guy has people killed.

I make a command decision.

"I could . . . uh, donate a piece."

Sidney frowns. "Donate? You mean give?"

"Yeah. You know, for the collection. Since it's your life's work."

"You cannot *give!*" Vicky Huang hisses, outraged, half rising from her chair. "Then it is worth nothing!"

Fuck. Apparently *giving* something to Sidney Cao is, like, some kind of face-stealing sneak attack.

"Well, no, it's still worth something, it's . . . you know, like, a deduction."

"A deduction?" Sidney asks, looking confused.

Wait, that's not right, I think. It would be a deduction for *me*, or for our foundation or something. Maybe.

"Well, I mean . . ."

I struggle to think. But even though I really tried not to have too much of the wine and the port and the rum, I'm either plastered or so fucking wasted from everything that's happened that my thoughts are going all over the place.

"So what happens with this collection when you die?" I blurt. "I mean *qu tai.*" Which is a nicer way of saying that.

Sidney leans back in his chair. Sips his rum. "I leave to my children. I have three," he confesses. "I can afford this."

Yeah, if anybody can afford to dodge China's one-child policy, it would be Sidney Cao.

"How do you know they'll keep it together? The collection, I mean."

"If I tell them to, they will," he huffs.

"But . . . how do you *know*? I mean, they could totally decide to sell off pieces of it after you're gone."

Sidney's eyes narrow. "Of course I can make this a condition of their inheritance," he says, and he sounds pretty pissed off.

It's another one of those times when I feel like I really stepped in it.

What can I say? There's got to be something. Think, I tell myself. Fucking *think*. Dude built a giant mall that looks like a pyramid. Or ziggurat. Whatever. In the middle of wherever we are, in some place that no one cares about.

I'm flailing around, and what I finally grab onto is this: "But . . . if this is your life's work, don't you want other people to maybe . . . you know, *see* it?"

Sidney seems to think about this. Puffs on his Cuban cigar. "Yes," he finally says. "My plan is someday build a proper museum. For the future, when Xingfu Cun is established as a business and cultural center for this region."

Weirder-ass shit has happened, I guess.

"Okay," I say, "so then it makes sense for you to . . . uh, create that museum plan now. As a nonprofit. And we can donate a Zhang Jianli piece to, to help support that. It will be a way to . . . to teach people about art. And to appreciate your life's work. For the future."

There's this silence that's as heavy as if someone tossed a boulder into the room.

Sidney takes another puff on his cigar. Sips his rum.

"Very interesting idea," he says.

AFTER SPENDING THE NIGHT in a bedroom that's bigger than my entire apartment, where almost everything in it is white—white carpets, white walls, white furniture, and a white baby grand piano (and I have to say, it's better than another bedroom suite I passed, which looked like a Disney-princess store exploded inside it)—I turn down Sidney's offer to stay and relax a few days in beautiful Xingfu Cun. "Many fun things to do!" he tells me over breakfast. We're back in the dining room, where a buffet's been laid out featuring a Chinese breakfast, an omelet station, fruit, pastries, and, for some reason, pizza. "We can ride horses or play golf. And of course we have karaoke and, if you like, paintball."

Karaoke or paintball, with Sidney Cao—I'm not sure which prospect creeps me out more.

"Thanks, Sidney, that's very . . . you know, sounds like fun. But I still have some . . . some business I need to deal with."

He looks disappointed. I don't know, maybe he's bored here and I'm a distraction. Or he just likes showing off all his stuff.

"Of course, of course," he says.

THEY'LL FLY ME WHEREVER I need to go, he tells me. At this point I'm not really sure where that is. I don't even know where I am, actually.

I could go back to Beijing. We've arranged to meet there in a week, Sidney and Vicky and me, after I've had a chance to talk to Harrison about the agreement I made. He may not like it, but I figure if no money's changing hands, at least we won't get ourselves any deeper in shit with the government.

"And as soon as we get our . . . our new business license taken care of, if there's other work you're interested in buying . . ."

Even as I say that, I kind of shudder inside. I mean, what would Lao Zhang think, about this guy buying up all his art and stashing it in his basement?

Sidney picks up his croissant with his chopsticks, takes a bite. "If you have any problems with the license, just let me know. We can help with that."

Which is another thing I need to talk to Harrison about.

"How about Shanghai?" I say.

SIDNEY HIMSELF DRIVES ME to the airport, in his Lamborghini.

"You like this kind of car?"

"Yeah. Sure. It's . . . very fast."

I'm plastered against the seat. The engine sounds like a cloud of hornets on steroids, and we're going so fast that I'm really glad there aren't any other cars on the road.

By the time we get to the airport, I'm drenched in sweat.

The jet waits for us on the tarmac.

"See you in Beijing." Sidney clasps my hand at the foot of the boarding ramp. "But please come and visit again soon."

"Thanks," I say. "I'll do that. And, uh . . . thanks, for . . ." How to put it? "Picking me up. And everything."

"My pleasure."

WHEN THE FLIGHT ATTENDANT leads me to my seat, I see my duffel bag, rescued from the Guiyang hotel, sitting on the couch across the aisle.

IN SHANGHAI I CHECK into this crazy old hotel, the Astor House, built in the nineteenth century, on the north end of the Bund. I've stayed here before, and I like it because it's actually not very expensive and the wood floors are so old that they're slightly sunken from a century and a half of footsteps.

I don't know that many people in Shanghai. My main connection here is Lucy Wu, and she's in Hong Kong. Or who knows, maybe Vancouver. But Shanghai is a big rail hub and air hub. I can get just about anywhere from here pretty easily. And there are so many foreigners that no one is going to notice me.

I was guessing Xingfu Cun is maybe in Anhui, since that's where Sidney's company was based originally. Wherever it is, it's a short flight to Shanghai. We left Sidney's mansion at 11:00 A.M., and I'm already settled in my hotel room at just past 2:00 P.M.

There are things I need to do. Things I need to figure out.

I start by calling my mom.

"Oh, hi, hon! Where are you?"

"Shanghai. I'm . . . uh, finishing up some business."

"Just so you know, the toilet's all fixed now, and everything else is fine. Andy says he knows someone who can work on the ceiling in the guest room. You know the plaster's falling down?"

"Yeah." I hesitate. "So . . . uh, did my friend John bring a dog over?"

"He did! She's so sweet! He said you found her on the road?"

"Something like that."

"You know, he really is nice. I think he really likes you."

"Maybe," I say. "But the dog, the dog's okay?"

"She's fine. I'm giving her the antibiotics like I'm supposed to. And John recommended a vet here to check on the wound, so we're doing that. I'm taking her in tomorrow."

"Great," I say.

AFTER THAT I SPEND some time on the Internet. Check my email.

I check a few other things, too. I have an idea, about that American guy, Buzz Cut. The one from the warehouse.

I find out what I need to know. And when I'm done, I know who I need to call next.

I stall for a while, go downstairs to the hotel bar, have a beer and think about it. Because this could go very wrong and leave me in a worse situation than I'm in right now.

Here's the thing: Those guys, the American guy and the Chinese guy who left me in that warehouse in Guiyang, they wanted me dead. And by now someone's found those bodies, the two guys that Sidney's men killed.

They know I'm alive.

And the American guy knows who I am.

Companies like Eos hire private security. Some of them even hire private intelligence. Like GSC, the company my ex-husband works for.

I've tangled with those guys before. Some of them, they're connected.

Private contractors. OGAs. "Other government agencies."

You try to figure out, are they government? Are they private? And what I finally decided was it doesn't really matter anymore. They're all part of the same fucking thing.

Last year those kinds of guys—contractors, OGAs, whatever you want to call them—got me in a lot of trouble. And they warned me. Told me if I stepped out of line, there'd be consequences.

A company like Eos is so powerful that it can buy anything it wants.

We will be watching you. We'll be listening to you. There's no place you can go where we can't find you. So don't try to run. There's no such thing as running.

Living in China, where you know you're being watched, I sort of accepted it. Okay, fine. Most of the time I pretended surveillance wasn't there.

When I found out it was my own people too . . . well, that pretty much sucked.

You better be smart. You start acting stupid, there's not much I can do.

It's not like I *meant* to be stupid. I was just trying to do a favor for a friend, right?

Yeah. Right.

"DOC MCENROE. I WASN'T expecting to hear from *you.*"

"Yeah, well, I wasn't expecting to be making this call."

I hear Carter cough on the other end of the line. He always seems to have some kind of cough. I don't know whether it's because he smokes or just because he's living in Beijing, where air is sort of a solid.

"So what do you want?"

I have to hand it to Carter: he doesn't pretty things up.

Carter works where my ex does, at GSC. I wouldn't call him a friend. At one time he was the opposite of that.

"I need a favor," I say.

I lay out the situation. What I need to know.

A pause. A phlegmy cough. "And I'm supposed to do this for you why?"

Because you helped me before, I think. Because you acted like you were on my side, at least a little.

Because you know what you and your buddy did was wrong.

But I don't say any of that.

"Maybe I've got something to trade," I say.

CHAPTER THIRTY

CARTER WANTS TO MEET face-to-face. I don't like that idea. Sure, I called him. But I don't exactly trust him.

It didn't take him long to find out what I wanted to know. At least that's what he claims.

"You pick the place," he says. "I'm not having this conversation over the phone."

"When you get to Shanghai, call me. We'll pick a place then."

If he's going to fuck me over, turn me over the Eos people, I'm not going to make it easy for him.

"Fine. I'll be down tomorrow."

He calls me around 4:00 P.M. the next day. "Okay. Where?"

There's a fancy bar down on the Bund that I went to once with Lucy Wu. Not really my thing, but unlike the expat dive bars I generally go to, it's the kind of place where you'd have a hard time causing trouble.

Besides, now I even have the outfit for it.

I TELL HIM 6:00 P.M. and make sure I'm there first. It's a bar/restaurant on the first floor of one of the restored European buildings that line the Shanghai riverfront. Sunk a little below ground level, so it's got that dark, almost speakeasy vibe. I scope out the place. I mean, it looks okay, but what do I really know about this spy shit? There's some foreign businessmen having cocktails and overpriced scotch. A couple of elegant Chinese women wearing little black dresses. Accent lights glow against the black-and-red walls.

I seat myself at a little table against the wall, where I can see the entrance and I'm not too far from the back exit, then order a beer—some new Chinese microbrew made by an American and an Australian. It's not bad.

I don't have to wait too long before Carter shows up.

He spots me pretty fast. Comes over to the table and looks me up and down.

"You're looking kinda fancy," he says, pulling out the chair opposite and sitting down heavily.

I shrug. "Yeah, well, don't get used to it."

He looks the same. Middle-aged. Ginger hair going grey. Freckles. Blocky body in a cheap suit.

"How much am I gonna overpay for a tequila in this place?"

"Too much. It's on me."

He chuckles. "You're really moving up in the world, Doc."

"If you say so."

He pounds his tequila and orders another one. I sip my beer. I'm trying to be smart.

"So tell me," he says after the second tequila arrives. "What's your take?"

"My take?"

"Tell me what you think is going on. And then I'll tell you what I know."

I sigh. I mean, I could be wrong.

Here goes nothing.

"I think this guy Han Rong worked for Hongxing Agricultural Products, like he said. But I don't know that he really quit because he was all . . . outraged or whatever by what Eos and Hongxing are doing."

Carter stares at me with a neutral expression. Drinks some tequila. "How come you say that?"

"Because . . . I don't know, the dude's a weasel."

He nods. "Okay. So then what?"

"Could be a lot of stuff. Like maybe he's helping to fuck up Eos here in China so whoever's paying him, some other company, can get a leg up with all this GMO crap. Or he's still working for Hongxing, even. Hongxing decided they wanted to fuck over Eos and steal the patents for whatever it is they're working on together, raise enough shit about Eos in the international press that Eos just gives up on whatever it is they're doing here. Make them the bad guys. And whoever, Hongxing or some other company, can take over the market here, for now."

All the while Carter stares at me, eyebrows half raised, expression a blank. I feel myself flush.

"Something like that," I mutter.

"Not bad." Carter lifts his hand to call the waitress. "Go on."

"Okay. I'm not sure about this next part. Well, I figure Eos knows what Han Rong knows. About the three seed companies."

"What do you mean?"

I sip my beer. "The American guy said, 'We know the source of the leak now.'"

Carter nods, fractionally.

"The place in Guiyu, maybe that was for real," I say after the waitress leaves. "I mean, as an address for a fake business. Or a place they could drop shipments to distribute to other stores or to farmers. It's not like officials or whoever would probably check up on them, right? Who'd go looking for a seed company in Guiyu? Nobody goes there unless they have to."

I think about the camera at the storefront in Dali. They were waiting for someone. Someone like me.

"The store in Dali, it was a setup. A trap. They were just waiting to see who took the bait. When I showed up at the warehouse in Guiyang, they were expecting me."

"What about your pal Jason?"

"He's not my pal," I snap. "I never even met him."

"Jesus, you're touchy," he mutters. "I mean, how far do you think he got?"

And this is where it gets tricky. Because even if I can trust Carter not to screw *me* over, I bet he'd love to get his hands on Jason. To collect the bounty on his head.

"I'm not sure. I'm guessing that he got as far as Dali," I said. "But if he went to Guiyang, he never visited the warehouse. That's what they wanted to know when they caught me. If I knew where he was."

"And do you?"

"Like I said, no."

"Okay."

Our drinks arrive. Mine's a Coke. For once.

"Well, I gotta say, Doc, from what I found out, you're pretty close. I can't tell you for sure whether it was a faction in Hongxing or some other group of assholes who wanted to fuck over Eos. Whichever it was, Hongxing closed ranks and they're sticking to the original agreement with Eos. Who knows why? Maybe they're scared of Eos's firepower. Or maybe they think they can make more money working with Eos than competing with them. You know these Chinese companies. Most of them can't innovate for shit." He tosses back his tequila. "So whaddaya got for me?"

I sip my Coke. "I already gave it to you."

His face gets that mean look I remember. "Nice. Here all this time I thought you might be playing fair."

"Hey, I did some checking. You guys work corporate security

for another big biotech company. Maybe *you* might wanna fuck with Eos a little. Help secure some market share here."

"What if we don't?"

I shrug. "Up to you. I still told you some useful stuff. You wouldn't have known where to look if I hadn't. Besides, you didn't tell me anything I didn't already know."

At that he chuckles. "Okay. So you knew it already. Then what is it you really want?"

The way he's looking at me, with that little smirk, arm draped over his chair back, he's not going to help me. I'm pretty sure I've wasted my time, or worse.

But I already took it this far.

"Those guys, those guys from Eos. They were gonna kill me. I've already got enough people on my ass. I don't want to be looking over my shoulder for them, too."

"And you think I can do something about that?"

"I think you know them. You or somebody else at GSC. That's how you got your intel about Eos. And, I mean, they knew *me*. Where'd they get *that* from? Somebody at GSC, right? What was it, a couple of you getting together in a bar, swapping stories? You tell them about that fucked-up head case you threatened and bullied and beat up last year? Or was it . . . I dunno, a little horse-trading? Like you like to do."

Silence. Carter's doing that stare again, trying to psych me out, I figure. Well, fuck him. I can play that game, too.

He blinks first.

"You still haven't told me what you want," he says.

"I need for you or somebody to tell them that I'm not going to cause them any problems. That this isn't my fight. I was just trying to do a favor for a buddy. That's it."

He's quiet again, but he's not staring at me. Instead he fixes on his tequila.

"Okay," he finally says. He still won't look at me.

"Thanks." I'm so surprised he agreed that I don't know what else to say. "You want another tequila?" I think to ask.

He shakes his head. "Look, Doc, you're not gonna fuck me over on this, are you? Because yeah, I know those guys. And they're assholes." Now he does look at me. I'd say he seems more annoyed than concerned, but whatever. "So say I talk to them. It's gonna be hard to call those dogs off the scent. The best thing you can do? Give it up. Don't give them a trail to follow."

"Okay," I say. "Gotcha."

I DECIDE TO LOOK for soup dumplings. They're supposed to be a Shanghai specialty, and I've hardly had any dumplings since I left Beijing.

Just those ones with Creepy John. And the dog.

Anyway, the famous place is over in some tourist area near a temple, but it's not close and I'm tired. Plus, my new outfit may look cool, but it's not quite warm enough for the forty-something-degree weather outside. I ask the hostess about dumplings when I pay the bill for my drinks and Carter's tequilas, and she tells me there's a good place not far from here. I find it, tucked on a little street just a few blocks away. Your basic cheap Chinese restaurant, white walls, plastic tables with plastic covers, a couple of fish tanks in the window. I order some dumplings, including the soup kind that come with a plastic straw so you can suck up the hot juice.

I'm aching tired. Seeing Carter again, talking to him, it's made me think about too much other shit I don't like thinking about.

What I try to think about, while I'm eating, while I'm limping back to my hotel, is what do I do now?

Go back to Beijing, I guess. I mean, that's the only thing to do, right? Hope that Carter can call off the dogs.

Which makes me think about Dog Turner. I wonder if he's out of the hospital.

What the fuck is it with dogs anyway?

I get back to my hotel just after 8:30 P.M., and all I want to do is crawl into bed.

Except maybe I'll check my email first.

Nothing new from Natalie. Of course, it's like, what—4:30 A.M. in San Diego right now?

I think I'm going to hate writing that email. Or making that Skype call. The one where I say, *I took it as far as I could, but I didn't find Jason.*

Come on, I tell myself. How many people would've done as much as I did? I mean, I almost got killed.

I also found a dog. And had that crazy night with John. But that's not stuff I should be thinking about.

I wonder if Langhai's posted anything new?

Don't even look. What if he has? Are you really going to go there? I could just check.

I go to Youku. Look up Langhai's account. And there it is. "Kaili Dreaming."

Don't even watch it, I tell myself. Just don't.

Of course I do.

It's another tourist video, kind of like "Dali Scene" but more impressionistic, I guess. Jagged mountains draped in mist. Villages made up of wooden houses with peaked roofs. Emerald terraced hills. Dudes in round bamboo peasant hats, plowing fields with water buffalo. Old ladies wearing silver collars and embroidery. People dancing. Old men holding out bowls of something . . . wine? And there's these flags, ragged white banners with red stains tied to wooden poles stuck in grass-covered mounds, some fluttering in tree branches. All through it this weird music—pipes, I think, and high-pitched voices.

The last couple shots are of this valley, a stream running through rice paddies, a roofed wooden bridge, a waterwheel.

The End.

No credits. No "thank you" to hotels or businesses.

The video is so beautiful. I figure the place can't really look like that. All that unspoiled nature and those pretty, hand-carved villages and people dressed up in their groovy ethnic outfits and all. No place I've been to in China really looks like that. Like some tourist's fantasy.

WHEN I WAKE UP the next morning, the same soundtrack I fell asleep to is still playing in my head.

I shouldn't go there. It's a bad idea.

Give it up. Don't give them a trail to follow.

Can I go there without leaving a trail?

I do a little Googling. Find out that Kaili is the capital of a minority autonomous region in Guizhou Province. The capital of which is Guiyang, where I just was. Where I went to the warehouse.

I lie in bed, and I'm aching all over. Really hurting.

I add it up: What happened in Guiyang, that was just the day before yesterday.

The bed at Sidney Cao's French palace was a lot more comfortable than this one. Too bad about the whole "Sidney Cao is a batshit crazy obsessive stalker and murderer" part.

Fuck.

I sit up, scoot to the edge of the bed. My whole body feels like it's cramped up. I can barely stand.

Percocet. Coffee.

I plug in the electric kettle, make myself a cup of Starbucks VIA, and collapse onto the desk chair. Hold the cup in both hands and sip.

You can't go, I tell myself. You can't. You could lead them right to Jason. Plus, you could get your ass kicked even worse.

What you do is, you turn over the information you have to Dog and Natalie. Let them know about Jason's video channel. They can try emailing him. Maybe he'll write back.

It sucks, though. I got so close. Found out all kinds of shit. Followed every lead.

Except this one.

And I don't want to give up. I don't want to quit. Don't want to let those Eos fuckers stop me.

I want to complete the mission. Act like I'm not afraid, even if I am.

But I can't.

I sip my bitter, grainy coffee.

I could take an overnight train to Beijing, or I could fly, but given the way I'm feeling, which is beat to shit, used up, and tossed by the side of a road, I'm not much in the mood to travel.

I try to decide, should I be worried about the Eos guys? About Buzz Cut? I mean, in the long run they're a problem. Another entry on my list of powerful people that I've managed to piss off.

In the short term?

They don't know I'm in Shanghai—that is, unless Carter fucked me over.

I'm sure they know how to find me in Beijing.

At least I have friends there. People who can help me. Like Harrison. And . . . well, Creepy John.

I'm really not sure that I want to go there. Asking a guy who works for the DSD for protection?

Talk about getting in bed with the wrong people.

I'll go home tomorrow, I tell myself. Try to get my shit together so I can front like everything's normal to Mom and

Andy. Set up a meeting with Harrison to discuss the whole Sidney Cao situation. Move forward. What else can I do?

It's too bad Lucy Wu isn't in town, because it would be nice to hang out with her. Discuss art or something. Funny. I never would have thought that I'd end up working with her. Being friends, even.

I look at my fancy outfit draped over one of the chairs and think maybe I can pull it off. Put on those clothes and be that person.

Ellie McEnroe, Art Gal.

Hah. What a joke.

I mean, okay, I've learned some stuff. It's, like, I know Lao Zhang's art is good. I just don't really know *why*.

It's powerful. It makes me feel something. But *how* it does that I still don't really understand.

I read art magazines, Web sites, all that, just so I can fake my way through conversations with people who know more than I do, who are experts. But a lot of what I read—all this intellectual stuff, the theories—I don't know what they're talking about.

I haven't read anything or even thought about it since I started chasing Jason.

Harrison takes me places, tries to teach me stuff. I could try harder to learn on my own, I guess. To really *know*.

Complete the mission, right?

WHAT I DECIDE TO do is go look at art.

I mix and match my pricey jacket with jeans and a faded T-shirt. I pack my sweater, just in case, although it's warmer than yesterday. Have another cup of coffee and another Percocet. Nothing like a little caffeine and narcotics to start your morning right.

I can do this.

I go to Mogushan, your basic collection of art galleries in a bombed-out factory complex. The art's okay, I guess, but nothing really strikes me. But I find a fun T-shirt place, with designs ripping off CCP icons—praying hands clasping a Little Red Book. Another proclaiming WE LOVE TIANANMEN SQUARE!

I sit and have a beer at a little café when my leg starts hurting. It's better, though. I mean, back to where it was before Guiyu, meaning pretty fucked up. But it's a pain I can live with.

After that I visit the Shanghai Museum. Classical Chinese art. Scrolls. Landscape painting. Pottery. Calligraphy. It's beautiful. I spend a lot of time there in the hushed gold light, just looking.

When I'm done, I find some soup dumplings at a little dive not too far from the museum, and then I go back to my hotel.

This wasn't a bad day, I think. I could keep doing stuff like this. Having days like today. It's not a bad life, right?

Maybe it's even a good one.

I open a beer I snagged at a mini-mart and flop down in the desk chair. I figure I'll do a little Web surfing and email before I sleep.

There's an email from an address I don't recognize: SparkleOn77@yahoo.com. I open it.

Hi Ellie it's Natalie. Writing you from hospital. Doug still here. Docs not sure what's going on. He's confused and agitated. Asking a lot about Jason. Just wondering if you have any news I can tell him. Thanks for everything. Sent from my iPhone.

Fuck.

I'm not ready to write this email. I'm really not.

Hi Natalie. Re: your question, it's a little complicated, but I've got some good leads for you. Probably better if we discuss on Skype.

I hesitate.

Really sorry to hear that Doug's still in the hospital, I type. "*Hope that the docs get what's going on with him straightened out soon. Best, Ellie.*"

I SLEEP, BUT I don't sleep well. Maybe I'm missing Sidney Cao's bed. Maybe it's the pain in my muscles. Plus the crazy dreams I'm having. For some reason there's these frogs all over the place. Twitching and jumping. I'm trying to walk down a street that in my head is in Yangshuo, even though it looks more like the electronics village in Guiyu, and the frogs are everywhere, and I step on a couple, and they crunch under my foot.

I wake up in a sweat.

6:00 A.M.

I lie in the bed for a while, but I can't get back to sleep. I think about drinking another beer. I think about taking another Percocet.

Finally I get up and make a cup of instant coffee and open up my laptop.

Not too many emails. The usual spam. A nice note from Palaver and Madrid, buddies of mine who hooked up during our deployment and got married, like in Vermont or someplace seeing as how they're lesbians, had a kid. Stayed together.

Nice to see things working out for someone.

I think about my mom and Andy.

No way. No way that will last.

I'm thinking about that, and I look at the next email. The subject line is "Hi," and it's from Jason88.

No one I know.

I get this little shiver between my shoulder blades. Open the email.

I heard you're looking for me, it says.

CHAPTER THIRTY-ONE

FOR A MINUTE ALL I can do is sit there and stare at the screen.

I heard you're looking for me. That's all it says.

And *Jason.*

I drink some more coffee. Try to think. How did he get my email address?

How do I know it's even him?

Okay, I tell myself, okay. I handed out my card to a bunch of people in Yangshuo. He could've gotten my email address from any one of them. Even if he only had my name, he could've looked me up. I'm easy enough to find on the Web, what with the art business and charitable foundation and all.

But I can't know for sure that it's him. Buzz Cut could've set up the account, emailed me to see what I'd do.

I think about it, and I type, *Where did you get my email? How do I know you're who you say you are?* Hit SEND.

After that I heat up some more water, make myself another cup of coffee. And wait.

It takes about an hour before a reply from Jason88 hits my inbox.

*A friend of mine you talked to gave me your info. I'm not saying
who. You could tell somebody else and get them in trouble.*

*You call my brother 'Dog.' You hooked up in Iraq, at Mortaritaville.
He told me about it, how he felt bad, but how you guys are still buddies.*

I feel my cheeks flush, but it's not like anyone's around to see
me. Shit, what did Dog tell him? About how we fucked in the
laundry trailer? Not exactly one of the classier moments of my
life, even if I was only nineteen at the time.

*You want to talk to me, you know where I am. Don't bring anybody
with you.*

I sit there, staring at the message on the screen. Gulp some
bitter coffee.

*I don't know where you are. And your brother's the one you need to
be talking to, or Natalie,* I type. *Not me.*

I try to think—what else should I say? Beg the guy to come
home to the States? Where he's a wanted ecoterrorist, with the
FBI on his ass?

Doug's not in great shape, I type. *He just wants to know you're
doing okay. He thinks the charges are bullshit. He wants to help.*

Which is also bullshit. Not that Dog doesn't mean it. But
that a guy who's as fucked up as Dog, who can't think straight
and is currently in the hospital, who's lacking a million-dollar
bank account—how the fuck is he going to go up against the
machine that's out looking for Jason? That wants to grind him
up and throw him in jail for twenty years at least?

Look, we caught a terrorist!

I want to help if I can, I finally type. *But I don't know where
you are.*

Which is more or less true. I only have an idea.

I hit SEND.

And get back: *Requested action not taken: mailbox unavailable (state 14).*

Well, fuck.

I search Help and find out the message means that the mailbox he was using is probably closed.

So the guy writes me an email. Answers once. Closes his account.

Leave it alone, I tell myself. You don't know for sure it's Jason. Okay, he knew some things about me and Dog, but there are ways someone else could have found that stuff out. Hacked our emails. Listened in on Skype. Found some mutual buddy of ours and just asked. I mean, who knows?

Even if it's him, does it make sense to risk it? Risk leading Eos to Jason? Risk getting those fuckers back on my ass?

Don't give them a trail to follow.

I think about all this, and I have an idea. Maybe it's a really bad one.

I have a cheap cell phone I carry with me, ever since what happened last year. No GPS. No regular account. No way to trace it to me—I buy new SIM cards and minutes when I need them.

Just in case.

I wait an hour and use it to call Vicky Huang.

"I have a big favor to ask Mr. Cao," I say.

"OF COURSE, OF COURSE!" Sidney's gotten on the call himself. "Certainly I can help you with this." I can picture him smiling on the other end of the line. "My jet is your jet."

YEAH, I TAKE SIDNEY Cao's jet to Guiyang. I'd take it to Kaili, but the airport there isn't finished yet. I sit in the leather seat, sip some crazy overpriced Bordeaux, eat filet mignon, and think, Fuck, well, that's another Lao Zhang painting I'm probably going to have to give Sidney for his private museum. I drink some more wine, and I think, This whole thing—the jet, the palace, Sidney's World—it's the stuff Lao Zhang likes to skewer in his art, and here I am, going along for the ride.

I realize something else. I haven't logged in to the Great Community for . . . days? Weeks? How long has it been? Sometime in Yangshuo.

I've hardly even thought about it all.

I guess because I've been getting my ass kicked in the real world. The electronics dumps in Guiyu. The bird sanctuary. New Century seeds. My mom. Creepy John. The dog.

Except—it occurs to me as I'm sitting in a leather seat on a private jet, sipping this crazy-good, way-overpriced wine and eating my filet—what's "real" about any of this? I think about Guiyu, about Wa Keung and Mei Yee and Moudzu, about how they live.

This relates to the kid who fixed my laptop . . . how?

How did I get here?

Don't think about it, I tell myself. Think about the mission.

I GET TO GUIYANG at around 1:30 P.M. The white-gloved flight attendant waves good-bye to me as I limp down the boarding ramp, the hangar for Shining Star Aviation in the background.

I take a taxi to the Guiyang train station. Just manage to catch the 3:00 P.M. train to Kaili. It gets me there at 5:30 P.M.

The Kaili train station, not your first- or even second-tier-city train station. It's this dumpy two-story building, ceiling fans hung by skinny poles from a whitewashed concrete ceiling, smelling like decades of cigarettes and piss. I push my way through the metal-grilled gate, stumble down the shallow cement stairs, out to the curb, blinking. Into another city where I don't know where I am or what I'm doing.

Kaili looks kind of small, I think. The train station doesn't even have a real parking lot, just some spaces in a half circle out in front. A little chilly. I turn up the collar of my jacket. Stand there, daypack on my back, duffel on my shoulder, looking for a cab. Not a lot of traffic. Some blocky white buildings. It hardly feels like a city at all.

IT'S A CITY, BUT a small one, for China, wedged into a space blasted out of granite mountains. Modest storefronts mostly. A larger indoor mall advertising brands I've never heard of that sits across what looks like the center of the city, where a bunch of streets run into each other, forming almost a circle. Occasional signs in English that make no sense, like 300 SEATS OUT OF PRINT WATERFRONT MANSION. It might be for real estate.

"*Ni shi naguo ren?*" the cabbie asks. Where are you from?

"*Meiguo.*" I am too tired and too fried to have this conversation now.

"Oh, American! I haven't met Americans before. Not too many come here. Welcome you to Kaili!"

"*Xie xie ni.*"

"Every day is a festival in Kaili, have you heard that saying?"

His accent has a lilt to it, like it's Irish Chinese or something. Mandarin isn't the native language here.

"I haven't. I don't know very much about Kaili."

The cabbie grins. He's a few years older than me, small, receding hair. "Then I'll tell you, every *third* day is a major festival."

Good to know.

★ ★ ★

MY HOTEL IS THIS cheap place that I'm guessing used to be government-owned, and maybe it still is. There's thousands of hotels in China that look like this: chunky, maybe ten stories, faded white walls, long halls, broad wooden railings, gilt trim. Worn red carpets. The kind of place where there's a piece of paper stuck on the door of my room that says, "*HINT! Honorific Guest, please give the product cash to stage to take care of, before sleeping invite anti the lock the door lock, the door bolt comes the door bolt, close the window and put on to put the, otherwise, the risk is complacent. Camp Dish Guest House.*"

Inside, it's two beds, a pressboard desk with a TV, an electric teakettle, and musty white curtains.

Not bad for twenty-four bucks, I tell myself.

I do what I always seem to do every time I find myself in a city I don't know, half asleep and half hungover: throw my stuff on a chair, kick off my shoes, and collapse on the hard bed. Sleep.

I WAKE UP TO gunfire.

I'm on the floor before I know it, crouching by the side of the bed.

Firecrackers. It's firecrackers, dumbass.

You'd think I'd be used to that by now, living in China, but they still get me every now and then.

I haul myself to my feet and hobble over to the window. The firecrackers are still going on. Maybe a new business opened up. Maybe there's a wedding. Maybe it's part of today's festival.

I need to check out the places in Langhai's video. See if anyone knows him. But first I need to figure out where those places are.

I have to decide how I'm going to handle this.

Lunch, I decide.

★ ★ ★

MY HOTEL IS UP a little hill. I head down it. With my knit hat on and a sweater, I'm pretty comfortable. It's funny, because Kaili looks like a lot of other small Chinese cities. A little run-down. Lots of concrete and red brick, round grey roof tiles. Maybe a few more trees. But there's something kind of pleasant about it. I'm not sure what. It feels relaxed, I guess. Not so many cars. The air is clean.

I wander down a narrow street with no sidewalks. There's a market here, tables selling fruits and vegetables, meat, tofu, spices. Noodle stalls. I'm tempted to stop at one of those, but I keep going. I hear people talking, and I don't have a clue what they're saying. It doesn't sound like Chinese at all. Kaili is the capital of the Miao and Dong Autonomous Prefecture—at least that's what the book in my hotel room said—and I guess most of the people here aren't Han.

And then I hear this crazy music. It's like . . . I don't know how to describe it. Pipes. A drone. High-pitched women's voices. I mean, I've heard plenty of Peking Opera, and it's nothing like that. This slips into my head. That musician who used to live across from Lao Zhang back in Mati Village, he'd love this stuff, trance music, with a beat.

As I approach the intersection, I see the parade.

It's not a big parade. Just a line of musicians and singers. The men are wearing, like, bell-bottomed pants with embroidered trim. The women, red-embroidered skirts and silver headdresses, big silver necklaces that drape over their chests like floppy collars. The men carry these pipes fringed with red yarn and ribbons, and the pipes are so tall that they brush the leaves of the trees.

Is this the every-third-day big festival, I wonder, or just the normal daily one?

I follow them.

They go through a gate, weaving into a parking lot. I think it's a restaurant. Or maybe restaurants—there's more than one building. Lots of restaurants are like this in China, where you have different levels of service and price. Private dining rooms for special groups. Public rooms for everyone else.

With the musicians and all, I'm guessing they cater to tourists.

Straight ahead is a one-story building painted a kind of greenish turquoise, with a mural on the front that's this psychedelic design of dragons and flowers, so intricate that it makes me dizzy.

Or maybe that's because I haven't eaten.

I go inside.

YOU KNOW, THEY'RE PRETTY used to foreigners in most of the places I've been in China, but not here. Everyone stares. It's like I'm some kind of celebrity or something, maybe the kind that gets loaded and ends up on the cover of the *National Enquirer.*

Then the hostess, who's wearing an outfit that looks like the female musicians', except without so much silver, breaks into a smile. "Welcome, welcome!" she says, and indicates a table. *"Qing zuo!"*

I sit. The other customers check me out. They seem friendly anyway. A lot of smiles. They're small, most of them, short and trim. I never think of myself as tall or big, but here I am.

"Rice wine." The hostess has returned with a younger waitress in tow, who's bearing a small clay jug and a cup, like a sake cup, on a tray. "Local specialty. Please, try a little." At least I'm pretty sure that's what she says. Her Chinese is hard for me to understand.

I'm not crazy about Chinese wine, but I don't want to

be rude. "*Xie xie*," I say. "I am interested in trying local specialties."

She pours me a cup. And it's good. Kind of sweet, but not syrupy, and without the chemical burn of *baijiu*. "Very good to drink," I say, and she pours me another one.

Great. Is this one of those situations where if I don't drink, I'm being incredibly impolite and they'll hate me? Maybe I should go ahead and risk being hated, considering that I am on a mission here.

I drink it. The mission's not going to happen till after lunch, right?

I have a fish with sour cabbage and pickles and sesame-flavor tofu, some more rice wine, and it's all really good. A couple of guys at the next table ask me where I'm from. "Beijing," I tell them. They laugh. "Your Chinese sounds like a Beijing person," one of them says.

What brings me to Guizhou? they want to know. Vacation, I tell them. "I've heard Guizhou is very beautiful."

Oh, yes, they tell me, and proceed to rattle off a list of places I need to visit: Xijiang Village, Langde Shang, Shiqiao, Zhaoxing Dong Village, some cave whose name I miss, and Huangguoshu Waterfall—"biggest waterfall in Asia."

"Many things to see in Guizhou," one of them tells me. "You should stay here awhile."

I nod. But there's not much chance of that.

"I saw this video about Kaili," I say. "Very beautiful places. If I showed you, could you tell me where they are?"

I RISK SWITCHING ON my iPhone. The GPS is off, I tell myself. So is the Bluetooth, and I have a VPN installed on the browser. What are the odds that someone can find me, just because I turned my phone back on?

I really have no idea. I never did figure out how the Suits kept tabs on me last year.

Buzz Cut, though, he can't know what the Suits know about me, right?

Assuming Carter didn't fuck me over.

I'm suddenly feeling like drinking more rice wine.

"Is that a new iPhone?" someone asks. "How much does that cost? Very expensive in China!"

Another time, I'd maybe try to explain American cell phone company contracts, but not now. "I don't know. It was a gift."

I find the video and play it for the crowd.

CHAPTER THIRTY-TWO

I SET AN ALARM, get up early, drink some coffee. Go downstairs at 7:30 A.M. and meet the driver I hired yesterday.

The places in the video, they're all near Kaili, I'm told. Most of them famous, at least around here. Xijiang, the Thousand-Family Village. Shiqiao, known for its handmade paper. Other places whose names I don't remember but that I have written down on a piece of paper.

"Can we visit them all in one day?" I ask the driver.

He looks at my list, compiled by the folks in yesterday's restaurant. Frowns. "Maybe a day and a half."

"I don't have a lot of time."

"We can try to hurry."

WE GO FIRST TO Xijiang. It's a tourist trap, with a hundred-kuai entrance fee, but a beautiful one. Wooden buildings with carved doors and windows, rising up a hillside in layers, like a beehive. Wooden signboards shaped like butterflies. A quiet river winds through the center of town. Stone streets. Noodle stalls and souvenir stands. And ATMs and a place to buy phone cards. We enter at a long wooden bridge, grey roof tiles supported by wooden poles, carved beams, a balcony up on top, and are greeted by lines of old men and women, singing and playing pipes, offering shallow bowls of rice wine, which I'm wishing were coffee given how early it is. I have a cup anyway—you know, to be polite.

I see a sign for a coffee place, but it's closed.

I wander around the town for a while, up the hill to the next level, until my leg starts aching, and then I sit and try to think it through. I watch a small group of Chinese tourists pass by, led by a guide wielding a pennant flag. Thankfully, no bullhorn.

Would Jason be in a place like this? A Disneyfied Miao Minority village? With entrance gates and ticket takers?

I know *I* wouldn't be, if I were him.

I limp down to the teahouse where the driver waits.

"Let's go," I say.

WE DRIVE A WAYS. To Shiqiao, a village where they make paper by hand. The mountains look just like the video, I think. Jagged and draped with mist. Those white banners, whatever they are—grave markers? prayer flags?—they're everywhere. Stuck into the earth. Tied onto tree branches. Some of them have red dots in the middle, the edges blurred by the bleed of the paint into the white.

I walk through the main street of the village, green mountain rising behind it. It's quiet. There are walls made up of unmortared, uneven grey brick. A satellite dish on an old tiled roof. New wooden houses here and there, with fresh window carvings. I can smell the wood sap. Bunches of yellow corn hang in the eaves. A rooster and chickens.

I glance inside one wooden building with an open front. There's a young guy in there, bending over scarred wooden troughs, and it smells like wet paste, like kindergarten. He's making paper, I guess.

No sign of foreigners, other than me.

★ ★ ★

WE DRIVE UP MOUNTAIN roads. The air smells like pine and mist. Rice paddies spill in terraces below us. A lone peasant in a round hat ambles along the side of the road, carry pole with wire baskets full of cabbage on either end draped across his shoulders.

I can't really take it all in. All this . . . I don't know, nature or whatever. Yangshuo was stunning, but not like this. Not wild.

I keep expecting the director to yell "Cut!" and stagehands to drag it all away.

We keep driving.

We stop at a village. Have some late lunch. Women weave at this village, at handmade looms. They want to sell me cloth and silver bracelets. I buy a simple bracelet, to be polite. Out on the main street, there are men crouched by birdcages. "The birds fight," the driver explains.

I don't really get this. They look like songbirds.

"They take them out of the cages?" I ask.

"No."

So . . . what, it's a sing-off?

I never do find out.

Finally we come to a village that starts in a valley, winds up a hill. Wooden buildings, like Xijiang's, but not as fixed up. Bunches of corn and peppers hanging in the eaves. There's a fancy wooden bridge with three shingled roofs crossing a stream, and something that looks like a waterwheel made from bamboo and old logs. A few of those prayer flags, or grave markers, or whatever they are, stuck in mounds on the hillside.

I recognize this place from the end of the video.

"I want to take a walk here," I tell the driver.

★ ★ ★

I HOBBLE ALONG THE stone path. Shallow steps lead up into the village. Chickens and a dog and an occasional cat scamper by. But it's very quiet. Hardly any people. An old woman who sits out on her stoop working on some embroidery. An old man smoking a pipe. Something snorts and snuffles in a shuttered, dark bottom floor of one of the old wooden houses. A pig? A crazy person? Who knows?

Farther up the path, the village widens out into kind of a plaza. There's a bunch of buildings, some in the familiar white tile and cement stained by green mold. A school, I think, and maybe a police station or a village government building. There's a basketball hoop off to one side. Black-and-white paintings of Karl Marx, Mao, and Deng Xiaoping hanging on the two-story school building. Still no kids. It's practically a ghost town.

I keep walking up the path. I hear a couple drifting notes of a wood flute, shaky, like the person doesn't really know how to play it.

Here's a brick-and-wood building with a cross on top. A Christian church, I'm pretty sure. Farther on, another plaza, surrounded by more wooden buildings, and wooden benches shaded by a peaked roof. There's a pole in the center, with a carving of what looks like a cow skull stuck on top.

"This is where they do the old dances," someone says.

In English.

I turn, and there he is.

Jason/David/Langhai.

CHAPTER THIRTY-THREE

IT'S WEIRD SEEING HIM after all this time. His hair's lighter than the photo I have—bleached, I guess, but cut short. He's clean-shaven, and his cheeks have lost some of that fullness. He looks thinner and older.

The eyes, though, they look the same, toffee-brown with those flecks of gold.

"I'm Ellie McEnroe," I say.

"I figured." He's holding a wooden flute, and he uses it to gesture toward a bench at the far end of the plaza. "You want to sit? It's a nice view."

"Sure."

I follow him over to the bench. He's wearing jeans and a battered North Face jacket, probably counterfeit, though it's getting harder to tell.

He sits, facing away from the plaza. He's right: The view is amazing. Below us is a valley. Terraced fields climb up the opposite hill, and they're different colors, all these shades of green, some of them white, like maybe they're planted with flowers. I can't really tell from here. There are clumps of dark trees among the fields, a cluster of wooden houses. White smoke rises up from a controlled burn, meeting the white mist drifting down from the peaks. And those torn white flags on crooked sticks, fluttering in the breeze.

"You're a friend of my brother's?"

"Yeah. From the Sandbox." I mean, he knows that already, right?

"Why've you been looking for me?"

"Doug asked me to," I say. "He's not doing so good. And he's worried about you. He wants you to come home."

Jason makes a sigh of a laugh. "Yeah."

It's almost like he doesn't care. But I don't know how much he knows, about what's going on with Dog right now. If he didn't get the email I sent, maybe none of it.

He fingers the wooden flute. I hope he isn't going to start playing it.

"So . . . is he worse?" he finally asks. "Or is it just the same old tragedy?"

I can feel myself bristle. It pisses me off, hearing him talk like that. What the fuck does Jason know about what Dog went through? About what *any* of us went through? Sitting on his ass in some coffeehouse playing his flute.

"He's in the hospital. He's had some seizures. They're not sure what's causing it."

Jason doesn't say anything. He's looking at the valley below us. Maybe at the peasant in the field across the way, plowing through the mud behind a water buffalo. Just like they've been doing it for the last five thousand years.

"And he wants me to come home. Why? So I can get what's coming to me? Go to prison?" He laughs again, and now it's hard. "He can go off to Iraq and Afghanistan and fight for oil or whatever. And that's fine. That's patriotic. Me fighting for the future of the planet? I'm some kind of deluded, stupid freak."

"He doesn't think that."

"How the fuck would *you* know?"

"Because he told me, dickhead," I snap back. "He said he thinks the charges are bogus."

"That's new," he says. "I guess it's true, brain injuries change your personality."

"God, you're really a little turd," I say, and I have to admit I'm surprised. I thought he was going to be different. You know, idealistic and all.

I mean, shit. I nearly got killed chasing after this kid.

"Yeah, that's one of Doug's nickname's for me." He grins slightly.

"Fine, whatever. You're fighting for the future of the planet. You still can't go burning people's shit down."

"Tell that to the people in Afghanistan we blew up with our drones."

"Okay, I'm done." I stand up, slower than I'd like, waiting for the spasm in my leg to ease up so I can walk out of there.

Mission accomplished. Fuck you, asshole.

"I didn't burn anything down," he says suddenly. "We had a plant in our group. FBI or Eos security. I don't know which. He got people pumped up. Kept pushing everybody. That night we went to the Eos facility, it was supposed to be a nonviolent action. Stickers and stencils. I still don't know what happened. I think he set the fire himself."

"Burned down his own company's lab? Destroyed company property?"

"Sure, why not? It's just one facility. They had all the data backed up. They do that, they can discredit the movement, put a bunch of us in jail, make everyone think it's okay to treat Greens like terrorists—"

I'm getting that hollow feeling in my gut again. The one I get when I'm hearing something I don't want to hear, because I know it's true.

"We threaten them because we're telling the truth, and they can't stand that. They don't want people to know. They just want to keep poisoning the planet and counting their profits, and that's all they give a shit about. Not about you, not about me, not about a bunch of farmers in China, or India, or the US. We're fucking roadkill to them."

Jason's rigid, tensed up, ready to fight. Now I see the passion that drove him into the mess he's in. The kid I thought he was.

And then he just deflates.

He's too young to look this exhausted. This defeated.

Then I remember how *I* looked when I was his age.

"Anyway, I can't go home," he says.

"Yeah. I get that."

We sit and watch the farmer in the paddy below us, slogging through mud behind his water buffalo, against that backdrop of emerald hills covered with white flowers. I think I can smell them, the flowers, a hint of sweet in the sharp scent of pine.

"He's probably using a shitload of pesticides," Jason says.

"So why did you want to meet me?" I finally ask. "Is there something I can do? Something you want me to tell Doug?"

He turns to me, frowning. "I didn't ask you here," he says. "I knew who you were because some friends of mine told me you were looking for me."

And now I'm getting that prickly feeling between my shoulders. Like someone's got me in his sights.

"I figured you were . . . I don't know, maybe working for Eos," he continues. "Working for somebody." He shrugs. "I just don't care anymore."

"I'm not," I say, and I'm looking around, looking for Buzz Cut, looking for hajjis, for whoever might have followed me here.

But there's no one. It's utterly quiet, except for the wind blowing through the leaves, like a faint shuffling of cards.

"Listen," I say, "someone spoofed your email address. Said you wanted a meeting with me, and that I'd know where to find you. I figured out where you were through your Langhai videos. And the way I got here, I don't think anyone followed me. But . . ."

I take another look around. At the silent plaza, at the cow skull on top of the pole. At the mountains, the mist, the fluttering white flags.

"I don't think you should stay here," I say.

"Fuck," he says quietly.

I expect him to . . . I don't know, react. Freak out. Bolt, grab his stuff, and head out of town.

He fingers his flute, like he's going to start playing it. Then shrugs. "It's not like I have a lot going on. I'm teaching the village kids some English. I'll miss that."

"Sorry," I say, and I mean it. "But if you're trying to hide? Maybe this isn't the best place."

"You think there's a better one?" He's looking out over the hills again. "Where can you hide anymore?"

"Maybe some place that's not in China, for a start. Or a place in China that's bigger. A city, like Guangzhou, or Shanghai, where there's a lot of foreigners and you won't stand out."

"A city like Guangzhou or Shanghai's the last place I want to be." He turns back to me. "The way we're going, who knows how much longer there'll even be places like this left? I want to be in them while I can."

I get it. I stare out over the hills, at the cultivated wilderness, at the people living on this land who aren't living that differently from how they did hundreds of years ago.

Except they probably have Internet.

"Okay. But at least get yourself as far away from Eos and Hongxing as you can. Away from here, or anyplace you posted as Langhai. And for fuck's sake, delete those videos."

"No."

"No? *Seriously?*" I want to grab him by the shoulders and shake him, hard.

"If they catch me, if that's what I'm leaving behind, then I want them out there." He manages a smile. Cute, almost cocky. "Maybe I'll hop the Great Firewall and cross-post them to YouTube. Think I'll get more hits?"

Stubborn as Dog's been about this whole mission? I'm thinking it runs in the family.

Okay. If he wants to stay here, I'm not going to be able to talk him out of it. But I feel like, after everything that's happened, I have to try to do something. Something positive. I don't know what.

"I'm going back to Beijing," I finally say. "I'll see if there's something I can do to help."

He snorts. "Like what?"

"I don't know, like . . ." I think, suddenly, of Moudzu and Peach Computers. Of Moudzu's parents, who'd hoped I was a reporter.

"I know some journalists back in BJ. I can talk to them. See if someone wants to do a story. It could be a big one."

"I guess it couldn't hurt," he says. The way he says it, I'm guessing he doesn't think it'll help.

"In the meantime, seriously, get yourself someplace else. And set up another email address. Email me when you're settled. Just don't say who you are."

"What do you want me to say?"

"You'll think of something. We'll figure it out from there. How to get the evidence to me. Backups of the videos. Just in case you . . . decide to delete them or something."

In the distance I hear some of those crazy pipes, like I heard on the street in Kaili yesterday. Drums. And now high-pitched singing.

"Festival tonight," Jason says. "Why don't you stick around?" He smiles, a little hesitantly. "You can tell me about Doug. You probably know a lot about him I don't."

I shake my head. "I'd like to. But I'd better not. Stay, I mean."

Now I stand up, muscles between my shoulders twitching. I'm feeling like I've already stayed too long. Like someone's coming for us.

"Remember what I told you," I say. "And . . . write me. Okay?"

He nods.

Who knows if he's listened to anything I've said?

Me, I'm getting the fuck out.

I take one look over my shoulder as I reach the path that leads out of the plaza, into the village. See Jason sitting there, his back to me, his shoulders slumped, staring at the rice paddies below.

CHAPTER THIRTY-FOUR

I WHITE-KNUCKLE IT ALL the way back to Beijing.

I luck out and get a seat on a train that leaves Kaili at 1:30 in the morning. I don't particularly care where it's going, I just want out of here, and I don't want to go back to Guiyang.

As it turns out, the train goes all the way to Beijing, but it's a thirty-two-hour ride.

What I do is, I get off at Changsha instead, eleven hours later, just after noon. Go directly to the airport, which takes about an hour. I miss out on the flights that leave around 2:00 P.M. but manage one departing at 4:00 P.M. that gets me into Beijing just after 6:30 P.M.

I don't think the Eos guys have access to whatever system it is that my passport gets entered into when I buy a plane ticket. But even if they do, if they think I've been looking for Jason in Changsha, all the better.

From the Capital Airport, I catch the express train that hooks up to the Beijing subway and transfer to the 2 Line. And from there it's just a few stops to the Gulou station.

As I ride up the escalator and emerge onto the familiar corner, see that goofy bronze statue of kids playing surrounded by half-dead bushes, I feel this rush of relief and affection that's better than a drink.

Home.

I fumble for my keys, expecting my mom to open the beige metal door before I manage to open the second lock. But when I open the door, there's no one home.

No Mom. No dog. Just the hall light left on.

I look around the kitchen and see a doggie water dish. An empty food bowl drying in the dish rack. There's a bag of Iams kibble and cans of dog food in the pantry.

So they're just out someplace, I tell myself. She left the hall light on because she knew she'd be getting back after dark. It's not even 8:00 P.M. yet.

No need to get all freaked out over nothing.

I TAKE A SHOWER. Change into a fresh T-shirt and pair of jeans. I'm wiped out, and what I really want to do is crash on the couch. Wait for my mom and the dog to come home. Hope that she doesn't ask me too many questions about where I've been and what I've been doing, because no way I want to come anywhere close to having that conversation.

Two things stop me from doing this. One of which is that I'm really hungry.

I go to the dumpling place a couple blocks away on Jiu Gulou Dajie. Choose mutton with chives and spinach with eggs and wolf them down doused in vinegar, a little soy, garlic and hot chili. Wash it all down with a Yanjing beer. I'll take this over Sidney Cao's gourmet gorge-a-thons anytime.

Well, except for maybe the wine. That shit's pretty good.

THERE AREN'T THAT MANY *hutong* neighborhoods left

in Beijing, but most of them are still within the Second Ring Road, and there's a bunch between the Drum and Bell Towers and the Lama Temple. I take the subway to the Lama Temple stop, get off, and head west.

This area's gotten popular the last couple of years. Not like Nanluoguxiang, all tourist bars and T-shirts and Mao-morabilia, not quite yet. There are a number of restaurants and bars, though, some with live music, some with wine, and a couple of weird dives. I'm heading for one of those. It's on a little alley southwest of the temple, a shoe-box-size place that's painted matte black, the walls graffiti-scrawled with fluorescent markers. They have strong infused cocktails stored in glass jugs and good imported beer. Also free wireless.

Even with the VPN, I don't feel comfortable doing what I'm about to do in my own apartment. Not after everything that happened. Not when I have no idea who's watching me.

I sit in the darkest corner at the rough plank table, boot up my laptop, and log on to the Great Community.

It's night there, too.

I'm not sure what's going on as I wander through the square. Floating signs for an art show. A bigger one for a rave. The SexChat Club is lit up, individual bobbing lights representing the number of avatars who've signed in.

The corn statue, the one Sea Horse was building . . . how many weeks ago? It's still there, but it's changed. The giant ears of corn have rotted, black gaps among the kernels, some kernels swelled up to the point of bursting, like tumors. There are more dead bees lying belly-up around the corn. A few of them have shriveled, like they've been dead for a long time. The only thing that's the same is the baby. Rosy-cheeked and chubby. Bearing a basket of rotting, poisoned corn.

I head to my house. As always, the three-legged dog runs

toward me, barks, and wags its tail. The orange cat sleeping on the stoop wakes up and purrs.

Funny. I have a real dog now. Maybe I should get a cat. Kang Li has a few to spare.

While my avatar sits on the couch and waits, I order another beer.

Finally, when I'm about ready to pack it in and head home, Monastery Pig—Lao Zhang—knocks on my virtual door.

NI HAO, he types. HAO JIU BUJIAN. Long time no see.

SORRY, I type. BUSINESS HAS BEEN A LITTLE COMPLICATED.

Lao Zhang's avatar sits on the couch next to me.

Where to start?

I MET A BILLIONAIRE WHO WANTS TO BUY SOME OF YOUR WORK, I type, but that's as far as I get before Lao Zhang drops the bomb.

I'M COMING BACK TO BEIJING, he says.

YOU CAN'T, I tell him. THERE'S NO POINT. THINGS ARE BAD HERE NOW. THE GOVERNMENT'S SCARED. ESPECIALLY WITH THE LEADERSHIP CHANGES COMING UP NEXT YEAR. ANYBODY THAT WORRIES THEM, EVEN A LITTLE, THEY'RE HASSLING. THEY'RE ARRESTING ARTISTS.

I type that bit in caps, hoping he'll get it.

I UNDERSTAND. BUT I HAVE NOT DONE ANYTHING WRONG.

AND YOU KNOW THAT DOESN'T MATTER!

IT WASN'T RIGHT FOR ME TO PUT YOU IN THE PLACE I DID. WHERE THEY ARE COMING AFTER YOU INSTEAD OF ME. I DIDN'T THINK YOU'D HAVE THESE PROBLEMS. I THINK MAYBE THINGS ARE NOT GREAT, BUT THEY WILL NOT BOTHER FOREIGNERS THIS WAY. I WAS WRONG.

NOT TOTALLY WRONG. THEY AREN'T GOING TO ARREST ME. I—

I stop there. Because what I'm about to type is that I have a friend in the DSD. Creepy John. Who wants to protect me. And there is no way I want to get into that whole situation right now.

ANYWAY, MAYBE WE CAN SETTLE THE PROBLEMS IF I COME BACK.

ARE YOU CRAZY? THEY'RE GOING TO WANT TO KNOW WHERE YOU'VE BEEN. WHAT YOU'VE BEEN DOING. THEY'RE GOING TO SAY YOU LEFT THE COUNTRY ILLEGALLY. THAT YOU'RE WORKING WITH FOREIGNERS. THAT YOU'RE A SPY. I MEAN, WHO KNOWS?

MAYBE I HAVE NOT LEFT CHINA. MAYBE I HAVE AN EXPLANATION. I AM JUST WORKING SOMEPLACE. IN THE COUNTRY. LIKE TAOIST MONK LIVING IN CAVE TO WRITE POEMS. I DON'T KNOW ABOUT PROBLEM. NOW I DO. SO I COME HOME TO FIX.

THEY'LL PUT YOU IN JAIL. IN A BLACK JAIL. OR WORSE. DON'T DO IT.

ALREADY DECIDED. His avatar stands up. SEE YOU SOON.

Fucking great.

I SIT THERE AND have another beer and a shot of one of the infusion things, something involving vodka and ginseng. Thinking about all the times I was missing Lao Zhang and wishing he were here. And now all I can think about is how much I'd rather he stayed away.

Not because of Creepy John, I tell myself. Because it's not safe.

I DECIDE TO WALK home. Get in some PT. Maybe clear my head a little. Hah, I think. With the shit that's going on, not much chance of that.

It's chilly out, but not too bad. I'm okay with my knit hat and my collar turned up, and the cold hitting my face is like a shot of espresso. Not that I really want to sober up. Lao Zhang coming back . . . I can't even start to figure out what that's going to mean. Or how I feel about it. Or what the consequences will be.

It's 12:30 A.M, the Hour of the Rat in Chinese astrology. Maybe that's why I like this time of night, me being a Rat and all.

I keep heading west, down the dark alleys just south of the

Second Ring Road. It's quiet here, and I need that right now. When I get to Beiluoguxiang, I'll go down to Gulou Dong Dajie, the main street that leads back to Old Drum Tower Road. There used to be a *hutong* route all the way across, but the military complex they put in the center of the quarter ruined that. I wonder if they did it on purpose, putting a butt-ugly reminder of who holds the power in the middle of this little piece of old Beijing, with its hipster bars and rock clubs and funky galleries and boutiques.

I turn onto Beiluoguxiang. You'd think with the way Nanluoguxiang's gone from cool to trendy to commercial that the northern end of the street would be hipper by now, but it's not. A lot of the little grey buildings are empty, shuttered. Dark. Like this one. Old flyers for an "Evolution Rave" flaking off the painted-over windows, but there's no music now. No sign of life.

I hear something—a skittering on the pavement to my left. I look. I swear I see the hindquarters and tail of a rat, disappearing up the alley, into a crack in a grey wall.

Then a heavy step behind me and a man's chuckle.

"You just make it too easy."

CHAPTER THIRTY-FIVE

HE'S GOT ONE ARM wrapped around my neck. His other hand grips my wrist, and he twists my arm up against my back so hard that it feels like my shoulder's going to pop out of its socket.

"You scream, I'll break it," he says.

I'm thinking I should scream anyway. Because I recognize his voice. Buzz Cut. And then Carter steps into my line of sight.

But there's no one around that I can see. And if there were, would anyone help?

I think about the self-defense stuff I learned. It worked against Russell. But against this guy? And Carter?

Fucking Carter. Seeing him is like a punch in the gut.

"You took the bait," Buzz Cut says in my ear. "You saw him, I know you did. And this time you're gonna tell me where he is."

"Or what?" I manage.

He gives my wrist an extra twist. The surge of pain almost knocks me off my feet. Except of course this asshole is holding me up.

"We'll think of something. Carter, give me a hand."

Carter steps out of the shadows. It's too dark for me to see his face. I lash out with my foot, kick Buzz Cut in the shin, try to stomp on his foot, but he tightens the arm around my throat, lifts me up so my toes just brush the ground, and I can't breathe. I land a slap to his crotch, not hard enough to take him out, but enough so that he grunts and jerks forward and my feet are back on the ground. I see Carter at Buzz Cut's side, and I think he's going to grab me, but instead he smacks Buzz Cut on the shoulder.

"What the *fuck*?" Buzz Cut yells. The arm around my neck loosens. "You son of a *bitch*!"

"Yeah, yeah," Carter mutters.

I take in a few gulping breaths. The hand clutching my wrist releases. I stumble away.

"You're fucking dead," Buzz Cut says, slurring the words.

I turn. See him stagger backward, fall against the grey brick wall of the abandoned club. "I'm gonna . . ." he stutters. "I . . . fuck . . ."

His knees buckle, and he collapses, landing hard on the dirty concrete.

"Jesus, Doc," Carter says, and I don't need to see his face to know how pissed off he is. "I told you these guys are assholes. Couldn't you have just dropped it, like I said?"

"I . . . I was going to." I look down at Buzz Cut. He's not moving. He's still breathing, though. I think. "What did you . . . ?"

Carter turns his palm up. He's holding something, a dark tube the size of a large-caliber bullet or a small cigar.

"What . . . ? Why . . . ?"

He shrugs. "I tried to play *Let's Make a Deal*. I thought we had one. He said he just wanted to talk to you. But I know this guy, and like I said, he's an asshole. So I figured I'd better make sure." He nudges Buzz Cut with the toe of his sneaker. Buzz Cut mumbles something and curls up like a cat trying to take a nap.

"They had guys staking out your apartment," he continues. "So as soon as you came back into the frame, we were on you." He shakes his head. "What the fuck, Doc. You have to go wandering down dark alleys half drunk in the middle of the night?"

"I . . . It's Beijing. It's . . . it's my neighborhood. It's safe."

"Sure, if you aren't in the middle of some dangerous fucking *shit*. You're gonna play in this playground, you'd better learn the rules. Unless you got a death wish or something."

The two of us stand there for a moment, listening to Buzz Cut's quiet snores.

"What are you gonna do with him?" I ask.

"I dunno. Probably just leave him here. It's not like he can bitch and get me fired."

"But . . . he said he was gonna kill you."

"Let him try."

Seeing Carter standing there, I'm thinking that in a battle of the badasses, I would not bet against him.

"He's got his people. I've got mine. And he was out of line." Carter shrugs. "Let's get out of here."

WE GO TO A little *hutong* bar I know run by these Mongolian brothers. My throat hurts from being choked and all, and I could use a beer. It's a cool place, and one of the brothers has a couple of cats he adopted who live there. They like to sleep on top of the crooked bookcases and climb the tree in the middle of the tiny courtyard. Tonight it's not too crowded. We sit in a corner against the wall, curtained off by a battered wooden screen.

"You need to stop drinking so much," Carter tells me, pounding his shot of tequila.

I laugh. "Yeah. Right." I'm drinking Harbin beer.

"Hey, *I'm* not the one who's on everybody's shit list. That would be you."

He doesn't even know the half of it.

I don't think.

"So why'd you help me?" I ask.

"We had a deal," he says, not looking at me. "If you're gonna horse-trade, you need to be an honest actor. Which that dick was not." He chugs his Erdinger and laughs. "Nice having an excuse to leave him in a gutter."

There's more to it than that, I'm pretty sure.

I study him. He's close to my mom's age, maybe a little younger. I never thought about that before, about what kind of life he has when he isn't being a corporate spy/thug.

"Oh, man, don't tell me I remind you of your daughter or something."

He draws back. His face twists like he's smelled something bad. "My daughter is a straight-A student in college," he says, sounding pissed.

"Okay, okay. So not that."

He leans back in his chair. Crosses his arms above his belly. Smiles a little. "More like this crazy Polish girlfriend I had in Estonia. Into vodka and meth. Fucking nuts."

I hope he's joking. Because of the many places I do not wish to go, this would be high on my list.

"Don't worry," he says. "I've outgrown that kind of shit. So should you."

"Yeah, whatever." I drink my beer. Pet the black-and-white cat when she winds around my legs.

"What happens if I go to the press?" I finally ask.

"How the fuck should I know? Probably nothing. But hey, you wanna try, I'm not gonna stop you."

I get us another round of beers and a couple shots for Carter. We drink for a while.

"It might help," Carter mutters.

"What?"

"Getting the story out there. Embarrassing Eos. You're already in their sights. You go public, you might get too hot for them to touch." He drinks some more. Seems to consider. "Or . . ."

"Or what?"

"You make your own deal. Tell them you *won't* go to the press, if they leave you alone. If anything happens to you, the information gets released. You know. Preemptive blackmail."

"What do *you* think I should do?"

He shrugs. "Depends on what you want."

I think about it. Think about Jason, and Sparrow and Kang Li. Moudzu and Peach Computers. Then I think about the utility of saving my own ass.

"You know what?" Carter says suddenly. He rests his elbows on the table and leans forward. Like he's about to share a big secret.

"I don't want my daughter and her kids, if she has them, eating that GMO shit." He slams his shot. "What kind of a world are we leaving for them anyway?"

I'm pretty sure he's drunker than I am.

"I don't know."

His voice drops to a whisper. "My daughter's pre-med."

"That's really cool," I say.

I STAGGER HOME.

This time when I fumble for my keys, a dog starts barking from inside, toenails scraping against the metal door.

My mom opens the door before I can get my key in the second lock.

"Oh!" She breaks into a smile. Reaches out to hug me. I just kind of stand there. The dog dances around her legs barking.

"Calm down, Mimi!" my mom says, grabbing the dog's collar. Her hair's frizzed out, and she's wearing pajama bottoms and a T-shirt that she must have gotten in Yangshuo, a yin-yang symbol against those freaky mountains.

"Mimi?"

"That's your friend John's name for her."

I step inside. See Andy sitting on the couch in front of the TV, blinking blearily. He, too, is wearing pajama bottoms and a T-shirt.

"We were watching a movie," my mom explains. "I guess we fell asleep."

"It's pretty late."

"*Ni hao*, Ellie," Andy says. "Your vacation was good?"

"A blast."

"Blast?"

"*Hen hao wanr.*" A lot of fun.

The dog nuzzles my free hand.

"Hey, you remember me, dog?" She sits and thumps her tail. "I guess you do."

She looks good. Her coat shiny and clean. "John had her groomed," Mom explains. "He's been back to visit her. I think he's attached." She grins slyly. "Maybe not just to Mimi."

I roll my eyes, scratch the dog behind her ears, the ruff of fur around her neck. Feel the collar. Leather, good quality, with a brass buckle and studs.

"John says you can change her name if you like. He just needed one to register her here in Beijing." She smiles. "He wanted to take care of that for you."

"Right."

Knowing John, I'll bet he microchipped her.

Andy slowly rises from the couch. Stretches and yawns. "I let you two sleep now." He passes by my mom, taking a moment to smile at her. My mom smiles back, and I think she's blushing.

He pauses by the door. Clasps his hands together and bobs his head in my direction. "Welcome home, Ellie. Have a good rest."

This strikes me as pretty funny.

I LIE IN BED, and tired and drunk as I am, I don't fall asleep right away. I feel Buzz Cut's arm against my throat, and my shoulder's throbbing. Another injury to add to the tally.

It'll heal, I tell myself. And I don't know, maybe it was worth it.

I completed the mission. I didn't wimp out. Maybe I didn't accomplish much. I didn't exactly talk Jason into coming home. But at least I can let Dog know he's okay.

And I'm thinking maybe I *will* go to the press. I know a couple of reporters. Harrison probably knows more.

I'll have to think hard about what I want to tell them. How much I want to put myself in the story.

As little as possible, I decide. It's Jason who needs to be the story, not me.

And yeah, maybe it won't do any good. Jason and me, Moudzu, Sparrow—we're all pretty far down on the food chain compared to who we're up against. Just grunts in some generals' wars.

Worker bees. Ha-ha.

But I think about what John said to me once. About how it's hard to change things. About how most of us can only do something small. But how, if enough of us try, maybe we can connect all those small things together.

Do something great.

Or who knows? Maybe not. But I might as well try. What else am I going to do?

Tell the Great Community, I think. Let them know what's going on. They can spread the word, too.

I hear scratching at the door. A low whine.

"Really, dog?" I mutter. She scratches again. "All right, all right." I switch on the nightstand light and shuffle over to the door.

Mimi sits there, staring up at me, her gold-flecked eyes wide. Her tail starts to thump.

"Okay. You can come in."

I limp back to bed. The moment I'm in it, the dog scrambles up. "Seriously? Come on. This is *my* bed, not yours."

She snuggles against my side. Nuzzles my hand. I swear she's being cute on purpose.

"We're not going to make a habit of this, right?" I scratch behind her ears, under her jaw, around her neck. My hand feels the brass tag, which has gotten tucked under the collar. I straighten it out. Then pull it around so I can read it.

On one side it says MIMI, followed by a telephone number— my iPhone. On the other side, two Chinese characters: 秘密

Pronounced *mi mi.* Meaning "secret."

I start laughing. I can't help it.

With Lao Zhang coming back, I'm not sure how long the secret will hold. But it's one I can keep, for now.

ACKNOWLEDGMENTS

There are so many people that I need to thank for *Hour of the Rat* that I really don't know where to start.

So, in no particular order:

The folks at Soho Press—publisher Bronwen Hruska, Mark Doten, Paul Oliver, Meredith Barnes, Rudy Martinez, Janine Agro, Simona Blat, Rachel Kowal, and in particular, my editor, Juliet Grames. I am extremely fortunate to be working with a group of innovative, ethical, and passionate people who care very deeply about the books they put out and the authors who write them. Plus, they are just plain fun to hang out with. That goes for Soho authors as well. A more convivial bunch of writers you won't find anywhere. The Soho Criminals, guys. It's on. I'm buying that bass ukulele.

The Random House sales team, whose smarts, enthusiasm, and mad bowling skills are greatly appreciated!

My many writer friends, the people I can go to who understand exactly what I'm celebrating or freaking out about. The Wombats, the Purgies, Pitizens, and a special shout-out to the Fiction Writers Co-op, a group whose combined knowledge, experience, generosity and talent continues to astound me. My fellow Sisters and Misters in Crime, SoCal and NorCal, and the SoCal and NorCal chapters of Mystery Writers of America. And, especially, Noir at the Bar Los Angeles—what a fantastic community of writers and readers!

Maryelizabeth Hart and the crew at Mysterious Galaxy San Diego and Redondo Beach. While I'm at it, a sincere "thank you!" to the independent bookstores of America. Thank you for being here, for fighting the good fight and for providing a much needed "third space" where we can come together as a culture and as a community.

Librarians—you, too! Libraries were where I learned to love books. You enrich our society immeasurably, providing invaluable community resources at a time when communities really need you.

Writer friends who especially helped me with this book: Dana Fredsti, Bryn Greenwood, and Jenny Brown. THANK YOU! (That's in caps because I'm shouting it from the rooftops.)

China friends—you guys keep me coming to Beijing in spite of the air that's trying to kill me. Your help with Mandarin and other research questions was invaluable. Plus, thanks for all the dumplings! Si Fuzhen, Dave Lyons, Kate Ba, Brendan O'Kane, Jeremiah Jenne, Yajun Zhang, Allison Corser, thank you. Tim Smith, my "brother," thank you twice.

My Los Angeles crew, who helped me through a pretty tough time in my life: Jim Bickhart, Joe Touch and Gail Schlicht, Holly and Mick West, John Amussen and Drea Bailey, Pete Sloman, David McCallen, and especially Ebbins Harris.

Tim Hallinan, I'll see you at the Novel Café.

Ryan McLaughlin, my web designer, who's always so much fun to work with and approaches each new tweak with enthusiasm and creativity.

Kerrin Hands—I keep winning the cover lottery—again, I score!

Ben Lucas, Tommaso Fiacchino, I love a business that has introduced me to great folks like you.

Jane Johnson, we will have those margaritas! Thank you for your support and your belief in me as a writer.

Pilar Perez, for the margaritas and for providing a wonderful writing refuge in a beautiful place.

Jennifer Hubbard—for sparkly purple you know what.

Jon Hofferman, Mimi Freedman—for Buffy nights.

Billy Brackenridge, for Rafanelli and sushi. But not together.

Dana Fredsti (again) and David Fitzgerald, for general moral support.

Bill, Carol, Chris, and Merrilyn Galante—for general awesomeness.

Richard Burger, whose very thorough reads of the manuscript picked up all kinds of things, China facts, language, misplaced periods—thank you so very much. Also, for all the fun we've had while traveling together. Western Guizhou calls. Soon, my friend. Very soon . . .

Nathan Bransford, for the rice-farming info, and for believing in me in the first place.

Debra Baumann, my go-to for information and fact-checking about GMOs and other agricultural subjects— thank you for your sharing your knowledge and passion, and for the wonderful work you're doing in your secure undisclosed location somewhere in California . . .

The fine folks at Curtis Brown: Brianne Sperber, Stuart Waterman, Kerry D'Agostino, Holly Frederick, Dave Barbor, Ginger Clark, and most especially, Katherine Fausset, for your patience, support, good humor, and friendship. It's such a pleasure working with you.